COPS AND C

I. K. Watson is the author of two other novels: *Wolves Aren't White* and the acclaimed gangster novel, *Manor*. He lives in Hertfordshire.

Also by I. K. Watson

Fiction
Manor
Wolves Aren't White

Non-fiction
Quality is Excellence

COPS AND OTHER ROBBERS

I. K. Watson

FOURTH ESTATE • *London*

This paperback edition published in 1999
First published in Great Britain in 1998 by
Fourth Estate Limited
6 Salem Road
London W2 4BU

1 3 5 7 9 10 8 6 4 2

A catalogue record for this book is available
from the British Library.

ISBN 1–85702–847–3

Typeset by Palimpsest Book Production Limited,
Polmont, Stirlingshire
Printed in Great Britain by Cox & Wyman Ltd, Reading

for my wife, Alex,
who put up with the nightly plot disturbances.

Prologue

It began with the Ice-cream Man. It seemed like a lifetime ago. He'd just passed his inspector's exam and was acting up. Memory played tricks. Memory and bad dreams.

The London streets steamed with the devil's breath. Red was the predominant colour. Red neon shimmered through the rain. He stood, soaked, staring at the wooden door, its flaking green paint turned to the colour of shit by the light.

He felt numbed, detached, in the ethereal world. He saw himself move forward in slow motion, his hand reach out to wave at the uniformed officer beside him, the double-handed steel ram rise up, the hot rain drip from the red-painted steel as it came down to split the door from its lock. He only heard the drumming of the rain and the screaming sirens as the door fell open. But that wasn't really the start. He could go back further than that.

It began two days earlier with a missing girl, Sharon Keaton. A search in derelict buildings where you could come to serious grief. Raw knees and aching backs, moving forward on hands and knees, moving everything that could move, searching for a tiny blonde hair, something she dropped, a footprint. The sergeants and inspectors joined in. Cut-backs had something to do with it, but they wanted to help. When kids were involved everyone pulled out the stops.

The photograph of her still scarred his mind. It had been all over the television. A fresh-faced six-year-old looking out impassively over the incident room. She had disappeared in the early afternoon. One minute playing with dolls on the front lawn, the next gone. Into thin air. No witnesses. No strange cars parked nearby. Nothing. Just a hole left by one little girl, and her mother's screams of panic.

And then the specific things to be done, the screenings, the pulling out of known offenders, the perverts, flashers, paedophiles, interviews, house-to-house calls, searches of waste ground, of empty factories and warehouses, dustbins and

1

culverts and cracks in the earth, any place big enough for a little girl to hide, or be hidden, and all of it urgent because of the creeping feeling, the gut knowledge that experience brings, that the longer it went on, every passing hour, lessened the likelihood of finding her alive. A shit job. Everyone agreed.

And then they had him. The Ice-cream Man. Paul Baker. It was thanks to a list of schedule one offenders spat out by the computer and the sharp eyes of a copper who spotted some magazines under his stairs. The Ice-cream Man. He used to live on Argyle. The place was condemned. He had lived there with his nan before she died. It was from there that he went out to buy ice-creams for the little girls. The press coined the name. When he got out of prison the council moved him to a one-bedroom flat in Telford Avenue. That's where the sharp-eyed copper visited him, just to check his alibi. If he hadn't left the magazines filled with photographs of children lying around, it wouldn't have been so easy.

His previous was five years earlier. A sympathetic judge had taken his lack of social support into consideration and given him six. After four he was back on the streets. When would they learn that one in four child sex offenders were at it again within six months of their release? With him it took longer, but the result was the same: another missing girl.

If the kozzers had it their way, that judge would now be hauled up to share the new sentence.

Argyle. The green door of the derelict festered and bled and opened into darkness. And the nightmares began.

Part 1

Chapter 1

'Do you know how you know if your marriage is still good, Rick?' Sam Butler asked.

'Yeah, when you don't think about it. It's like your body. If you're not aware of it, it's probably all right.'

'No, no. I'll tell you how. It's knowing you still get excited when you see your wife walking towards the house instead of away from it.'

He looked across to make certain Rick Cole was still attentive, then went on, 'I'm in love with my wife. I still get excited when I see her walking up the path.'

Cole grunted. 'You'll get over it.'

'I don't believe that.'

'Believe it. Nothing lasts. Life is like a self-service restaurant. You see what your mate's got and you think, I fancy some of that. Then, after a while, the meal on your plate seems pretty unappetising. That's the real world, fast-food, mad cows. Believe it.'

Butler frowned unhappily. 'Bollocks.'

Burn-out is the fashionable word. People from the professions love it. It's a white-collar disease, the twentieth-century cop-out. Toffler hit it on the head. Something to do with too much information, too many images for the brain to handle. Maybe he'd had a look at the future and got lost on the Superhighway.

Sam Butler was showing all the symptoms. Jaw muscles flickering, blowing hot and cold, fidgety, going off on tangents. His problems started at home. Didn't they all? He was getting the rough end of his wife's discontent. She was approaching forty and beginning to panic. He never mentioned it, but things like that got around the office faster than a dose of Asian flu. And those Asian bastards got everywhere.

They'd been in the car over an hour, parked up in a row of others. Surveillance: they were watching the entrance of a Paki shop over the road. It was mid-afternoon. The sun blazed

5

and exploded off windscreens and chrome. The windows were down but it was still suffocating. The smell of sweat and stale cigarettes. Worse for Butler, because he didn't smoke and the ashtray was starting to overflow with JPS butts.

'Last year, me and the wife . . .' Sam Butler started up again like a lawn-mower on a Sunday afternoon. He paused and his eyes softened, remembering a time when his marriage was better. He corrected himself, '. . . the wife and I, that is, went on a trip to Denmark, one of these mini cruises. Three nights, one ashore. Esbjerg. Poxy place. Cold people. Funny, the further north you go, the colder the people get.'

'Maybe it's got something to do with the temperature.'

'I doubt it. That'd make us pretty friendly, and the Italians, those greasy bastards, even friendlier. And that's bollocks.'

'I thought all those fjords were supposed to be beautiful. The stuff that picture postcards are made of.'

'Fjords? Fjords?' He shook his head.

'No fjords?'

'Flat, boring. Like Dungeness without the power station. And that place is pretty boring even with the power station.'

Cole made an effort and said affably, 'I'm surprised.'

'Terracotta roofs and flat grassland and Hans Christian Andersen. He was big over there. And booze—'

'Expensive. I heard.'

'I'd say. About twice the price it is here. Even the duty free on board was more expensive than Sainsbury's. There's got to be a fiddle going on in that duty free business.'

'Tell me some place there isn't a fiddle going on. Waste of time then, eh? The trip?'

Butler nodded thoughtfully. 'The point is, about one in the morning we were walking back to the boat. No traffic. Not a murmur of traffic, but people were walking home from the pubs and restaurants. We came to this pedestrian crossing – red and green lights. The red was blinking. Everybody stopped. You couldn't see a car for a mile each way, but everybody stopped and waited for the green. A full minute or more. Can you believe that?' He shook his head. 'That's law and order for you. That's a civilised country.'

6

'You mean no one crossed even though the road was clear for a mile each way?'

'Exactly.'

'Including you and Janet?'

'Right. When in Rome, all that.'

'That's stupid.'

'It's conditioning.'

'I bet if you'd made a move, everyone would have followed.'

'I don't think so. I think the locals would have been offended.'

'It's crazy.'

'It's Denmark.'

'Remind me not to go there.'

'The only draught you could get was lager.'

'Schoolboys.'

'Piss.'

'Probably.'

Sam grinned. It was the first time Cole had seen him smile in a couple of months. Ever since his marriage started to rock.

They watched the shop some more. Butler's features fell away to worry again. His natural look. He saw Cole's glance and admitted, regretfully, 'He isn't going to show, is he?'

'Maybe.'

'Bastard.'

'Maybe you got the wrong SP. How reliable was it?'

'It was good,' he said coldly.

'Maybe someone warned him off.'

'Warned Conners off?' His lips tightened contemptuously. 'If he was warned off, then it leaked from the office. That's not likely.'

'Oh yeah? What about your gossip?'

'He's hardly likely to warn him, is he? Not after giving me the whisper in the first place.'

'Maybe your snout thought it over,' Cole said, seriously. 'Got cold feet.'

Butler shook his head. 'No, no that doesn't work. He'd like to see Conners nicked. They aren't friends. He's got pins in his lower jaw to prove it.'

'Do I know him?'

'Are you kidding?'

'Suit yourself.'

'Oh, bollocks.' He sighed, then said, 'Smiley, you know Smiley?'

'Smiley? The Smiley married to Jill what's her name, the model?'

'The same.'

'Jesus. Villain, yeah, we all know that, but grass?'

'Surprised?'

'Yeah, surprised. She earns a fortune. What the fuck's he mouthing off for? He doesn't seem the type.'

'That's Jack shit. There never was a type.'

'Oh yes there was. Even the low-life think they're the lowest. They've got less standing than the nonces.'

Butler sighed. 'We wouldn't get very far without them.'

'That's true.' Cole glanced at his watch then flipped on his mobile. 'We'll give him another ten. That'll make him forty-five minutes late. That'll make it one – closing time.'

Butler nodded. Cole was right. Conners wasn't going to show. They were wasting their time. Butler's whisper from Smiley came in just before ten. Conners was going to have a go at the small post office counter at the back of the Paki shop. Conners always worked alone, so Detective Superintendent Baxter reckoned the two of them along with a couple of armed response units hiding round the corner and cars ready to seal off each end of the road was enough. They only used more than five cars when they tackled a lone female suspected of being an illegal immigrant.

Cole said into the mobile, 'D'you hear that?'

The voice of one of the armed kozzers crackled, 'Got you, Rick. Ten minutes. Someone should have a nasty little word in the ear of whoever gave you this crap. I could be parked up over the park. It's lunch-time, the girls are coming out of the offices. We could be watching them strip off in the sun.'

'Consider it done,' Cole said, and flicked off.

Butler pulled a face and inhaled deeply. There was something on his mind. Eventually, he said heavily, 'I think Janet's having an affair.' He gave Cole a quick sideways glance.

8

'You're joking. Janet? Never. I don't believe it. Not unless she's changed a lot since I last saw her. Christ, she's right out of the bottom drawer. Even the thought of it would iron out the creases in one of her pleated skirts. She's a Welwyn Garden City woman. They don't have affairs up there. They're too busy with the charity shops.'

'I'm being serious. I think she is.'

'Go on, tell me.'

'Little things. I know we've been going through a rough patch, but she's taking more care over her appearance. Puts perfume on even when we're staying in. She's distant, not really there.' He turned to Cole and pulled a face. 'You know about these things. You went through it. What were the signs?'

'I didn't get any. That's why it came as such a shock. My sign was a suitcase in the hall and a car waiting for her outside.' That wasn't absolutely true. With hindsight, there'd been a few indications, but nothing much.

'Well, I'm getting signs.'

'Let me get this straight, Sam. Because your wife's started to use perfume and her mind's on other things, she's having an affair?'

He struggled, then, 'Yeah.'

'You don't think it's something else, like, for instance, she's trying to get your attention?'

He frowned. 'But she's the one who's distant. It's her attention that lapses. And she sings.'

'She sings?'

'Yeah, bloody Carpenters, Beautiful bleeding South. She actually listens to the words and sings along. It's an affair.'

'Because your wife sings she's having an affair? Is that reasonable? I mean, if she was coming in at one in the morning with her blouse on back to front, or if there were love bites on her arse that you didn't put there, then yes. But singing? Carpenters for Christ's sake. Give me a break.'

'I haven't seen her naked in two months.'

'Oh, well, that is a sign.'

'You think so?'

9

'No. Maybe not. She's just trying to kid you that she's got love bites on her arse. To make you jealous.'

Butler grunted and smiled again. Twice inside an hour. Not bad. Cole should be a counsellor.

The ten minutes were up. The mobile stuttered.

'Yeah?' Cole answered.

'That's ten. Is he closed?'

'Yeah,' he replied, as he watched the sharp-faced, scrawny owner of the shop throwing the bolts on his door.

'We're off, then. Bollocks.'

'Yeah, likewise.' He turned to Butler. 'That's it. Show's over.'

'It never started.' Butler grimaced. 'What now? Back to the fort?'

'You can face Baxter on your own. I've got things to do. You'd be better off looking up your gossip. Find out what the hell went wrong. At least then you'll have an answer to Baxter's question.'

Butler shook his head and picked at his nose with thumb and finger. 'Maybe you're right. Drop me off at the Grove. I'll find Smiley, then make my own way back.'

'Give him a hard time,' Cole instructed. 'More than a nosebleed.'

Cole turned the key; the Rover purred. BAe had sold it to the Krauts and made a fortune and someone in the MoD had smiled as it all worked out. A few hundred yards on he dropped Butler off and watched him walk away. A slightly stooped figure with sagging shoulders. One of life's victims. A loser. He'd come into the job to get a house and a bit of security. But free housing was in the past now. The Tories had scrapped the allowances for new recruits. A constable he knew was left with just over forty quid a week after shelling out for his bills. That was a recipe for moonlighting or corruption. But did he say Sam was a victim? Well, he had also got lucky. His parents died and left him set up. He didn't need a police house any more. He didn't even need the odd backhander to make ends meet.

*　　*　　*

10

Cole arrived back at the station at six and walked into a celebration. It would have taken place in the canteen but the place was being disinfected after an outbreak of salmonella had put most of the night duty in bed.

The air in the operation room was smoky and stale. A NO SMOKING sign wavered in the blue-grey haze. Plastic cups from a drinks machine covered every available surface; most of them were being used as ashtrays. Some of the ash had spilt on to paperwork that lay in untidy heaps on the single pedestal desks and the four-drawer grey steel filing-cabinets. There were a dozen people in the room, half of them uniformed, more than half of them smoking. Everyone's attention was tuned into the voice of Detective Superintendent Baxter and the sad figure of the man who stood next to him, DI Russell Ward. After thirty-five years, twenty of them in CID, he was retiring. His smile was fixed and false. He wasn't looking forward to enforced idleness.

Everyone liked Ward. Even the chief superintendent had come downstairs for this one. He stood next to his deputy, his spotless hands clasped in front of him, his eyes on the squares of floor carpet, flicking from one cigarette burn to another as though joining the dots to form a picture. Like the others, he waited for Baxter to finish his history of Ward's achievements. For a while, it seemed that every case he'd ever worked was going to get a mention.

Some more wooden tops, the beat uniforms, piled into the room, perhaps smelling the booze that would soon be handed round in paper cups. They could smell booze faster than a sniffer dog could find another dog on heat. They stood behind the chief, perhaps at his invitation. But Cole doubted it; the chief wasn't known for his sensitivity. In fact, he was about the most dispassionate man he'd ever met; dispassionate and rather unpleasant, characteristics that seemed to be fundamental requirements for senior policemen.

He glanced across at Detective Constable Hazel McLintock. Apart from one or two of the women police officers who hadn't become muscle-bound by working out, she was the only thing worth looking at. She was a new face. She'd done her training at

11

Shotley, near Ipswich, and got a transfer from Suffolk. She was very screwable, wide hips, good legs, but she didn't like Cole. That much was obvious from the casual glance that arrowed his way. It was tipped with paraquat. Cole guessed that she'd been listening to the others.

A big white-faced clock on the wall ticked loudly. It had been a long day. Sitting in the car for two hours listening to Butler had made it longer.

Baxter was finally winding up. 'So it gives me great pleasure, Russell, to present you with this token of our appreciation. Perhaps in the years to come you'll find it in the bottom of a cupboard, dust it off, and then remember some of the good times we shared together . . .'

Cole caught the policewoman's eye again. Her look had been quizzical, as though weighing him up. Now she looked away. Her lips tightened fractionally.

The thick frame of the station officer appeared at the door. On television cop shows he would have been called the desk sergeant. For the real kozzers that was a constant source of amusement. Or irritation. Where did they dig up their advisers, for Christ's sake?

A tear threatened in Ward's eye as he held up his canteen of glinting cutlery. 'Thanks, everybody,' he started and was immediately cut short by a sudden burst of applause. Baxter had gone on too long. They weren't going to let Russell Ward eat into any more drinking time. The smoke eddied as hands smacked the air. Even the chief's stern features broke into a smile as he reached to shake Russell Ward's outstretched hand.

Cole remained impassive, not joining the party, an outsider. He guessed there were only two people in the room even aware that he was there. Sam Butler was trying to catch his attention. DC Hazel McLintock gave him another quick, curious glance. The sort that said the Yorkshire Ripper had more of a chance of putting space between her knees. No doubt she was wondering about his dark secret and why he had transferred from the Yard. She probably concluded that it had to be above board, that the chief, for all his faults, wouldn't countenance anything less than that.

12

Sam Butler caught up with him in the corridor.

'Did you find your snout?'

Butler shot him a stony look. 'Smiley's in the casualty unit at Hilltop. He's very poorly.'

'Go on?'

'Assault. He reckons it was a mugging. Since when do muggers kneecap a victim? He's been well and truly seen to. He could only see me out of one eye. His other had been closed with what the hospital thinks is oven cleaner.'

'Oven cleaner?'

'Needless to say, he hasn't got a clue who attacked him.'

'Sounds like you'll be needing another mouthpiece.'

'Tell me about it.'

'You think it was Conners?'

Butler shook his head. 'No, Conners doesn't police this manor.' He glanced up and said confidently, 'It was Mason. I'm sure of it.'

Keith Mason was an old-fashioned gangster with powerful friends; a traditionalist, he believed in respect through fear and was into just about everything – loan-sharking, illegal gambling, racketeering, prostitution, illegal immigration, VAT evasion, credit-card fraud, drugs, money-laundering – but proving it was something else again. Conners worked on his manor. Almost certainly he divvied up on blag returns.

'You going to see him?'

'What's the point? He'll have an alibi as tight as the chief's wallet. Anyway, Smiley won't press charges.'

Cole nodded. Butler was right. Mason was too slippery to be caught out that easily.

'You still think the whisper came from here?'

'Certain of it,' Butler said.

Cole watched him walk off down the corridor, heavy feet slapping at the linoleum. He shook his head and allowed himself a resigned smile. It was barely noticeable, more in the eyes than on the lips, but it was there.

Treacherous old thing, life. You couldn't count on it at all. Just like a meal in a fast-food restaurant.

*　　*　　*

The sun that had made life uncomfortable as the police watched the Paki shop had moved further west and angled in through the windscreen of another car to catch the short blond hair of the man behind the wheel. It drenched his pale features and washed them of colour. It picked up a few specks of dust on his police uniform. The radio stuttered with police messages. There was an accident on the High Road causing a tailback. He listened to the messages but remained impassive. His attention was focused on an old woman across the road. She used a walking-stick and held a scoop and was pulled along by a small wiry black-and-white dog.

He checked his watch. It had just turned three thirty. The woman had turned the corner toward Barnwall School. In a few more minutes the road would be filled with the flight of shell-shocked teachers making their move before they were blocked by the steady exodus of the kids.

He took a few deep breaths, trying to calm himself, and wiped the sweat from his hands on his uniform trousers.

Then he saw her.

She was first out, as was customary, rushing home to get her homework done so that she could go out again.

He'd been passing her all week. On occasion he'd stopped to chat, told her that he was keeping an eye open. They'd had reports of a flasher in Lovers' Wood. She'd thought that was funny. His willingness to tell her such things impressed her. 'Don't go spreading it around though,' he'd said. 'That's confidential. Wouldn't want to cause a panic.'

He waited until she was close, then called through the open passenger window, 'Jane.'

She moved towards him, swinging her bag, a smile of recognition spreading over her scrubbed features.

'You look like you're in a hurry to get home. Climb in, I'm going your way. I'll drop you off.'

The radio chattered again. A woman's voice, 'OK, Mike, I'm on to that.'

Jane West climbed in, easy and confident. 'You're sure it's no trouble?'

'No trouble,' he reassured. 'Seatbelt.'

14

She settled back in the passenger seat. Now that she was beside him she seemed smaller, not worried exactly, as she wondered whether she was doing the right thing, but fragile. He noticed her slender hands gripped together on her lap as she bunched her school skirt, the ridge of knuckles. The material rode up over her bony knees. Her legs were covered in tiny fair hairs. He wondered what it would feel like, rubbing his hands up, beneath the pleated skirt, and felt himself stir.

'Seatbelt,' he repeated.

After a while she spoke. 'This isn't the way.' Her voice was fractured, caught in her throat. Concern narrowed her eyes. 'I live the other way.'

15

Chapter 2

DI Rick Cole motored across to the outskirts, to a small two-bedroom semi, garden front and rear, attached garage, situated halfway along a quiet avenue of identical buildings. A street lamp flooded the front of the house with orange light and turned the garden into something strangely vulcanic. The council had put up the light last year. It hadn't been necessary – someone was having his pocket lined. He locked the car and walked to the front door, noticing again that the grass needed cutting. Life was a bitch. A FOR SALE notice with a black horse on it left an oblong shadow on the lawn. As his key slid into the Yale it reminded him of another time.

Six months earlier Jenny had broken the news. He'd arrived home late from another 2–12, and found her sitting in the bay-window. The curtains were open and she was flooded with the orange light from the new street lamp.

'I'm leaving you,' she had said.

It was typical of her; no preamble, straight to the point, go for the jugular. She hadn't even looked round. She just heard his glass tinkle on the sideboard. Her eyes, slightly hooded and tired, still focused on the front garden. She sat with her legs drawn up under her chin and her arms wrapped around them. She wore a navy pinstripe trouser-suit, ready to go out.

'I thought about a note,' she went on. 'But that wouldn't do, would it? Not after eight years. I'm not running away, I'm retreating in an orderly fashion, undefeated. I'll regroup, but not here. Not with you.'

As he poured a long scotch he noticed her cases, two of them side by side next to the hatch, locked and strapped. There was something very final about them, about the planning that had got them there.

There had been signs, but it had nevertheless come as a bombshell. Perhaps he had been inattentive, thinking that things were ticking over. Since his move from the Yard, ever since the inquiry that had created the space between them, they had made love just a couple of times, both disastrous. She had even suggested he see his counsellor again. He put it down to his new shift patterns and the tension the move had created. He hadn't really been aware that her nights out with friends had increased, that she'd become increasingly irritable and was often strangely abstracted, that the sharing part had slowly disappeared.

Looking back, part of it was down to the move from the Yard, but really it had been going wrong before that. It was his job. The move hadn't made much of a difference to that. Different faces, that was all. The job. The thing you married. But the catalyst, he discovered a week later, was a certain USAFE lieutenant from the 513th Airborne Command based at Mildenhall. For some months, the lieutenant had been attached to Whitehall, a coordinator or something, and that was when Jenny met him, just around the corner from her branch office. But now he was back in Mildenhall; they had to plan ahead to get together, and he was waving a front-door key in Jenny's face. It wounded Cole. Somehow, if no one else had been involved, it would have been an easier pill. He thought about going after them, knocking four kinds of shit out of them for the feel-good factor, but he had got himself together just in time. It didn't matter. His pride would eventually get over it.

The marriage was eight years old, no children, just an abortion because they didn't want them yet, and the house to show for it, so it could all be civilised, painless and quite simple. She paid him two grand because of the negative equity and signed the house over to him. There was nothing friendly about it. Only anger, and, after a while, sadness.

'I hate this,' she had said. 'I hate it. I go to bed alone, I sleep alone, I wake up alone. It's not a marriage. You haven't touched me for months. What's happened to us? Even on your days off you don't come near me. I got used to your anti-social hours, the quick changeover and the constant fear. Years ago. We learned to live with it. Christ! It becomes a way of life. I stood by you at the Yard, even though I knew you were making a mistake. But since then you've changed. You've lost something. When we were first married there was a confidence about you. I loved that. But now, even when you're here, you're somewhere else, on some stupid job. A policeman's wife! I was warned. Weren't we all? But it's not just that. Police work reaches into every corner of our lives. There is interference in almost everything we do. Coppers aren't normal, are they? I don't know why we expect them to be.'

She stood up and folded her coat neatly over her arm. At the door she hesitated. Her step faltered. The cases pulled on her arms.

'I never minded you being a policeman,' she said, lamely. 'I just didn't want the house turned into the police station. Understand?' She paused, waiting for a response. When it didn't come, she nodded to herself, resigned, and added reluctantly, 'I'll ring you.'

He swallowed a large measure and looked across at her. The Teacher's burned a hole in his chest. He smiled tightly, and said quietly, 'Don't bother.'

Later he was to regret saying that, but at the time it sounded right. He turned back to the bottle. Before he had refilled his glass the front door had slammed shut and somewhere on the road a car revved.

He shook the memories away, closed the door behind him and flipped on the hall light. There were two letters, one from his father and a gas bill. He dropped them, unopened, on a small black lacquered telephone table. In the living-room he drew the curtains and poured a drink. The room seemed empty, not lived in. There was a layer of dust on the TV screen and on the Toshiba music stack. For a moment he wished he'd gone to the White Horse. In there his colleagues would still be laughing, telling blue jokes and flirting outrageously. He flicked on the television for some sound, any sound.

Coppers aren't normal, she had said.

They eat it, sleep it, breathe it. If they could fuck it they'd do that too. They see things no one should see, they hear things no one should hear. Their day is spent knee-deep in filth and corruption and hatred and violence with perverts and molesters and rapists and murderers – and they take the filth home. It invades their homes, their lives, the innocent parts of their lives. And it invades those around them. It makes everything dirty and

18

suspicious. Everything is taken seriously. There is no such thing as a relaxed discussion.

He opened the letter from his father. Everything was fine. His mother was well. The weather in Mablethorpe was good. Were they going up there for Christmas? Did he know the duty situation yet?

His parents didn't know. One month had grown into another and then six and he still hadn't got round to telling them. Maybe next week. He would have to tell them before winter set in, for that was when the annual visits took place. Once the garden had died down and didn't need its daily watering.

He reloaded his glass and carried it into the shower. The water fizzed at him, stabbing at the grime on his face. He turned up the temperature until it was almost unbearable, enjoying the pain. The steam felt heavy in his chest.

. . . and there's a smug look about you all, especially the younger ones, especially the plain-clothes. You're proud of it, the power, strutting like peacocks. There's a smell about you all, a deep, dark secret. You've caught the evil, it's contagious. You're dangerous, all of you. That's why you don't have any friends outside the force. That's why you can't communicate with real people. It can't be any other way . . .

He cleared a patch of mirror. Water streamed down from his short black hair. Stubble darkened his chin. Shadows spread out like bruises beneath his eyes. Blue eyes that looked back at him, mocking, wild now as the booze took hold. He was thirty-six. He looked older. He watched himself as he emptied his glass and felt the alcohol burn away some more tension.

'There's a smell about you,' he said aloud, and smiled. 'A deep dark secret.' The smile spread until it pulled his lips apart. Suddenly he felt comfortable, remarkably confident and at ease. For a moment the image of Hazel McLintock ghosted back. He tried to concentrate on it. Bending her over and lifting her skirt.

The telephone rang in the hall, blanking the thought. It held that curious urgent tone of the unexpected night-time call.

He left a trail of footprints on the green landing carpet and

19

down the stairs. Water droplets zig-zagged down his hairy chest and stomach, sparkling in the cheerless hall light. His penis shrank, caught in the cooler air that curled in from the bottom of the front door. He needed a draught excluder. Something else that needed doing. For a moment he'd forgotten the house was up for sale. He'd forgotten that Jenny had left.

'Yep?' he said into the telephone.

'Where's your bleeper?'

He recognised the station officer's lazy low drawl. It sounded almost friendly. Perhaps that was unfair. Sergeant Mike Collier had always been amiable.

'It's on the sideboard. I was in the shower. And it's where's your bleeper, Guv. Remember? What's happening?'

'A missing girl. You'll love it.' He laughed, then added seriously, 'Maybe not. We're a bit short on the ground. Half the shift have still got the shits and most of the others went to the party and are now pissed out of their tiny brains. And Rick, you better pack your insect repellent.'

'Let me guess. Richmond Park Estate? Who's the wooden top?'

'John Knight.'

'Is Baxter aware?'

'No. Inspector Knight got hold of DS Butler. It was Sam's request that you be bleeped.'

Cole sighed. 'He would, wouldn't he? How long has she been missing?'

'Over eight hours.'

'Age?'

'Twelve.'

Cole thought about it. Eight hours wasn't long, not for a twelve-year-old. She'd probably gone off with a friend, broken open a booze cabinet, fallen asleep.

'Right then, give me an address.'

'Churchill Place. Number twenty-nine.'

'Low-life. Bet you there's three kids, two killer dogs, video, Sky dish, income support and *Sun* newspapers piled in the hall.'

'Tory voters, you mean?'

20

'Something like that. Tell John I'm on my way. And get Sam to meet me at the nick, will you?'

'Will do. Catch you later.' Collier rang off.

Cole finished his drink and, still naked, enjoying the freedom and brush of his bollocks, poured himself another.

Chapter 3

In most towns and cities it was not unusual for children to go missing. They were almost always found within fifteen minutes or so, more often than not before the police reached the scene.

Just after eight, as Russell Ward's retirement party got serious by moving to the White Horse, Sheerham's printer was woken by Command control at Scotland Yard.

SER NO. 814. 2035, CLASS 80, 91.

MESSAGE – We have a missing 12 yr old female – Jane Karen West, who failed to return home from school. Mother visited school and possible friends – no trace. Mother back home at 29 Churchill Place, Richmond Park.

Informant – mother, Mrs Lee West, using neighbour's phone 324151.

At Sheerham police station the duty officer tapped in his response.

Action – at 2043 by 4211. Resource sent CB1.

CB1 was Charlie Bravo One, an Astra hatchback panda, driven by PC 7231 Wendy Booth. So far it had been a quiet evening, but it hadn't really started yet. Friday nights got going after nine, then became one of the busiest nights of the week. PC Booth was on the last shift of her long week, responding to calls from divisional, patrolling the outlying areas of the town, waiting to catch the early boozers, the tobacco-stained businessmen who went straight from the office to the pub. Wendy Booth was twenty-seven. She'd been in the force for eight years and on driving duties, which she preferred, for the last three. She loved catching the businessmen, especially the younger ones, the pompous bastards.

She was parked up in a lay-by when the message came through. Whenever it was a domestic, or there was a child involved, they wanted her as back-up. The interesting jobs went to the men. The information registered – missing girl at Richmond Park, please respond. The address sank in. Wendy pulled a face and said, 'Shit.'

Richmond Park was the roughest and poorest part of town, a sprawling, run-down council estate that needed levelling, preferably with the occupants still inside. It was all terraced rows and tower blocks, alleys and car-lined roads. Houses were neglected, the windows cracked and boarded. The tower blocks were a mugger's paradise, full of dangerous walkways. The lifts were invariably out of order, the paint was peeling and the walls covered in graffiti. Kids ran wild. Louts, next year's prison intake, huddled together, staring contemptuously, calling you a cunt and meaning it. The police were losing the war, and until someone recognised that poverty and desperation were the main causes, they would continue to do so. It was the one place in town where Wendy would have preferred a partner.

She tossed her cigarette from the window and reached to the glove compartment to check she had a set of missing person forms, then drove unhurriedly to the estate. It took her five minutes to reach Churchill Place, a row of terraced houses, and she parked outside number twenty-nine. The road depressed her. Narrow, grey, tiny front gardens, mostly turned over to concrete slab where old cars leaked rust and oil. Weeds that thrived on the sulphates grew through the cracks. A few kids played by a wreck. Otherwise, the place seemed quiet. Three overweight women, thighs threatening to explode through worn leggings, stood by the ugly red-painted door of twenty-nine. Wendy thought that their bulging bodies, slouching postures and lack of any dress sense were an insult to women everywhere.

She brushed cigarette ash from her uniform skirt, checked her face in the mirror, then pressed the Cyfas. The code 05 logged her arrival at the scene with divisional control. It was timed at 2052.

She picked up the forms, secured the car and approached the women. 'Mrs West?'

The woman holding the door slightly open nodded. The others stayed put.

'PC Booth, Sheerham. Has Jane turned up yet?' From the expressions, Wendy already knew the answer.

Mrs West shook her head. From the car, the women had seemed unconcerned. Closer, Wendy saw the worry, the fight against creeping panic.

'Is anyone else home?'

'No. Bill's still out searching.'

'Bill?'

'My husband.'

'Is he on foot?'

'In the car,' she said.

'Can we talk inside, Mrs West? I need to write down some details.' Wendy turned to the others and said, a little formally for their liking, 'Are you neighbours?'

They nodded together.

'Perhaps you'll come back in a few minutes?'

'Yeah, sure,' one of them answered coldly, and they stood back.

Wendy followed Mrs West into the house and closed the door. The hall was tiny. At the far end, beyond the stairs, was a small kitchen. A door on the right led to the lounge. Everything was clean and tidy. Not even a magazine out of place. Wendy was surprised. She could take some tips from Mrs West in the housekeeping department.

'Tea? Do you want some tea?'

'No, thanks. We better get these details down.'

Mrs West sat stiffly on the couch, her hands wringing in front of her ample waist. Wendy sat in the one armchair and spread the forms on a polished glass coffee table.

'Mrs West—' she began.

'Call me Lee.'

'OK, Lee. Is Jane your only child?'

'Yes.'

'What time was she due home?'

'School finishes at three thirty. She's never later than four.'

'Is that Barnwall School?'

'Yes.'

'What's that, about fifteen minutes' walk?'

'Yes, but you know, sometimes she dawdles with friends. But she's normally in by four at the latest.'

'You went down to the school? What time was that?'

'I've got a cleaning job I finish at three so I can be here when she gets back. Five, about five.'

'Who did you speak to at Barnwall?'

'The PE teacher was still there with five-a-side. He got the caretaker. We looked in her class and checked the toilets. He was going to check the rest and phone Mavis, my neighbour, if he found her. Our phone's out of order. Bill tried to put an extension upstairs, but he messed up the wires. We're waiting for the telephone people to—'

'The school caretaker?'

'Yes.'

'Do you know his name?'

'Dave somebody.'

'You came straight back here?'

'More or less. I checked the streets on the way. I had to make sure she hadn't come back. She hasn't got a key. Baldwin. That was it. Dave Baldwin.'

'And Bill, your husband, is driving around the estate?'

She nodded.

'How long has he been gone?'

Lee's bottom lip began to quiver. 'Ever since he came home from work.' Her eyes welled up. Her voice rose. 'I'm sorry, I'm sorry.'

'Come on,' Wendy said, in her best consoling voice, which really wasn't very good. 'I'm sure everything will be fine. You OK?'

A sniff, then a brave nod.

'What about Jane's friends?'

'There's a few, they go around together, all from her class. Jenny's on the estate, so's Rachael and Zoë. They haven't seen her. She left them at school. Sometimes they rush back to do their homework so they can get out again before tea.'

'You went to see them?'

'Before I went to the school I phoned Zoë and Jenny. Rachael's on the way so I called in there.'

'Has she ever been late before?'

'Once or twice. You know what kids are? But I've always managed to find her. At the playground or at Jenny's.'

'Is Jenny her best friend?'

'No, that's Rachael. But Jenny manages to talk her into things, if you know what I mean?'

'I know. Is there anywhere else she's likely to go? A relative, perhaps, even if it's in the next town?'

'No, no one. She's never been this late. Never more than six thirty. Not without me knowing. I just know something's happened.'

'Come on, let's fill in the form.'

'Oh, I forgot, Bill's checking the hospital, too.'

'That's always a good idea. Now, I need a full description and the other details again, just to make sure I haven't left anything out.'

Four hours. It wasn't long. Not when you're twelve years old and having fun. For parents it was a lifetime. For police, it was about the time it started to get serious. With eleven- and twelve-year-olds, depending on the family, four hours was about it. After that, things started to get more ominous by the hour.

It was 2135 when PC Wendy Booth sat in her car and sent in a detailed description. A light-blue F-registered Lada with rust patches on the wings pulled up behind her. A heavy-set middle-aged man got out and met Lee on the doorstep with a comforting but despairing hug. Wendy watched them as she finished her call, then climbed out of the car.

'Mr West?'

'That's right.' He had a deep cockney accent. His tie was loose at the collar, top button undone. Wendy noticed his creased black trousers were slightly turned over at the waist.

'No sign of Jane?'

He shook his head. Strands of hair that he used to cover his bald spot came undone. His eyes were bloodshot, filled with concern. His thick arm was around Lee's shoulders.

'I've got more people on the way here. We'll cover the whole estate. I know it's difficult, but it really is early days. Unless you can think of somewhere Jane might have gone, I think you'd be better off staying here with Lee. I'll be back soon. We'll keep you posted.'

He nodded silently then turned to lead his wife into the house. The neighbours were watching and speculating. Groups of teenagers were beginning to muster. The word had got out. The younger kids were pulled in off the street. Strangers were given the evil eye.

Police responses gained momentum. Beat officers arrived to search on foot, and more pandas moved in to comb the streets. Calls went out to the taxi and mini-cab firms and more importantly, to the bus and train stations. Local radio was contacted.

The divisional computer recorded the action as it was reported.

2151 by 4211 – 7231 checked out school with caretaker D Baldwin. No trace.
2151 by 4211 – 7269 checked Walkern Rd/Scouts' Hut/Mill End.
2152 by 4211 – 7231 checked along Colney Rd bordering Lovers' Wood. No trace. No trace at King George off-licence.
2152 by 4211 – 7231 joined by 6899 to cover Lovers' Wood.
2152 by 4211 – CB3 7111 checking bus depot.

At 2217, PC Wendy Booth pulled up outside number twenty-nine again. After checking the school and then Colney Road, she had been joined in the car by the skipper, Sergeant Mike Wilson. He was tall, slim, forty years old. All boots, bollocks, and baggy uniform, was how Wendy described him to her female colleagues. His face was friendly, big nose, soft eyes, easy smile.

Bill West opened the front door before they reached the step. His wife stood watching from the lounge. There was a horrible look of anticipation on her face. Wendy smiled quickly, reassuringly, and heard the tiny murmured sigh of relief.

'There's no news yet,' she said. 'This is Sergeant Wilson.'

'Hello, Mr West. It's a worrying business all round. We've got an army of people looking for her.'

27

West held open the door. 'Are you coming in?'

'Yes, yes. Thank you.'

The officers followed West into the hall. Sergeant Wilson went on, 'The thing is, there's a standard procedure when children go missing. We've got to have a look in the house.'

West nodded glumly.

'And the garden, I'm afraid,' the skipper went on, reassuringly. 'Just to satisfy ourselves that she's not hiding somewhere. I'm sure she isn't. You will have looked already. But we have to go through the motions. You can imagine the red faces if she's found, say, in the shed?'

'I understand,' West said.

Wendy wondered if he did. The fact was, most disappearances turned out to be domestic matters. Most crimes against children were committed in their own homes.

'While we're having a look around,' Sergeant Wilson said, 'I wonder whether you have a recent photograph of Jane? Could you dig one out?'

'Tea?' Lee West blurted. 'Would you like some tea?' There was something in her voice, a pleading quality, as though she needed something to do.

'That would be very nice,' Wilson said, with genuine gratitude and even more wisdom. 'The stuff they serve at the station, well, you wouldn't call it tea. With and with for me. What about you, Wendy?'

Wendy smiled. 'Milk, no sugar, thank you.'

Lee gave them a quick little smile and shuffled into the kitchen. 'I'll put the kettle on, then find a photo.'

'What do you do for a living, Mr West?' Wilson asked, casually.

'I'm in the stores, over at Dixons. Nowadays beggars can't be choosers.' West indicated the stairs. 'Look, help yourselves, will you? Her room's the first on the right. There's a chair up there I use to get to the attic. If that won't do you, I'll get the steps from the shed.'

'Don't worry about the attic,' Sergeant Wilson said. He left West nodding reflectively and climbed the stairs behind Wendy.

'He's not daft,' Wendy murmured, as they entered Jane's bedroom.

It was small, and spotless like the rest of the house. Posters of Liverpool FC and the latest pop groups were blue-tacked to the walls. It was a typical child's bedroom, if a little neater than most: a single bed, matching quilt and curtains, dolls and a teddy sitting on the pillow, clothes hanging neatly in a white MFI wardrobe, others folded in a matching chest of drawers. The desk and chair were probably too small for Jane, but she still used them. School books, pens and so forth were piled on the top. On the chest was a mirror, comb, brush, some cheap perfume and hairspray, and a selection of ribbons. In another drawer they found a packet of Sainsbury's sanitary towels.

'How old is she?' Wilson asked.

'She was twelve last month. You don't have daughters, Skipper?'

'Two boys.'

'Well, for your information, menstruation can start from age eight or nine. Although eleven or twelve is about average. I didn't start till I was thirteen.'

'Right,' he said, and turned away. 'Right.'

Wendy saw his red ears and smiled at his discomfort.

He changed the subject. 'I didn't notice any photographs of Jane, did you?'

She shook her head.

'There's usually a school photo or something on the sideboard. We've got half a dozen. Dust traps.'

'There's not much dust in this house, Skipper. Maybe Lee's avoiding dust collectors.'

Five minutes later, they sat in the lounge holding cups of tea, trying not to let them rattle on the awkward saucers. They were more used to mugs.

'What now?' Bill West asked, stonily.

'I'd like to check the boot of your car. And that's it really.' Sergeant Wilson gazed down at the school photograph Lee had put on the coffee table. 'When was this taken?'

Mrs West was momentarily flustered. 'In May, or, yes it was, May. I remember.'

Bill West said, 'Well, when you've finished with the car I'm going out again. I can't stand sitting here waiting.'

Sergeant Wilson nodded. He understood how necessary it was to be doing something. He glanced across at Lee, then back to her husband.

'PC Booth, Wendy, is going to hang on here for a while, if that's all right with you. I'm going to get this photograph copied and circulated. I think it's a matter of waiting now. We'll hear something soon.'

Lee West shook her head and lifted her hands to her face. Suddenly she had lost it, and she wept uncontrollably. Her husband sat on the fat chair-arm and put his hand on her shoulder. When she looked up her eyes were red and wet and her quick breaths were punctuated by short squeaky sounds of unbearable anguish. 'Please tell me she'll be all right. Tell me. Tell me. Oh God, please tell me.'

Chapter 4

Sergeant Mike Wilson had a nasty feeling about this one. It was true that it was early days and that Jane West would probably turn up at a friend's house, unharmed and very apologetic, but there was a creeping feeling in his gut that things were not right. He suspected his sense of unease came from the parents, Bill and Lee West. They were sensible and responsible and, from what he had seen, they had brought their daughter up to be responsible, too. Experience told him that Jane wasn't the sort to go off on some impulsive adventure.

He used the car radio to pass on his misgivings to Inspector John Knight.

'All right, Skipper,' John Knight said from the stale, smoky atmosphere of the ops room. 'I'll bring in CID.'

By midnight, a specialist search team from OSD – Operational Support Division – had turned out and, using Dragon lamps, were combing Lovers' Wood. The force helicopter, sanctioned by an irate and sleepy Chief Constable from his warm bed, went up to further illuminate the area. Dozens of roads and other likely locations had already been checked by officers on foot or the pandas.

One report came in about a car and a man acting suspiciously near the wood: a white Maxi and a white man wearing blue overalls. The log recorded him as the first SIM – strange in manner.

Apart from continuing the search, there wasn't much more to be done until first light. Then it would be public address systems and appeals to passers-by, and the start of the house-to-house inquiries. First, though, it was necessary to interview the parents again and establish beyond any doubt that there were no problem areas in the family, that Jane's disappearance was not another domestic – an argument, a runaway, or worse. This interview was down to CID.

Rick Cole arrived back at the station in the early hours of Saturday morning. The summer dawn was still two hours away and the moisture in the grass sparkled, caught by the stark street lighting. Cobweb hammocks covered the bushes and small conifers around the almost deserted car-park. He went in through the brightly lit doors of the front entrance. As he entered, Mike Collier peered through the door at the back of the empty reception.

'No Fred West jokes, please.'

'Right you are. Morning, Rick.'

'Morning, Mike. Is it? I'm losing track of time. What's happening?'

The station officer shook a heavy head. 'One SIM, nothing else. Sam's in the ops room with John Knight.' He added the surname because there were three Johns in uniform.

'Who else have I got in?'

'DC McLintock.'

Cole grunted as he walked past and noticed the sergeant's wry smile.

In the ops room the uniformed inspector brought him up to date. It seemed that he had covered everything but now, sharing Sergeant Mike Wilson's concern, he was passing it over to CID. A bit on the early side, perhaps, but standard procedure.

After the briefing, Cole turned to Butler, who was perched on his desk. 'Get over to the parents, Sam. Count the dust mites: family, friends, the whole ball game. Take Hazel McLintock with you. Where is she?'

'Canteen, Guv.'

'They've finished fumigating then?' He flashed a rueful smile then, 'When you've finished, leave her there for an hour and let her get a feel for the place.'

Sam Butler glanced at his watch, then nodded gloomily. Cole saw his look and knew exactly what was going on in the sergeant's mind. He wanted to be at home, keeping an eye on the shadowy figure dipping into his wife.

Once Butler had gone, Rick Cole moved into his office, lit a cigarette and left the pack within reach on his desk, then lifted the phone. For the next twenty minutes he would do the rounds, calling in all the available detectives from the stations within the division, leaving just a bare minimum as cover for each location. When that was done, armed with coffee from the machine in the corridor, he began a manual log, a prelim to a computerised HOLMES that would take over if it became a major incident.

When that was done, he lit another cigarette, his sixth in the last hour, and picked up the photograph, the eight-by-six school photograph of Jane Karen West. Small-boned, she looked more like a nine-year-old. The youngster looked out sheepishly from beneath a dark fringe. There was a half-smile on her lips, a slight apprehension in her brown eyes. She was neatly turned out, hair brushed and shining, white shirt crisp and spotless. An attractive girl, Cole thought, in an impish, tomboy sort of way.

DS Sam Butler found Hazel McLintock in the canteen. She followed him down to the car and climbed in the passenger seat of his midnight-blue Escort. Her skirt rose tantalisingly over her black-clad knees until she brushed it down. Butler noticed, but pretended he hadn't. As he started the car, he said lamely, 'How do you get on with Ricky Cole?'

'That's a funny question, Skip.' There was a smoker's huskiness to her voice that he found endearing.

'I get the feeling that you don't like him.'

'I've no complaints,' she said defensively. 'I haven't had much to do with him.'

'That's a bit formal, isn't it?'

'He's got a heavy reputation. I heard you were acting up when he came. You must have been disappointed.'

The detective sergeant smiled evasively. 'He's a good copper.'

'Maybe. But if you must know, I think he lives on the edge, and that's a dangerous place to be.'

'Hot-blooded? Cole?'

'I know it doesn't seem to fit, not at first glance, but he's always so unemotional – unnaturally so. Last night, at the station, everyone else was giving it some, showing DI Ward a proper send off – including me, and I've only known him for a few weeks – but not Cole. Christ, even the chief came down for a drink!' She paused for the right words then went on, 'I get the feeling that one day . . .'

'Go on?'

'One day he'll explode. It's just a feeling. I'm probably well out of order. But I'd categorise him "store in a *cole* place and away from naked flame".'

Butler gave a contemptuous snort.

'Then there's the gossip.'

'You're referring to the Yard? Few people know what went on down there, except for the people involved, and most of them won't be doing any mouthing off for their own safety. No one knows. Understand? Any feedback you get up here is mostly bollocks. It was your average case, but it happened to involve a Masonic Lodge and a major cover-up. He didn't need it. He played by the rules, not the unwritten ones, and got shat upon from a great height.'

'It sounds like you're defending him. I know you're friends.'

'Not at all. And we're not friends. We're colleagues. But I do happen to admire him. I'm putting the record straight, that's all.'

'He grassed a lot of officers. Where does that leave loyalty?'

'Tell me, Hazel, tell me straight. Would you stand back and watch fellow officers break the law? I'm not talking about speeding or smoking a little grass or even moonlighting. I'm talking major league. Corruption at a high level.'

She narrowed her eyes. 'I don't know.'

'Then you shouldn't be in the job. But I don't believe you. You'd report it. The same as I would. The same as Rick Cole did. And you'd live with the consequences. The public image of us closing ranks no matter what had better be bollocks. We'll leave that to the medical establishment and the church.'

She nodded. Embarrassment burned her cheeks.

'I'll tell you something else. Even he's not sure that he made the right decision any more. And that's down to the way he's been treated by people like us. I can see him jacking it in and walking away. To lose a cop like Cole would be bloody criminal.'

DC McLintock thought about it as they drove on. What

Butler had said made sense but it didn't make her like the DI any more. There was something about him, an aloofness, an irritating arrogance, that set him aside.

The road curved west, towards the estate.

DS Butler and DC McLintock met Sergeant Mike Wilson by his car outside number twenty-nine.

'Hello, Skippy,' McLintock said.

'Don't call me Skippy, Hazel. Sarge, Skipper, Mike, even bastard if we're on first name terms. But not Skippy. It undermines my authority.' They shared a weary middle-of-the-night laugh. It was an ongoing joke. Sergeant Wilson turned to Butler and went on, 'Let me go in first. I'll prepare the ground for you. OK?'

Butler nodded and glanced at DC McLintock at his side. As she watched the skipper move into the house she looked pale and drawn. Given normal circumstance they were both reaching the end of their shifts. Now they would see the first fingers of dawn, perhaps even the sun itself.

Sergeant Wilson found the others in the lounge. He explained to Mr and Mrs West that CID had taken over and would like to go over the details again.

'Tea,' said Lee West, struggling to her feet. 'I bet they'd like some tea.' Before he could object she was on her way to the kitchen.

He turned to PC Wendy Booth who sat, dark-eyed, in the armchair, and flicked his head towards the door. She stood up and straightened her skirt.

'OK,' the skipper said to Butler as they exchanged places, 'it's all yours. She's putting the kettle on.'

Sergeant Wilson opened the passenger door of the panda and stood aside as Wendy approached. 'Come on, girl. I'll drive. It's time to go home. You should have knocked off hours ago. Me too. CID can have it now. We've done our bit.'

For DI Rick Cole the incident made a change from the crashing routine of general police work, diary updates, work rosters, vehicle logs and so on. The school photograph of the fresh-faced youngster brought back memories. As he sat at his desk he felt a twinge of regret as the past came back in waves. Memories sweeping past and being replaced by others in a never-ending sequence. It was down to tiredness. His mind still wanted to dream.

A chief super had stood at the window, looking out from the Yard. His voice had been flat. 'Some of these men have spent a lifetime in the job, but that's not the point. We can't afford a scandal of this proportion, and that comes from the top. Our credibility is already suffering. Even now, we're hovering just below child molesters and just above Tory politicians. It's got to be sorted internally, that's the official line. No argument. Apart from that, think of all the low-life they've put away that will be screaming corruption – unsafe convictions.' He shook his head sadly, but it wasn't convincing.

'So what happens, then?'

'They retire. That's the top and bottom of it. None of us like it. But for the sake of the job—'

'I don't believe this.'

'You're right, Rick. There is no justice. But at the end of the day, we've got to do what's best for the job. They all know they've been collared, and we'll go out of our way to make sure they're pretty bloody uncomfortable. We'll drop a few hints here and there, let a few wives and families know why they've taken early retirement. They'll be no easy jobs waiting in civvy street. It'll be three pound an hour in security. We'll make sure of that. Let's just call it our own special brand of justice, shall we? It's not the kind we want, it's not at all ideal, but it's the only kind we've got.'

The Ice-cream Man had started it. In a curious sense, the horror of that had pitched Cole against the system, had led him to take on his colleagues.

One of the kozzers at his side used the double-handed ram. The wood splintered, the door crashed open.

They found her in the dark, tied up, crusts of dried blood on her skinny legs and fresh blood running down her thighs. She was cowering on a filthy mattress, naked, shivering, terrified.

'I want Mummy. I want Mummy.'

The words still haunted him.

Chapter 5

Saturday morning crept slowly through the windows of number twenty-nine and threw its bleak murky light onto the remnants of the despairing vigil. Teacups, sandwich plates and ashtrays full to overflowing littered the front room. Lee West had tried to sleep but hadn't, had instead sobbed into the darkness, dying. Now she was up, busying herself out of necessity, her stinging eyes trying to conceal the pain of her twisted gut and the panic and turmoil of her thoughts. Bill had been up all night. The police had been in and out.

While the others went to work, DS Sam Butler and DC Hazel McLintock called it a day and went home to bed.

Armed with the details given by DI Rick Cole at 0800, a dozen detectives who had come from various stations in the division joined their uniformed colleagues and mounted a house-to-house. OSD moved from Lovers' Wood into nearby fields. The footpaths and roadsides between Barnwall School and the estate had been checked during the night, but now, given the light, they were searched again. Vans fitted with public address systems covered the roads of the estate, appealing for information. Officers set up at the school entrance, waiting to interview every parent, child and teacher who might wander by. With the exception of the gym, the school was closed for the weekend, but the head teacher and some of her senior staff had turned up on the off chance to see if they could help. They opened the canteen and brewed up for the officers who stood in a small group by the school gates.

There was still time. You had to keep reminding yourself that in the UK 43,000 children ran away from home every year and most of those returned within a day or so. There was still time, but not much. They were approaching the point when the last slim hope they had of good news would pass. Had Jane stayed with a friend overnight, she would arrive home during the next hour or so, bewildered at all the fuss.

The SIM, the man in the Maxi, responded to the appeals

and called in at the police station on his way to work at 0820. Saturday morning overtime earned him time and a half and he was keen to get on. He was a fitter at Arlington Metals and had climbed out of his car for a leak by Lovers' Wood. He hadn't seen anything suspicious, only an old lady walking her dog, lead in one hand, scoop in the other. She was the woman who had told the police about him in the first place. His drive from the factory to his home took about fifteen minutes. He'd clocked out normal time and fifteen minutes later arrived home to his wife and children in time for the six o'clock news. He was logged as the first TIE of the inquiry – traced, interviewed and eliminated.

Alleged sightings began to come in – two or three in Hertfordshire, one as far afield as South Wales, dozens locally. Each was logged, assessed, and placed in order of merit.

Just after nine, Assistant Chief Superintendent Bob Deighton wandered through the incident room and into Cole's office. He was a tall, thin man, working out his time in cost-effective management.

'Do you need any support, Rick?'

'No, sir. Everything's in hand. I'll give it half an hour then call in the HOLMES team.'

Deighton nodded. There was no point in declaring it a major incident until they were certain the girl hadn't stayed at a friend's house. For that very reason he had delayed sanctioning the drag of a pond in Lovers' Wood. The underwater team, like the division's helicopter, was financially crippling. 'What's the latest?'

'OSD scaled down at about three. They picked it up at first light, a sector search working out from the school.'

'What about the family?'

'Nothing at all amiss. Just about as good as you're going to get. Sam was impressed.'

'OK. We'll use room four.'

Room four was the sergeants' rest room.

'They'll love you for that. It's the third time this year they've been kicked out.'

'Can't be helped. HOLMES can set up next door. The

38

indexers can start moving in. I'll give it till nine thirty, then inform the chief that we've got a major incident.' He glanced at the photograph now stuck to the pinboard behind Cole's desk and shook his head. 'How old is she?'

'Twelve.'

'She looks younger.'

Cole nodded.

'They usually look older.'

Detective Superintendent Tony Baxter was head of the Serious Crime Squad based at Sheerham. Over his wholemeal toast and boiled eggs, with his *Daily Telegraph* propped against the tea-cosied pot, and his wife rattling at the sink, he listened to the early bulletins on the local news. He already knew about the missing girl. Bob Deighton had phoned him after leaving Cole's office. Even though Cole seemed to have everything covered, the assistant chief super didn't share Baxter's confidence in his detective inspector. Not that Baxter liked the DI – he didn't.

For a moment, he watched his wife as she went about making up a packed lunch and wondered whether he should go in. Beyond her, through the window, the sun was struggling through the grey. The day was already planned. A gentle motor across to Felixstowe, a meet up with his brother and his family, then the beach and the fairground later. A few pints, some shellfish, and no alarm clock in the morning. The kids had been looking forward to it all week. Baxter had five of them, three of whom were still at home and young enough to get excited at the prospect of the big dipper. The two older girls were at Swansea University, no doubt on another sort of ride. He hoped that the occasional spliff was the only thing they tried. Nowadays, no matter how you brought them up, you could only hope.

He ran through the possibilities. The girl had run away, was staying with a relative or a friend, was hiding somewhere, had been hurt, unable to get help, or was lost. They were the easy options. The others were now more likely. She'd been abducted, held against her will, sexually abused, murdered.

Take your pick. But it hadn't come to that yet and, until it did, or for another day at least, Baxter decided that Cole could continue as SIO – senior investigating officer. If all things remained even, on Monday, a mere forty-eight hours away, he would assume the mantle of responsibility.

His children came down and took over the table. Ten, twelve and fourteen; Mary-Anne was the youngest. The boys fought over the cornflakes, spilling the box. Baxter looked over his paper and they cooled down. Controlling them was easy. A raised eyebrow would usually do the trick. But Mary-Anne was different. She had a streak in her that was wild and Baxter adored it. Shielded by the paper, he glanced at Mary-Anne and tried to imagine the horrors that Mr and Mrs West were going through. Trouble was, because of his business, he didn't have to imagine them. There wasn't a lot that he hadn't seen during his service, but the case that still froze his heart was the Ice-cream Man, the major that Cole had led just a few months before being transferred to Sheerham nick. Baxter had seen the details. Paul Baker had used a knife to increase the size of the underdeveloped vagina. After the mutilation and rape the youngster had still been alive when Cole found her. She had died the following day in the General Middlesex intensive treatment unit. On more than one occasion, when he found himself looking at Cole, he wondered how the case had affected him. You couldn't wipe the memory of that kind of evil. There was no magic door that you could close at five in the evening and then open at nine the next morning. The images of horror stayed with you, day and night. Not up front, that would be too much to bear, but they were always in the background, brought back by the sight of a youngster, perhaps walking alone away from her or his protector. Unfortunately, there was a tendency to become over-protective. You had to fight that all the time. If you didn't, the shields you put up, the restrictions, were likely to become suffocating. In the end they would destroy the very thing you were trying to protect.

His wife wrapped the final sandwiches in clingfilm. She insisted on using it even though, a few weeks earlier, he had warned her of the dangers; something he'd read, something to do with the chemicals in it soaking into the food. 'That just leaves the flask. Then we're all ready for the off. Look, the sun's broken through.' She pointed over the sparkling apple trees in the garden at the swelling orange disc that promised a fine afternoon.

The sun swept away the early grey and once again the day turned warm. The sergeants' room was cleared and furnished with desks, chairs, filing cabinets, main frames and Nobo boards. What they'd got so far was pinned up around Jane West's photograph. More uniformed and plain-clothes officers were brought in from around the division. An underwater team began to drag the pond in Lovers' Wood. An information desk was set up to look after the media interest. The Sunday papers, going to press in the next few hours, wanted their front-page stories adorned with pictures of the girl. For rather dubious reasons, the head-and-shoulders school photograph was not good enough. They wanted a full body shot, playing with friends in the park, or better still, a family shot taken during their last holiday, swimsuit would do nicely. Civvy support staff set up in the incident room and a full HOLMES team of trained indexers moved in next door.

DC Hazel McLintock started another shift at two. DS Butler caught her as she explored the new incident room.

'Hazel, you all right?'

'Don't I look all right, Skipper?'

'You look tired.'

'So does everybody else around here.'

'I'm going to upset you.'

She sighed. 'Back to twenty-nine?'

He nodded. 'There's been a uniform with them since you left. You're to take over again. At least she serves a great cuppa.'

The idea was depressing. Hazel wanted to be involved in the search, not parent-sitting. But it was typical of force thinking. She knew it hadn't been Butler's decision.

'All right, Skipper.'

'What, no arguments?'

She shook her head. 'No, I'm not in the mood for arguments.'

Sam Butler watched her walk off along the corridor. Accepting the decision without a protest wasn't like Hazel at all. He wondered if everything was all right with her, whether she had problems at home. If she did, well, she had something in common with him.

By the time DC McLintock reached the Wests' the dragging of the pond by the underwater team was complete. They found dozens of curiosities but no body. Lovers' Wood and the surrounding area of wasteland was logged as searched.

Lee West had the family photo album out. The uniformed officer was quick to change places with the detective.

'I'll make you some tea,' Lee said. Hazel followed her into the kitchen. 'I heard they had frogmen in the pond.'

'They didn't find anything,' Hazel said, trying to sound positive. 'We have to believe now that Jane is being held somewhere. That doesn't mean she's been hurt.'

Lee grasped at the smallest hope. 'There's still a chance, isn't there?'

'A good chance.'

'These men who take young girls . . .' Her voice trailed off, but Hazel knew what the question was.

'Quite often they snatch them for the thrill. They don't actually do anything. A day or so later we find them wandering the streets, unharmed.' The scenario was unlikely and the detective knew it, but it was important for the parents to keep hope alive.

During the afternoon, there was a general winding down, the search was losing its momentum; the novelty, if it could be called that, was wearing off. They were coming down from the high, the buzz, and wasted adrenalin left them lethargic. It always happened that way. You went all out for the first few hours and then, out of fatigue, or through lack of new ideas, you pulled in the reins.

As Rick Cole carried another coffee to his desk, he found Marsh's deputy waiting for him. Bob Deighton, as stiff as the chief, turned from the window and said, 'Of course, we

42

still have nothing to suggest that the girl's disappearance is a criminal matter. It's not against the law to run away from home. She'll turn up in King's Cross, on the streets.'

'I don't think so, sir,' Cole said, flatly.

He knew that Deighton was weighing it up, snooping on behalf of Superintendent Billingham, Baxter's uniformed counterpart. Perhaps he was keeping notes for Baxter himself. He guessed that Baxter would have toyed with the idea of making an appearance.

Cole explained, 'From what we've found out, and we've spent quite a bit of time with parents, friends and teachers, none of the usual pressures that mark a runaway are evident. She's a happy kid. Unusually so. Her school work's good; she's doing famously at the senior school; she's getting enough space from her parents; and she's having a helluva good time with her friends. You've only got to spend ten minutes in the house, even less in her bedroom, to realise that there's nothing much wrong there.'

'Boyfriends?'

'Casual, lads from school.' He paused to light a cigarette, then stressed, 'She's a bit young for that, in her ways as well as her age. There's no one in particular. Occasional film or a Big Mac, and then in a group, boys and girls together. She keeps a piggy bank in her bedroom. It's still got what's left of her birthday money in it. Twenty quid plus some shrapnel. If she was doing a runner, that's the one thing she'd take. And another thing that DC McLintock came up with – if she was running away she wouldn't go to school first and she certainly wouldn't run away in her school uniform without taking a change of clothes. Which she didn't.'

Deighton turned back to the window. 'So there's not much more to be done, then? We wait.'

'That's about it. OSD have covered what they can, including a double search of the wood. The house-to-house has covered the estate and the houses overlooking the school drive. It won't be long now before it's wound down. We're getting big media coverage in the morning, front pages. TV and radio have already picked it up.'

43

'I heard some of it.' Deighton moved slowly to the door. 'Keep me informed, Rick. I'll be here for another hour or so. About five.'

Cole's nod was thoughtful and cold. His door swung shut. He took Deighton's place by the window. The hot weather had browned the patch of grass that he could see and, even though they had been watered daily, the border flowers were drooping. He finished his coffee, pulled a bitter face, and aimed the plastic cup at the waste-paper bin.

Perhaps Deighton was right and Cole's gut feeling unfounded. Perhaps Jane West would turn up. On the manor there had been over fifty disappearances reported in the last year. Among them, a thirteen-year-old had turned up at a friend's house two days later. A four-year-old had wandered through an open front door and was found forty minutes later playing in a nearby park; a two-year-old was taken by his father after magistrates gave custody to the mother. He was recovered less than two hours later. Then there were a number of kids 'in care' always taking off from their various homes, schools, foster placements and so on. They might disappear for a week at a time.

Cole returned to his desk. There were still a few things to tie up. The details needed circulating to the other forces, and to the national charities and organisations who concentrated on missing persons. The Sally-Anns, for instance, kept an eye on the London main line terminus stations. Apart from that, it was down to the sightings that were still coming in, responses from the earlier media coverage. So far they had proved fruitless, but none could be ignored. Then there was the list of schedule one offenders, child sex offenders living on their patch who the police kept tabs on. Officers were already working through the list of addresses. The police played a waiting game with these men. Half of them would offend again, a quarter of them within months of their release. Leopards didn't change their spots. As far as the police were concerned the sons of bitches should have been put down on day one.

The uncertainty was there, but it hadn't yet had enough time to destroy them. Not like the long-term disappearances. After enough time the constant ache, the nightmares, the need for a resolution, became all important. They would sooner have a body than continue in the vacuum.

There were moments when Bill West had to console his wife. He was turning out to be stronger than Hazel McLintock had anticipated. She'd seen very little sign of emotion from him. But his silence was unnerving, his thoughts locked up. She could see the anger, the throbbing jaw, the narrowed eyes, and she expected that sooner or later he was going to lose control. But at the moment, while his wife needed him, he kept himself together.

A PC relieved her at eight o'clock and she spent the rest of her shift in the incident room, running through past missing person files. There had been two in the right age range in the last ten days, both male, both run away from the child-care unit at Witton. They were found in town and returned to the unit within twenty-four hours.

She knocked off at midnight. As she hit the corridor, DS Butler and DI Cole emerged from an office in front of her.

Butler said, 'We're going over to the White Horse for a quick one. We need a drip feed. You coming?'

She glanced from the skipper to Cole. She'd been heading that way herself, knowing that a number of her colleagues would be there. Day or night, you could always guarantee that. She nodded briefly. Their step barely faltered and she caught them up at the reception door. Cole went through first and held it open. As she passed she noticed his aftershave. Old Spice. It reminded her of her dad. She was surprised that she liked it.

The curtains were drawn, the front door locked, and they used the side entrance. There were a few faces in the one bar left open, mostly coppers.

Without hesitation, Cole paid for a round. They carried their drinks across to a small table.

Butler said, 'In 1915, the buying of rounds in a pub was illegal. You could go down for six months.'

Hazel gave him a disbelieving look. 'Why was that?'

'The authorities wanted to cut down the consumption of alcohol.'

'And? Did it work?'

'No. It just produced a nation of tight bastards. People living in Essex keep the tradition going. And the Scots, of course.'

'I was born in Essex!' she said.

'You're the exception.'

'Huh!' She glanced at Cole. Apart from ordering drinks he hadn't spoken a word since leaving the nick. She wondered whether having her along had inhibited him. He lit a cigarette without offering them around. She lit one of her own, lower tar in any case, and turned back to the sergeant as he addressed her again.

'You're a bit of a stranger in here. What's brought this on?'

'I thought I'd see how the other half lived.'

'I don't live here very often. Drinking at this time of night is a sad man's game – and the sad woman's, of course.'

'Of course.'

'This is a serious waterhole. You can smell the anonymity. The good thing about it is its indifference. There's no danger of being found out because no one cares.'

In the White Horse day and night didn't matter; little natural light passed through the aged windows with their coats of city grime – the acid rain and city fumes had turned the glass into something else. The pub's exterior gave no impression of its depth; two bars had been knocked together, separated by thick stanchions. The ceiling was beamed with old timber. There were a couple of unwelcome gaming machines near the door and at the far end narrow alcoves for courting couples. In between were a few tables but at this time of night not many were in use. Serious drinkers mostly stood.

Sam Butler looked at his watch as the sounds of distant thunder rumbled, and said gloomily, 'I better be getting back. It sounds like there's a storm brewing.' He finished his drink and stood up stiffly. On the way out he acknowledged some other faces in the room.

Hazel stubbed out her cigarette. 'He's under the thumb,' she said, flippantly.

46

Cole looked up, 'What, Sam you mean?'

Hazel had finished her drink. For a few moments she sat in uncomfortable silence, then thought to hell with it. She collected her cigarettes and lighter and lifted her bag.

Through the smoke Cole said suddenly, 'Hazel, wait. I'm sorry, I haven't been good company. If you haven't got to rush, I'd like to buy you another drink.'

She eased her weight back, dropped her bag over the hook of the chair and folded her arms. 'I'm in no rush.'

He nodded. 'Same again?'

'Please.'

She watched him move to the bar. In his dark suit he looked slimmer, taller, but very much the model copper. He would never get away with undercover work.

When he returned he said, 'I know you checked the At Risk with CPU but it suddenly occurred to me that it might be worthwhile speaking to the Wests' GP. They often get a feel for things but are reluctant to bring in Social Services.'

'Don't you ever turn off, Guv? There's nothing wrong with that family. I'd stake my life on it.'

'When did you join up?'

'How experienced am I, you mean?'

'If you like.'

'Seven years ago. You?'

'Christ! Nearly eighteen years now.'

There were a lot of things she wanted to ask him, particularly about the business at the Yard, but there was no way. Even though the alcohol was thawing some of her tension, she was far from at ease. It was the first time she had spoken to the DI informally. Up until a few minutes ago she hadn't even liked him. He had always been cold. Now she was reviewing her opinion.

'You were saying about Sam?'

'Oh yes, that he rushed off a bit sudden. There are rumours.'

Cole nodded. 'I heard. My wife used to say that all coppers are damaged goods. That they should come with a health warning.'

'She sounds the sort of person I'd like.'

'She probably meant policewomen as well.' He smiled genuinely and lit another cigarette. He offered over the pack.

She shook her head. 'I'll stick to mine. Then I won't get complaints about my coughing keeping him awake.'

'You too?'

'He goes away Monday for a week, so he can catch up on his sleep. Actually he's going on Sunday in time for Monday.'

'That makes sense,' he said. He toyed with his glass.

She realised that he was nervous.

'I don't have to worry about things like that any more.'

'I heard.'

He glanced up and met her gaze. 'It seems that every kozzer on site is either on the rocks or screwing around.'

'It's a hazard of the job. It was the same where I came from, and I bet you it's the same all over.'

'Maybe.'

'Anyway, the further up the ladder you go, the less you find it. Take the super, for instance.'

He nodded. Baxter was an exception, the others just careful. They didn't mess on their doorstep. 'What does your husband do?'

'He's a senior social worker with children and families.'

'Local?'

'Yes.'

'Mm, I think I recognise the name. Nigel McLintock, isn't it?'

She nodded.

'Yes, I've met him in court. Did you move down here for his job?'

'Yeah, you could say. We moved house some time ago. An hour each way became too much for me.'

'I'm not surprised.'

She levelled her gaze. 'So you met my husband?'

He nodded. It was coming back. 'It would have been just before your transfer. Four or five months ago. Child abuse. Good old Jehovah's Witnesses.'

She recalled Nigel mentioning the case. Jehovah's Witnesses believed that children were a present from God. They closed

48

ranks tighter than anyone else; dealt with the problem internally. Before the paedophile was allowed to mix with the children again, he had to stand up in the Kingdom Hall, admit his guilt and promise there would be no recurrence. They'd borrowed the idea from the Catholics.

They spoke for a few minutes more without really saying anything and then called it a night. 'We're over the limit,' he joked, as they headed for their cars, catching her by surprise. 'We better get a taxi home.'

'Yeah,' she said, and shot him a smile. 'I'll go and whistle one down. I always wondered why they stopped issuing whistles.'

'Thanks for the company. I enjoyed it.'

She hesitated, then said quickly, 'You're welcome, Guv.' And she knew without any doubt that they'd do it again.

Chapter 6

The two Baxter families set up a barbecue on Felixstowe beach. The women cooked. Last time Baxter's brother, Henry, had tried it, the chicken portions came with tourniquets and threatened to poison the lot of them. After lunch and the necessary doze, Baxter began to get uncomfortable in the hot sun. He glanced around for some respite. The others seemed happy enough, the women chatting away like there was no tomorrow, his brother still snoozing contentedly, the kids playing on the stony beach.

He sat up and watched the five kids giving a ball some stick. Four boys and Mary-Anne. She was tall for her age, taller than the boys, but painfully thin. The bones jutted out of her shoulders and hips. Behind her scrawny frame, short, dark boyish hair and pretty face, there lurked a headstrong character that belied her ten years, eleven months. She could be as stubborn as her mother. Her school reports always said cheerful, likeable, lively, can be a little boisterous at times. That just about summed her up.

Baxter shook his head, freshly astonished at her physique; all arms and legs, bony knees and elbows. Considering the girth of both Baxter and his wife, he guessed his youngest child must have been a throwback to some distant part of the family. His other children were on the heavy side. It was only severe diets that had brought the eldest girls into shape and his sons had never bothered. They were just younger versions of Baxter. His brother's two lads were heavy too, and older than Mary-Anne at twelve and thirteen, but she held her own, beating them to the ball, coming out of the rough and tumbles on top. Her swimsuit was slightly too small, and left the briefest strip of material covering her bony groin. Baxter felt a stab of annoyance that she wore it; she seemed oblivious to the fact that it was slightly revealing. She had another costume in her bag that fitted perfectly.

The boys accepted her as one of the lads and she was

completely at ease in their disorderly struggles, not yet aware of her sexuality or theirs. Her mother had discussed such things openly, as had the school, and Mary-Anne had been disappointed at not having been the first of her group of school friends to reach menstruation.

'She should have been born a boy,' Henry said, as he saw Baxter watching. Tony Baxter was two years younger than his brother, but looked a good deal older. He also carried an extra three stone, mostly around the middle.

Baxter adjusted his spectacles to watch the youngsters play and nodded his agreement. 'It would have been a lot less trouble,' he muttered. Mary-Anne had arrived unexpectedly. They'd already got rid of the girls' cast-offs, confident that four children were quite enough.

Henry laughed. They had had the conversation many times, that the boys were less of a problem than the girls.

Baxter continued, 'And if the others are anything to go by, it won't get any easier.' Whenever his two older daughters came home from university, and that was more often than Baxter had anticipated, they had a way of rubbing their mother up the wrong way. It took her days to get over their flying visits. Restless, he glanced at his watch for the third time in as many minutes. The barbecue was safe, the women were still rabbiting, and he'd finished the paper. He caught Henry's eye and nodded towards the boozer.

Henry agreed, climbed to his feet and dusted sand. 'We're just popping over the road,' he said to the women. They barely paused in their conversation.

The last time they'd got together had been at their father's funeral, seven months earlier. The Baxters had never been a particularly close family; perhaps his father being in the forces and the globe-hopping from posting to posting had put paid to that. No grass ever grew under their feet, no lasting relationship. So when they parted, started families of their own, as much as they made promises to each other and to themselves, they were rarely drawn together more than once or twice a year, and then only for a fleeting visit. Even when their parents were alive, such visits were infrequent. There was never a family home, as such. Never the warmth and certainty of belonging that he'd seen in his wife's family. As soon as she walked in it was as though she'd never been away. When Baxter had walked into his parents' house, he always felt like a visitor, sometimes unwelcome.

They talked for a couple of hours, mostly about the old days, and the alcohol unlocked some hidden intimacies. When they arrived back, the women were packing up and the children were changing.

'The kids have had enough, started to get chilly.' Baxter followed his wife's glance to the sky. One or two ominous clouds had shouldered in across the sun. 'We thought we'd wander down to the fairground.'

Baxter nodded and helped to pack the barbecue. His wife held a wide towel around Mary-Anne while she changed out of her swimsuit. At one stage it parted and flashed the white strip of her behind as she pulled up her knickers.

'Be careful,' Baxter snapped, and saw the dark, reproving look from his wife.

'For goodness sake, Tony,' she said and secured the towel. 'She's a little girl. What on earth's the matter with you?'

He glanced about at the other family groups, searching for the unhealthy glance, the suddenly averted gaze. But they were getting on with their own business. If they'd noticed his daughter's nakedness, they weren't interested.

'All done?' his wife asked Mary-Anne, before folding the towel. Baxter was conscious of her curious look as she stuffed the towel into a bag, and felt slightly embarrassed. His suspicions were heightened by the missing girl, he knew that, but he couldn't help it. He was getting paranoid, seeing danger in the most unlikely places. Perhaps it had something to do with being a mature father; he had been forty-one when Mary-Anne had arrived. But he knew that was a nonsense. It was down to the job, the thing you married, the thing you took home. He knew that the beach was one of the favourite haunts of the paedophile. And with their telephotos they could take their snaps from a mile away. Nevertheless, for a moment he was angry with himself. But he couldn't shake the feeling of mistrust. He knew how many paedophiles there were out there, lurking in the shadows of every town and village, their eyes flitting to make certain they weren't being watched while they took their furtive little glances.

Baxter was an early bird. On Sunday morning he rose at six thirty and left his wife in bed. He'd been up twice in the night. Thunder had woken him and once awake he realised his stomach was groaning. He blamed the mussels and jellied eels they'd eaten at the fairground. Over some tea, for an hour before the house stirred, he read the papers. The tabloids had got hold of Jane West's photograph. The school photo issued by the police had not been good enough and they'd presumably paid or talked Mr and Mrs West into releasing some holiday snaps – beach shots of Jane. Innocent enough, if it hadn't been for the cynical reasoning of the editor. Sales. The tabloids' contribution to child abuse. There were few details that hadn't already been released. One of the papers ran an article about missing children. Sensationalised it. Highlighted the sexual details. Used pretty faces, suggestive poses. They were supposed to deal with the truth. In Baxter's view, they added to the problem more than any film or TV show. At eight, when he heard running water in the bathroom, he checked in with the office.

They had run out of ideas. Now they depended solely on public support and it wasn't a good day for that. On Sunday people walked around with their eyes closed.

Chapter 7

About two hours after the bedroom light went out on Sunday night Tony Baxter's telephone rang. It became part of his dream. Even though his wife had to lean over him, she got to the telephone first. She left the receiver off the cradle and shook his shoulder.

'What? What?'

'The phone,' she said as she shuffled her wide behind and settled back on her own side. 'Aren't we ever going to get a whole weekend off?'

The irritation in her voice sobered him up. He was vaguely aware of the wind and rain rushing against the window. He raised his shoulders to the headboard and lifted the phone.

He said abruptly, 'Yes, what is it?'

'Sorry to disturb you, sir.'

The voice was familiar. Baxter tried to fit a face. It was probably one of the late shift reserves doubling up with the switchboard.

'DI Cole asked me to call you, sir.'

'Talk to me, son. What's happened?'

'We've found a body.'

Baxter sat up straight. His head was woolly. The brandy, medicinal, had caused it. He'd been half-expecting the news, yet still it wouldn't register. His frown became almost painful. 'The girl?'

'It's a girl. That's all I know.'

'When?' he asked quietly.

'Just after midnight.'

Baxter glanced at the green fluorescent hands of his bedside clock. He nodded into the phone and said quietly, 'I'm on my way. Half an hour at most. Give me an address.'

'It's more of a map reference, sir. In the middle of some allotments not far from Richmond Park estate. You'll need a compass. DI Cole is on his way.'

He took the details then placed the receiver carefully on the cradle.

His wife sensed that it was serious and opened her eyes.

'What is it?' Her voice was sleepy.

'Go back to sleep, sweetheart.' He swung his feet onto the carpet and rooted around for his slippers.

'It's too late. I'm awake now.' She watched him fight the arm of his dressing-gown.

'They've found a body.'

'Oh God, not the girl?'

'It sounds like it.'

She struggled out of bed. 'You shave,' she said. 'I'll make you some toast.'

His unsettled stomach groaned at the prospect. 'No, no. Just coffee.' He moved into the bathroom and heard his wife's heavy footfalls on the stairs.

Ten minutes later he was dressed and sitting at the kitchen table. The wind sent some heavy raindrops against the dark window.

'It's not a night to go far in,' his wife said, as she put toast and coffee before him. 'Two storms in two nights. What's happening to our weather?'

'I told you not to bother.'

'You can't go out without something inside you. Not on a night like this.' She licked her finger and dabbed his chin. 'You've cut yourself.'

'Yes. I tried not to.'

His wife hovered and he was forced to eat.

To his wife, Tony Baxter was protector as well as provider. He was protecting society from evil. She looked upon him with pride. As he stood to go and brushed crumbs from his suit she felt like saying 'Go and get the bastard', but she didn't. She'd never use such a term, even when she lost her temper, which wasn't often. Now she watched him through the door and into the stormy night. She closed the door behind him and, with difficulty, threw the security bolt. Once again it was a safe place, a den, shielded from the ugliness of the outside world, a copper's house.

As Tony Baxter drove through the heavy rain to the location he'd been given, he thought about Jane West's parents and the awful business of giving them the details.

There wasn't much happening on the roads. A few late revellers made their way home and the odd milk float rattled past, milkmen starting their double rounds, fighting the weather and the slippery bottles.

DI Cole had just returned to the office after finishing his rounds when he heard another rattle of thunder. The water boards must have been jumping for joy at the thought of storms for two nights on the trot.

Nothing much had happened during the day, the search had all but petered out, and he had taken the opportunity to visit the stations nearby, checking on the prisoners and whether there was anything he should know about. The only newsworthy incident came from Carrington Road. There had been a stabbing during the early hours of Sunday morning. A low-life had been stabbed on the steps of the old theatre. He was in hospital and officers had been there most of the day waiting to interview him. But tonight had been quiet. Sunday nights invariably were. When the news of the discovery came through he sat down at his desk and forced himself into finishing his coffee before making his way purposefully to the ops room.

'Where's DS Butler?'

'He's on his way to Churchill Place,' the reserve said. 'He was going to pick up DC McLintock. He was going to drop her home.'

'She's at the estate?'

The reserve nodded.

'Get DS Butler for me.'

A few moments later he was through to Butler's mobile.

'Sam?'

'Rick?'

'Yeah, you heard?'

'Yeah, it's been all over the radio. One of the pandas filled me in.'

'Get Hazel out of there. Give it to her in the car. Not a word to the Wests, not at the moment.'

'Understood.'

'I'll meet you at the allotments in Nelson Lane. Fifteen minutes.'

'Right.'

Once Cole had signed off, Sam Butler pulled his car into a lay-by. He wound down the window and gulped in the damp night air. Drops of rain hit his face. For a moment he shivered, then he took a handkerchief from his pocket to wipe away his tears. He felt absolutely gutted. Things didn't usually get to him, not like this. He'd been on child murders before. Perhaps the emotion he had wasted at home, the uncertainty, had finally caught up. He composed himself before reaching forward to start the car again.

Ten minutes later, Hazel McLintock was sitting beside him. Her jacket was spotted by the rain. He hadn't gone into the house. She had come out to the car, and saw his face for the first time once she had fastened her belt. In the pale illumination, a mix of green dash and orange street light, she took in his swollen eyes.

'What's happened?'

'We've got a body.'

He saw Hazel's face cave and pulled the car out quickly in case the Wests were watching from the window. He parked up round the corner and turned to her. She wept silently into her hands. Her shoulders shook. He wanted to reach across and touch her, console her, but was afraid she might interpret it the wrong way and his hand made only half the space between them before he withdrew it. Instead he took out his handkerchief and offered it across.

'Thank you,' she sobbed, and glanced up. Her mascara had run. She used the mirror.

'Cole wants us to meet him at the allotments. We'll go in together.'

'Are they certain? Have they got ID?'

Butler said gently, 'Come on, girl, of course it is. Think about it. It's time for automatic pilot.'

She wiped her eyes and nodded. 'You're right. But it's going to take a long time to learn how to smile again, Skippy.'

'Don't call me Skippy,' he said.

The clouds hung low over the allotment site; streamers broke away and fell to earth. The site was situated on Nelson Lane which ran east to west along the northern edge of the Richmond Park estate. The lane was seldom used as people preferred to keep to the streets running through the estate, where the lighting was better. It offered them a sense of security.

Four police cars had drawn up, flashing the area with a mixture of blue and white light. Tail lights added a touch of red and orange. A couple of sergeants and half a dozen PCs stood about, huddled beneath their capes, waiting for instructions. Most of the wooden tops were moaning like hell at the timing and the weather, until they saw her, and then everything went from their minds. They began to cordon the area and put up a canvas tent around the body. Shoes and boots picked up thick soles of mud. Someone arranged battery and lights. DI Cole and DC McLintock met Detective Superintendent Baxter on the grassy verge just inside the main gate. Cole had sent Butler back to the station – someone with at least a stripe had to man the fort. One of the uniformed sergeants led them along the dripping path between the glistening plots of growing vegetables and the occasional black mound of rotting horse manure toward the eerie wash of light.

As they approached, the photographer began using his flash. The air above the forensic tent and the tent itself lit up in powder blue. The screen was pulled aside and the civvy doctor emerged. In the stark light he looked flustered as he snapped his bag together. He saw their approach and paused. Baxter was in the lead. Raindrops ran down his face and dripped from his chin. He acknowledged him with a slight nod.

'Hello, Tony,' the doctor said. 'This is nasty. Very nasty. I've seen nothing like it.'

Tony Baxter wiped his spectacles and replaced them. 'Is it Jane West?'

'Female, eleven or twelve,' the doctor went on, as though he hadn't heard.

'Is that it?'

The doctor shrugged, clearly shaken, and added, 'I've con-firmed she's dead for you.'

Baxter narrowed his eyes. Behind him Cole glanced at the DC and flashed her a sympathetic smile. He realised she wasn't handling it very well. Nothing up front, just a slight overblinking of the eyes, but it was there. But maybe he was wrong. Maybe it was just tiredness, or the rain that was hitting them face on.

'It's too late for jokes,' Baxter said, sharply. 'Cause of death?'

The doctor shook his head, then, 'No idea, you'll have to wait. It seems like strangulation, but it's too early. You'll see what I mean.'

'Time of death?' Baxter asked.

The doctor tried a quick smile. 'Don't be silly.'

Baxter raised a resigned eyebrow.

The doctor relented. 'Two hours at least, four at most. We'll get a better picture later.'

Behind them a van from the funeral services pulled onto the grassy verge and began to sink. It would eventually deliver the body to the mortuary. 'Christ, they're quick off the mark,' Baxter said. 'Business must be bad.'

The doctor nodded. The SOCOs, the scene of crime offi-cers, had scarcely begun their work. That was beside the HO pathologist who would want to carry out his own tests. The van's headlights flared in strands of the doctor's thinning hair and threw his face into darkness. 'They'll need a child's body bag,' he said. 'I'll see you in the morning.' He trudged off towards his car.

Baxter watched him go, then turned to Cole and the DC at his side.

'Right!' he said brusquely. 'Let's see what we've got.'

A uniform hesitated before lifting the canvas flap. Baxter frowned.

'What is it, Mills?'

Sergeant Mills nodded tentatively toward DC Hazel McLintock. In the stark light she looked washed out and fragile.

She recognised the sergeant's reluctance and slightly annoyed, said to him, 'I'm a big girl now, Skipper!'

59

Baxter shot her a glance then turned back to the sergeant. 'Let's get on with it.'

'Right you are, sir.' Sergeant Mills shrugged and lifted the flap.

The three of them piled into the enclosure, Superintendent Baxter first, Cole and McLintock together. A SOCO, on hands and knees, turned to check out the interruption. Baxter stood motionless, open mouthed, taking in the scene. Cole and McLintock arrived either side of him.

'Oh, shit,' DC McLintock said and turned back, catching the knowing told-you-so eyes of Sergeant Mills as she went.

Baxter stood there swaying.

Over the years, policemen become immune to shock. Through necessity and while still PCs, they become indifferent to almost all scenes of crime, from the stinking decomposed body crawling with bloated maggots to the traffic accident which might have reduced a body to squashed tissue, sinew, blood and bone. Baxter had been in the force thirty years and in that time he'd witnessed many terrible things but now, surprising everyone and himself most of all, a combination of a dodgy stomach, Sunday night's Chinese and barely digested toast and coffee made him violently sick.

Cole backed out of the enclosure and saw Hazel McLintock standing a few yards distant. Her eyes were tightly closed and she was taking deep breaths. She faced the rain as though it offered some relief.

Cole caught Mills's thin smile as Baxter coughed and spluttered. 'You think that's funny?'

Mills shook his head. 'Funny? No. Call it the thrill of *schadenfreude*, if you like. It's always a pleasure, even at this time of night, to see ones peers come unstuck.'

Chapter 8

At eight the next morning, unbroken cloud stretched away in every direction. It seemed to hang lower over the estate, washing what little colour there was out of the concrete and brick. Twenty-nine Churchill Place was quiet, the curtains still drawn. The air was heavy. It felt like lead on the chest.

DI Cole looked across at Hazel McLintock and said, 'You OK? Do you want a minute?' He tossed a cigarette end from the car window. In the back the police grief counsellor waited to get on with it.

Hazel shook her head and confirmed, 'I'm all right.' Like Cole, she had managed to grab a couple of hours sleep, but it hadn't been restful. The images of night had refused to fade. Anticipating the first call of the day hadn't helped either. She had spent the few hours at home alone. Nigel had gone off to his conference and the house was strangely marked by his absence. She had cried herself to sleep. The emotion, barely suppressed at the SOC, poured out on to her pillow. She wasn't the only one to feel that the police had failed. Many policemen experienced it, even though it was a ludicrous sentiment.

As they travelled over to the estate she wished that it had been Detective Sergeant Butler beside her. She couldn't share her feelings with Cole. He seemed cold and formal, as if their conversation on Saturday night hadn't happened.

'Right,' Cole said, checking back with the counsellor, Debbie Freeman. She nodded and opened her door.

As they walked along the path a neighbour peered from her front-room window. Cole knocked. Bill West opened the door. He was unshaven, his shirt undone, revealing dark hair sprouting through a string vest. He didn't know Cole or Freeman but he recognised DC McLintock behind them. He nodded slowly, anticipating bad news. It was a guess and nothing more for there had been a complete news blackout during the night. Only the late editions, coming out after nine, would carry the news that a girl's body had been found. He stood aside to let them in.

In the living-room, Lee West's brother and sister-in-law sat stiffly on the sofa. They had motored up from their home in Devon on Sunday. Their expressions were fearful as West led the police officers in. The woman immediately grabbed her husband's hand with both of hers.

'This is Doreen, Lee's sister, and her husband Colin,' West said. 'My wife's upstairs.' As he spoke he heard footsteps on the stairs. He turned to see Lee West standing in the doorway.

She looked at Hazel, then at Cole, then she screamed. The shriek, as painful as any sound the detectives had heard, cut through the stillness, and for a moment took everyone by surprise. Suddenly Lee West had gone; they heard her cries in the hall then the front door opening.

'Quickly,' Cole said. Hazel sprang to the door, but Bill West made it first as he raced after his wife. He caught up with her on the path. She had fallen, or collapsed. Now she was beating the concrete with her fists. Her knee was grazed, blood spat across her knuckles. Bill West knelt beside her, holding her tightly. He couldn't say anything. His own throat was blocked. Instead, gently, he rocked her against his sagging chest.

At the door, Debbie Freeman turned to Doreen. 'I think you ought to call the doctor out.'

Doreen indicated the neighbours who stood in the next door garden, having heard the screams. 'They've got a phone,' she said. 'Ours is out of order. I'll ask if I can use it.'

Debbie nodded.

Cole knelt beside Bill West and helped Lee to her feet. Slowly, taking her weight, they led her back into the house.

Hazel McLintock fixed her expression as she closed the door behind them. Her lower lip trembled and she fought to control it.

They lowered Lee onto the sofa. Bill West stayed with her, his arms holding her close. He looked up, his face ashen.

'Tell me?'

Cole said quietly, 'This morning, early.' He shook his head.

'How, tell me how?'

'It's too early to tell. I'm very sorry.'

'Where is she?'

'She's at Hilltop. I'd like you to drive over there with me, if that's possible.'

West held onto his wife, rocking her against his chest. Leaving her was going to be difficult.

Colin suggested, 'I can go, if you like.'

'No, sir. I'm afraid the coroner will insist on a blood relative. Perhaps your wife—'

West interrupted sharply, 'I'll do it.' Suddenly his mouth opened in a grimace, his eyes screwed up and squeezed out the anguish.

Hazel turned away. In the front garden she lit a shaking cigarette and inhaled deeply. Angrily, she flicked away a stray tear in time to see Doreen walk back down the path. She held a bunch of wet tissues to her eyes. 'The doctor's on his way,' she said as she struggled for composure. 'Is there anything else I can do?'

Hazel tried for an answer but in the end just shook her head.

'I understand we have a suspect?' Chief Superintendent Marsh said as he glanced at his deputy, Bob Deighton. A wry humour fluttered from his eyes; his thin lips remained tight.

Before him, Baxter wondered whether he'd missed something. A frown spread out above his spectacles.

Marsh went on, 'Someone who likes Chinese takeaways?'

Baxter caught on and nodded slowly. 'Very good, very good,' he said, but he wasn't smiling. He found no humour at all in the events of the night.

Marsh said quietly, 'You'll be taking the mantle of SIO. Will you keep Cole on to assist you?'

Baxter was surprised. He waited, non-committally. When nothing further came he said, 'Well, Jim Gregory is back this morning.'

Deighton frowned. 'I thought I saw him on Friday.'

Baxter confirmed, 'He popped in to wish Russell all the best.'

63

'Oh yes, of course.'

Marsh looked up and said seriously, 'We thought Cole handled himself rather well over the weekend. We, Bob and I . . .' He glanced at his deputy for confirmation, '. . . are not entirely in the dark as to what is happening downstairs, contrary to popular opinion.'

'Meaning?'

'Let's just say we've kept an eye on the caseload distribution. Would that be fair comment?'

Baxter nodded reluctantly. He accepted the censure but he had to remind himself that every copper, Marsh included, had come up through the ranks. But Marsh didn't seem to live in the real world. Baxter was still certain that Cole was only passing through, using the place as a stepping-stone. A good copper maybe, but he'd never become a team player and in Baxter's eyes that was fatal. Police work was team work.

Deighton flexed his thin delicate fingers and said, 'I hear she was wearing make-up?'

'She was. The rain messed it up.'

'Make-up?' Marsh frowned.

Baxter explained, 'Powder, rouge, foundation.'

'She made her face up?'

'Or he did.'

Deighton shook a bewildered head. 'Rouge? Is that still used?'

Baxter shook his head. 'Only by the old girls, apparently.'

Marsh sighed. 'It's like something out of Hitchcock. *Psycho*, Anthony Hopkins.'

'Perkins,' Deighton corrected him. 'Anthony Perkins played Norman Bates.'

Marsh nodded slowly as though bringing the film to mind, then said, 'Yes, so it was. What about this chap who found the body, Michael Grant?'

'As good as gold. A pensioner on his way home from the George. He passes the allotments at the same time every night, a few minutes after the pub closes.'

'And what about the ritual aspect? I take it the emphasis is on the occult?'

'Well, it's hardly common farming practice, is it?'

'I don't know so much. Bob reminded me that in some rural areas it's custom to stick rats on the top of fences.'

Baxter glanced across at Deighton. He held onto a contemptuous smile. 'She wasn't stuck on a fence and this isn't a rural area.'

'Well, what do you think?' Marsh's voice turned chilly.

'I think we've got another Peter Pickering out there. Remember him? He subjected a fourteen-year-old to torture, rape and murder, and he took his time.'

'Similarities?'

'Tied up, raped, strangled, hacked to death with a kitchen knife.'

'He's still inside?'

'He was in Ashwell with Ian Brady but I understand he's been moved to Arnold Lodge, a medium-secure unit. There's serious talk of him being released within the next few months.'

Deighton seemed appalled. 'It's outrageous. Never mind Pickering, one is bound to ask about the mental state of the people at the Home Office. Even the Home Secretary.'

'Did he have previous?' Marsh's interest picked up.

'As long as your arm,' Baxter put in. 'Five months before he killed Shirley Ann Boldy he was released from serving a nine-year stretch for sexual attacks on two girls. Before that he'd spent years inside for similar assaults.'

Deighton shook his head and said quietly, 'We're wasting our time, aren't we?'

'It would appear that way,' said Baxter.

Marsh looked down at the papers on his desk. 'That's always been the case,' he muttered. 'Nothing's changed.' The meeting was over. 'Keep me informed, Tony.'

Shortly after Bill West left for the mortuary with Rick Cole and DC McLintock to formally identify his daughter's body, Detective Superintendent Baxter called together his team in the incident room. He confirmed that Cole would be his deputy and that either he or Cole would hold daily briefings at eight in the morning and seven in the evening. DI Jim

Gregory, on his first day back from leave, would also join the management team. The superintendent went by the book, the formatted management policy book. At the end of the inquiry it would contain every decision that had been taken. Meanwhile there were things to do, the gathering of evidence, what the police called trawling. It meant starting again – house-to-house, pulling out past offender files, giving out descriptions, press conferences, questions, talking to neighbours, allotment holders, people living near the SOC or the school.

At the mortuary, Cole and McLintock stood aside while the attendant uncovered the girl's face. Bill West seemed to fold and had to brace himself to stop his knees from buckling.

'Oh, my baby,' he muttered. 'Oh, my little baby.'

In the waiting-room, while Hazel organised a panda to take West home, he turned to Cole and said abruptly, 'I don't want her cut, d'you understand? No more. Please.'

A softer look fell onto Cole's features, the gentle eye of a practised bedside manner.

Hazel McLintock noticed it and shot him a curious glance.

Cole gently reassured him. 'Don't worry, sir. They won't need to do much. Just confirm cause of death, that's all.'

He had told the lie many times. It wasn't upsetting to tell it again.

Some miles to the south east, a mobile police incident room was positioned on the allotments. A blue-and-white-striped cordon POLICE DO NOT CROSS laced its way around the perimeter of the allotments and fluttered like bunting in the breeze. Two PCs stood at the gate, guarding the area from unwanted visitors, including a few plot holders who took the exclusion personally and threatened to complain to the council, while fifty other officers raked at the vegetables and the long grass that edged the plots. Police sniffer dogs and their handlers began their searches. They were looking for clothing, a weapon, anything that might be significant. In the air, one of two twin Squirrel helicopters based near Epping, equipped with nightscope and thermal imaging cameras to search for footprints, had been criss-crossing the area for most of the

66

night. More officers were on the way, drafted in from nearby districts. Inside the canvas SOCOs dressed from head to toe in white continued their work. They used tweezers and tiny brushes as they went over every inch of ground. They were looking for hair or flakes of skin, perhaps a gob of phlegm or a spot of blood; perhaps, if they got lucky, a footprint. A few people from the estate had gathered to watch in the narrow lane, and a journalist from a local newspaper hovered with his photographer. The nationals would be down later to vie for position with the television news crews. All they had got so far was that a girl's body had been discovered and there would be a statement later in the day. They had put two and two together. It had to be the missing girl from the front pages of the Sundays. The one in the polka dot swimsuit.

Chapter 9

The station crawled with senior policemen. The commissioner and his assistant, playing host to the neighbouring division's élite, descended on Sheerham like unwelcome gatecrashers, and for a while they took over. Chief Superintendent Marsh, his nerves blotching his grey features, served them coffee and led them into the briefing room. The idea was that they were lending support; in reality they were getting in the way.

Bob Deighton caught Baxter on his way to the parade room where the joint briefing was scheduled, and pulled a dismayed face. It was almost unheard of, plain-clothes trespassing on Superintendent Billingham's domain.

'The feeling upstairs is that the girl's death was part of a ritual. The commissioner thinks it might be a good idea to involve the Yard's occult specialists. The chief agreed with him.'

'Of course he'd agree with him,' Baxter groaned. 'Bloody marvellous. Inputs from bloody racialist figureheads and paper pushers. Where did he dream that up? Occult! We're already swamped with experts, aren't we? Our resident psychologist thinks we're sitting on the main paedophile ring in Britain. Every time a kid's involved we've got psychologists and social workers pointing to devil worship rings in the Outer Hebrides. What is it with these people? What's happened to the old fashioned child murderers, like Brady, Hatch, Armstrong, for Christ's sake? Specialists do little but interfere, Bob, you know that. Their field is so narrow that people lose their way, miss the obvious.'

Perplexity spread on Deighton's face. 'It was only a suggestion, even if it did come from him.'

Baxter tried to relax. He was tired and on edge. The autopsy hadn't helped. Nor had the anti-diarrhoeal drugs he had bought at Boots on his way back from the mortuary. He gave a resigned sigh. 'Well, unless they've got a specific MO on impalement and teethmarks, we'll keep it simple for the time being.'

'Impalement? I thought she was tied to the cross?'

'She was, but she had been skewered by something else, a dildo, something.'

Disgusted by the idea, Deighton shook his head.

'Let's work through the basics before we get too involved along specific lines. We'll have a day or two of fundamental detective work and see what we've got.'

Deighton nodded. 'It's your show,' he said. 'But they're there if you need help. Just keep them in mind.'

At six o' clock the parade room filled up. The uniforms outnumbered the plain-clothes six to one. The guests sat with Marsh; Superintendents John Billingham and Tony Baxter were slightly to one side beneath the Target Criminal board. There was space between them, a sort of no man's land complete with barbed wire and land mines. Bob Deighton made a late entrance and sat on the end of the row.

The parade room was Billingham's territory. He didn't like the invasion by CID, even though it was Marsh's idea and he usually agreed wholeheartedly with everything Marsh came up with. Baxter was on his feet. He gazed across at the chief's guests then turned back to the assembly and raised his eyebrows.

The tension was broken. A few tired smiles tugged at the faces of the senior men who recognised his shrewdness. Although he only caught it in profile, even the chief smiled quickly.

'Right,' Baxter said. 'Firstly, we're keeping stumm on this, a total news blackout on the details.'

It was always difficult to know how much to give to the newspapers. Too little led to speculation and hysteria; too much could damage the inquiry and encourage the nutters to come out with claims that they did it. And there was the danger of copy-cat killers, waiting for the blue touchpaper of tabloid description. It was an ugly, dangerous world.

Baxter turned to Cole at his side. 'OK, Rick, let's have it.'

Cole nodded and addressed the assembly. 'Jane West, twelve years old, adolescent, rebellious, absolutely one hundred per cent normal. Attractive, likeable, happy, everything to live for.

Home, parents, relatives and friends seem, on the face of it, and to use DS Butler's sentiment, as good as you can get. We'll have another look, but I don't expect to find anything amiss.'

Most people in the room knew just how infrequently children were murdered by strangers. Since the war, the numbers had remained remarkably constant, just five a year. Statistically, the children most likely to be murdered were babies under a year old, more often than not by parents or family friends.

Cole went on, 'First reports from HO forensics in Huntingdon. The timber that she was tied to was your average deal. It's found in any builders' merchants and probably in the rafters of your own houses. An inch-wide chisel was used to taper the end that went in the ground. For what it's worth, they carried out a similar operation and found that it took ten minutes to complete. Still worthwhile, though, to check out the merchants. We're looking for something over six-foot-three of three-by-three, and a two-foot cross-section of three-by-one.' He paused to flip a sheet of paper over his clipboard. 'This is what we've got so far. The ends of the timber were cut by a circular saw, teeth shape and size available et cetera. What it does mean is a lot of shavings. Keep that in mind.' He paused again, read ahead, and pulled a face. The words on the page sharpened the memory. 'The victim was tied to the cross. Why? The obvious answer is that whoever did it wanted the body found. Why? Semen left on the body and the possibility of mass screening suggests to me that we're not looking for a local man. On the other hand, the area is off the beaten track, hidden round the back of the estate, which indicates local knowledge. So maybe someone who moved away from the area.'

Baxter interrupted. 'Another possibility has been suggested . . .' For a moment he turned and glanced at Deighton who shuffled uncomfortably in his seat, '. . . that it was part of some occult practice, a ritual.'

Cole shrugged. 'It's certainly worth considering.' He went on, 'Death was caused by suffocation, probably during a forced act of oral sex. There was slight damage to the throat. She had been sodomised. There were teeth marks on the body. Some time after death an instrument, at the moment the most likely contender is one of these giant-size dildos, was rammed into the vagina with sufficient force to destroy a number of internal organs.'

Cole paused and glanced up. There were some pretty shocked faces out there that had heard the details for the first time. Jaws tightened, eyes fixed on him and on the enlarged photograph of Jane West just behind him.

'The victim's face had been made up; lipstick, rouge, foundation, the works. The make-up hasn't been fully identified yet, but it's an old range, no longer on the market. Scanning electron microscopy gives us traces of lead on her arms and legs and amounts of silica under her fingernails and in her hair and mouth. Analysis of other debris taken from her mouth and from the rest of her body will follow later. Bruising on her arms is consistent with being held tightly, perhaps during the sexual assault. Working with Bone's Law on the width and length of the fingers and the flesh cushion, we're looking for someone between five-nine and -ten and one-forty to one-sixty pounds, right-handed. Rope burns, not bruising, on the victim's wrists and what was left of the flesh on her ankles is not consistent with being tied in a restraining fashion, and not caused by being fastened to the cross. In other words, she was tied up after death. Why? Why tie up a dead person? More black magic? Some fetish I haven't heard about? Necrophilia? The pathologist is pretty certain that the injuries to the victim's feet and lower legs were caused after being fastened to the cross, which was perhaps as much as two hours after she died. He estimated over twenty powerful blows with something like a miniature baseball bat. Perhaps a child's bat.' He studied the pad again. 'Where am I? A trace of linseed oil is present in the rectum area. Partially undigested remains of chilli pizza, salad and garlic bread and a small amount of chocolate were found in the stomach. Death occurred between two and three hours after the meal. Lactic acid accumulation in the muscles and other time of death tests indicate that she died between ten and twelve. Therefore she ate between seven and ten. She had also consumed a fair quantity of white wine. We hope to get a make on this later. So, we've got a picture of those last hours. She was given a meal with wine and even chocolate. If she'd been harmed before that it didn't stop her eating. After the meal, what was the final, or possibly only attack, took place and resulted in death. The body was then transferred to the field and tied to the cross. After that the mutilation of the legs and feet took place. We can be certain that these actions were planned in advance. The choosing of the site, the knocking of the cross in the ground, the fastening of the body to it, knowing that it would be found, these weren't just spur of the moment actions. There has to be a reason.'

Cole turned another sheet and went on. 'Fibres. A number of fibres were found on the victim's hair and in her mouth. They are green acrylic fibres, uniform in both length and thickness, associated with the process called flocking. They have a melt test temperature of 225 degrees Fahrenheit. Huntingdon think they come from an ICI range of carpets. More info later. The rope used to tie her to the post is what they call twisted hemp, very common, on sale in most gardening or do-it-yourself stores.'

Cole dropped the clipboard to his side and let his gaze wander across the room. 'Right, not a lot, but enough to get on with. Keep the ritual idea in mind but don't let it get in the way. Add takeaway pizzas, builders' merchants and carpet shops to the door-to-door. We're extending the search area around the SOC to five hundred yards and the grid system to one hundred. That's it. I've done.'

He turned to Baxter and nodded. Baxter glanced at his uniformed counterpart and asked, 'Anything to add, John?'

Billingham scowled.

'Then that's it,' Baxter said.

Chief Superintendent Marsh got to his feet as Baxter left the room, and went into a huddle with his guests and senior uniformed officers. As far as the chief was concerned, he agreed with the commissioner – the uniforms were the real policemen.

The evening management meeting took place in the police

canteen over Formica-topped tables, where the distinctive smell of fried food eased through the closed shutters to the kitchen, along with the faint odour of disinfectant that had been used over the weekend. They went over the statements and family details.

The meeting was low-key and subdued. There was a child murderer on their patch; by comparison, other criminals became insignificant. Overnight, the police had become everybody's friend. Liberalisers, lefties and civil liberty organisations had become public enemies. Some things could never be forgiven. This was one of them. Murder for gain, or out of jealousy and hatred, could be understood, labelled, given a life stretch, and with the exception of those involved, could be forgotten. But the murder of children was another matter. The evil lingered on in the mind. That through lust alone someone was able to step aside from humanity couldn't be understood. The gravity, the sheer enormity of the offence, committed for sexual gratification, was beyond belief. There was a monster on the loose – real, in the street.

Tony Baxter knocked off at nine thirty and went home. His wife would have his dinner waiting, ready to be nuked. With the exception of potatoes that microwaves hadn't mastered, he wouldn't have known the difference. He ate the meals put in front of him. He didn't taste them. Given the noises emanating from his stomach, he knew that keeping this one inside him for any length of time would be a major achievement.

Rick Cole had the key in his front door when he heard the telephone. He made it on the third ring and sat on the stairs to answer.

'Rick?'

For a moment he thought it was Jenny and his chest fluttered, then he picked up on the accent. 'Hazel?'

'Yes, I'm sorry.'

'It's all right. I've just this moment got in. What's wrong?'

A slight pause, a little catch of breath, then, 'I shouldn't have

73

called. Everyone else is either in bed or with their husbands or boyfriends. I've been back an hour and can't settle. I've been sitting here feeling sorry for myself.'

'That's a game for one person.'

'Tell me about it.'

'It's getting to you?'

Silence, hesitation that destroyed the possibility of a lie.

'Are you all right?'

'No, I'm not. The PM was the last straw. The way her little face folded when he pulled the scalp forward . . . I thought I'd handle it.'

'Where's . . . I'm sorry, I've forgotten your husband's name?'

'Nigel.'

'Yeah.'

'He's in Manchester all week. I told you about it in the boozer, remember? Of course you don't. Why should you? A conference on child abuse. Don't you just want to laugh?'

He grunted and murmured, 'I'm not laughing.'

'I expect you're knackered. The last thing you want to do is console a distraught DC.'

'I'm all right. You want to talk?'

'Do you mind some company?'

'Shall I come over?'

'I'll come to you. Twenty minutes. You're sure you don't mind?'

'Taken aback, that's all. I'll put the coffee on.' He hung up and sat there for a moment to clear his thoughts. Taken aback wasn't quite right. He was staggered by the sudden turn of events. Suddenly he made a move. Things needed doing. Shower, tidy the place up, he had a guest coming.

The door bell rang early. Cole opened the door a few inches. Around it she saw the dark hair on his chest and smiled. His body was washed in the orange street light, his hair dishevelled and wet.

'You said twenty minutes.'

'I meant ten.'

Hazel McLintock looked different. She wore track-suit bottoms, white trainers and a white woollen sweater that hugged her neck. For a moment he seemed indecisive before opening the door wide.

She walked into the surprisingly bright hall. He closed the door and headed for the stairs. All he wore was a pair of navy-blue boxer shorts. He waved a hand toward the living-room and muttered, 'In there. Give me a minute.'

She tried to hide her speculative smile and watched him climb the stairs two at a time. The rumble and slosh of a washing machine came from the kitchen. The door to the passage was open. An ironing board stood propped against the work surface. Two shirts hung on hangers from the cupboard-door handle.

She moved into the living-room. The street light poured across the bay window until she drew the curtains and turned on the light. The light bounced off an empty whisky bottle by the chair. A glass stood on the chair-arm next to an open text book. *Roman Britain.* An overflowing ashtray lay on the floor next to the bottle. A few newspapers were scattered about. All remnants of the last time he'd spent a few hours at home.

Copies of the confidential twice-weekly *Police Gazette* lay beneath the gas fire. The air was filled with stale smoke. There was dust on the TV screen and the PVC top to the music stack. She took in a couple of photographs on the sideboard, one of an old couple, the other of Cole with his arm around an attractive woman. She guessed it was his wife. She sat down on the sofa just as Cole appeared at the door. He had dressed, jeans and sweatshirt, and brushed his hair. But he hadn't shaved and his jaw was dark.

'Coffee,' he said and disappeared again. She heard cups rattle, the washing machine begin its final fast spin. By the time the spin finished Cole was back carrying the drinks.

Hazel sat on the sofa, her legs drawn up beneath her. She looked tired, but comfortable and at home. She reached for her drink and held onto it with both hands while she sipped it. The steam dampened her nose. She gave him a resigned little smile of acknowledgement. 'Surprised?'

'Yes,' he said. He moved the glass and sat in the armchair opposite.

'So am I. A couple of days ago you'd have been the last person I'd have wanted to see.'

'That much was obvious. What changed?'

'The boozer, I suppose. I realised you were human after all.'

He smiled.

'And this morning. Seeing you handle the Wests.' She sipped some more coffee then shot him a speculative glance. 'I saw the For Sale notice. You're moving?'

'Maybe. Getting a buyer isn't easy.'

'Where will you go?'

'I don't know. I haven't really thought it through. But after Jenny left selling up seemed the right thing to do. For a while I just wanted to start again. Does that make sense? Now it's not so important.'

She nodded.

'What about you?'

'Me?'

'Yes. Do you think you made the right decision transferring here?'

She fell in and smiled. 'Now it's not so important.'

He recognised a slight regret behind her half-suppressed laugh. 'Have you thought about a family yet?'

'I've thought about it,' she said, seriously. 'I think Nigel quite likes the idea, or did. But children aren't the answer. That's what makes me laugh when I get called to the domestics. If a kid's involved give it to Hazel. Half the guys in the squad have more experience with kids.'

Cole knew exactly what she meant. There was no answer to it. Women always copped the shout when a child was involved. But it was for the child's sake, not necessarily out of prejudice.

'In the boozer I got the impression you weren't happy,' he said, not wanting to get dragged into sexism. 'You mentioned Sam's problems as though you shared them.'

'I don't think my husband's screwing around like Sam's wife, but if he did I don't think I'd mind. But he thinks I've let him down. He wants the non-judgemental wife bit – an outlet for

76

the day's events, the placements that have broken down, the battered wives, abused children, the incompetence of the local police.'

'Judgemental. Christ, that's a social worker's word if ever I heard one.'

'He doesn't realise that when I get home I'm already OD'd on wrecked lives and grief. The last thing I want is to hear more of the same. They don't get on with it, social workers, they just moan about why they can't do this or that. They think they're the only ones suffering the financial restrictions.'

Cole knew exactly what she meant. He'd been there. Many a time he'd fought to produce some reaction to minor everyday tragedies. Jenny had never been fooled.

She went on, 'I listen to my friends' misfortunes or the details of their lives – a new outfit, the freezer on the blink – and I'm just blank. The truth is I'm not interested. Is that selfish?'

He stood up and pulled a fresh bottle of Teacher's from the sideboard. 'I need some of this. What about you?'

She hesitated over her coffee then set it aside and nodded. When he was settled again she asked, 'What's with the history book, *Roman Britain*?'

'Just an idea. When I got home last night, or rather, this morning, I couldn't sleep. I remembered a time in history when women were impaled. It was in Boudicca's day.'

'You think there's a connection?'

'That's jumping the gun. And Jane West wasn't impaled, she was just tied to the stake—'

'She was in a way.'

Cole pulled a sceptical face and shook his head. 'No, Jane's murder is about sex, power, all those old clichés. Some bastard out there is getting off on the idea of us knowing what he's done. An evil, mental bastard. Definite contender for a door left open and a short-sighted screw. He's looking to read all about it in the tabloids.'

'In that case he'll be pretty pissed off.' She swallowed a large measure. 'Maybe it's not such a good idea, keeping the details from the media. It might make him act again.'

'Let's hope we can catch him before he does. I know it

77

seems a long time, but she was only murdered last night. Just twenty-four hours ago. We'll have him. The checks will throw him out.' Cole spoke with a confidence that he didn't really feel. So far, with the exception of some grit, fibres, a blood group of O-positive which had been confirmed just moments before he left the office, and the Bone's Law description which could fit half the men in the country, they had very little to go on. In most major crimes you either had a good suspect in the first day or so, or you resigned yourself to a long and often unresolved investigation.

'You were SIO on the Ice-cream Man, weren't you?'

He nodded slowly, reluctantly. 'I was at the Yard, working with the child pornography unit. Going through the lonely hearts columns. It's still the favourite place for these bastards to advertise. Believe me. Man requires woman, likes dogs and children. You've read them.'

'What happened?'

Cole sighed. In his mind he had lived it a thousand times. 'Paul Baker was just the start,' he said. 'He'd gone down five years earlier for indecent assault and abduction. The profile threw him up. We found the girl, Sharon Keaton, a six-year-old, in a condemned house on Telford Avenue, a place Baker used to share with his nan.' Cole's eyes narrowed to slits. The memory was as sharp as though it had happened yesterday. 'Photographs we found at the house led us to a local photographic lab. I tell you, warnings should go out to mums and dads about taking nude shots of their kids. The lab was making copies and selling them on to paedophile rings. We got names and addresses from the lab. One of the addresses led us to the centre of the child porn industry at that time. Videos, magazines, photographs, you name it.'

Cole thought he had been immune to it all. He'd had the daily inoculation, the reports, the photographs. But there were one or two things to come that shocked him. The booze had loosened his tongue.

'The videos were filled with child rapes, the real thing, abuse that was beyond belief. We tried to match the faces with our missing kids. Nothing. And yet there were dozens of them. It

78

was a police surgeon that came up with an idea. He recognised the cries from some of the children. To us they were just cries and screams. But he heard a word or two hidden in the cries. They were from eastern Europe, former Yugoslavia, Bosnia, Croatia, anywhere where the parents were desperate enough to get their kids to safety. The photographs were flashed to the agencies over there and before long the whole thing blew up. The parents had paid money to have their kids moved out. They went via Spain or France, hidden in containers, seven or eight at a time, boys and girls aged between five and ten, and they arrived at a warehouse on the outskirts of Amsterdam. Most of them would do just about anything to stay alive. Others were forced into it. Videos were produced by the thousand, magazines by the hundred thousand, passed to distribution centres around the world. Ours was just a small outlet.'

She nodded sadly and glanced at her watch. She finished her drink in one, felt the warm kick in her throat and said, 'It's time for me to go. I don't want to outstay my welcome.'

For a moment, he thought his description of the investigation had been too much for her. 'It's no problem. We've still got the best part of six hours.'

'That's what I mean. I've got to try and get some sleep. Thanks for the company.'

'That was my line, wasn't it?'

She smiled wearily. 'Something like that.' She placed her glass on the side and moved to the door. He followed close behind, catching her perfume.

'You better get a cab. You're over the limit.'

'Yeah, yeah,' she said.

Once she had pulled away, he poured himself another drink and sat down in her position, seeing the room from her vantage point. Apart from the dust it didn't look too bad. Not for a single man.

During the last few days the detective constable had got under his skin. It had started at Russell Ward's retirement, he supposed, when he noticed her glances in his direction. Since then, he had thought about her more and more. She was a

79

puzzle: friendly, but in a formal sort of way. There was a line she was refusing to step over – just little hints here and there. It was almost as though she was weighing things up, going through the process of making up her mind about him. The more he thought about it, the more he decided that the PM had just been an excuse. She wasn't that upset. She had used it to see him.

In the darkness of his bedroom, with only a faint streak of light curling around the top edge of the curtains, Cole realised he was finding it increasingly difficult to get her out of his mind. Somehow he had allowed her to become a permanent fixture. And he was enjoying the strange intimacy.

Part 2

Chapter 10

When the cashier was serving another customer, he looked at the magazines displayed on the top shelf. They were full of cunts. Spread open. You could see inside. Legs were wide. Bits hung out. Like bits of glistening pink shellfish. Rotting shellfish. You could smell it. Disgusting. The women pouted their lips, their smiles were filthy, trying to get you to do it to them. He knew. They couldn't fool him. Not for an instant.

When Father was alive he went with cunts like that. He was always out with them, spending his money. Mother was always short. She knew. He remembered her tears. When Father went out she used to turn to him. She needed comforting. He used to stroke the bruises on her stomach. She used to move his hand down across the fatty folds and into her hair. In those days Father was always short tempered. Often violent for no reason. On occasion, his father had hit him. Once his arm had been broken but they all agreed to blame it on a fall off his bicycle. Then Father died. It turned out to be a heart attack at the wheel of his car. A heart attack brought on by booze and cigarettes and not sleeping. And that left Mother with a seven-year-old son. She had Father's pension, but that didn't keep them. They should have had more than that. They should have had help. Mother had been in the same car. She came out of it crippled, bedridden at the age of forty, her legs and hips smashed beyond repair. Her feet missing altogether. He remembered her sores, horrible, smelly wounds that wouldn't heal. Oozing with pus. Like cunts.

He'd been in the car as well, trapped in the footwell of the back seat. It'd seemed like hours. He was all right. Just a little knock on the forehead as he was thrown forward, and a few bruises on his chest. That was all. But the seat was pressing down on him and he couldn't move as the well filled up with still warm blood and his mother's screams lanced into his head. The blood was warm and sticky against the side of his face. It had a sweet sickly smell. He remembered the great globules of white shimmering sparks as firemen cut the side of the car to reach him. He still had dreams about it even now. The smell of blood in a butcher's shop brought it all back.

Of course, social services provided help and his nan moved in. But when he left school, social services more or less finished, unless you wanted to pay for it. Nothing was free. Not nowadays. They just left you to get on with it. All they cared about was their budget allocation. Finances. His nan ended up in a nursing home, not knowing what day it was. Dementia, they said. Over the years, he'd seen it get worse. After that he stayed home, of course he did, to look after Mother. Hour upon endless hour with nothing to do but listen to her pain and grief. And clean up after her, that was part of it, clean and dress the sores. Wash her, bathe her, all over, including those disgusting bits. That was the worst part. When she needed comforting again, after he had cleaned her down there. Towards the end, when she was incontinent, the shit went everywhere. Filthy, smelly. All over her. He had to open her up, that horrible wasted flesh, just to clean her.

He used to sit in his bedroom at the back of the house, day in, day out, looking into the school playing-fields. He used to watch the football matches, and sports days, he liked those. And hockey. The girls playing hockey in their short green skirts. They wore green pants, too. He used to sit at his bedroom window, rocking backwards and forwards while he watched. He could see even better, make out the details, once he'd bought a pair of binoculars.

But the women his father went with were like those in the pictures. Their cunts were filthy, slack, corrupted by dirty virus-dripping cocks. Dried up, shrivelled, smelling like rotting fish. That's it! An Indian conspiracy. The Bombay duck was a dried up cunt. Cut out, dried, buried for fifty years, then served as a starter to chicken Madras. Just smell it. You'd know.

He couldn't bear the thought.

Used, disgusting holes.

Pus pouches.

But for the sight of his mother's he'd never seen a real live one. Not then. Frankly, he didn't want to see one, not a filthy

84

used one, dripping with cock spunk. No sir. NO SIR. His head shook violently, even at the thought. Ugh. It would be like looking at one of those photographs on the top shelf, but for real.

Photographs. The walls of his mother's bedroom were covered in them. Photographs and posters. They were taken when she was a young woman. An actress. They were pictures of her in various roles. Cleopatra, Salomé, things like that. He remembered the dressing-room. The smell of the greasepaint. When he was four or five she used to sit him in the corner while she put on her make-up. They used to play a game. She painted his face. Then she'd sit him on her knee and let him suck her tits till they stuck out like the rubbers on the top of pencils. She was there, a first-row name, with a whole career in front of her. Until the accident. How he used to love it. Exploring every nook and cranny. Under the stage was best, where they kept rolls of carpet and old sets.

It wasn't until the last few weeks of his mother's life, after the doctors told him there was no hope, that he began to plan.

Chapter 11

'I'm twenty-six, right? By the time I was twenty-six I was gonna be a fuckin' millionaire. What went wrong?'

'I'll tell you what went wrong, man . . .' A pause while Martin Brookes dragged on Caribbean black. 'Your career took the wrong turn. You got the wrong advice from the careers people. You should have gone into sales instead of consumables. How much you doing with me a week? Tell me?'

'I don't know. You should know.'

'You think I keep books?'

'How should I know?'

'Well, I'll tell you, from memory. It's up and down, I appreciate that, depending on your results, but on average I'd say one and a half, maybe two. Now, I don't know whether you've got another supplier, man, that's your business, but add that up and it comes to a lot of bread. Bread that could've been spent wisely. You take it from me at a discount, you sell it for a small profit. Next time, you buy more, your discount gets bigger, your profit gets bigger. Private enterprise. Conservative philosophy. Thatcherism. New Labour. Different faces, same ball game. Do unto others before they do you. That's how I started. You don't see me shooting or snorting the stock. Do you see me shooting or snorting the stock? No you don't.' Another half inch of weed glowed and turned to ash. 'Except for a little shit, you see nothing. Nothing at all. There's nothing to see. All those blags you're doing, for what? All wasted on this. I ain't complaining, don't get me wrong. You're a regular customer. But if you wanna know where you went wrong, that's it.'

'I used to juggle a bit now and then.'

'That was years ago, and that was weed, and who were your main customers? Schoolkids. Dinner money. That's not juggling, man, that's playing with yourself. How did it go? You sell a quarter and have an eighth for yourself. Rocky, fluff, all that second-rate shit. That's still happening today

in the playgrounds. That ain't what I'm talking about at all.'
His long hair whirled as he shook his head, then fell limply.
'And I'll tell you, Jay, smack is becoming fashionable again.
All these kids are taking it up to level out from coke and Es.
All these fucked-up ravers. And although thirty quid does 'em
for a weekend, in a year that'll be a grand or more. A retailer's
paradise.'

'Tell me about it.'

'It's true. It's building up again. We ain't talking about the
economy here. All that crap from Turkey almost saw us off.
Forty quid a gram, that's it. Three years ago it was ninety. Same
shit, same purity. Think about it. Everyone else is getting a rise
with inflation, we're going backwards. But now's the time to get
in on it. Things are looking up, believe me. It's coming from
Afghanistan via Yugoslavia, or whatever the fuck they call it
now, and Holland. Man, people are getting so pissed off with
Es, and who can blame them? Stimulants are yesterday's bad
news, like the Beatles, like the Royal Family.'

Jason Hackett shrugged and pulled the window net aside.
He gazed out of pin-point pupils as he absently picked at
a crusty red scab on his arm, flicked it away towards a big
rubber plant in the corner, then said suddenly, 'Fuck me! I
haven't seen so much plod in one place since the miners' strike
back in . . . fuck knows.' His brain was dulled as the heat surged
through him.

'There's a kid gone missing. I heard just before you got
here.'

Hackett continued his gaze out of the seventh-floor tower-
block window. Down the road, in Churchill Place, police cars
flashed blue lights. 'Fuck me, there's another bastard one
pulled up. When was the miners' strike?'

'Search me.'

'It's not you being searched that fuckin' worries me. I'm the
one going to be walkin' out of here.'

'About twenty years ago, not more than that. You would
have been six. Edward Heath's three-day week. Was it three
or four?'

'No! No! Not that fuckin' one. When the kozzer got half a

87

ton of concrete through the windscreen, off the bridge, you know? That one.'

'Oh, that one. That was more like ten.'

'Yeah, that's more like it. I knew it wasn't twenty. I'm not that fuckin' old.'

'The other one was better. I was into your game then. Till I learned better. That guy turned out to be my fucking hero. Heath. Edward Heath. Turned all the fucking lights out, didn't he? I'll tell you, it was a fucking dream. Disneyland. Demi Moore's snatch. Better than a semi-detached on a windy night. Better than a conservatory with a piss-poor Yale. We scored during that fucking show. One street, Edgemore Lane, you know it? We did more than six fucking jobs before six in the evening on one fucking night. They hadn't even got home from work. Still trying to find their way in the fucking dark. They were the fucking days man!'

'Before my time,' Hackett said, gloomily. Brookes had never been in his class, not in thieving. About the only thing Brookes had ever mastered was a bit of plastic bottle he used on a Yale, sliding the curved edge between lock and frame. Schoolboy stuff. He heard the clink of metal and turned from the window.

Martin Brookes sat cross-legged before a long coffee table doing the weighing. Scales, a little shovel, plastic bags, he looked like a chemist. He glanced up and said, 'Don't go wasting this. When it came to me it was fatal. Fucking pure. I'm talking about the Virgin Mary's hymen, man. Nothing less. Same supply that snuffed those people over the Cross last year. That's the trouble, there's too many amateurs playing with it. They haven't got a fucking clue.'

'What have you used?'

'Menatol. What else? It should cut back to about ninety-five, man. Since when have you known me to use anything else?' Brookes tossed his head back in mock anguish. 'These bastards cutting with baking powder and bleach are giving us conscientious sorts a bad name. They sieve in the cut, pull out a bit of personal, and what are you left with, tell me? Fuck me, they're worse than bank managers. It's like stealing yards at a throw in. There ain't no honesty left in this country.' He was a remnant from the sixties, the Jesus look, long blond hair, beard to match, bluish lips that looked like a prossie's snatch, tight blue jeans, Imran Khan's muslin shirt and three rows of poisonous beads. He tossed a cellophane envelope onto the table. 'That's it.'

Hackett had already fixed. He knew how good the shit was. He felt good, mashed, ready to melt into the foot-deep pile of the shag carpet. His jacket sleeve was still riding his arm, his personal needle back in its case, tucked away in his pocket. He turned back to the window. His movements were awkward, drunken. 'Fuck me, they've brought a couple of dogs out now. A kid, you say?'

'Yeah, kid from the local school. Been missing since school ended.'

Hackett glanced at his watch. The seconds ticked in slow motion. Time throbbed like an orgasm. Einstein blew on this smack before jotting down his theory. 'That's only a few hours. Bit fuckin' premature, isn't it? She's probably round the bike sheds gettin' seen to.'

'There's some bent evil bastards running around. News is full of missing kids nowadays.'

'I suppose. Still, I don't think I'll go back through Churchill. Fuck that. I'll go the long way round.'

A woman walked in from the bedroom. Hackett watched her reflection in the window. Everything had slowed up. She seemed to move in single frame. She was in her thirties, dishevelled blonde hair spilling over her pale face. She wore a white bathrobe tied loosely at her waist. Her eyes were dark with shadow, her lips a dash of red. She stooped down behind Brookes and draped her arms over his shoulders. Even her reflection in the window showed up more tracks than White City. She fumbled for a straw and aimed for a little heap of coke he kept separate. Hackett had watched him trample on it earlier. A line of dust disappeared and she threw her head back and staggered to the sofa. The robe parted. The fluttering white V of her pants gave him a little kick. If Brookes hadn't been around he would have fucked her, no questions asked. He'd

89

have climbed right inside and swung on her fuckin' G-spot. His thoughts came drowsily.

'Did you hear what happened to Smiley?' Brookes asked.

'What, Jill Jackson's Smiley?'

'Yeah, that one. Is there another?'

'I see her in the paper the other day. Doing this see-through number, you know? On the catwalk. Tits, if you call 'em tits, swingin' around. Seemed to me they were just nipples without any tits. Still, that's the thing, init? Small tits are this year's fashion. If they could use twelve-year-olds they would. Fuck me, I've got bigger tits than most of them. Jill Jackson's are bigger, least her nipples are, but not by much.'

'I saw it.'

'Fucking legs on that, though. Tell me how someone like Smiley could pull somethin' like that? I don't know.'

'Charisma.'

'What happened?'

'He's in hospital.'

'Yeah?'

'Yeah, this afternoon. Mason had him seen to, that's the word. Apparently he slapped his wife about.'

Hackett turned from the window, astonished. 'Smiley slapped Mason's wife about?'

'No, not Mason's wife. His own fucking wife.'

'He slapped his own wife? He slapped Jill Jackson?'

'Yeah.'

'And Mason put him into hospital?'

'Yeah. Mason said if he wanted someone to slap around to go and pick up a tom, that's what they're paid for. He doesn't like to see women hurt. If you got a problem you should talk it out, go to fucking Relate or something. He sees himself as the guardian of family life.'

'That's a fuckin' surprise.'

'Yeah, I suppose it is. It certainly surprised Smiley. Mind you, there was this other rumour.'

'Yeah?'

'Yeah. That Smiley going ape and slapping Jill about was down to booze, pissed out of his head. And he hit the booze

90

because he'd grassed to the filth. Scared shitless, he was shaking so bad he thought he'd got Parkinson's. So, really, whether Mason tucked him up for knocking his wife about is questionable. If that wasn't the case, he's got to face it again when he gets out.'

'When's that likely to be?'

'Well, that depends how quickly he learns to walk with plastic kneecaps and see out of one eye.'

Hackett winced. 'It was grassin'.'

'You think so? With Mason you never know. He can be unpredictable.'

'Definitely. Even Mason wouldn't do that for just slappin' your own wife, even if it was Jill Jackson. He probably didn't even know her.'

'Oh, he knew her. He's been shagging her for about six months, off and on.'

'Oh shit. Did Smiley know that?'

'Course Smiley knew. Everyone knew. Everyone thought Smiley was happy about it. Saw it as some kind of honour that Mason was shagging his wife. Till now. Now we figure that's why he mouthed off.'

'Jesus.'

'That's the way it goes. Mason's an old timer. You don't fuck around with people like him. Fuck me, man, it wasn't as if it was something important. It was only his wife.'

'Jill Jackson.'

'Think about it. Smiley didn't see her as Jill Jackson, did he? He didn't see her body like the rest of us see it. To him it was like fucking . . . his wife. Like, you live in Folkestone, you don't go to the fucking beach, do you? You live in London you don't visit the Tower. Know what I mean? Same difference. While the rest of us wank just dreaming about her, he'd give it a poke and not know the difference. Sooner sit up and watch the late movie. See what I mean?'

Hackett tossed a banded roll onto the table. Brookes picked it up, pulled off the band and began the count. A few moments later he nodded and Hackett stashed the wraps in the inside pocket of his lightweight jacket. Next to his gear.

'Right then, you going to see me out?' he said as he stole another glance at the woman's crotch. The dark hair spilling from the elastic of her pants was stiffening him up. If he stayed much longer he'd be walking around as if it was flag day.

Brookes caught his furtive glance and said, 'You know the wife, Connie, don't you?'

Hackett gave his head a quick shake.

'Oh, I thought you'd met. If you like you can take her in the bedroom. Call it a fucking discount. You're a good customer.'

Hackett weighed up the odds and decided against. He didn't like the look of the tracks, some of them flared, next week's abscesses. Shared needles, all that shit. He didn't want to die before he'd made his million. Beside that, the way he'd been lately, he'd have trouble getting a length together. That was a long term problem with smack. It always had been. A wank was all right, but the real thing put it to bed. Funny that. But that's how it was.

He shook his head and moved to the door. The woman raised her head from the sofa, glared at him, then sank back.

'Now you've hurt her feelings,' Brookes said and smiled thinly. 'Be careful out there. Snowball's on the loose.'

'Eh?'

'George Orwell, *Animal Farm*.'

Hackett nodded. 'Right,' he agreed, but he hadn't got a clue.

'Stay cool, man,' Brookes said sadly, sixties-style.

The door closed and left Hackett in a gloomy corridor. The walls were covered in marker pen: floating balls attached to upright dicks stuck into mouths or split figs. If it hadn't been for the teenage titles given to each sketch he wouldn't have known the difference. One looked very much like the other. But they proved that the world was full of fucked-up people. He headed for the lift, then remembered it was out of order and hit the stairs. The stink of urine came up from the basement. Down there, at night, people pissed on discarded condoms and syringes, aiming among the crumpled shapes of sleeping alkies and tramps.

He went out the back way, over the ground-floor railings, away from the commotion and flashing police lights at the front. He kept to the shadows, and made his way to the side street that led him out of the estate. It was always a pleasure to leave Richmond Park.

Twenty minutes later he let himself into his first-floor bedsit on Carrington Road. The entrance was directly opposite the Carrington, the old vaudeville theatre. The place had been used as a bingo hall and a year ago it had been boarded up for good. Agents had been trying to sell it. There had been interest, but no offers. The pigeons had taken over, filling its carved stonework with nests and the pavement below with bird shit.

His bedsit was large in comparison to others, but shabby, badly needing a paintbrush. The ceilings were high, old-fashioned, bordered with plaster coving. None of your polystyrene crap. At the far end was a small kitchen, beside it a smaller bathroom.

After sniffing just a dab he hid his week's supply behind a piece of loose Polyfilla that looked as though it had been used to fill a hole on the rotting window frame. Five minutes later he was out again, crossing the busy road towards the theatre. Clouds were stacking up, snuffing out the evening sky, bringing forward the dusk.

Joseph Pullin was waiting for him. He was propped up in the doorway, half-concealed by a couple of wide pillars. His sleeping-bag and blankets were rolled up. It was Friday. On the streets it was the worst night of the week. World War Two. Lager louts, alkies, crackheads scoring for Glasgow Rangers, any one of them would have kicked him for fun, a few of them to make off with his gear. It was still early, but Pullin had been on the streets long enough to know how to survive. You find your patch and you guard it with your fucking life. If the others thought you were a nutter so much the better. That's why he kept a couple of bottles, cider and meths, the nutter's mix, in plain view beside his stash. Not many people messed with a nutter. Nutters didn't give a fuck. That made them dangerous. Even the brain-damaged fuckers from Scotland kept their distance.

'All right, Jay?' he asked in a phlegmy voice. 'We're in for some rain. Perhaps it will clear the shit off the pavements.'

Hackett lit a cigarette and nodded. He offered one across. Pullin accepted a light and pulled deeply. 'Ta,' he said, and coughed.

Pullin was sixty-two but with his weather-smacked face and slightly stooped shoulders, always hidden summer or winter by a thick overcoat, he looked older. Surprisingly, considering he'd lived in the doorway of the theatre since it closed, he was clean and looked reasonably well fed. Not like the other homeless you tripped over, who really looked the part. His face was reddened by the elements and, when he could get it, real booze, not the show he kept by his gear, but he knew where to get the hand-outs – the free meat and veg, the clean clothes, a shower and shave. He knew where the Sally-Anns set up for the food and which leisure centres opened for the showers.

Hackett nodded towards the twin telephone kiosks to the left of the theatre. 'Anythin'?'

'No, not a thing.'

They had a little contract. Pullin had been taking messages for the last few months in exchange for the shrapnel in Hackett's pocket. It rarely came to more than a couple of quid a time. And if Hackett was short then it never came at all. The older man accepted it. Just recently Hackett and Pullin had been enjoying a good spell. The night before last it was heavy coins, almost a fiver.

The sky darkened. Pavements crowded up. Alcohol turned to laughter and raised voices. Carbon monoxide thickened into a haze. Traffic started to choke the worn out road.

Hackett glanced at his watch and said, 'If you want to shake a leg or do some shoppin' I'll hang around for a while.' The old man often used the twenty-four-hour Paki store a hundred yards down the road. He seemed reluctant. Hackett nodded and slipped a fiver across. 'Go on, take it. It's been a good week.'

Pullin accepted the money but remained hesitant. 'Thing is, Jay, there's this tart.'

'You've got a tart?'

'No, not me. Not exactly. I'm a sort of father figure, see?' He rubbed the white stubble on his chin. 'Thing is, told her I'd be here. Don't suppose she'll come back but . . .'

'I'll tell her you just popped out. She can wait.'

'It's not like that. If she don't see me here she won't come across. It's like, she's scared.'

'Everyone's scared. It's a fuckin' scary place out here.'

'Look, I'll hang on. I can always go shopping later, take the gear with me.'

'And lose your place.'

'Well that's always a chance, isn't it? At least I won't get shat upon.' He pointed to fresh pigeon droppings.

'You're worried about her?'

'Thing is, Jay, Black Benny's been sniffing around. I wouldn't like Benny to get his hands on her. She's too good for Benny.'

Black Benny, a second generation West Indian born in Tottenham, a vicious little toerag, waited at King's Cross station for youngsters who arrived from the northern cities. He was everybody's friend, feeding them up with free crack, until they needed it, which wasn't long, then he put them to work around the Cross or in the red rooms behind his mini-cab shop. Ten quid blow-jobs and twenty quid pokes. The kids didn't last very long. That's why he needed a regular supply.

Hackett shot the old man a strange look.

'What?'

'I'm surprised at you, that's all.'

'I know what you're going to say. Said it to myself. Don't get involved. There's no place for friendship on the streets, not when you're trying to survive. Yeah, I know. I know. You're on your own, every man for himself. There's a war going on out here. Grab what you can and to hell with the others.'

'Well then?'

'Well then, she's a little belter, not that that's got anything to do with it. I'm too old for that shit. But I suppose I'm getting paternal in my old age. I worry about her. She's vulnerable.'

'She's trouble. You don't want trouble with Black Benny, do you?'

'I don't want trouble with anyone, let alone Black Benny. She said she was eighteen, come down from Nottingham. From what I could gather she's been living rough for a couple of weeks. I showed her where the DSS was but they sent her round to Youth Employment.'

'Then she ain't eighteen, is she?'

'I realised that. Good grief, I realised that. She didn't get a penny out of them. Advice yes. Go back home. But that was all. Damned people didn't even tell her where the hostels were.'

'Most of them are closed up.'

'I know that. So she starts talking big. She was going to sell the *Issue*, get a squat. She really hasn't got a clue. I suppose it's her innocence I find endearing. It brings back a memory of the past. Just a fleeting memory. It's almost sad. It's so unusual to find innocence on the street. It reminds me of Sunday school. There's no pity on our street, Jay, no place for the innocent to hide.'

'If she's so innocent how's she find herself down here? How's she survived a couple of weeks? She ain't so innocent. She's taking you for a fuckin' ride.'

Twelve years earlier Joseph Pullin had been a school teacher. Until life turned on him – and that can happen to anyone at any time. When it does it strikes like a viper. He was suspended for thumping a particularly unruly student. His parents died within weeks of one another and he turned to the bottle. His marriage fell apart and his savings disappeared. When the bailiffs arrived he got on a bus to London. Disappearing behind the capital's glitzy lights was an easy thing to do. The streets were full of people hiding away, covering tracks, trying to rub out the past. His was just another face. Another fucked-up, blistered face.

The telephone rang from the kiosk.

Pullin raised his hand but Hackett was already on his way. The ringing was almost drowned by the noise of traffic. He moved fast. He didn't want someone from the crowded pavement getting there first.

'It's me,' he said into the dirty instrument.

'Hello you, this is me. What's happened to your secretary?'

Hackett recognised Patrick Wall's voice as it travelled from Heathrow airport. 'I've given him the night off. You all right?'

'Not bad, not bad. You'll like this one. Oak Road. You know Oak Road?'

'It's ringing a bell.'

'So it should, my son. It's pretty exclusive. Luggage was the bollocks. The cost of their suitcases alone would buy my place.'

'A fuckin' duffle bag would buy your place, Patrick. Address?'

'Oak Road, number fifteen. He's a doctor.'

'How the fuck d'you get that?'

'Clocked it, my son, on their outward bound labels. Dr and Mrs W G Singh. Travelling with their son, aged at a guess, about fifteen.'

'Sounds promising. Curry merchants. I like a spot of curry. Oak Road on their labels?'

'They're not that stupid. Had to queue up behind them on the check in. Clocked their receipts, insurance, passports. Even got his inside leg measurement. They're off to Acapulco for fourteen nights, and get this, club class.'

'It does sound promising.'

'Be in touch.'

Hackett hung up and let the crowd carry him back to the theatre steps. He climbed them, moving out of the rush, and then saw the girl. Or at least the back of her.

In her baggy clothes, oversized bomber jacket and creased jeans, her thin frame and long legs made her appear taller than she really was. Her thick-soled black shoes pushed her up even more. She was no more than five-seven or -eight. She held onto a bulky holdall. He noticed the long brown hair trailing down the back of the jacket. She stood legs slightly apart, facing Pullin.

Pullin caught his eye.

'So long, Joe.'

'Jay, just a moment.'

Hackett turned back.

The old man waved a hand at the girl. 'This is Greg.'

'Greg?'

97

The girl turned to face him. Girl, woman, something in between. She didn't look old enough to vote. She said easily, 'My parents named me after seeing their favourite film star in *Roman Holiday*. I was going to be an Audrey. I should have been.' Her voice was unaffected and held a trace of the north.

Hackett grinned and said, 'Greg's good. I like Greg. Who was the film star?'

'Audrey Hepburn.'

'You've lost me.'

'He was pissed when the certificate came round the hospital. He could only remember that Gregory Peck was in it.'

Joseph Pullin had called her a little belter and he'd been right. Without a scrap of make-up and looking like she hadn't washed in days he could see why Black Benny was chasing after her. Full lips parted slightly, dark oval eyes looked him up and down and seemed to dismiss him before focusing on something behind him. She was clocking the faces on the street, obviously wary. As she turned back to Pullin, Hackett mouthed silently, 'Trouble', and the old man grinned and flashed his tobacco-stained teeth.

'Catch you later,' Hackett said, and turned to the road. As he dodged the rushing vehicles he wondered whether Pullin and the girl were watching after him. Of course they were, he thought. No doubt about it. Absolute fuckin' certainty.

The rain held off but the threat was building by the moment. The air was saturated, the cloud ceiling low, shot through and glowing with dirty yellow light.

He parked in a side street just off Oak Road. He'd nicked the car, a green E-reg Nova, half an hour earlier behind Wood Green bus station. People going to the West End parked there and caught the underground the rest of the way. It would be at least midnight before it was missed, which gave him over an hour.

Massive oak trees climbed above the detached properties, far enough away that the roots didn't interfere with the foundations. You needed walking shoes just to get around some of the gardens. The road was lined with copper beech trees and clean pavements and tall fences concealing immaculate lawns. Trees hung over every fence, real trees, none of your council house conifers. The cars, two or three to a house, were Jags and Rovers, top of the range Escorts, the occasional Volvo. This was director and management territory, broadsheets, dishwashers and daily cleaners. Maggie Thatcher's autobiography, still unread, lay in a position that visitors couldn't miss. The size of the television screens had come down, fourteen inches, eighteen max, some hidden in cupboards. There wasn't a satellite dish in sight. Lots of burglar alarms and dog shit, poodle and Jack Russell size, but no satellites.

He kept to the silent springy surface of the bowling-green lawn. For these people Sunday mornings involved Black and Decker. Lots of it.

It took him five minutes to suss the alarm systems at number fifteen, traditional magnetic reed switches wired up to a self-contained bell positioned fifteen feet up a side wall. Short of finding a ladder there was no chance of getting to it – not that he wanted to. The days of filling the boxes with shaving foam, if they ever existed, were long gone. He guessed there'd be something else inside, ultrasonics, microwave, shit like that. There were protection lights over the front door and round the back, activated when the reflected transmission was altered by a moving object.

Small windows were his favourites. If you didn't want additional grief you avoided double-glazing like a black man's pocket. Nowadays, most burglaries took place during working hours when houses were empty – amateurs had moved into the profession. Desperate people who needed bread for junk or food for their families. Smashed glass and forced locks and get out quickly, without even having a good snoop for valuables. They hadn't got a clue. The thought of meeting someone inside frightened them half to death. Hackett was a professional. The thought of smashing glass and rushing a job never crossed his mind.

The most vulnerable point, the one he preferred, was not a small high-level window, but a ground-level one at the side of the building. It was double-glazed. He smiled at his previous thoughts. It had a small encapsulated magnetic reed switch inserted into the framework. Difficult if someone was home because it meant a little noise, but he would have taken it on anyway. With the house being empty it was piss easy. His pencil torch found the half-concealed edge of the switch. It was activated by a separate magnet fitted to the window. When the magnet and reed were pulled apart more than six mill, the magnetic field was lost and all hell would break loose. That was the principle. It meant you couldn't open the window.

After you've scored a pane of glass you need to tap it on the other side for a clean break. Tap it score side and you've every chance of smashing it to hell. Using a plunger and pulling the glass towards you keeps to the principle.

Very carefully, Hackett positioned his bag on the path beneath the window and took out glass cutters, all-weather Sellotape and a wide plumber's plunger. It amused him that for just a couple of quid he could beat technology. Mind you, what he'd find inside was still to be seen. The only thing he was sure of was that the room he could see through the window, a sort of laundry-come-boiler room, was unlikely to be fitted with any expensive gear. It took him seconds to score the outside glass. He didn't bother with the tape to muffle the crack. Instead, he held the glass with the plunger then gave it a sharp tug. There was a muffled snap as the glass broke. The tricky part was to stop the first section of glass hitting the second. He eased it back towards him, using the plunger as a makeshift handle. Very carefully he placed the pane of glass on the grass at the side of the path then went through the routine again. It took him less than three minutes. His final task was to remove the sharp edges of glass from the bottom frame and cover the fresh break with tape. This was sufficient to stop any sharp edge catching him on the way through. He was left with a tunnel-shaped hole about eighteen inches high and the same across. He shoved his gear inside, making certain not to put any pressure on the frame – it wouldn't take much to move it six mill – and then went head first, arms outstretched, and slithered onto the floor of the laundry room.

He gave himself a minute in the darkness, straining to hear in the silence. He'd never got over the buzz of entering a house, the heady flush of adrenalin. He was addicted to it. Some robbers had no alternative: there was nothing else they could do. Others actually enjoyed the danger. Hackett was one of those. Even while he was inside, sharing an eight-by-eight and living on the steamed shit they called food, he was getting off on the memory of the last job.

Eventually, he flicked on his pencil light and began to explore. Amazingly, the house was clean. He sussed that out by working back from the control box in the hall. No electronic fields, no infra-red, not even a pressure mat, nothing. He was surprised and mildly disappointed. Lugging his soft, bulky absorption mat had been a waste of time.

He went through the house systematically, following a routine that came with years of experience. The only room he left alone was the bathroom. From the others he took anything that looked the part and wasn't bulky. He left videos and computers to the amateurs, the opportunist thieves and kids. It was always a thrill going through the woman's room, peeling back her intimate secrets, the underwear, the pill, the occasional sex aid. He never messed a house up – that wasn't his style. In a drawer he found some very tricky sparklers, including a set of pearls which looked like the real thing. He moved into the master bedroom in the hope of finding some credit cards. He looked through the chest and wardrobe and was about to leave when the side of a briefcase caught his eye. It was under the bed, half-concealed by the overhanging duvet. It was the glint of polished black leather that shone for just an instant in the narrow beam of light. He pulled it out and emptied it on the bed. He sorted through papers and stationery and tentatively moved the other contents with his gloved hand. He put two prescription pads in his bag, then moved his torch closer to examine some labels on the side of half-a-dozen small white boxes. They were boxes of the tranquilliser temazepam or what the punters who mixed them with scag called jellies or wobbly eggs.

He smiled and shook his head. 'Now that is a fuckin'

result.' It was silly, really, because they were still available on prescription, but it was something for nothing. Something unexpected. Like grabbing three lemons on a fruit machine that would give you your money back.

On the manor, Ray Marshall was the fence. He was known as the jeweller, although his shop was filled with bric-a-brac. 'I'll give you two grand for the lot,' he said confidently. 'Some of it's rubbish, but I like the necklace.' He was short and stocky, knocking fifty. His gaze held a disconcerting intensity.

Hackett concealed his surprise and said, 'I'll think about it.'

'What do you mean, you'll think about it?'

'If they're worth two grand up front they're worth a second opinion.'

'Two and a half, and that's only 'cos I know you. Two and a half. That's it.'

Hackett collected the stones together. 'I'll still think about it.'

'Tell you what, I'll give you a grand for the necklace on its own.'

'I'll let you know, all right?'

'It's not fuckin' all right. Round here you deal with me.' Marshall rubbed a fist into the palm of his other hand. 'OK, if that's how you want it.' The voice held a touch of anger, not disappointment. Hackett was seeing another side to the jeweller and it made him nervous.

He left Marshall gazing thoughtfully at the telephone and heard the old-fashioned brass bell on the door as he pulled it open. As he went quickly along the pavement he held onto the bag in his pocket. There had been a threat in the jeweller's voice. For a moment, as the crowds came at him along the pavement, he felt a stab of panic in his chest. He told himself that he was being unreasonable, that it was his imagination, but he couldn't shake it. His pace increased. One thing he did know: two and a half up front meant that what he carried was worth four times that amount if he shopped around.

He cut across town and called into Weidenfeld's. For insurance purposes, he explained as he laid out the pearls. The

102

old Jew behind the counter didn't believe a word of it. He examined the necklace under a magnifying glass and then an eyepiece before laying it carefully on the counter.

'It's quite exquisite,' he said. 'A lovely piece.'

'Well, well?'

'Well, for valuation I normally charge five pounds. Show me the rest and I'll waive it. Stupid I'm not. A long time I've been in this game. A lot longer than you. Don't worry. I don't buy secondhand and, more importantly, to other people I don't pass on details of clients. Understand?'

Hackett nodded and carefully emptied his small cotton bag. Weidenfeld examined each item in turn, licking his thin lips. Eventually, he said, 'A very nice collection you've got yourself here. I take it they'll need to be broken up?'

Hackett nodded and said, 'Yeah. I should think so.'

'There's an alternative. You could export them. You could think of that.'

'Are they worth the trouble? We're talkin' a few grand, aren't we?'

Weidenfeld grunted. 'A few grand? A few grand you say? I would say it's more like twenty grand. Is that a few?'

Hackett held on to the counter. 'You're jokin'?'

'That's something I never do. Young man, if you're interested, and it's up to you, I can give you a telephone number. Someone who exports quality merchandise like this. An agreement you'd have to reach. A share of the profit, he would obviously want. Understand?'

'I'll take the number,' Hackett said.

'You'll phone him?'

'I'll phone him.'

'This evening would be a good time. After, say, seven.'

'I'll do that.'

'He'll expect your call.'

When Hackett left the shop his elation was tempered by his earlier encounter with Marshall. By the time he reached Carrington Road he'd convinced himself that he had used the phone to lay on a mugging. Nevertheless, he couldn't help congratulating himself. What a result. Most jobs would make

103

just a few quid, a ton if he was lucky. People just didn't leave twenty grands' worth of jewellery lying about. There had to be a catch. For a moment his step faltered. He even wondered whether Weidenfeld had been mistaken.

It was Saturday, knocking lunch-time. A football crowd, looking forward to a pre-season friendly and already lubricated, had started to muster, flicking abuse at anything that moved. Red and white scarfs flapped in the warm breeze.

He hit his bedsit, still cautious, still paranoid, and stashed his bag in the window frame. He left his smack untouched and snorted two tracks of candy instead. He needed a stimulant. He needed his wits about him. He needed a good voice for the match. He went into the bathroom, splashed cold water and examined his bloodshot eyes. For an instant his expanding brain pushed them out and he took a step back. 'Fuck me,' he said, as he thought about the twenty grand. He saw the spreading smile in the mirror and leaned forward. 'I would fuck you, you bastard,' he said happily.

He wiped himself down and jumped into a new pair of jeans. He'd lifted them a couple of days earlier from the new outfit on the High Street. A plastic bag lined with tinfoil hid the tag from the electronic eye. He even winked at the cashier as he went by. He checked the window frame again, just to be on the safe side, dismayed that in his part of town it was necessary to do so, then, bins on to save his brain from exploding, he went out into the noon sun, feet off the ground, hovering, ready to take on Ray Marshall's muggers, ready to take on the fuckin' world.

Chapter 12

Jason Hackett celebrated his good fortune in the Red Lion. Four pints of IPA, some mad-cow disease in a bun and a couple of double malts set him up. He went to the pre-season friendly with ten thousand others and celebrated some more as the home team beat Stoke City. He was high but it had nothing to do with the dope. At the ground there were fewer kozzers on duty. He noticed things like that. The poor bastards were all out looking for the missing girl. Not that he felt sorry for them. The pigs deserved everything they got and more. A public address system had been set up outside the ground and was broadcasting appeals to the swelling crowd. Had they seen anything? Did they know anything? Were they near Barnwall School at any time yesterday?

Yeah, yeah! Like he was going to tell them.

From the ground it was back to the pub and a few more pints. This was a normal Saturday routine when the team played at home and there was no way he was going to change it, no way he was going to be singled out. His mates were there, flushed with the team's win. He wanted to tell them about his result, but managed to fight off the booze and keep it to himself. As the day progressed the threat from Ray Marshall faded as though it had been a dream. About six, and then again at seven, he sniffed some more, but started to look forward to getting home when he could really score. Snow was for footballers and pop stars with shit for brains and chipolatas up their ring pieces. Crack, that was different. Fuck that. He'd tried it, of course, till the bubbles were coming out of his nose, but it was too sudden for him, too stark, he'd started seeing himself as a Liverpool supporter. When that happened he knew he was in trouble.

The telephone was in the pub corridor opposite the toilets. People brushed past, fastening flies with drunken fingers, trying to pat away the splashes. He kept his voice down.

'I recognise your voice,' Weidenfeld said.

'Suppose you do. I didn't expect to hear yours. Where's your friend?'

'I am the friend, but I don't buy at the shop. Are you interested in my proposition?'

'Yeah, what's the deal?'

'The deal is you'll have to trust me.'

'Trust a Yid? Are you on pork scratchings or what? You're takin' the piss, right?'

'That's an offensive term, young man.'

'Takin' the urine doesn't have the same ring.'

'Not that . . . Oh, it doesn't matter. Why do I bother? Yes, you'll have to trust me.'

'No way. I'd sooner trust a Frenchman's dick. Are you kiddin'? I don't even know you.'

'I don't know you either. You could be part of a set-up for all I know.'

'Me, a grass? You are fuckin' mental!'

'I don't know. Stranger things have happened.'

'Yeah, on fuckin' *Star Trek*, that's all.'

'I'll tell you what I have in mind, then it's up to you. I'll give you three grand for the merchandise then it's a fifty-fifty split on what I can get for it.'

'Oh Jesus,' Hackett murmured. He just knew he was getting shafted. 'When would I get the rest?'

'Monday I have it, Tuesday mmmn, Wednesday I can probably make the sale, so Thursday. Not before Thursday. That's the earliest.'

Hackett tried to conceal his disappointment. He didn't like it at all.

'There's an alternative.'

'Yes?'

'I'll give you six thousand for the lot and you walk away.'

He thought about it, the bird in hand, all that, and liked it better. 'That sounds more like it. Where do I deliver the goods, if I decide?'

'You know my shop? There's a little café, Linda's, three doors up. I have breakfast there on Monday at eight. If you're there, fine. If not, fine also. I'll carry with me two envelopes.

You must decide which one to take. If you're not there by quarter past eight then that's the end of it.'

'I'll be there.'

'Good. I'll look forward to seeing you.'

'Right.'

'So, next year in Jerusalem, eh?'

'Come again?'

'It doesn't matter. I'll see you on Monday morning.'

Hackett hung up. His mood had taken a dive. The conversation with the Yid had done it. The thought of spending more time with his footballing friends was suddenly depressing; getting legless, orbiting the girls for nothing in return and for him there never was, had lost its appeal.

Hackett arrived home at something to nine, threw the bolts on his door and, mixing in a little crushed jelly, did some cooking. He filled his needle from the teaspoon, gave it a shake to let it cool, then applied a little pressure to get rid of the bubbles. Bubbles aren't so cool. He wrapped a cord, held one end with his teeth until his vein ridged, then carefully, finding a spot that wasn't bruised or scabbed, he slid in. He pulled back fractionally till the brown, shitty coloured liquid turned pink, then slowly pressed in a dream. He lay back while his troublesome thoughts disappeared. Anna Ford was on the portable with Jill Dando. He thought about a duo but lost it and concentrated on Anna. As he sank into the warm embrace of his duvet Anna Ford was flashing her beautiful eyes, telling him the news, that everything was all right, all right, spreading her legs so that he could climb inside her and hibernate for a thousand years.

Thunder woke him. The hot weather had stacked up the clouds again and this time it was more than a threat. Rain pelted at his window. But was it the thunder that stirred him? Above the rumble of nature and the throb of traffic, he heard a girl's faint scream, and then some shouting. His mind was muddled. The portable was still on, winking shadows across his scabby walls, some black-and-white crap filling the early hour schedules. John Wayne in a white hat. Almost a silent picture.

He struggled from the bed and realised the fly of his jeans was undone, his dick hanging out like a poor man's pocket, empty and shrivelled. He vaguely remembered a wank before falling asleep, something to do with Anna Ford, but there was no damp tissue on the floor. It obviously hadn't worked.

He turned off the TV, then went to the window and drew back the nicotine-coloured nets. Across the road, on the theatre steps, there was some heavy drama. Through the fizz of bouncing rain he recognised Joseph Pullin in his overcoat. He was pulling at the girl's hand, trying to hold her back, as another man, a big black bastard, tried to pull her away. She seemed to be all arms and legs. She had changed her street clothes for a tank-top and black miniskirt. He heard the raised voices but they weren't clear. A few pedestrians stopped to watch, some of them huddled together beneath straining umbrellas. Suddenly, the black man turned. There was a scuffle and Pullin hit the floor. In that moment the girl legged it. She made the dark alley that ran down the side of the theatre. The black man, Hackett was sure it was Black Benny, went after her. His black leather coat sparkled, caught by the lights of passing traffic.

Even as Hackett moved to the door he told himself to stay out of it. It was every man for himself. The city was no place for friendship. It was the only way to survive.

Cars swerved to miss him, one screeched to a halt, skidding on the wet surface, and a spotted dickhead riding a black cab called him a wanker. He was right, of course.

A few people stood around Joseph Pullin; one of them knelt beside him. When Pullin saw Hackett's face he tried a smile but it fell off to a grimace. Rainwater washed down his old face. His eyes blinked madly. His greatcoat was soaked through.

'He's done me,' he said. There was a smudge of red on his chapped lips, turning pink as it mixed with the rain. 'He's done me, Jay.'

Hackett pushed the other man aside and moved closer. He eased Pullin's hands back off his chest and peeled the thick coat aside. Blood was staining his jumper in a serious place. He turned to look up at the horrified faces. The rain stabbed

108

at his eyes. He felt it run beneath the collar of his sweatshirt. 'Will one of you go over there to the phone and call a fuckin' ambulance,' he said. There was a moment's dithering, then two women took off. He turned back to Pullin.

'Promise me something?' Pullin said. A red bubble burst on his lips and flecked his nose. It was washed away almost immediately by the fierce rain.

'You know me, Joe. What is it?'

'The girl,' he whispered.

'I told you she was trouble. Didn't I tell you? Didn't I? You didn't listen.'

He grimaced again, his eyes began to slip. Hackett shook him. 'Stay awake, Joe. Stay awake. You can hear the ambulance. Can you hear it?'

'Oh, shit, I'm so cold. Jay? Jay?' He lifted a hand and tugged Hackett closer.

'I'm here, Joe.'

'The girl. Promise me?'

'OK, I'm noddin' my head. Can you see me noddin' my head?'

'It's gone dark. I can't see a fucking thing. I'm frightened.'

Pullin's eyes closed. Hackett shook him again but there was no response.

One of the two bottles beside Pullin's bedroll was nudged over by a stray foot in the pressing crowd. It rolled across the wet concrete and came to rest against Hackett's leg. Hackett glanced up and slowly, picking up the bottle by its neck, he got to his feet. The man who had accidentally knocked the bottle over took a step back and murmured an apology.

Hackett pushed a path through the crowd of people and ran to the alley. It was dark and steaming. Spouts overflowed from a building on the right. Cardboard boxes were turning to mush; pallet stacks and galvanised bins were black shapes. He started down, careful where he trod, trying to miss the hissing puddles. He heard a distant ambulance and then a police siren.

He'd gone fifty yards when the alley branched behind a tall office block. Security lights that had been left on threw a dim light ahead of him. Through the slanting rain he saw the two figures before he heard them. They were about twenty feet in front of him. Black Benny, facing away from Hackett, held the girl by her wrists.

Hackett didn't think about it. If he had done he would have walked the other way. He covered the distance in moments, splashing through a deep puddle and, before Black Benny had even turned to face him, he brought the bottle down on the back of his head. He heard the crunch, felt the bone give, and thought he'd killed him. Benny groaned, blood splattered, and he went down like a sack of shit.

The girl backed up against the rough brick wall. Her dark oval eyes were wide and fearful. Water splashed around her feet and threw mud up her legs.

Hackett said, 'What's you name? Jack? Jim? Fuck it. Fuck it!'

'Greg. It's Greg.'

Benny was stirring. He struggled onto his knees then went over again like a shot pig, his face half-covered in mud, his eyes blinking wildly. A single line of blood ran down from his hairline.

A shout came from behind. Hackett wheeled round. Two men had turned the corner, both of them the same colour as Benny, Nescafé without the cream, just blurs in the rain, and they were eating up the distance.

Hackett pushed the girl. 'Run!'

She didn't need telling. Even in her thick-soled clumpy shoes she went like the clappers and he had trouble staying with her.

'Fuck it! Fuck it! Fuck it!' The words came with his every breath. Why the fuck had he got involved? Why hadn't he just settled back and waited till Monday, done the deal, and got the fuck out of it until things had calmed down, until he was back in Ray Marshall's good books?

As they hit the next corner Hackett glanced back. The two men had stopped and were helping Benny to his feet.

He turned to the girl. 'Keep goin'. We've got to disappear for a while. Those people are fuckin' dangerous, believe me. Is there any place you can go?' He saw the desperation in her eyes as she shook her head.

'You're not going to leave me, are you?'

'You can't come with me. I don't even know where I'm goin'. I'm fucked up now. They might have recognised me. They certainly know you.'

'What then?'

'Keep walkin'. I'm tryin' to think. I need to think. My name ain't fuckin' Len Jones.'

'Who's Len Jones?'

'He's a guy I know. He's good at fuckin' chess. At workin' things out. Pawn to fuckin' queen's knight four, or somethin'. Know what I mean? I ain't him. I fuckin' should be. Then I wouldn't have all this grief. I'd be fuckin' his wife instead.'

They made another corner. At the top of the alley a main road flushed with light; a few cars roared past. He knew it was going to be difficult. Benny had a lot of faces on the street. Too many to make getting lost easy.

Voices came from behind them, travelling along the crumbling brick.

Ahead of them, just before the road, three waste bins waited for collection. Hackett pointed to them. 'Let's get out of this alley.'

'Over the wall?'

'We'll be fucked on the pavement. You got any better ideas?'

He clambered onto a pile of slippery boxes that collapsed under his weight and pulled himself onto the nearest bin. He reached down and pulled her up beside him. The top of the wall was just a foot above his head. He hauled himself up, said 'Fuck it!' and jumped.

He landed heavily on a spongy mud surface. It knocked the wind out of him. He got to his feet. The girl hung above him, holding onto the wall with her fingertips. He grabbed hold of her bare legs and she let go. Her weight took him by surprise and she fell on top of him. Her knee belted him in the jaw. He bit his tongue and tasted blood.

They lay propped against the wall, their legs sunk into the mud, listening to the voices as they grew louder, so close now it was difficult to believe they were separated by the brick. In the dim light he put a finger to his lips. She nodded, wide-eyed, hardly daring to breathe. The voices grew fainter, then were lost altogether in the sounds of traffic. He gave it another minute or so, then said, 'You all right?'

She nodded. 'Where are we?'

'Back of the theatre. The stage door's on the main road.'

Before them, a patch of black earth spread to the dark walls of the old building. No shrubs or flowers, just a sterile place heaped with junk, cardboard boxes, old timber and broken furniture. It looked ready for burning. Beyond the pile was a door.

As they approached she asked, 'Is it derelict? It looks empty.'

'Yeah, it's been empty for a year. This is a fire exit.'

It was a double door, the bar handles chained, the paint flaking.

'You're going to break in?'

'Well, I ain't goin' to stand out here all night. I'm soaked. And I'm not climbin' that wall again, that's for sure.'

She stood back, wringing her hands together, and watched as he selected a length of timber from the pile. It might have been part of an old rafter, about six feet long of three-by-three. He approached the door, jammed the length of wood behind the chain and levered back. The chain held but the bar handle snapped away with a loud crack.

He glanced back at the girl. She looked petrified. Her face was plastered with mud, her long hair in strings around her neck. She looked like the geezer in the first sound movie, but she was too frightened to make any sound. He gave the silence a minute before easing open the door.

They entered a dusty corridor. The place was in total darkness. Hackett edged forward, feeling his way along the wall, then he turned back and whispered, 'Stay here.'

He saw her nod.

He moved forward again. The darkness was lifting. Light from the office block squeezed through a few high windows. It was just sufficient to illuminate curtained passages and more doors. Five minutes later he returned, closed the door, and switched on the passage light. He saw the bewilderment in her grimy face. Goose bumps had spread along her arms as she wrapped them around her chest. She shivered.

'Don't worry, the place is empty.'

'Someone will see the light.'

'No they won't, not from the back. They must have kept the electric on to show people around. The place is for sale.'

Relief, or something like it, brought a long sigh. He noticed her skinny knees knocking together. She made the wall and let it take her weight.

'You all right?' he asked.

'I feel so weak and shaky.'

'When's the last time you ate somethin'?'

'This morning. I had a cake this morning.'

'That's why you're shaky.' He glanced at her skimpy wet clothes, the miniskirt and tank-top that left her navel naked. 'What happened to your gear? Your other clothes? You had a coat and bag.'

She shook her head. Her dark eyes levelled. 'I had to leave it when Benny saw me. I couldn't run with it, could I?'

'You ran to Joe?'

'I didn't know anyone else.'

'What's your name? Greg? Well, Greg, you fucked him good and proper.'

Her lips trembled.

Hackett waved a throwaway hand. 'Fuck it, it wasn't your fault. Black Benny's an evil bastard. Always has been. You weren't to know. Your mistake was gettin' off the train at King's Cross.'

She sniffed.

'You're most likely comin' down with a cold or somethin'. Should have kept your coat no matter what.'

'What are we going to do?'

'We? Did you say we?' he scowled, then relented and threw her a winning smile. 'For a start, I'm goin' to make you a cup of coffee.'

'Coffee?'

'Yeah. Someone, probably the caretaker, has left some gear in one of the dressin'-rooms. We'll brew up. That'll sort you

113

out. We're safe here. No one works a Sunday. Not this time of Sunday mornin' anyway. We'll just hang out for a while.' The thought of his scag over the road tightened his lips. 'Benny will look for us for a while then give up. These black bastards have no stayin' power.'

'What then?'

'Then we split, girl. You'd be wise to get back on a train and head back to where you came from. Where the fuck do you come from?'

'Nottingham.'

'Oh yeah, Joe did mention it. Robin Hood, all that shit. I was in Nottingham once, for a few months. Nottingham DC.'

'DC?'

'Detention Centre. When I was younger.'

'I used to go riding in Sherwood Forest.'

'No kiddin'?'

'Yeah.'

'You had a horse?'

'A giraffe.'

'I meant, why the fuck did you leave?'

'My mum was giving me grief.'

'As much as Benny? That's what you gotta weigh it against.'

She shrugged weakly. He led her along the corridor, through a curtained entrance, into the auditorium. He left the curtain open so that the light swept in from the passage. They stood to the left of the stage. He grabbed her hand and pulled her up the steps. Her heavy shoes left mud on the wooden boards. She stood for a moment, wide eyes sliding across the vast hall of seats, up to the ornate balcony. Most of it was dark but she could make out the shapes.

'This is the bollocks, isn't it?' he said.

'I always wanted to be on the stage. I did a bit at school, you know? Shakespeare and stuff. It was the only thing I liked at school.'

'There you go, then. One of your ambitions already tucked away at your age. Come on.'

She followed him across the stage and down the far steps into another passage. It was dark. She ran to keep up. He opened the first of a series of doors. The room was about twelve feet square, complete with battered dressing-table, mirror, chair, screen, a small hand-basin, and a row of empty hangers. On the dressing-table was an electric kettle, coffee, sugar and a half-empty bottle of milk.

'Whoever used it hasn't been gone long,' she said.

Hackett frowned. 'Why?'

'The milk's fresh.'

'Well, whoever it is, maybe the caretaker, is well and truly tucked up in bed by now. If he's got any sense that is. Who'd be out on a night like this? We'll be gone before he puts his slippers on.'

'There're no cups,' she said. 'I can't drink out of a kettle.'

Hackett gave her a sharp look. 'You are a bit of a one. I ain't surprised your old mum fell out with you. Just sit there. I'll go and find some.'

He had a quick look in the next room. It was similar to the first, same set up, no cups. He tried the third room. The door was locked. The key hung in the hole. He unlocked it, pushed open the door and reached in to find the light switch. As he did so a vaguely familiar odour grew more pungent. His nose twitched. It reminded him of the smell in a butcher's shop, sawdust and blood and offal. There was a green mattress on the floor and a small bag overflowing with clothes. On it was masking tape, rope, an old magazine and a single photograph, slightly crumpled.

Hackett approached the mattress and picked up the photograph. It showed a schoolgirl, maybe a fifth former, sitting in the back seat of a car. Her school skirt was around her waist, her knickers around her knees, stretched tightly because her legs were open to reveal her slick.

'Fuck me,' Hackett said. He folded the photograph and stuffed it in his back pocket. He made it just as the girl appeared at the door. He picked up the magazine.

'What have you found?' she asked.

He flicked it open as she approached and uttered, 'Bloody hell!'

'That's disgusting,' she snapped. 'They're little girls.'

'And boys. Ugh!' He threw it to one side. Even he was shocked. It was then that he noticed the spots on the edge of the mattress and on the dusty floor. He stooped to examine them. He touched one with the end of his finger and rubbed the substance between finger and thumb.

'It's blood, I think,' he said. 'Someone's had a nosebleed.'

'It doesn't look like blood.'

'It turns this colour after a while.'

'It doesn't look like blood,' she repeated nervously. 'But I don't like it, Jay. All this stuff, rope, tape. It looks like someone's been tied up.'

Hackett frowned. The thought of the missing schoolgirl flashed into his head. The photograph burned through his pocket.

'Yeah,' he said. 'Maybe. I wonder.'

'I'm hating it. It's frightening me.'

He moved quickly across to the door. In the passage he turned back to her. His voice lowered to a whisper. 'OK. OK. I'm not happy about it myself. It's a creepy bastard place. Just right for a pervert. We'll leg it over to my place and hope Benny didn't get a look at me. You ain't stayin', mind. Just a while. Right? Just to dry off. Till the mornin'.'

'Right,' she said and relief softened her features. She climbed the stage behind him.

The Sunday dawn was still an hour away. The traffic had dwindled; the clouds still tossed but the rain had petered out; the odd drunk rolled by, muttering curses at the moving pavements. In shop doorways bodies stirred and empty bottles clinked together.

They ran quickly across the glistening road like fugitives, heads tucked away in shoulders, bodies bent, as though somehow being an inch or two shorter was going to make a difference. He closed the glass door behind her and pointed to the stairs.

'First floor.'

'Don't you have a lift?'

'I've got my own,' he said. 'Absolutely. Right?'

Chapter 13

While she used the bath he took the opportunity to cook. When she came out of the bathroom in a cloud of steam he'd got black rubber between his teeth and the needle in his arm.

'I hope you don't mind. I washed my clothes and hung them on—' Her mouth dropped open. 'Oh my God, you're—'

'Diabetic. Right?' He relaxed the rubber and slowly emptied the syringe.

'You're kidding?'

'Sort of.'

'Oh my God, why didn't I know? Why didn't I guess?' She wrapped her arms defensively around a massive cream bath-towel and took a step back.

He sank into the bed, caressed by angels, and heard his own voice. 'You're too good to be true, you know that? Don't tell me you haven't seen someone take a dig before. I don't believe you.'

'I've never seen a needle. I've seen dope, spliffs . . .'

'You've been down here three weeks. You've been on the streets, right?'

She shook her head. 'Only for a few days now and again. A friend put me up when her boyfriend was on nights. It's only one room. His shift changed. I had to get out.' She looked around, composing herself. 'I've got to drink something, and eat.'

'Help yourself.' He waved toward the tiny kitchen. He was sinking deeper into the bedclothes. His heaven. Ready to hibernate. Anna Ford's snatch, or something as warm. 'There isn't much. Cornflakes, bread, I don't know. Have a sort out. While you're at it, I'll have some coffee.'

She nodded, still shocked. 'I left the water in the bath. It's a bit dirty.'

'That's all right,' he said, and made an effort to get up. He stashed his gear then stumbled past her. 'The tank don't hold so much. I'll use it to have a wash.' At the door he turned back to her. 'You're havin' me on, right?'

'About?'

'About the dope?'

'No, I've never even tried it.'

'Well, I don't know.' He shook his head in wonder and took another step before pausing again. 'How old are you? Joe said eighteen, then seventeen. But Joe's eyesight wasn't so hot, not since he got his glasses nicked.'

'I'm fifteen,' she admitted and brushed past him into the kitchen. 'Sixteen next month. And your water's getting cold.'

'Yeah. Fifteen. That's more like it.' He closed the door behind him.

In the bathroom he used her water and cleaned his teeth. Something was happening to him. It was the first time in days that he'd cleaned them and God knows how long since he'd used the bath. The water was a muddy colour but it got rid of the green mould on his bollocks. She'd hung her clothes from every ledge, fixing them with whatever she could find, shampoo bottles and packets of soap that he'd lifted from Sainsbury's. He saw her pants hanging from the high window-ledge. He pulled them down and used them to wipe his face, before letting them brush over his penis. He smiled at the novelty then hung them up again. Five minutes later he yelled, 'You've got my only towel.'

'Well, you're not having it.'

'Use the sheet under the duvet and give me the fuckin' towel.'

Quickly, making sure that he wasn't peeping around the bathroom door, she exchanged towel for sheet and threw the towel to his outstretched hand. A minute or two later he emerged zipping up his jeans, shirt undone to his waist, exposing his white skinny chest.

'That's better,' he said, and lay back on the single bed. His eyes felt heavy. He watched the girl eating. She'd made herself a crisp sandwich. Prawn cocktail. Her nipples poked through the sheet. He could just make out the darker circles. A contentment spread over him like a warm blanket, an old friend. He hadn't got a care in the world. Fuck Black Benny. Fuck all the black bastards. His door was bolted, he'd got a certain six grand stashed in his wall, he was clean for the first time in days, he'd got a little belter to look at and if she stood up he might even get a peep at her fluff. The sheet was pretty thin. If not, well, he'd still got the photograph in the back pocket of his jeans. What else did he need?

'What is it?' she asked with her mouth full. She'd noticed the glazed, distant look.

'I'm whacked out, that's what. But I feel good.'

'That's the stuff you've just taken. You'll be dead by the time you're thirty.'

'Thirty. Yeah, that's what I figured. That's another four years, a lifetime. Thirty'll do me fine. Who want's to be forty anyway? Nobody. That's the truth. Forty is a sad age. Fuck me, back in the ancient times people used to die at forty. Think about that. See the old guys eyein' up the young birds. Give 'em a pint and they think they're the bollocks. Till they drink it they just hide in the corner, terrified. I never wanna be forty. Fuck that.'

'What would you say if I asked to try it?'

'I'd tell you to go fuck yourself. To start with it would make you throw up. Probably. It often does the first time. And secondly, what I got here is top-grade gear, high quality. Even a little dig might damage you, or anyway, it wouldn't do you any good. I'd have to cut it so bad it would be criminal. I'd never be able to look at myself in the mirror again. A bit like my old man. He was a total arsehole, but he always said that a man who put dry ginger or anythin' else into malt whisky hadn't got class. It's a bit like that. Right? Know what I mean? It all comes down to class.'

'I don't like injections anyway.'

'If you want a buzz, I've got a bit of dust left. I mean, you just sniff it. It's fuck all, really. A bit of fun. It's like an E. It's like speed, uppers, bennies. They're all stimulants. They wouldn't do you any harm. Not unless they're spiked. Contaminated. Know what I mean?'

'What are you using?'

119

'Me? Fuck me, I use anythin'. Mostly scag. Sometimes speed. Depends how I feel at the time. I mean, sometimes I'll even have a sniff just to keep me going between digs. I've used everythin' known to man, and a few beside.'

'What about grass?'

'The weed ain't a score, girl. It's a pastime, like watchin' a video or somethin'. A Disney. Not even an eighteen. Even then there's a major difference between what you get. Most of the shit around is crap bog Moroccan, a rip-off. The best is skunkweed, Dutch skunk. That's the best. Or if you want hash, then Manali. That's good.'

'What's it feel like? The scag?'

'You don't want to know about needles. Get my drift?'

'Stay away from needles?'

'See, you ain't just a pretty face. Right. Stay away from them. Sniff, smoke, swallow if you want, but don't inject. Unless it's crack. Don't even smoke that bastard stuff.'

'But what's it feel like?'

'Fuck me, girl. What's it feel like? Go and see fuckin' *Moon . . . Moonraker . . .*'

'Uh?'

'You're right. That's wrong. That's James Bond, init? I mean *Trainspottin'*. Crap film, I mean, you'd need to be livin' on the shit to understand what's goin' on. But the old fuckers in the papers say it's brill because they like to think that they're cool. Know what I mean?'

'I saw it, on video.'

'Then you know what I mean.'

'They said it's like coming multiplied by ten or a hundred.'

'That's bollocks. It definitely don't give you a hard on. If you're really into it, the opposite is true.'

'But he took men's mags into the room, to masturbate.'

'Yeah, well, the geezer who wrote it had his head down the fuckin' pan, didn't he? Listen to me, scag destroys dick faster than married life, so I'm told.'

'So what then?'

'It's more like livin' in the world of your favourite dreams. And they ain't wet.'

'But you always wake up?'

'Most of us wake up. Then you gotta think about the next, and the next, and nothin' makes it easier. And you'll do anythin' to make the score. Anythin'. Right?'

He lit a cigarette, sipped his coffee and watched her closely. Even with her long hair plastered to her scalp, and looking as though she hadn't slept for a week, she was bloody gorgeous. A dream.

She sat cross-legged on his carpet, swamped in the sheet. Strands of her hair stuck to her neck. In that position, in the sheet and with her dark, oval eyes, she looked like a Gandhi type, quite beautiful, with a definite trace of Paki or Indian in her. He chuckled at the novelty. He knew it was part scag.

She pushed the plate aside and glanced up. A fleck of something, crisp or crumb, stuck to her lower lip. Her quick tongue flicked it away. She looked at him curiously. 'Joe mentioned you.'

'Me?'

'Don't get big-headed. We talked about everything and everyone.'

'What'd he say?'

'That he'd known you for a year. That you were the strange young man over the road. The only one he trusted. It was funny listening to him speak like he did, so well, with that upper-class accent. And him, homeless. A down-and-out. A tramp really.'

'He called me strange?'

'He said you lived by a code. Look after yourself, don't get involved. It was the only way to survive. If that's the case, why did you help me?'

'I shouldn't have done. It was a mistake I'll probably regret. I done it for him.'

She sighed, flicked her tongue again and said, 'Well, do you regret it?'

He pursed his lips and took his time. 'I've got a feelin' I'm goin' to.'

She grinned. 'OK, I'm ready.'

'What, you want to try it? You mean it?'

121

'Why not? After what happened tonight I might as well. Just a bit, just to let me see.'

He shrugged, pulled his legs round and sat at the top end of the bed by the curtained window. He took out a small cellophane bag and re-sealed his hiding place. He held it up to the light. There wasn't much left. He looked across at her. 'You sure about this?'

She shrugged quickly and nodded. 'Yeah, I want to try it. Just a bit.'

He used the little glass table and chopped at the powder with a razor. Eventually, he stroked out two thin lines of dust. 'There isn't much but it should do you.' He left a straw on the table and lay back on the bed to watch, mildly amused.

Tentatively, on all fours, she approached the small table. She gave him a little glance then picked up the straw and bent over the tracks. Carefully, she stuck the straw into her nostril and practised, holding the other nostril closed and inhaling in quick little sniffs.

'Like this?' she asked.

Hackett grinned at her performance. One line of dust disappeared into the straw. Her eyes watered and she blinked madly. She swapped hands and went through the routine again, practice first, then the dust, then the blinking and the wild shake of her head.

'Oh. Oh,' she said. She dropped the straw, pinched her nose, wiped her eyes and turned to face him, finding her former cross-legged position. 'Oh my God, I can't believe it, I can't believe I actually did it.'

'Can you feel anythin'?'

Disappointment crossed her face. 'Nothing. Yes I can. Yes I can. Tingly. At the top of my nose. Like I'm going to sneeze.'

He finished his coffee, then leaned over the bed and placed the mug on the carpet.

'I need another drink,' she said as if seeing his mug had reminded her. 'My throat's gone dry and I feel a bit woozy. Do you want some more?' She struggled to her feet, collected the mugs, lifted the bottom of the sheet over her arm and walked toward the kitchen. The sheet had become a sarong. She did look like an Indian. But hang on a minute. The put-putters were into saris, not sarongs. Hackett's eyes narrowed in concentration. That's right, the Pakis wore sarongs. The Pakis. Or the tarts in the South Seas. *Mutiny on the Bounty.* All that. Maybe those islands were off Pakistan. They were all over there somewhere, the other side of the map, south.

When she returned with the coffee he asked, 'Did you do geography at school?'

'Not much. It was all into humanities. We more or less decided ourselves. Teacher didn't give a toss, not really.'

'That's terrible. Classes too big. Cut-backs. Half-price teachers. Sometimes I wish the IRA had finished the job with those robbin' bastards. Brighton, remember? Still, things will get better now Tony's in. Anyway, I bet you don't even know where the South Sea Islands are, do you?'

'Course I do. I'm not that thick. In the Pacific – Polynesia, Tahiti, the rugby player, what's his name, Tonga, and Pitcairn, you know? Mel Gibson.'

'All right, all right, I know. Saw the film. All the tits. Near Pakistan, ain't it?'

She shot him a curious look. Her eyes had turned even darker, the pupils dilated. Her tiredness had gone and she felt suddenly elated. She drank some coffee, placed the mug on the carpet and crawled toward him on all fours. The sheet opened and he got a peep of hanging breasts; tiny nipples, like pink iced-gems, those little round biscuits with blobs of icing sugar on top, faced southward. They swung gently. He wrenched his gaze upward to her face. What he should do, he told himself as she moved closer and he got a whiff of soap, was jump on it and fuck it there and then. No messing. But somehow, even if he could get it into gear, his word to Joe Pullin got in the way. Not only that: he'd be too nervous to function. He couldn't remember the last time he'd been this close to a girl. Never mind alone with one.

She placed her arms on the bed and rested her chin on her laced fingers.

He said, 'So tell me about the grief with your mum, then?'

'Oh God, not that. Don't remind me.'

'I'm interested.'

'We just didn't get on. I couldn't do nothing right. Nothing. The atmosphere was so bad, slanging each other every night, Dad and Steve, my brother, losing their rags . . . It was impossible, unbearable. Understand?'

'So you took off?'

'I thought about it for a long time. It wasn't sudden.'

'Did you tell 'em you were goin'?'

'They wouldn't have let me. No chance. I wouldn't have made the front gate. I just legged it while they were at work.'

'So they'll be worried about you?'

'Yeah, well . . .'

'I think you should phone 'em, maybe. Let 'em know you're OK. It's good to talk.'

She laughed and wagged a finger. 'I know, the fat geezer, Michael Caine.'

'Wrong.' He pulled a know-all face. 'Bob Hoskins.'

'Oh yeah, that's the one. I always get them mixed up. Weren't they in a film together?'

'Yeah, *Zulu*, I think. Hoskins played the chief coon, but that's not important. What's important is you phonin' your mum and dad.'

'Maybe I will. I was going to go to Newquay, you know?'

'With all them spaced out surfers. *Baywatch*.'

She giggled. 'Yeah, and me Pamela Anderson.' She paused and said seriously, 'A mate of mine, a bloke I met at a club in Nottingham, he does some deckchairs down there, said I could work the summer.'

'So why did you end up here?'

'I hitched it down. I told you about me mate living in Turnpike Lane? Well, I thought if I could get here, I'd be able to get a lift to Newquay easier. Nothing goes to the south-west from Nottingham, does it? I mean, nothing goes from Nottingham at all.'

'I suppose. I went that way once. Exeter. It's warmer down there. Closer to the sun.'

'You could come with me.'

'Yeah. I don't think so.'

'You haven't got a girlfriend?'

'I've had girlfriends. Just no time nowadays.'

She raised her eyebrows and he felt suddenly self-conscious. It was like talking to a bleedin' copper who didn't believe a thing you said. Suddenly he was pissed off. He'd saved her life, given her a roof, let her use his towel and fed her. Now she was taking the piss.

'Course you've had girlfriends,' she said quickly, recognising his mood swing. 'I didn't mean it that way. It's just that your room here hasn't got any feminine sort of gear. No tablecloth or little mats. No ornaments, glass pigs, no Mills and Boon on the table.'

'Mills and Boon?' He laughed and she breathed relief. He was back with her again.

'It's true.'

'It's obvious, isn't it? Guy livin' on his own hasn't got time for all that. Dust collectors. That's what all that is. You'd have to be dustin' every day. I had a girlfriend a couple of years ago. Debbie somebody. She was all right. But we didn't get on.'

'Did she live here?'

'Live here? No. She stayed here, off and on. A day or so at a time. That's all.'

'What caused you to split up?'

'I don't know. She just stopped comin' round. Bollocks.'

'Yeah, that's best. I'd go out with you. I would. If you got your teeth fixed and some half-decent gear. I wouldn't mind.' She flashed him a daring smile. 'I feel like, totally awake, like I want to do something mental, like go to a rave, dance all night.'

'Look!' He pointed to the window. Dawn was breaking over the top of the curtains. 'There isn't any night left.'

She looked back at him. He was washed out, his hollow features were pale, his eyes, pinholes, were bloodshot and smarting.

'You're right,' she said and stood up. 'You ought to get some sleep. I'll sleep in the chair.'

'No, no you won't,' he insisted. 'You'll sleep in the bed. No arguments, right? You've got to get a decent rest 'cos later, in the mornin', you've got to make yourself scarce. Black Benny's still out there. And he'll still be lookin' for you.'

The memory produced a frown. 'And you,' she murmured. 'He might be looking for you.'

'Doubtful. If he'd recognised me he would have been knockin' straight away. So there you go. You've got to get on a bus or a train, right away from here. Go back home. I'll sleep in the chair.'

They woke at midday. She'd used all the milk making the coffee. He thought it had tasted different. Milky. While she dressed he went down to the Paki shop.

'You heard about Joe?' The ragged-faced rag-head gave him a grave look.

'I heard,' Hackett said, sullenly.

'The word is he's going to pull through. Punctured lung, loss of blood, serious but not too serious. He's a very lucky man.'

Hackett glanced up at the gaunt thin features and the flicking, dark, disbelieving eyes.

The Paki went on, 'There was a girl, you know? When there's trouble there's always a girl. Without fail. Do you know who she was?'

Hackett shook his head and placed the milk and a packet of horseshoe-shaped buns on the counter. 'No, I heard nothin',' he said. 'What are these?' He nudged at the buns.

'Cakes. French cakes. You see, I've decided to go all continental. EEC. All that. All the girls, the secretaries, they love them. Cakes for breakfast is what the French do. Sophistication, my friend.'

'I ain't your friend. Fuck that. But I'll take 'em,' Hackett said. He thought he'd impress her.

He walked back carrying the milk and buns at his side. He'd read the label but he still couldn't pronounce the word. Croissants. What sort of fucked-up word was that?

Out of breath from the stairs, he opened the door, took a step into the room and said, 'I've got some—'

126

The door slammed shut behind him and he looked into the grinning faces of two men. He recognised them from the alley. The plastic bag hit the floor. The milk spread out on the thin green carpet. He looked over at the girl. She was on the bed, shrinking into the corner, knees drawn up defensively, brown hair cascading over her white tank-top, eyes as wide as he'd seen them.

He looked back at the taller man and uttered, 'Shit, it's the missin' link.'

The man, bull-necked and as wide as Devon Malcolm's off day, dusted down his black suit and said, 'No, it isn't, you're wrong. Jason Hackett, isn't it? Jay for short? Well, Jay, you're very funny. Benny, now, he don't think you're funny at all. He ain't so cool at the moment on account of half his head is still plastered all over the Carrington. No, man, cool he is not. In fact, I'd say he's pretty well pissed off with you. Seems you fractured his skull. Bandaged up like the Invisible Man. He's still in hospital. They won't let him out. Think about that. I only got to talk to him an hour ago myself. Poor man doesn't even know what day it is. But he remembered you, Jay. Oh yes, he remembered your ugly face. And yep, he's pretty pissed off with you.'

His big hand spread out and shoved Hackett in the chest. He was sent backwards into the chair. He stayed put, his eyes not moving from the man. 'My name is Johnathan. It's been my pleasure to have known Benny for many years. You could say that we are friends, like brothers. And I can't tell you how much it saddens me to see how he looks now. You hit him just a little bit too hard, Jay. In fact, right now his teeth are chewin' on his own haemorrhoids. Can you imagine what that's like for a man with Benny's constitution? I mean, his flatulence is well known. Anyway, that's why Big Billy Moses here – oh, I'm sorry, I forgot to introduce you. Moses, this is that little piece of white shit that put our friend into hospital. Where was I? Oh yes, with Benny being kind of indisposed, he feels a headache comin' on, he asked Moses and me to see you personally and extend his warm regards.'

Suddenly there was a gleaming switchblade in his hand,

snapping and menacing the air in front of Hackett's face. The polished steel caught the light and flashed in his eyes. For an instant he saw his own reflection. It looked pretty nervous.

Moses was younger and casually dressed, black leather jacket, tight jeans and immaculately polished lace-ups. Dreadlocks hung down like clumps of twisted cobweb. He was much shorter than Johnathan but his muscles still bulged through his clothes. He produced a roll of brown masking tape and began to wind it around Hackett and the chair. The final wrap was around his ankles.

Johnathan looked casually about the room. 'My, my, how the other half live. Jay, I hope you forgive me for saying this, but this is a shit-house. Man, you live like a pig.' He clicked his tongue two or three times. His eyes fell onto the bed, at the girl cowering in the corner. He made out he'd only just noticed. 'Well now, what have we got here? Jay has got himself a prostitute. That is a surprise.'

Hackett stuttered, 'She ain't a tom.'

Johnathan raised his knife and slapped it into the palm of his hand. 'Now, there's one thing I cannot abide, and that's someone lyin' to me. Liars are scum, 'cos they make life so difficult. You just don't know what to believe.'

'I ain't lyin'. She ain't a tom.'

The knife flicked again. Moses pulled off some more tape and stuck it around Hackett's mouth, wound it around his head three or four times.

'That's it,' Johnathan went on. 'I'll hear no more wicked lies from you. Of course she's a scum pussy. You think I believe that you could get a woman without paying her? Now, man, that is beyond belief. That is science fiction. That is Isaac Asimov. Jay, Jay, the only way you could get your leg over for free would be by visitin' the morgue. Am I right? Oh, I'm sorry, you can't speak. Just nod your head. I'll get by with that.' He smiled and turned back to the girl. 'So you got yourself a pus bunny. What's her name? Is it an odd name? A boy's sounding name? Greg maybe? Did I hear you say Greg? Well now, that's a coincidence, 'cos my good brother, Benny, has first refusal on a dirty little slag called Greg. Now ain't that a mother-fucking coincidence? I mean, Greg, on a girl, don't seem to fit so well. There can't be that many Gregs around.' He wagged the knife again. 'I wonder, it just crossed my mind, you know? That we might be talkin' about the same little piece of ass here? What do you think? Nod your head if you agree.'

Hackett didn't move. Over the tape his eyes were wide and fearful.

'I think I saw just a faint nod there, Moses. I believe I did. Did you see it too?'

Moses nodded and smiled. His black white teeth flashed whiter than any white man's. And somewhere in there there was gold.

Johnathan continued, 'See, I gotta be sure about this, 'cos, well, I'd hate to take the wrong little slag back to Benny. Could you imagine his disappointment if I did that? I mean, after all, after his bad day last night, if the wrong girl turned up he'd really go off Sundays in a big way, wouldn't he?' He put his hand on Moses's bulging shoulder. 'Now, Moses here, he's got a heat-sensitive self-propelled guided missile that can find a prostitute at a distance of fifty yards. Seen it in action myself. It locks onto that red hot prostitute pussy and off it goes like a guided dildo. There just ain't no stoppin' it. Show the man, Moses.'

Moses's smile turned to a smirk as he slowly unbuttoned his fly. Hackett's eyes widened even more in disbelief. He struggled helplessly against the tape. Moses's penis came out like a dark German sausage. Even slack, the end of it protruded from his hand. Five diamond studs glinted around his foreskin.

Johnathan said, 'Now, you probably ain't seen a black man's dick before, so all you got to go on is rumour. But I can tell you, Jay, that even among black men, that is a bit special. Yes, sir. You can see they don't call him Big Billy Moses for nothin'. He's real proud of that. If I owned it I'd be proud of it, too. Yes, indeed. With that chopper he can part the waters of the Old Testament, the Red Sea itself. In fact, Moses ain't his real surname. His birth certificate reads Colin Justice MacInnes. Named after my good brother, the writer of such famous works as *Absolute Beginners*. You probably saw the film. What a piece of shit that turned out to be. Anyway, the story goes that even as a boy he'd developed in an abnormally big way, and his Ma took to callin' him Moses, on account of she saw it as some kind of miracle. Now let me see, about five years ago, when he was just nineteen, the nickname Big Billy came about because of his height. He never grew more than five-foot-three tall; all his growing was going on down below. People were too frightened to call him Small Billy, 'cos he's a bad mother-fucker. So, Big Billy it was, and it's kinda stuck ever since. Are you taking all this in, Jay?'

Hackett struggled some more, but he was stuck fast.

Johnathan nodded. 'Yes, I do believe you are.' He turned to Moses. 'Now, Big Billy, is that thing picking up any strong signals? My, indeed, I can see that it is.'

It had grown while Hackett watched and now protruded through the tunnel created by both of Moses's hands.

'Well, Moses, I think it's time to lock on.'

Moses smiled and approached the bed. For an instant Greg shrank back but then, realising she was about to be cornered, made a dart to the side. She stumbled and he managed to grab an ankle. Her sudden scream was cut short by a back-hander across the face. She fell face down on the floor. He grabbed her other foot and twisted her around, onto her back. Her long hair covered her face until she flicked it aside to show her blazing eyes. Her jaw firmed up in determination and she kicked out to loosen his hold. He grinned, held her legs together one-handed and lifted her almost clear of the floor so that she faced away from him. Her head and shoulders remained on the carpet, her chin bent into her neck, her slender arms splayed out either side. She grabbed at him and dug her fingernails deep into his ankles. If he felt any discomfort he didn't show it. Her short skirt fell to her waist. Her legs seemed incredibly long and thin. She let go of his ankles and frantically attempted to push her skirt back to cover her pants. He simply lifted her higher and held her out, almost at arm's length. He moved his free hand down to the back of her skirt, grasped a handful of material and wrenched it upward. She gripped the skirt at the front, holding on for all her worth. He wrenched again and smiled at the sound of stitches coming apart. She seemed to hang in the air, suspended, like some piece of meat on a rack, her ankles still clamped together by his massive hand. Even as her skirt and pants were pulled up to reveal her white behind she held onto the front of her skirt. He tugged again, with more force, and the material slipped through her fingers. She cried out and tried to cover her suddenly exposed crotch. He pushed the skirt and pants over her knees, changed hands when they reached her ankles, then pulled them off her feet and threw them to one side. They landed in a heap next to Johnathan's handmade Italians.

'Stop!' she shouted. 'Let me go!' Each word was ground out. She gave up trying to cover herself and clung to his shoes, trying to twist round so that she could get her teeth to his legs. He kicked her in the back and she let out a sudden gasp, her chin once again angled into her neck so that she looked straight up towards her own feet. She felt his penis moving between her legs, the icy touch of the polished diamonds, then she saw it, the head, poking out above her own pubic hair. Panicking now, she struggled again, writhing and twisting her body in a hopeless attempt to free herself.

Moses went down onto his knees. Her back hit the carpet but he kept her legs in the air. With his free hand he reached around her legs and grabbed her throat. Her eyes filled with terror.

'You listen here, girl. One more sound, just one little sound, and I'll use a knife on your face. Understand me, girl?' He let go of her neck and smacked her face. 'Understand?'

Holding back her sobs as her breath came in quick little bursts, she nodded.

'That's better. Now don't forget, otherwise I'll have to cut you real bad. I might even have to cut your pretty little nose off.'

He moved his hand away from her face and grabbed hold of her legs. He forced her knees apart and placed his head between them so that her legs bent over his massive shoulders.

Johnathan glanced at Hackett's fiery eyes and smiled. 'Now, tell me, Moses, is that clean, or is that the worn filthy hole of a scum bunny?'

131

Moses leant forward, squeezing his head down between her quivering thighs. 'Well, boss, from this angle I ain't so sure that Jay ain't been tellin' you the truth all along. It could be.'

'That's interesting, Moses, and surprisin'. Yep, I must admit to being somewhat surprised. Is there any way you could be sure?'

'Well, boss, I suppose . . .'

'Go on, Moses, I'm listenin'.'

'Well, at a push, if you think it's necessary, I suppose I could do a quality control check. It'll mean checkin' the fit.'

Johnathan smacked the switchblade into his palm again. 'Like an old-fashioned trial, you mean? If she's tight, then Jay was telling the truth, but she'll probably shout out in pain and you'll have to cut off her nose. But, if she's worn and loose, and she don't shout, then Jay was lyin', and that means I'll cut his throat from ear to ear. I cannot abide liars. So, yes, I do think this unfortunate trial is necessary.'

Moses extricated himself and pushed her legs aside. He held her around the neck again and brought her face to within inches of his own. 'Listen to me, girl. I'm gonna fuck you. You might as well get used to the idea right now. It's gonna happen. You're gettin' fucked and there's nothin' you can do about it. So you might as well accept it and save yourself from gettin' hurt real bad. If you fight me or struggle then I'll cut your face. Now, this is how we's gonna do it. From experience I knows it's the best way.'

Her features collapsed in utter panic and she tried to pull away, shrinking from the abomination. Her mouth opened as if to scream but only a whimper emerged. She tried to shake her head but he held it steady.

He put a finger to his lips. 'Not a word, remember? Now, you go over there, lean over the bed and stick your ass in the air. You understand me?'

Her attempt to shake her head continued. He tightened his grip. His fingers dug deeply into her throat. She gasped. A tear squeezed from her eye. Her mouth opened and slobber hung from her top lip.

132

'I'm losin' my patience with you. I said, do you understand me?'

The shake turned into the faintest of nods. His grip stayed firm and choking. 'Now don't you even think about tryin' anythin', like runnin', or screamin'.'

Her nod turned into a feverish shake. The tears began to redden her cheeks and damp the round collar of her tank-top.

'OK then, I'm gonna let go of you, and I want to see you carry out my instructions to the letter.'

Johnathan pulled his eyes off the girl and glanced at Hackett. Hackett's eyes were narrowed in concentration. Johnathan couldn't work out whether Hackett found the girl's torment distressing or not. It crossed his mind that beneath all the tape the bastard was enjoying himself.

Moses let her go. Her breaths came in short bursts, each one caught in her chest, jerking her shoulders. For a moment she sat head bowed, legs clamped together, hands spread out to conceal her groin, then slowly she edged towards the bed. It seemed to take an age but Moses was satisfied to watch. Eventually, she reached the bed. Sitting on the carpet beside it, her legs drawn round, still pressed together, she buried her face into her hands.

Moses didn't move. He said ominously, 'That's not quite right, girl, and I think you knows it.'

Slowly she raised herself onto the duvet, clawing at it for purchase, until her behind was bent across the bed. Her knees remained on the carpet, the soles of her feet in plain view. Her feet were splayed but her knees stayed firmly locked together. She turned her face away from them. Before it was hidden from his view Hackett saw her embarrassment and shame.

Moses said, 'You're almost there. That's almost it. But now you gotta spread your legs. I want to see your asshole winkin' at me, and your little pussy, I gotta get a line on that. Understand?'

A shudder worked its way down her body and left her knees quivering. She drew them apart. Her buttocks clenched.

'We can see your asshole, girl, but not much else. Unless

you spread wider and raise yourself higher, then I'm gonna get mighty angry with you.'

She cried out loud.

'Did I hear something?' Moses said. 'Did you hear something, Johnathan?'

'I believe I might have done, Moses. But in this shit-hole it might have been a rat. It might not have been the girl.'

'Well, if she moves in the next few moments and follows my instructions, then I'm inclined to agree with you that it was a rat, but if not . . .'

She crept further onto the duvet. Her toes bent on the carpet and she raised her behind an inch above the bed. As she did so her knees came together again and began to knock.

Moses tut-tutted.

They heard her sob again and saw her legs shake even more. Her behind lifted higher.

'That's better. Thing is, your legs have somehow come together again. I think we need some air between them, girl.'

But for her trembling she remained motionless.

'I mean, I want you to open your legs! Tell you what, I'll make it easy. You do the splits till I tell you to stop. Go ahead, we's all waitin' on you.'

Her sobbing grew louder. Her feet edged outward, slipping on the carpet. They'd parted a yard before he said, 'That's it. That's better. You wouldn't believe the view we've got. All in all, it's one of the nicest little pussies I've seen in a long time.' He looked across and winked at Johnathan, then returned his gaze to the girl. 'Now there's just one last thing I want you to do. Usin' both your hands, I want you to reach round and pull your boat apart as wide as you can, as if you're openin' the door and givin' me a friendly welcome.'

Her shoulders shook. Her desperate sobs were muffled by the duvet. Her knees quivered and sagged.

Moses tut-tutted again. 'I don't believe you're gonna let me down after comin' so far. Do I have to remind you what's at stake here?'

Her legs firmed up immediately and her trembling hands moved.

134

'That's good,' Moses said.

Amusement flickered on Johnathan's face as Moses shot him another grin. He said, 'Kind of reminds you of a football club stag night, don't it?'

Hackett averted his gaze, not out of convention or shame. In the past he had paid to see such things. But those taking part had been strangers, and in the last few hours he had come to like the girl. Johnathan saw a tear slide down across the tape covering Hackett's mouth. 'Well, I'll be damned, and I probably will be, but that has surprised me.'

Hackett heard Moses again, 'Wider, girl. Now don't you go gettin' embarrassed on us.' He heard the girl's cry of despair, then, 'That's it. That's what I call a real welcome. Now just you hold it like that.'

The girl's sudden, painful cry, much louder than before, drew Hackett's eyes back again.

Moses almost covered her, his weight crushing her into the bed, his massive thighs between hers, his muscular buttocks glistening. Her legs seemed thin and pale against him. Her head hit the side wall with each forward thrust.

Johnathan leaned closer to Hackett and waved the switchblade under his chin. He said, 'It's time, Jason. It's nothing personal, you understand, but it'll make Benny feel a whole lot better.'

He'd barely spoken the last word when the door to the flat burst open and two black sawn-off .410 shotgun barrels pointed at everybody at once.

Chapter 14

The two men levelling the shotguns were bandits from the sixties, dark suit and tie jobs. They fitted the bill from their slicked-back hair down to their chiselled lace-ups. They were the right age too, past their sell-by, forty something, into mid-life crises and therefore dangerous as hell. They stepped aside and Keith Mason shuffled into the doorway.

Mason was short and round and thin on top. He wore thick lenses which magnified his round, pale-blue eyes. He was dressed informally, lightweight slacks and open-neck white shirt. He carried a lumpy M&S plastic bag.

Johnathan froze for an instant, then dropped the knife and backed up behind Hackett's chair.

Mason's eyes fell to the milk and croissants spilt from the bag where Hackett had dropped them, then flicked up to cover the room and came to rest on the bed. He spoke in a high-pitched voice: 'Get off the slapper and walk over here with your hands where I can see them.'

Moses struggled to his feet and dusted the wet patch on his jeans. 'All right if I do up my fly?' he asked and his face cracked into a worried smile. White and gold teeth beamed.

Mason turned back to Johnathan. 'Is that you, Johnathan?' he asked incredulously and screwed up his eyes.

'It surely is, Mr Mason.'

'What are you doing?'

Johnathan shrugged his broad shoulders. 'Well, I'll be honest with you, Moses here has been breakin' her in for Black Benny.'

'I heard he was hurt?'

'That is the truth.'

'So, she's a tom.'

Johnathan nodded. 'She surely is.'

'That's all right then.' Mason glanced at Hackett. 'What's the SP here?'

'Well, the girl's just part of it. This little toerag stole her and put Black Benny into hospital in the process. We're in the business of returnin' the compliment, so to speak, but, if you've got a prior claim, sir, then we'll gladly bow to your seniority.'

Mason nodded thoughtfully. Eventually, he said, 'As it happens I do have a prior claim. Take the slapper with my compliments, but Hackett, Jason Hackett, has got business with me.'

'That's fine.' Johnathan picked up the girl's clothes and threw them at her. 'Get into them, girl, and hurry it up. Let's not outstay our welcome.'

The shotguns lowered. Moses breathed a sigh of relief and took a tentative step towards Johnathan. They watched the girl stagger from the bed and fumble with her clothes. She shook like a smackhead in the forty-eighth hour. Her face was dark and blotched, her eyes lowered to the floor, not daring to meet their gazes.

Johnathan murmured, 'Kind of novel to watch a girl put clothes on.'

Mason grunted. They all knew his views regarding toms, and they weren't in any way complimentary.

Finally they were ready and Johnathan pulled the girl towards the door.

'If you should tire of Black Benny's small company, there's always a place with me,' Mason said.

Johnathan paused. 'I do appreciate that, Mr Mason. I really do. I'll give it some serious consideration.'

'You do that, Johnathan. Now get out of here.'

Moses followed him out and the door closed behind them.

Mason turned to Hackett. 'Hello, Jason,' he said. 'It looks like you've been having a bad day.'

His two minders checked the tape that secured Hackett to the chair. They waved an OK to Mason and moved aside.

Mason moved into the kitchen and tipped the contents of the plastic bag onto the drainer. As he unfolded an apron and tied it around his fat middle, he looked back through the kitchen door.

'I'm not a happy man myself, Jay. I know you'll sympathise with me. The thing is, all this increased kozzer activity while

137

they look for the missing schoolgirl is doing my business no favours at all. And now, on top of that, a business colleague of mine has been telling me that you've closed your account with him. I told him that I'd pop over and have a chat with you, see if we couldn't work things out. Better than that, I said, I'd even cook you some lunch. Not the kind of cooking that you get up to. I mean with real food. You look as though you haven't eaten in days.'

Hackett watched the man pick up various items. He began to chop up a big onion.

'Thing is, I'm into Ray Marshall for ten percent. I act as his, how do you put it? Agent? I act for most of the businesses around here. This is, after all, my manor. You know that, don't you, Jason?'

Hackett's nod was feverish, his eyes ready to pop.

'The goods in this case are neither here nor there. But there's a principle involved.' He tapped his wristwatch. 'See this, Rolex, gold, it's worth more than the result of your blag. But if it busted today I'd simply go out and buy another. I tell you that to illustrate that money is not the problem.'

Finished with the onion, he began on a couple of green chillies, chopping them finely, turning them to mush and then mixing them with some of the onion.

'I realise that you're not going to point the way to the goods without feeling some discomfort. I realise that. That's why I'm going to hurt you. Not badly, but enough to teach you a lesson. Don't worry, I'm not going to put you out of business. If I did that it would be bad for Ray Marshall, and in turn bad for me. You understand that?'

He carried a plate into the main room and placed it under Hackett's nose. 'Smell that. Strong, isn't it? It's the juices of onion and green chilli mixed together with a little cayenne powder. Cayenne is made from very hot red chillies. It's good with eggs and shellfish. But get some in your eyes, and by Christ does it smart. Get enough in your eye, especially when it's mixed up like this, then it's agony, I mean, sheer fucking agony. But it does wear off after a day or two. That's what you gotta keep telling yourself.'

Mason's minders watched impassively, almost bored by the proceedings. They had seen it all before.

Mason grabbed Hackett's hair and forced his head back, then very carefully, drawing open his left eyelid, he let the liquid trickle from the plate. Hackett blinked wildly as the cold juice ran down his cheek. Suddenly his eyes screwed up and a strangled noise came from his throat. He threw himself back in the chair and for a few moments rocked and heaved. Tears oozed out of his closed eyes. He settled down again, head bowed, eyes as tightly closed as he could get them.

'Hurts like fuck, doesn't it? What did I tell you?' Mason said and tugged his head back again. He prised open the eyelid. 'That's it, let's try a drop more.'

Hackett made a growling sound and his head shot back again, flicking drops of the liquid from his face.

Mason tugged the tape from his lips and said, 'Now you can talk to me, Jason, or just point.'

Hackett's voice quivered, 'In the window, behind the plaster.'

One of the two minders stood up and went casually to the window. He pulled the plaster aside, reached into the hole and withdrew the bag along with the digging equipment. He looked across and nodded.

'Good boy,' Mason said. He glanced over at the minders. 'OK, that's it. Short and sweet. Untie him and we'll be off.'

Hackett kept his eyes closed, not daring to open them. He felt hands tugging at the tape and suddenly his own hands were free. A few moments later he heard the door slam shut.

He fell to his hands and knees and felt his way into the bathroom. He reached up to the basin taps and turned them fully on. When the basin began to overflow he raised himself and dunked his head under the water. The cold water felt glorious against his burning eye. He wanted to stay there for ever. He changed the water three times before reaching for his towel. He dug out a wad of cotton wool and pressed it tightly against his eye, then went back into the other room and found a strip of the tape. He wound it around his head and stuck the patch in place. He returned to the bathroom and examined himself in the mirror.

He looked like a fucking horror film, the skin under his good eye bruised and flared, his cheeks hollowed and dark. He shuddered. He was going downhill fast. He made his way to the window. The sparklers had gone, he knew that much. His box of tricks had been tipped out and his smack was just a grey stain on the carpet. He let out a little cry and sank down beside it, trying to recover what he could on the glossy cover of a magazine.

He dusted up enough but lost a lot more. His hand shook as he cooked on the spoon, and shook more as he drew the liquid into the syringe. He didn't make the bed. He lay on the floor propped up against it, angrily smacking at the veins on his arm. He watched the needle sink, drew back some blood so that the liquid pinked, then plunged in. He withdrew and let the syringe fall to the carpet, then pressed his thumb against the tiny puncture. His lips drew back and his breaths shortened and his sobs came up from his chest. The room was suddenly big, the walls distant, echoing with the girl's voice, her tiny laugh, her catch of soft breath. He remembered lying awake listening to her breathe. He remembered thinking how pleasant it felt to have some company. He glanced across at the chair, upturned as he had left it, and the pile of tape beside it. He touched the pad on his eye. The red-hot pain was starting to dull. He was going to make it. He nodded to himself. He'd wait a few hours, settle his nerves, then he would smarten himself up, maybe change his jeans, maybe grab a bite to eat and then, and then, and then he'd think about it.

It was dark by the time Jason Hackett went out. The pavements were full and cars choked the road.

He had bathed his eye again and examined it in the mirror. There was no white at all, just blood-red. He repositioned his patch and stuck it in position by wrapping sellotape around his head. He had gone into the kitchen, to the box of tools he kept under the sink, and selected a hammer, one with a heavy steel head, long claws and thick wooden shaft. He had nicked it from Do-It-All. Now it was in his bag, along with his other equipment.

A hundred or so yards down from the Carrington theatre, and from the depths of a shop doorway, he watched the bright lights of the mini-cab firm opposite, the comings and goings, the cabs drawing up to the pavement, the customers crushing into them. Over the door the words 'Benny's Mini-Cabs' winked in red neon. Through the window Hackett could see customers waiting and a man behind the counter speaking into the radio. The shop catered mostly for blacks. The business fronted a dope and prostitution racket. The real business took place in the flat above. A door at the back of the small shop led up to the flat, as did a fire escape at the back of the building. Moses sat by the door at the rear of the shop. He was reading a paper, taking little notice of the customers filing in and out. Occasionally he'd open the door and let someone pass, or someone would walk out. Johnathan had climbed into a cab twenty minutes earlier.

Hackett wondered whether Black Benny would be in the flat. He doubted it. Given his headache he would still be in hospital or at home in Wood Green knocked out by painkillers.

He concentrated on the shop some more while nerves twisted his gut into knots the size of cricket balls. This wasn't like an ordinary job. There were some real villains over there who'd still like to get hold of him. Walk away! Walk away! he told himself, and repeated the old adage. There's no room for friendship on the streets. It's every man for himself. The girl meant nothing to him. He'd already done what he could, more than most. He'd saved her once. And Joe Pullin was going to pull through, so his word was not important. There'd be no ghosts coming after him. Walk away. But he knew he wouldn't. He was in love.

He crossed the busy road and made his way to the next turning. The door at the back of the flat was heavy and locked. He knew it would be. The old mortise would take more than a paper-clip. Even the key would struggle. Next to the door an old sash window looked into a dark room. He thought about the plunger but decided against and used his chisel. Within seconds

141

he was through to the catch and peeled about twenty coats of paint from it. He punched the catch open and used a screwdriver to prise the window up from the bottom. More coats of paint cracked and wood splintered. He waited a moment, then drew it wide. He climbed in and flicked on his pencil light. The narrow beam swept across a pile of junk, cardboard boxes, rolls of dusty wallpaper, broken chairs. He eased open a door, just a fraction, and peered around the edge. It led to a long, dimly lit passage. Patches of black mildew covered the wallpaper. Half a dozen doors led from the passage and at the far end a flight of stairs led down to the shop.

A door at the end opened and a woman emerged, swinging a towel at her side. She was in her forties, black, plaits, bright red lipstick. She filled the plum-coloured V-necked tunic she wore like she meant it. She sashayed on towards him. The tunic swished over her thighs. For a moment he thought she was heading for his door but then she turned to the door right opposite his. She paused as if sensing his presence, and swung round.

Hackett pulled the door wide open and leapt out. Her eyes widened and her mouth opened ready to scream. He pushed the hammer into her neck and pinned her against the door.

'Not a fuckin' sound, right?'

Her wide eyes looked ready to pop. She nodded feverishly, her eyes fixed on his patch. 'Right, honey,' she said. 'With the eye-patch I thought you was a pirate, that's all. Now don' you panic. It's your show. You can do whatever you like with me. You don't need that.' She glanced down at the hammer.

'Unless you want a smack with this . . .' he pressed the hammer harder until it marked her neck, 'you tell me where the girl is, the one they brought in today.'

He heard a splash and looked down as the carpet beneath her legs turned a darker colour.

'Look at that! You've gone and made me pee myself,' she said. She unfolded the towel and raised the hem of her tunic to wipe herself. He noticed her long fingernails painted the same colour red as her lips.

'The girl?'

She raised a nervous finger to the next door but one.

Hackett nodded. 'You go first,' he said.

She hesitated. 'It ain't a good idea, honey. She's with some-one.'

'Then we'll interrupt them, won't we?'

The woman shrugged and moved in front. She grabbed the door handle before looking back. Her eyes were dark. 'You sure you wanna do this, man? It could mean big trouble for you.'

'No, I ain't sure, but we'll do it anyway.'

She opened the door.

It was a small room with barely enough space to move around a stained mattress that lay on the floor. The man standing on the mattress had remarkably similar features to Moses, except that his dick was about six inches shorter. Shock registered on his face for just a fraction of a second as Hackett pushed past the woman and swung the hammer. The blow caught the man on the temple. For a moment he stayed upright with a look of disbelief on his face, then his face was washed with blood, and he collapsed.

The woman was frozen to the spot, horrified, her eyes not moving from the massive hole in the man's head. 'Shit!' she said. 'That ain't so cool.'

The girl lay on the mattress. She hadn't moved either. She was naked, legs splayed, finger bruises on her arms.

Suddenly Hackett was aware of the smell. Urine and spunk and sweat. Used condoms littered the floor. He pointed the hammer at the woman. 'Stay put, right?'

'Right on, honey. Don't you mind me.'

He took the towel and wiped the girl's legs. For the first time she seemed to recognise him.

'Jay?' She struggled to sit up.

'Come on, girl. We're out of here.'

'They've taken my clothes, Jay, they injected me.'

He nodded. 'That's how it goes. They fill you full of shit. It's been happenin' for ever.' He pulled her to her feet. Her legs were like jelly.

'What happened?' she said suddenly, focusing on his eye-patch. Her own eyes were tiny pin-points, slipping.

143

'I got somethin' in it.'

She sobbed. 'They did it to you?'

'Don't worry, I ain't blind. It just hurts like fuck.'

She began to sink. He held her up.

'I can't walk,' she said.

'Yes, you can. I'll help you.'

She glanced fearfully at the body beside the mattress.

'He ain't goin' to hurt you,' Hackett said.

The woman said sharply, 'Man, he ain't goin' to hurt no one no more. That's his thoughts you can see comin' out of that hole. You've killed the man. You know that? There's big trouble comin' your way. Big trouble.'

Hackett waved the hammer again. 'Will you shut up?'

'I talk when I'm nervous, mister. An' I'm nervous now.'

'I need your dress.'

'Take it, take it. It ain't my colour anyway.' The woman didn't hesitate. She lifted it over her head. She was left naked. She handed it over. Hackett helped the girl into it, then turned back to the woman. She was shielding herself, her arms wrapped around huge breasts.

'She's going to use the bathroom, right? I'll be in the corridor. Don't start screamin' for five minutes and you won't get this up your nose. Right?'

The woman nodded. 'Right. I'll just stand here and calm down. You take your time. It's no problem, honey. No problem at all.'

He closed the door and helped the girl along the passage.

'The toilet?'

'Forget the toilet. That was just to keep her trap shut.'

He opened the end door and pointed to the open window. He picked up his tool bag, stashed the hammer and pushed it through the window. Then he turned to help the girl. Moments later they were stumbling down the steps. He took her weight, forcing the pace, and they reached the corner.

'I think I'm going to throw up,' she murmured.

'Well, do it quickly.'

She sagged against a wall. He looked around. They were

144

alone in the side street. Tension began to claw at his chest. Any second now some big black bastards were going to come charging around the corner. He heard the splatter and then the coughs as she cleared her throat. He shot her a quick look. She wiped her mouth with the back of her hand.

'OK now?'

She nodded and reached out. Her arm hanging onto his neck, his arm around her waist, his other weighed down by the bag of tools, they moved forward again towards the bright lights of the main road.

'They all wanted a piece of the new white pussy,' she murmured. 'And they did it up my arse, Jay!'

'Yeah, sorry, I had to wait till dark and then some.'

'That's twice you've got me out of it. That's twice you broke your street code.'

'Yeah, well, I forgot to tell you somethin', right?'

'What was that?'

'Joe's goin' to pull through. He's goin' to make it.'

'That's good news.'

'How many were there?'

'What?'

'Back there. Geezers?'

'I lost count.'

'It don't matter. You're out of it. That's all that matters, right?'

'I'm probably pregnant a dozen times over. I probably got some horrible things. AIDS.'

'Nah, doubt it. They were all West Indian bastards. Black Benny wouldn't have Africans touchin' his girls, they're all fuckin' nutters. He'd turn white at the fuckin' thought. The only thing you'll catch off West Indians is rap music and a cravin' for sweet potatoes.'

They hit the main street and he felt slightly easier. Not much, for his patch was a winking billboard, but it was a whole lot safer than the side street.

'Where are we going?'

'There's a friend of mine, about the only place I can think of where you can get cleaned up. We can't stop for long. It would

145

be too dangerous. He has people in and out, if you know what I mean? But it'll do for half an hour.'

'How can you tell the difference?'

'Uh?'

'Between West Indians and Africans?'

'You count the crabs, girl. The Africans have got more. I thought everyone knew that.'

'Don't call me girl.'

'Where will you go, man?' Martin Brookes asked. He was putting in overtime, sitting cross-legged at his table, still weighing.

'I don't know,' Hackett said gloomily, as he looked from the window at the police activity in Churchill Place. 'Somewhere. A long way.'

'Overseas would be good, man. Scotland maybe. Or Newcastle.'

'They haven't found her, then? The missin' kid? The kozzers?'

'No. A police car drew up a few minutes before you got here, mind, and there was quite a commotion, till they took off like they were trying for a Malcolm Campbell.'

'Uh?'

'A new land speed record.'

'Oh, right. Formula One.'

Brookes frowned then tossed a bag of goodies onto the table. 'Do you want to fix now?'

Hackett shook his head. 'No, got things to do. More's the pity. I need one, I'll tell you that. I'll send you the dosh for this.'

'I trust you. Do you need any bread?'

'No, I've got enough to see us through a couple of days. But you can do us a favour?'

'Tell me?'

'Patrick Wall, you know Patrick Wall?'

'Yeah, he lives over your way.'

'Right. Shares a house with four others. Butt riders of the Bourneville Boulevard, all of 'em. Right? You wouldn't

146

catch me visitin'. Fuck that. But he's been campin' out over Heathrow, clockin' the baggage, givin' me the wink.'

Brookes nodded. He knew the routine.

'Thing is, I ain't paid him for the last couple of nods. You could sort that for me. A monkey should do. I'll get it back to you.'

'Stay cool, man. No problem.' Brookes glanced up. 'You don't have to rush off. Chill out here for as long as you want.'

Hackett shook his head. 'We'll get off. People know I need to dig. It's not a secret. They'll be checkin' the jugglers. They'll be round sooner or later.'

Brookes nodded. 'Maybe you're right.'

Connie came in from the kitchen and slumped on the sofa. 'She's bathed. I've cleaned her up as best I can,' she said sternly. 'And I've given her some knickers to wear. She should be going nowhere except the hospital. She's bleeding. She should have an AIDS test, hepatitis, all the other syphilis shit.'

Hackett nodded. 'We will, we will. When we get some place we will.'

She went on, 'I've forced her to eat some toast. It might settle her stomach.'

Brookes said, 'What did they shoot her with, man? D'you know?'

Hackett shrugged.

'A depressant, something to stop her moving around. Her eyes have fucking near disappeared. Has to be junk, man, probably with a downer.'

'That's what I figured.' Hackett turned from the window as the girl appeared. She'd brushed her hair and the bath had worked wonders, brought some colour back to her face. Even the purple tunic looked clean. 'You ready to go?'

'Yeah, I'm ready.'

He stashed the cellophane bag and picked up his working tools. He nodded his thanks to Brookes then headed to the door.

'Stay cool, man,' Brookes said, Woodstock-style.

147

Chapter 15

They found an all-night café called Elaine's about a mile from the estate and dived in out of a squall of rain. The sky was building up again; mountainous feathery-topped clouds shouldered in. He used the toilets and got rid of the patch. It was getting too many odd looks. Even the crackheads were looking at him twice. Not that his red eye fared any better – it was still fierce and the skin around it swollen. She had been shocked. There was still no white, just blood that seeped out at the corner. Out of it, together with his good eye, he watched the entrance for any sign of black heads.

He gulped at some coffee. 'What surprised me back there was how Mason reacted to Johnathan. It's well known that he hates the niggers, Black Benny included. It comes from him being Irish, I think.'

'How's that?'

'The Irish hate the blacks. You don't get any blacks in Ireland, do you? It's natural for them. That's 'cos they got black blood themselves and they won't admit it. Right? The old Africans moved up through Spain and landed in England. They mixed with the English natives, the cavemen. It's true. The Saxons came in, that's us, and they pushed the natives back over to Wales and then out to Ireland. That's why there's always been trouble between the Irish and us. They ain't pedigree. That's why.'

'He offered Johnathan a job.'

'I heard that. It's probably because Johnathan is westernised. If he was cut he'd bleed white blood. Havin' said that, it wouldn't surprise me to hear that relations between Mason and Black Benny have become a bit iffy. Maybe there's trouble brewin'. Gettin' hold of Benny's main muscle would make sense. Still, fuck them. We've got to make plans.'

Under the table, he pressed some notes into her hand. For a moment she seemed horrified.

'Don't worry, I ain't going to split. I've got things to do.'

'Then what's this for?'

'There's fifty notes there. That just leaves me enough for what I've gotta do. I want you to get a cab, a black cab – none of these bleedin' mini-cabs – down to Victoria. Right?'

'A cab down to Victoria.'

'Right. The bus station, Victoria bus station, do you know it?'

She shook her head.

'It's a big place. To the left of the main entrance there's a bank of toilets, right. You wait there for me. I'll be there.'

'When?'

'In the mornin'. Between nine and ten. Probably closer to nine. Check out the bus time. A long way, right? If you've got enough bread, then buy two tickets. One way.'

'Where to?'

'You choose, girl. A long way from here, that's all.'

She nodded thoughtfully, then said, 'My name's Greg.'

'I know that.'

'Then call me Greg. Not girl.'

'Oh, right. Now tell me what you're goin' to do?'

'Cab down to Victoria, buy two tickets, then wait for you by the loos.'

'Right.'

'You're not going to come, are you?'

'Listen, I'll be there. You've gotta trust me, right? Fuck me, there's no one else you can trust.'

'Where are you going?' There was a trace of panic in her voice.

'Someone walked off with my gear. I'm goin' to get it back. That's all. No big deal.'

Fear widened her eyes. 'That's all? You're going to get hurt again. I know it. Don't go. Please. Come with me.'

'I've gotta go, Greg girl. I've got to. No choice.'

'You do have a choice.'

'Listen, all my life I've been on the shit end of nothin'. The only chance I've ever had was the National Lottery. Fourteen million to one, know what I mean? I'm twenty-six for Christ's sake. I've got nothin', I've never had nothin'. I left home when

I was seven on account of my old man's benders, two fractured skulls and a busted rib. I didn't blame him. It was the booze. Fuck me, I loved him. Booze is natural, you either handle it or you don't. But it ain't your fault. It's like breathin' air. Blame don't come into it. You gotta have it. Before he got bad, lost his job, started boozin', we used to play football. Every weekend. He was my old man. He was my old man for Christ's sake. I loved him. I wouldn't have wanted my mam to kick him out. But the social gave her that choice. Him or me. Well, I didn't give them the fuckin' choice. I ran off, and I kept runnin'. When they picked me up I was put into care. I was moved from St Albans to Sparrow Herne, then Hounslow. That's where I learned the ropes. Hounslow. I'm twenty-six, yeah? And includin' a stretch at the DC in Nottingham, I've seen the inside of Wandsworth, the Scrubs, Pentonville and Highpoint. All I ever wanted was one result, one half-decent score. Just somethin' to set me up, a motor spares shop, or a little garage. Do you understand?'

She nodded slowly, almost wondrously. Her eyes had softened.

'I gotta go and do this. You buy tickets for any time after ten. If you haven't got enough bread then hold on for me. If I ain't there by ten, then . . . then you'll only need to use one of the tickets.'

'What's that supposed to mean?'

'It means that I ain't goin' to make it. Not for the want of tryin', mind you. You can count on that. I'll be tryin', believe me.'

'You'll be hurt. They'll kill you.'

He waved the idea away. 'It won't come to that. So that's it. I want you to walk out of here now, and pick up a cab on the street. I'll sit here and watch you.'

She placed her hand on his. 'Just make sure you get there.'

'I'll be there, Greg girl. Don't you worry about that. Now off you go before I change my mind and regret it forever.'

She stood back from the table and hesitated to look deep into his swollen eyes.

'What is it?'

150

'You're not what I dreamed of, Jay.'

He raised his eyebrows. His eye began to water again. He flicked away a red tear. 'What are you sayin'?'

'You'll be dead by the time you're thirty, and I want more than four years.'

He frowned.

'Do you understand?'

'I think I'm gettin' your drift. You're givin' me some kind of choice, right? One of them ultimatum things?'

'Yeah. But only if you get your teeth fixed.'

'Right,' he said. 'Right.'

Keith Mason's detached house overlooked the park in Mill Hill. It was surrounded by tall trees and a high brick wall. A single-storey annexe contained a heated swimming pool and sauna. Security was not a problem. Every villain in north London knew where it was and gave it a wide berth. Spotlights lit up the trim garden and gave the thick foliage a bluish wash. Vertical blinds on the massive front window were still open and bright light produced tracks on the spongy lawn. From the shelter of a camellia that spread back to the garden wall, Hackett settled himself and watched the movements in the front room.

Mason's wife of twenty years must have been away. He couldn't really see her agreeing to the house guest. He recognised the tall, sleek figure even from a distance. He'd seen her picture many times on the front of various magazines. Jill Jackson. Smiley's wife. While he was tucked up in hospital having his legs put back together, she was out having fun, spreading hers. She wore a long black number with side slits going on forever. She sank into the sofa, raised her knee and gave herself a dig between the toes, one of the few places where fashion models could score. She held up the empty syringe, shaking it in the air, and Mason took it off her.

She had him eating out of her hand. The man was dribbling all over her. It was understandable, in a way, but still surprising that a man like Mason could be treated like some kind of servant.

151

Hackett felt easy. There was no tension inside him, no sudden flush of adrenalin that he usually experienced when he went to work. Instead, determination actually steadied his nerves. He wanted this one. The consequences of failure, of being caught, didn't come into it.

The house lights went out, the flush of a cistern died, laughter and chatter from an upstairs room eventually ceased. In the rain, silent bats streaked across the garden, night insects jumped, an occasional lorry rumbled on the distant road. Two hours went by. The rain grew heavier. The occasional flash of lightning lit up the garden and thunder cracked from the fierce sky. Hackett stirred only occasionally to rub the stiffness from his body. Eventually, at just after four, when a wind came up to whip the rain and dawn was already a pale ghost, he went to work.

A stormy night was a robber's friend. The odd crash of breaking glass was taken for a milk bottle rolling off the doorstep, and wind in the rafters covered the creaking floorboards.

He'd already planned his way in, through the annexe. The slatted window, although high and narrow, was piss easy. They should be banned, he thought, as he took it to pieces.

Inside, the material surrounding the pool deadened his footsteps. The door to the house was locked, but with the annexe muffling any sound he made, it presented no problem. He removed the wooden batons that held the glass, then the thin layer of putty and tiny fixing nails and then, with his plunger, the pane of glass. There was just enough space for him to reach the bolts, top and bottom. He pressed the handle down on the Yale and opened the door.

He found his own goods immediately, left on the table in the hall. He spent the next ten minutes going over the ground floor rooms with his pencil light, but didn't add anything to his bag.

He was a professional. He was the best. He could walk on broken glass and no one would hear him. The words went around his head as he headed for the stairs. He went up carefully, spreading his weight, keeping his feet to the edges

152

of each tread. Checking just a yard or so ahead before flicking his light off, covering the distance then flicking on again for just a second. He searched the upstairs rooms, keeping the master bedroom until last.

Before he opened the bedroom door he shot the hinges and handle with Three in One and gave it five minutes to soak in. He inched the door open and went in on hands and knees. Someone stirred in the bed. Mason snored, a low quiet rattle. It wasn't loud enough to disturb the woman. The smack would keep her out of it for some time, especially if she'd brewed up with temazepam, like the girls who worked long hours often did. He used his pencil light, keeping it shielded, allowing just a glow to give him the bearings. He took in a few things. Jill Jackson's overnight bag, open on the plush carpet. Her underwear, expensive designer gear, lay on top. A thick wallet on the bedside table next to Mason. His Rolex glinted beside it. On the dressing-table was a jewellery box. He guessed that the sparklers inside belonged to Mason's wife. Jill's sparklers, ear-rings, necklace and bracelets, lay loose beside it.

Mason stirred again and turned over. His fat arm lay over the slight figure beside him. He exhaled deeply and the snoring stopped.

Hackett stayed put for a moment, until Mason's breathing settled down and the rattle started again. Then he made his move.

Ten minutes later, he was on the other side of the wall, counting out the contents of Mason's wallet. It was the best part of two grand. In the increasing dawn light he examined the jewellery, then added it to the bag containing his own. He hid his tool bag behind some thick bushes. He wouldn't need it again, so there was no sense lugging it back. He smoked a couple of cigarettes while he waited for more pedestrians, trying to control the elation that swept through him. At six thirty, when the early workers began to stir and the night-shift kozzers called it a night, he used a long-bladed knife to open the door of a G-reg Escort and tugged out the wires. Seconds later he was on his way, heading back to home ground.

*   *   *

Weidenfeld was in Linda's café at a quarter to eight. It was the sort of place where there was more grease spilt on the plastic tablecloths than was served to a whole wing at the Scrubs. He waved Hackett to an empty chair opposite.

'You're here already. Whatever happened?'

Hackett frowned.

'Your eye, terrible it looks?'

'Nothin',' Hackett said, wanting to get on. 'It's nothin'.' He pushed the bag onto the table. 'It's all in there. I'll take the six.' He kept a wary eye on the street beyond the windows for one of Black Benny's faces. Not that there was much chance of seeing one. The black bastards didn't normally surface until lunch-time. But there was just the possibility that they'd be kicked out to look for him – it depended on how pissed off Benny was.

'Such a rush,' the older man said. 'All the time rush, rush.'

'I'm in a hurry. Have you got the six?'

Weidenfeld nodded and spread his hands. 'Yes, I've got it.'

'There's some other gear in the bag. It's good stuff but it needs unloading at a distance. Your overseas friend. There's also a name and address in there. A geezer named Martin Brookes. Right? If there's any change, I'd like you to give it to him and he can send it on.'

Weidenfeld nodded slowly. 'You're leaving us?'

'For health reasons, right?'

'I understand.' He slipped the two envelopes onto the table. 'Take them both, young man. That's a total of nine thousand. Like I said, you trust me, and therefore, I shall trust you. Your friend will hear from me soon.'

Hackett stashed the envelopes and stood up. 'Be seein' you, then.'

'It's been good to do business,' Weidenfeld said, abruptly.

'Right,' said Hackett, and headed for the door.

He made Victoria at nine thirty. On his way in he saw the late edition headlines. The body of a young girl had been discovered on some allotments. He wondered whether it had been the girl from the Richmond Estate. The streets just weren't safe any more. Villains, bandits, robbers, psychopaths, they'd taken over. Now there were paedophiles crawling out of the drains, child molesters, child killers for Christ's sake. Something needed doing. The kozzers had lost the war. His thoughts stopped him outside the station. He took the photograph from his back pocket. It was creased, and some of the emulsion had flaked off, but the black-and-white image of the girl was still clear. It was no longer a sexual pose, there was no come-on about it. He saw the apprehension in her eyes.

He walked into the station shop and purchased a single brown envelope. He used the cashier's pen to write on the back of the photograph. 'Fowned in Carrington feater.' He wiped away his fingerprints with a tissue, then sealed the envelope and addressed it.

The girl was waiting for him, curled up on one of the slatted benches. When she saw him she sprang up and her grin spread wide.

'I didn't think you'd come, not really. Not really.' She shook her head.

'I told you I'd be here. Did you get the tickets?'

'Yeah, yeah,' she said breathlessly, fidgeting with her hands, wanting to grab his arm. 'There's not much change left.'

'Don't worry about that, girl, I mean, Greg girl. Right?'

She nodded.

'Where are we goin' then? And what time? I need a drink. I'm desperate for a drink.'

'Guess where?' she said, happily.

'What's this, *Mastermind*?'

'Go on, guess.'

He stuck a finger in the air. 'Newquay,' he said.

'Right,' she said.

'Right,' he said.

She tapped at the envelope in his hand. 'What's that?'

'I need to post it. Bollocks to the stamp. They can pay it the other end.'

She read the address. 'Inspector Cole, Sheerham nick. That won't get there. You haven't even got a postcode.'

'It does or it don't. I'll never know, will I?'

'Who's he?'

'He's a kozzer. But he's more like one of us.'

'How do you know him?'

'He nicked me twice, that's how.'

She shrugged.

'So, what time's the bus?'

'Eleven.'

'Come on then, let's find a post-box, then get somethin' to drink. You hungry?'

'I'd like a crêpe,' she said, and snaked her hand through his arm. 'If we can afford it. With lots of syrup.'

'Right.' He tightened his arm on her hand, not letting her go. 'You can have as many as you like. And tomorrow we'll be on that beach with all them spaced-out surfers.'

She hesitated and pulled back. 'I haven't got a costume. I haven't got a thing. I haven't even got a toothbrush.'

'Don't you worry about that, Greg girl. You let me, Jay, Jason Hackett, worry about that. I'll look after you.' He patted her hand. It felt cool and good, like a permanent fixture. With her other hand she pointed to a red post-box.

They wandered over. He lifted the envelope and hesitated.

'What's the matter?'

'I was just thinkin',' he murmured. 'This must be the first time I've helped the kozzers in my life. I must be gettin' middle-aged, civilised. Fuck me, I'll be votin' Tory before we know it.'

'You're joking,' she said. 'Please tell me you're joking?'

'I'll tell you twice. Yeah, I'm jokin', I'm jokin'.'

'Right,' she said. 'Just make sure you are. I couldn't live with anyone who voted Tory.'

He nodded and smiled contentedly. 'Yeah, right. Know what you mean. Corrupt, robbin', lyin' bastards. Just like the Labour!'

He let the envelope go.

Keith Mason opened his eyes as he heard Jill Jackson stir. In those few moments of awakening, while his thoughts were still doped by sleep, he noticed a strange, unpleasant smell in the air. He struggled to sit up just as the woman's scream pierced the room. He leapt out of bed, his thoughts still slow. He fumbled for his spectacles and stubbed his toe. Holding his foot and cursing, he hopped to where the naked woman stood, pointing down to her overnight bag. His pain disappeared and his mouth dropped open in utter disbelief.

The bag lay open on the thick carpet, her neatly folded underwear on top, and in the middle of a particularly sexy number she had worn the previous night was a small pile of fresh shit. Poking out of it, facing his way, mostly obscured by the dump, was the grinning face of his Rolex wristwatch.

Mason wrenched his gaze away and glanced first at the hole left by his wallet, then at the empty jewel box on the dressing-table.

'The mother-fucking cock-sucking cunt bastard fucking wanking bastard son of a bitch! I'll fucking tear his fucking throat out! I'll fucking kill him!'

Some seventy yards away, in the next house, an elderly couple enjoying a leisurely breakfast of grapefruit and boiled eggs over their shared *Guardian* newspaper heard almost every word. He lifted a blown white eyebrow and she licked a fleck of egg yoke from her delicate lips.

Part 3

Chapter 16

Discovering that someone had broken into the theatre had come as a dreadful shock. It had bent him double, like a kick in the guts. His breath had come out in a gasp of utter disbelief.

He'd followed his plan. Kept her there, secured, Friday night and Saturday. Until the police had made their checks. He knew they would. Single man, living alone, overlooking the school. He even took his photograph and treasured magazine to the theatre just in case they looked around. You couldn't be too careful.

A missing girl, they said. He saw them write his name on their forms. 'Hello, David. Have you seen anything? Do you recognise the girl? Were you in on Friday evening? Anyone hanging around?' They'd known him for years, ever since he was a kid. Some of them had even bought him drinks in the White Horse. He left the front door open. They could have walked in if they'd wanted to. In fact, one of them, a plain-clothes man, had a quick peep into his front room. He offered them tea, but they declined, satisfied to ask their questions and get on with it. Fools. They hadn't got a clue. But after watching them at the allotment, then getting back to the theatre, sweaty and excited, what a fright he got. For a moment his heart had stopped. Even in his state of panic he realised the photograph was missing. He had to retreat, think about it. Plan again. The sins of the father shall be visited upon the children unto the third and fourth generation. That was it.

Planning, planning, it was giving him a headache. He'd lost the theatre and in his fantasy the theatre had always played a part. The first act. The place his mother loved. A sort of homage. And, of course, the fall of the drop. The drop curtain was the one they lowered before the final act.

Mother always called him an angel. You're the angel of mercy, she'd say. You're my little angel. She called him that right up to the last day. He'd brush the few strands of white hair she had left and she'd call him an angel. My little angel. Not just any angel. Archangel. Then, after a little cough, she stopped breathing. Or rather, she didn't really stop, because the pause between her breaths had become so long, she just never took her next one. He waited for it. But it never came. Just silence. A strange cold silence. It made him shiver. Then he went slowly to the telephone and called the doctor. He didn't panic. He was in full control. Even the doctor was surprised.

Highcliff Girls' Junior School was much more up market than Barnwall. Opted out, so they got preferential treatment. The kids were smart in their mauve blazers and berets. These kids weren't from the estate. No, sir. They were from the well off end of town. Jews, managers, directors, police chiefs. But the skirts were similar, pleated, grey. There was something about them that was so provocative they sent goose-pimples along his arms. Loose, that was it. They were all loose so that the wind would catch them. Light-grey summer skirts barely covered their knickers, loose enough to flap upwards and get caught in the breeze and flash bits of knickers. And the girls were young enough to forget to keep their knees together. Sometimes they sat on the kerb, waiting for the bus, knees under their chins, white pouches covering their tiny snatches for all to see. Their tight legs were tanned and smooth, athletic, without an ounce of fat. They moved easily, throwing their school bags around, skipping the occasional step as they forgot they were no longer little girls. How old were they? Nine? Ten? These days, who could tell? The school entrance was common to both junior and senior. And the uniforms were identical, just filled out a bit more on the older girls. But they weren't kids, not in the old-fashioned sense. They were turning it on, attracting the boys. They knew all right.

From his position, just twenty yards from the bus-stop, he watched one girl in particular. He thought of the bony pubis not yet sullied by hair. Definitely no hair. That wouldn't do. Hair was full of woodlice and those crab things. Hair was the mark of old women, used and smelly. It was put there to hide the filthy cunt beneath. That's why the young girls didn't need it. They had nothing to hide. He'd worked it all out.

He watched the flow of traffic from the school; teachers retreating, parents picking up the younger kids.

It was time.

Chapter 17

Strong white light illuminated the heavy block lettering above the quiet glass entrance: METROPOLITAN POLICE, SHEER-HAM, DIVISIONAL AND AREA HEADQUARTERS.

DI Jim Gregory had pulled the night shift, taking over the IR while Baxter and Cole got some sleep. DS Sam Butler noticed his absence during the long early hours. A gut feeling, nothing he could put his finger on, led him down to the car and he motored slowly across to his own address, telling himself throughout the eight-minute drive that he was being foolish and unreasonable. He found DI Gregory in his hall and his wife on the landing. Gregory was peering into the hall mirror, fashioning a Windsor in his blue tie. His wife was forming a bow in the belt of her floral-patterned polyester dressing-gown.

DI Gregory drove himself to casualty. He needed five stitches on his broken nose. Butler made do with two sticking-plasters, one at the side of his eye, the other, a larger one, across the knuckles of his right hand.

A hall window had smashed. A neighbour dialled three nines. Four uniforms, enjoying every minute of it, turned out.

Detective Superintendent Baxter was furious, mostly because he heard about it from John Billingham, his uniformed counter-part, whose chilly sarcasm did not go down well, and because he knew without doubt that Billingham would be giving the full story to the old man as soon as he arrived. Butler was sent home to sort his life out. Gregory was called into the office and left the station half an hour later looking somewhat tense over the wide dressing that covered his nose. There was an unwritten rule – don't get caught – and he had broken it. Shagging the wife of a fellow officer was well out of order but shagging her when you were on duty and manning a murder inquiry was something that couldn't be forgiven. At the very least it meant suspension while disciplinary procedures took their course. Gregory's career was on the line.

At 0800, Baxter attended the joint management briefing

given by DS Scot and Inspector Knight in the parade room. Even without Gregory's stupidity, mornings were not his favourite time of day. He was like a reptile, he supposed. It took some hours of daylight, the warmth of the sun, before his benevolence was stirred. He sat beside a stiff-backed Superintendent Billingham beneath the target criminal board, which showed photographs or names and details of CRO men (men with criminal records) who were not wanted, but who were probably up to no good. Billingham wasn't happy either, but for different reasons. As far as he was concerned, CID was trespassing again. Marsh's insistence that they persevered with joint meetings was now beyond a joke. Innovation was one thing, it might look good when he wrote his next article for the *Gazette*, but the meetings were running into the time when officers should have been on the beat. He listened while the priorities for the day unfolded. Back to the beginning, the estate, the allotments, the victim's face flashed at everything in sight. Jane West's photograph was hitting the television again later, along with the usual appeals. A dozen officers were standing by to take any calls. They went over the details that had come back from Huntingdon, confirmation of the fibres and a few prints found on the body. Nothing relevant, at least not yet. Aldermaston had come back with the analysis of the dirt found in the victim's hair and under her fingernails. The silica was the local stuff widely used in buildings in the area; the lead was something called 206, used in old pipework and protective coverings. There was also a trace of mucor, a phycomycete which includes many common moulds; a class of fungi, a saprophytic whose thallus was a simple protoplasmic mass.

'What the hell does that mean?' Baxter snapped.

DS Barry Scot, who was standing in for Cole, cleared his throat and said rather coyly, 'It's a growth of fungi, Guv, that lives in moist warm air and absorbs non-living organic matter rather than being parasitic.'

'And?'

'The mould grows in dark places, attaches itself to damp brick and so forth. We could be looking for a cellar or a brick outhouse or garage.'

'Why didn't you say that, then?'

Baxter's mood was even worse than they'd anticipated.

On his way back to the office, Baxter paused at the drinks machine to pick up some plastic coffee.

'Worst thing ever invented,' he muttered irritably to DC McLintock as she waited in line.

Hazel flashed him a sympathetic smile. She appreciated that he was under pressure. With all the top brass in and out, the flak from the top floor was getting unbearable. The fracas involving Butler and Gregory hadn't helped.

Baxter spilt some coffee in the corridor and carried the rest into his office. On his desk were the series of SOC photographs. They caught his eye and drew him across. He had studied the pictures a dozen times, but familiarity made no difference to the feeling of revulsion that swept over him. He thought of his own daughter, very nearly the same age, and glanced at her photograph on his desk. He shook his head despairingly.

'A ritual,' he muttered, as he lifted his drink. Perhaps it was. Steam misted his spectacles, took him by surprise and as he put the plastic cup back on his desk in a hurry, he spilt coffee onto the photographs. 'Damn it! Sodding damn it!'

He took out a tissue and wiped the photographs but some of the emulsion rubbed off, leaving a brown mess. He was only vaguely aware that his door had opened and a figure stood framed in the doorway. He looked up and saw Rick Cole and interpreted the reproving look.

'You think this is funny?'

Cole raised his hands in mock surrender. 'Who, me?'

'You look like something the cat dragged in.'

'I was late to bed and I had an early call. Counselling duties.'

'Sam?'

'Yes, Sam. You know he's on the verge of a breakdown, Guv?'

Baxter frowned. Cole wasn't usually forthcoming. 'Go on?'

'I've noticed it for a little while. He suspected that something was going on for a few weeks. The pressure's been building.

His close involvement with the Wests tipped the balance. His reaction was out of character.'

'He doesn't need you to defend him, Rick. He assaulted a senior officer. No matter what the provocation, there is no defence. That's official. Unofficially, I'd have belted the bastard, too. Did you know about it?'

Cole drew up a chair. 'I didn't know about Jim. Frankly, I'm surprised. He always speaks highly of his wife and kids. I wouldn't have put him in the frame.'

'Me neither,' Baxter said, and sipped his coffee. 'I want a doctor's report on Sam before he comes back.'

'Then we might not see him for a while, and that's a shame.'

'Meaning?'

'In his situation work might be therapeutic. Getting back on the bike after a fall, all that.'

Baxter nodded reluctantly. 'It's going to make us short-handed. Gregory's out of it for the foreseeable future. You're going to have to pass some work up to me.'

'That'll make a change, Guv.'

'You have an endearing quality, Rick. I've only just noticed it.'

'Most people see it immediately.' Cole placed a brown envelope on the desk and slipped it across.

'What's this?'

'It came in this morning's post. I didn't come in here to discuss staffing problems.'

Baxter gave him a sharp look and picked up the envelope. He had never learned to read Cole at all. Sarcasm, humour, he couldn't work it out. It left him mildly irritated. Carefully, he withdrew the crumpled black and white polaroid photograph.

'It's already been dusted. It's clean.'

'What's this?' Baxter adjusted his spectacles. 'Porn?' He turned it over and read the back. 'Carrington?'

'The old theatre. There was a serious incident there on Saturday night. A tramp was stabbed on the steps. The local nick dealt with it. But that's not the point, Guv. Notice the girl's uniform, the school uniform?'

Baxter turned the photograph again and studied the picture. Much of the uniform was obscured by the girl's raised legs, but there was enough for him to recognise. He looked up. 'My God!'

'Barnwall School. Jane West's school. That girl looks a couple of years older.'

'Right, Rick, what's your plan?'

'Check out the theatre first. It's been closed for months. Then a visit to the school.'

'I agree. For the moment we'll keep it to ourselves.' He tapped the photograph. 'This might just be the break. And by Christ, we need something.'

'Right. I'll get on with it.'

He watched Cole leave, then tipped the rest of his coffee into the flowerpot on his four-drawer. The spiky cactus was thriving. He gave Cole a few minutes, then followed him into the IR.

DS Barry Scot had a forbidden kettle on the boil. Since the installation of the hated coffee machines they had been banned. A little rule that the chief super had dreamt up. Perhaps he had nothing better to do. Baxter found a mug next to Scot's filing-cabinet and helped himself to coffee and milk. 'Bloody life-saver, son.'

Scot nodded but remained slightly concerned as he watched Baxter lift the mug. The old man's habit of leaving a trail of coffee to his office door was well known.

DS Scot was a lanky six-footer in his late twenties. Fair hair, clean features, the son every mother wanted.

Cole called to him across the room, 'Barry, you're with me.'

'Right, Guv,' Scot said and stood from the desk. He gave Baxter's wavering mug a final glance, then followed Cole out.

Baxter finished his coffee and turned to DC McLintock. 'Give me a minute, will you, Hazel?'

The others in the room, a mix of DCs and DSs, glanced up curiously and wondered whether DC McLintock was in trouble. Hazel dithered before she reached for her jacket and followed the super from the room.

She had spent the last hour on the screen: records, all insertions to the person, impalements, wounding with spikes, spears, skewers, lances, bayonets, ritual murders, black magic, occult, devil worship. She had run out of 'search' titles. Her eyes were sunken and dark, her head reeling. Before the briefing she had spent half an hour on the collator's records, informal scraps of information kept on a card index system. The database was accessible to anyone listed on it. That wouldn't do at all. The information on the cards came from various sources: the National Intelligence Bureau sent the Notification of Convictions, other stations within the division sent messages that might be of interest, and local coppers picked up rumours and gossip. Some information was even lifted from the local rags. It was all there.

In his office, Baxter said, 'Sit down a minute.'

Hazel did so, formally, clamping her knees together. The concern stayed on her face.

'What's the matter, Hazel? Have you fallen out with the job?'

She frowned, bit her lip and took her time. 'Well, the serious side is getting to be a bit of a joke, isn't it?'

Baxter knew exactly where she was coming from. Cut-backs. Police murder files were overflowing with unsolved cases. Rates for domestics were cleared up at around eighty per cent, but what were known as 'stranger killings' were way down. The years of Tory rule had left manpower, cash and resources below the critical point. It was going to take years to correct the balance. Now if a crime wasn't solved in the first few days, it was put at the back of the pile, effectively forgotten. Limits to the number of officers used on a case, the overtime allowed, the mileage allowances and so on, were decided by the existing area budgets before the inquiry had even begun. But there were exceptions, to a degree. And child murder was one of those.

She went on, 'But really, the job's not changed. Since my transfer it's gone very well, better than I expected. I've enjoyed it. I actually like my work.'

'I noticed you in before time. Work isn't everything. Especially our work. At the end of the day, it's just a job. You do your work and you walk away.'

'That's just it though, Guv. It's not just a job, is it? It takes over your life.'

'Only if you let it. There has to be some place you can wind down. It's essential. Stop me if I'm teaching you to suck eggs. But if you haven't got somewhere to relax it'll break you.'

Embarrassment replaced the worry and she blushed.

He continued, 'You get hard, cynical. Hard things shatter easily. You've got to stay loose. I'm not prying, God forbid, just offering some fatherly advice. The job is full of knocks, you're in a no-win situation; you need something to balance it all.'

'I hear you, Guv.' She thought of Butler and his problems.

As if reading her mind Baxter said, 'I know you've been working closely with Sam recently. I don't want his situation getting to you, understand? How are things on the home front with you?'

She hesitated a moment too long. 'My husband's away at the moment, on a course. But things are all right.'

She wondered whether he gave the same advice to her male colleagues. She doubted it, but it didn't trouble her. Her mind turned to DS Butler. He'd been broken, but it had more to do with his wife than the job. Or had it, she wondered? Whatever, she would miss him and their conversations. She glanced at Baxter. The shuffling, overweight super had taken Butler's place. She felt perfectly safe with him. She enjoyed the Platonism, the total lack of sexual overtones. He *was* fatherly. She appreciated it.

'There's no problem,' she went on. 'But I take it you've been talking to DI Cole?'

'About what?'

'We had a talk yesterday.'

From the look on Baxter's face she knew she'd been mistaken. No one could be that good an actor.

'He didn't mention it,' Baxter said, seriously. 'He should have done.'

'Short of taking a drive back to Ipswich, Guv, there weren't many people I could turn to.'

'I understand.'

'Is that all, sir?'

'Yes. But just keep in mind that I'm here, Hazel. You don't have to keep your problems to yourself. And you don't have to drive all the way to Ipswich. Contrary to popular opinion, I won't bite.'

The theatre rose up from the corner of the busy street, sharply outlined against the bright sky. It looked run-down and deserted. Even though the pavements were crowded with shoppers the old stone produced an almost overpowering atmosphere of depression.

They left the car on double yellows and examined the heavy chain that wrapped around the door handles.

Cole said dryly, 'It might have been a good idea to phone the agents.'

'Maybe there's a caretaker knocking about. I'll check the back.'

Cole pointed to the wide steps. 'That's where the stabbing took place. Saturday night.'

'I heard,' Scot said, casually, and walked off.

Cole examined the area. If there had been blood, it had been hosed away. Or perhaps the heavy rain had taken care of it. He lit a cigarette and gazed at the buildings across the road. There must have been plenty of witnesses.

Two minutes later Scot appeared at the corner. 'This way, Guv,' he said breathlessly. 'No caretaker, but there's a door been forced.'

Cole followed him along a narrow path leading between the theatre side wall and the brick wall of an alley. They arrived at the rear of the building, skirted a pile of junk, and approached the door.

'Notice the timber, Guv?'

Protruding from old cardboard boxes and bits of old furniture were various lengths of three-by-three timber. One length, about six feet of it, lay near the door.

Cole nodded, his eyes sparkled. 'I would have, if you'd given me enough time.' His light-heartedness had something to do

170

with his mounting excitement. He pushed open the door. One end of the bar handle dragged noisily on the floor. Along the length of the long passage sunlight slanted in from the high windows, holding onto a million specks of dust. Their footsteps seemed loud on the bare wooden floor. Cole paused at the first curtained entrance and pointed to another further along the corridor. 'You take the top end. Find a way to the balconies.'

Cole drew back the curtain on the darkened auditorium. There was a bank of light switches just inside, at the side of the stage. He threw them on, four at a time, and watched the room light up block by stuttering block.

'Well, well,' he muttered, mildly surprised that the electricity was still on.

His gaze took in the rows of dusty chairs, then rose to the intricately carved balconies. He followed the wall around as the roof slanted down towards the stage and rested finally on the heavy curtains. He climbed the steps to the stage.

Scot's voice carried down from the balcony with a slight echo. 'An empty stage is eerie. There have been a lot of crimes committed on stage.'

'I take it you mean the story-lines, and not the inept performances?'

'Yes, I mean the stories; the crime, the cat and mouse, the red herrings, the copper working out who done it, and the butler never did.'

'If only it was so simple,' Cole said. 'Find anything?'

'Nothing. It might help if I know what I'm looking for.'

'Photographs, anything.'

'That helps.'

Cole moved to the far side of the stage and climbed down. He started along the passage to the dressing-rooms and pushed open the first door.

He moved in and looked around, faintly disappointed. He leant over the half-full bottle of milk and pulled a face. It was some days old and sour. Faded artwork on an old sectioned screen caught his eye. Scot, breathing hard, moved into the doorway.

'Nothing here,' Cole said and wandered out to the next room. Save for the drink making equipment, it was almost identical. 'There's no cups,' he muttered. 'Coffee, milk, kettle, but no cups.'

'I hadn't noticed, Guv. That's probably why I'm still a DS.'

Cole shot him a critical look before moving to the third door along. As it opened, a key fell to the floor. He stepped over it and stopped in the doorway.

'Jesus, this is it,' Scot said from just behind, pointing to the green mattress.

'Yeah,' Cole said, as he noticed the lengths of masking tape. 'You're right.' A shiver, an icy finger, caressed the length of his spine and for a moment, just an instant, all he saw was the green door swing open into darkness.

Chapter 18

The scene of crime officers moved into the Carrington. Their preliminary report would be made available in time for the evening briefing, but no one was in any doubt that Jane West's murder took place in the gloomy theatre dressing-room.

Along with Baxter, Cole was asked to update Chief Superintendent Marsh. Afterwards, he left Baxter with the chief. There were rumours that in the past the old man had been an absolute bastard, a stickler for the rule book; insubordination was a capital offence. It had only been PACE – the Police and Criminal Evidence Act 1984 – that had forced him to mellow. Before that, chief supers upward, and particularly chief constables, held the force in a dictatorial grip; they didn't need evidence of misconduct and the officer involved was not always fairly represented. A bad chief copper made life hell. Marsh wasn't bad, but he wasn't very good either, not when it came to backing his men.

In the IR, Cole picked on DS Barry Scot again. The others wondered if it was favouritism. 'Get over to Hinckley nick. They dealt with the stabbing on Saturday night. Pull all the details. I want witnesses. If necessary, put our own door-to-door on the flats opposite. Then get across to the hospital and talk to the victim.'

Cole glanced at DC James at his side. 'You go with him,' he said. He turned to DC McLintock. 'You're with me, Hazel.'

She was waiting for it, but she held back. She didn't want to appear too enthusiastic, even though her heart had missed a beat. She slowly pushed some papers aside, picked up her bag and slung her jacket across her arm.

In the car, Hazel turned to the DI. 'Baxter saw me.'

He was pleased she'd brought it up. He'd heard about it on the grapevine but hadn't known how to get around to it. 'What about?'

'He was worried about me.'

'He never mentioned it.'

She struggled with her words. 'I thought you'd told him about me turning up last night.'

'Why should I do that?' he asked, tentatively.

She shrugged. 'It just crossed my mind.'

'As far as I'm concerned, last night remains between us. You needed to talk. I was there. That's the end of it.' He glanced across at her, then nodded towards the dashboard. 'There's an envelope in there. Have a look.'

Her movements were almost formal, as though she was nervous. She reached for the envelope and took out the photograph.

'I see.' She felt uneasy, even embarrassed. The thought annoyed her.

'No, I don't think you do. That arrived in my in-tray this morning. Read the back.'

She flipped it over. 'The Carrington. So this is . . . Who sent it?'

'Good question.'

'I can't make out the postcode.'

'Already checked. South-west one. Victoria.'

'Who is she?'

'Another good question. The uniform belongs to—'

'Barnwall School.'

'Right. How old would you make her?'

Hazel examined the photograph. 'Fourteen, fifteen. It doesn't look as though she's being forced into posing, though. But there's something there. Petulance, insolence.' Her gaze fell to the girl's raised legs and she couldn't control another slight blush. She slipped the photograph back into the envelope and looked out of the side window, hoping the DI hadn't noticed. He had, and it tickled him.

Fifteen minutes later they met Betty Baldick, the head teacher of Barnwall School. She was a slim, mid-forties blonde, short and slightly stooped. She wore a flared, brightly patterned dress with shoulder pads and a wide black belt.

While Hazel showed her the top half of the photograph, Cole looked out at the playground. The younger kids were running

174

wild, the long summer holiday still not worn off. The older kids, trying to find a non-conformist look in slightly altered uniforms – skirts too short, trousers too baggy – lolled about the edges in little groups. Some of the older kids were known to him. When he and DC McLintock had walked through the playground they had eyed him suspiciously.

'Well, now, I don't recognise the face,' Betty Baldick said, in a business-like tone. 'Are you quite certain it's recent?' She shook her head in sudden exasperation and glanced up. 'Of course it's not. Look, the badge. For goodness sake, we haven't seen a badge like that in years!' Her dark eyes fixed on Cole. 'I think we'd better ask some of the longer-serving members of staff. They might remember her. She's a very pretty girl.'

'Good idea,' Cole said.

'Shall I take the photograph?'

Hazel held it firmly. 'No. If you don't mind, I'll hold onto it.'

Betty Baldick shrugged. 'Well, follow me. If we hurry, we'll catch most of them in the staff room.'

They got lucky. The science teacher, Keith Graham, vaguely remembered the girl, and turned up an old form photograph to confirm it. It was eight years old. Her name was Helen Klincewicz.

'That's a Polish name,' Cole said.

'I think it is,' Graham said, then raised his finger and stabbed the air. 'No, no, tell a lie. I do remember her. She was Irish.'

'Have you got an address?'

'Records, Inspector; archives, in the office next door.'

The address was on the other side of the estate and it led them further afield, to Hendon. Helen had married and moved out of the family home five years previously. Cole parked his car in front of a smart detached house and they walked side-by-side up a path winding between rockery to the door.

Helen Klincewicz had changed her name to Guest. She looked puzzled as Cole held out his ID. She was still in her dressing-gown, a spotted towelling robe with a loose belt. She clasped the soft material tightly to her chest.

175

'You better come in,' she said, nervously, as she checked the neighbouring drives.

Cole picked up two bottles of semi-skimmed from the step and carried them through behind Hazel. They were led into a spacious hall where a couple of chairs were arranged around a telephone table. Helen Guest let go of the gown to take the bottles and it fell slightly open to reveal she wore nothing beneath. As she carried the bottles into the kitchen her bare feet slapped on the parquet floor.

'You enjoy the job, don't you, Guv,' Hazel said, with a touch of sarcasm. She sat down in one of the upright chairs, her back stiff and formal.

'Yeah, I enjoy the job,' Cole said. 'Sometimes it's rewarding.'

She came back. She was twenty-three, dark-haired and very attractive, even without make-up. A flash of her green eyes could down a man at twenty yards.

Cole noticed Hazel's narrow-eyed look.

'How can I help you?' The Irish accent and a slightly breathless quality gave a lilt to her voice.

Hazel slipped the photograph from the envelope and watched Helen's eyes widen. Her slender hand flew to her lips.

'Oh, Jesus,' she said. Embarrassment flared on her cheeks.

Hazel said coldly, 'That is you, isn't it?'

Behind her hand the woman nodded.

'Who was the photographer, Mrs Guest?'

Helen shook her head, gripped her gown and shot a glance towards the staircase. She said, 'No, no. Where did you get it?'

'That doesn't matter,' Hazel continued.

'It matters to me.'

'We're interested in who took it.'

Helen pointed at the photograph. 'Tell me, is that against the law?' She looked at Cole. 'Is it?'

'No, Mrs Guest, it's not against any law that I know of. There was a time when it might have been. But nowadays it's pretty tame. When it was taken, and I'm guessing about eight or nine years ago, then you were probably under age. If that's the case, then the photographer could be liable to a number

176

of charges, but frankly, that's not why we're interested. The photograph was found at the scene of a murder.'

'Oh, Jesus, not the little girl?'

Cole nodded.

Helen's face lost its colour. 'I'll tell you what I'll do.' She paused, reached out and touched his arm, a gesture that momentarily delighted him, then went on quietly, 'Can I get back to you?'

Cole looked at the stairs, then at the curiosity on Hazel's face, then he nodded.

'Right. Do you know Sheerham police station?'

'I do.'

'I'll expect you at four. Please don't be late.'

She gave him a quick little nod of gratitude. 'I'll be there,' she said and sighed relief. It emerged like a catch of hot breath. 'Thank you for understanding.'

'It goes with the job,' he murmured.

Hazel looked on, perplexed.

Helen opened the door and repeated, 'I'll be there. Four o'clock.' Her gaze lingered on the car.

As Hazel walked past, Cole noticed her tight expression. As he climbed into the car Hazel said sternly, 'What was all that about, Guv?'

'Christ, Hazel, we interrupted her, them, whatever. She wasn't going to tell us a bloody thing with someone listening in from the top of the stairs. And I doubt very much whether it was her husband or he would have been down.'

Hazel was shocked. She shook her head. 'I didn't realise,' she uttered.

'Why would you?' Cole said. 'You were too busy giving her the evil eye.'

'What's that supposed to mean?'

'Nothing, nothing at all.'

He wasn't going to get into the female competitive bit. Not a chance. But he was still surprised that Hazel hadn't noticed the glow on Helen's face, that secret glow of sex. To Cole's mind, there was nothing more beautiful.

* * *

177

Back at the office, Barry Scot reported that the stabbing victim hadn't seen his attacker or anyone hanging around the theatre and the doctors had refused him permission to upset the patient with further questions. He was now working down a list of possible witnesses supplied by Hinckley nick. Reports came back from the agents who were dealing with the Carrington. Cost-cutting meant that security was limited to checking the exterior of the building only. The door at the back was only checked once a week. It meant that whoever used the place before the forced entry had a key. The SOCOs had already issued a prelim. Damage to the door was recent, at the best guess no more than sixty hours old, which put it at some time on Saturday night. The rusting process on the bare metal of the broken bar handle, not yet visible to the naked eye, along with mud from the garden and the alley carried into the passage on two sets of shoes, had given them that estimate. The milk was older than that, three or four days, and the dried blood about the same. The blood matched Jane West's. There was more to come, but he'd have to wait.

Cole issued more instructions. He wanted the security people interviewed, the whereabouts of all keys to the building obtained, and the holders TIED. Fingerprints were numerous; those on the kettle and other recent imports were given priority. So far the results were negative. He spent half an hour updating the HOLMES team before he was called to the front desk. Helen Guest had arrived promptly at four and was causing something of a stir in reception. Cole was still finding the arm of his jacket as he reached the front desk.

Helen Guest wore a pinstripe suit; the skirt was the shortest he'd ever seen. Her crossed legs and the navy-blue high-heel that tapped at the air drew eyes like pins to a magnet. Half the uniforms on site had made excuses to talk to Sergeant Mike Collier. Her green eyes lit up as she recognised Cole.

Cole shook a sad head as he glanced from the PCs to the sergeant. Turning to the woman he said, 'There's an interview room along here. You'll find it a little less crowded.'

One or two of the constables made suggestive noises. Helen Guest knew exactly what was happening and seemed to be enjoying it. She flashed Irish eyes at the watching uniforms and followed Cole along the corridor. The policemen leaned over the desk to get a final glimpse.

Cole closed the door to the small room. Hazel McLintock was already waiting. 'You remember DC McLintock, don't you? Please have a seat, Mrs Guest.'

'Call me Helen, please. I'm sorry about this morning.' She looked from Hazel to Cole.

He flicked her a no-problem smile and raised his hand in a throwaway gesture. 'Don't worry about it.' He tried to clear his mind of the image of her draped in the dressing-gown and went on, 'The photograph?'

Hazel took it out and lay it face up on the desk.

'Yes, the photograph. It's all really embarrassing. I never thought I'd see it again. I wish I hadn't. I was so young.'

'Can you tell us about it?'

She looked at Hazel, her expression inviting sympathy. 'I was at school, obviously. Fifteen. I did something very stupid.'

'Go on?' Hazel said.

'Before he retired, my father was a GP. Dr Klincewicz, from the Richmond Park surgery.'

'I know it. But your father was before my time. It's Dr Carter now.'

'That's right. Anyway, foolishly, and I have no excuse, I took one of his prescription pads and copied his signature. Then—'

'You sold them?'

She looked worried. 'Not really sold. More like swaps, really.'

Cole smiled. 'For what?'

'A little weed, you know?'

He agreed. 'I know.'

Hazel sighed, irritated. 'And whoever you gave them to filled in drugs like temazepam and other tranquillisers?'

'Yeah, I suppose he did,' Helen said.

'Do you know what they use them for?' Hazel pressed, coldly. 'They call them jellies or wobbly eggs and mix them with heroin.'

179

'It was a long time ago. It was a silly thing to do. I know.'

'So what happened?'

Helen smoothed out her sleeve then raised her hand to the neckline of her jacket, running her fingers slowly up and down. Cole found the movement quite disconcerting. She glanced at him. Her easy smile promised him the world and everything in it.

Sternly, Hazel repeated, 'So what happened, Mrs Guest?'

'What happened? Yes, I'll tell you what happened. I was nicked, that's what. One of your lot nicked me outside the school. Someone must have grassed on me.'

'A uniformed officer?' Cole asked, fidgeting uncomfortably.

'Yeah, in a car.'

'A panda?'

'No, no, it wasn't a panda. But it was a police car. It had a radio.'

'Did he arrest you?'

'Not exactly. We were going to find my parents. He was going to pull my father out of evening surgery.' She paused and lowered her eyes. 'We never got there. I begged him not to. My father would have killed me. He took me over the lakes. You know?'

'Fairland Lakes?' Hazel confirmed.

'Yeah.'

'What happened exactly, Helen?' she asked, a little less severely.

'He said he wouldn't touch me. All he wanted was some pictures, like that.'

'Did he touch you?'

'No, I'll give him that. He kept his word. He talked dirty, but that was all.'

'So, he got you to climb in the back and he took pictures. Is that it?'

'That's it.'

'He didn't touch you?'

'No. With hindsight that was a surprise.'

Hazel took a deep breath.

180

Cole cut in. 'Mrs Guest, would you recognise the officer again?'

'It was a long time ago, but yeah, I think so. He wasn't your average copper.'

'Why?'

'He was very thin, and his features were sallow. I remember thinking that. Coppers are usually well-built and they have more confidence than he did. I can't see your average copper letting me off so lightly, can you?' Her eyes melted him again. 'It has been my experience with coppers that they like to go all the way.'

Cole tried to suppress a grin.

'See,' she said to him. 'You know, don't you?'

'I'm sure I don't, Mrs Guest.'

'Call me Helen,' she said. 'In fact, you can call me any time.'

Trying to compose himself, Cole said, 'DC McLintock will take you along to records. She'll show you some mug-shots. Let's try and put a face to the uniform.'

Helen glanced at her watch. 'Fine.'

'Have you ever seen him since?'

She shook her head.

'What about before the incident?'

'No, never. I'd have remembered him.'

'Did you mention it to your school mates?'

'Some of them, of course.'

'You never heard of anything like that happening to any of them?'

'Not at all. Listen, this won't go any further, will it? I mean, I won't end up in court as a witness?'

Cole shook his head. 'That's an awfully long way off. Let's find the man first. Worry about that later.' He turned to Hazel. 'Right, I'll leave her in your capables.'

Hazel nodded and said, curtly, 'If you'd like to follow me, Mrs Guest.'

As Hazel led the woman further along the passage the corridor filled up again. Hazel shook her head in despair and ushered Helen quickly into records.

* * *

181

'A copper!' Baxter erupted. 'That's all we need.'

'She's spent two hours going through the PITs. If he's in the job, he's not at Sheerham.'

'It could be anywhere. Hinckley's favourite. Try there, then pass her over to records. Eight years is a long time. Eight years ago my hair was mostly dark. Find him and we've got ourselves a prime suspect. I'm on my way to Marsh. I'll give him the news. He won't be happy.'

'I've sent a copy of the photograph to FO. I'm hoping they'll come up with something on the car. With a little luck the back window will be unique.'

Baxter grunted.

'We've had some more in from the theatre. No trace of lead or damage to brickwork. The crap under her fingernails didn't come from the Carrington.'

'So she was some place else first?'

'Or after. There's more. No trace of perfume on the mattress and there would have been if she'd been on it.'

The pathologist's report had mentioned perfume on the body. Lots of it. Its identity remained a mystery.

'So he snatches her, he takes her to the theatre, then somewhere else, then the allotments?'

'Maybe. We'll see.'

Baxter nodded slowly, and headed wearily for the stairs.

When Cole applied to join the police force, the medical involved placing his feet on footprints marked on the floor, and touching his toes while three stern members of the examining board, sitting behind a table, looked up his bare arse. At the time he thought the procedure was to keep gays out of the job; anyone with a winking arsehole didn't even get to sit the written examination. Later, he found out that it was part of the indoctrination; people who wouldn't totally submit to the system were kept out. After he'd been in the job a while he promised himself that he'd never submit to that sort of indignity again.

Cole knocked off late and called on Sam Butler before driving home.

Over a scotch, Butler said, 'Janet's staying with her mother for a couple of nights. We'll see.'

Cole nodded reflectively. As far as he was concerned, that was a mistake. If they had any chance of a future, then togetherness had to be a part of it from the start. The idea of needing time to think was just putting off the inevitable.

Butler changed the subject. 'I've been thinking about Conners and who leaked the information. The whisper came in mid-morning, remember? And who was there at the same time, who came in to say cheerio to Russell?'

'Gregory.'

'That's the man. He left almost immediately.'

'Forget it, Sam. You're clutching at straws. It's not important at the moment. You and Janet are. Anyway, Gregory's history. The best he can hope for is a transfer.'

Cole spent half an hour with his grounded colleague before motoring home for a restless night going over the day's events and making mental notes for the next. At one stage he glanced at the telephone and half wished that the DC would phone him again. She'd moved closer. He'd noticed the spark of jealousy in her eye during the interview with Helen Guest and he'd enjoyed it. She was on his mind when he went to sleep and still there when the dawn woke him.

Chapter 19

The briefing on Wednesday morning concentrated on SOCO information. In prominent position on the board was the photofit, or rather, the computer image, of Helen Guest's photographer. The personal identity photographs, the PITs, kept in records, had been a waste of time. A copper, she had said. A uniform. But it was eight years ago and he could have come from any number of districts. But his information regarding the prescription pad indicated local knowledge, and therefore Sheerham nick. Finding him became the main objective. There was still a lot of work to do.

Jane West had been held in the Carrington dressing-room before being moved, tied up, sexually abused and slaughtered. Finding a match on the fingerprints had so far proved fruitless.

Catchem, the national database on sex crimes and killings of girls and young women, had come up with an offender profile. They hadn't yet been told of Helen Guest's police connection. Police investigators, especially the older men, treated psychologists' profiles with more than a little disdain. They were just exercises in probabilities and speculation, hardly worth the paper they were written on, and certainly not worth the expense. Baxter was an old-fashioned copper; he hated psychologists with their university degrees and self-importance almost as much as he hated computers. He knew what was coming even before Margaret Domey, the resident police psychologist, stood up with the Catchem report. The killer would have trouble with his mother, the father would be either absent or abused him. His mother might have laid him. He'll be between twenty and forty and be a lorry driver, or a van driver, or a rep – someone with transport. The child-murderer Robert Black had used a van to snatch his little victims: everyone else would do the same. The killer knows the area well, at some stage he lived or worked here. His sex life is inhibited. He wanks himself silly watching porn, in this case, schoolgirl porn.

We'll find a stack of it at the back of his wardrobe. He might be disfigured – cross-eyed, acne, scarred, burned – this is his way of getting back. Maybe the young girls laughed at him. It would take them three sheets of A4 to get there, but that's it. As far as he was concerned, profiles often had a negative value; even though everyone knew they were just an assist, the details remained in the mind, and suspects were sometimes excluded because they didn't fit.

Margaret Domey knew about Baxter's reservations and shot him a dark look before she began. She was in her thirties, dressed in a trouser suit, with short hair and little make-up. 'The killer is a resident with a lot of local knowledge. And he must have access to a vehicle.'

Yes, yes, Baxter thought irritably. Do get on with it, woman, and let us get on with the police work. There was something about Domey that put him on edge and raised his shoulders. She had a way of talking down to people in a voice that came straight from her well-stacked, tightly buttoned chest. It seemed to miss her mouth altogether.

She went on, 'He is organised, prepared, precise and systematic. He sticks rigidly to his plan. Even the sexual abuse was almost ritualised, one thing at a time, building in tempo, and this after keeping her alive and feeding her on chocolate and pizza for over two days. So, for two days he barely touched her. And then, once she was dead, he destroyed her sex organs and then bludgeoned her feet until they were unrecognisable.'

Baxter sat a little more upright. What he was hearing wasn't new. But the way in which Margaret set it out was quite emotionless. He had seen her in action before, but never so controlled.

'Here, a grotesque fantasy has been played out. He's imagined it many times, getting off, refining the plan, the selection of victim, the abduction and the attack, and then his manipulation of the authorities, the police, in parading his results. The whole thing from beginning to end has been thoroughly planned. He firmly believes that he is beyond our reach. Getting caught is not a possibility. That means, in all likelihood, that he hasn't been caught before. He won't show up on any past offender

185

files. Organised killers like this tend to fall into the older age group, around thirty-five to forty-five. And almost certainly he's done it before. No one starts with this kind of experienced attack. He's worked up to it with other, lesser, offences. Jane West was taken in broad daylight, with lots of people around, and yet we have no witnesses. Proof enough of the killer's efficiency. She was murdered in a systematic way and then hung in a place guaranteed to be found. The sequence of events suggests preparation and practice. It suggests experience in planning and organisation – perhaps through his work. But he won't be a team member. He's very definitely a loner.'

She turned over a sheet then glanced again at Baxter. 'How am I doing?'

He was shaken, suddenly embarrassed. A murmur of derision, especially from the uniforms, went around the room. Baxter's views were well known. He smiled awkwardly and nodded.

She went on, 'We're looking for someone who lives alone, or with his parents, not married. On the surface he seems intelligent but slightly reticent, especially when dealing with women. He finds it difficult to speak to them. Young girls are different. With them there is no threat; older girls shy away from him, perhaps because of a scar or acne, that sort of thing. With regard to relationships, he is immature. I know my next point will be scoffed at, but indulge me. His family are probably lower-middle-class, and his mother is overbearing. His father is a strict disciplinarian and keen to criticise, and has probably rejected him. His humiliation at the hands of his father has led to an almost unbearable desire to dominate. The only things available for him to dominate are the weak and innocent. A lot of his time is spent alone, indulging in his own fantasies. It wouldn't surprise me to find that he is a church-goer. For him, ritual is important. And there is a very definite religious connection. It's one of Catchem's major points. The legend of Tammuz, the sacred king sacrificed annually in the temple at Jerusalem. A Jewish month is still named after Tammuz. The chosen victim was generally a holy man who was stripped and impaled between heaven and earth, crucified for the sake of the earth's fertility. It was a tradition. The surrogate king sacrifice. The cross, the allotment, fertility. Get it?'

Baxter cut in, 'Am I looking for a Manson figure, then? Someone who believes he's the Messiah?'

Margaret didn't like being sidetracked. She half turned to address the superintendent.

'The ritual factors, the virgin, the insertion – for that read impalement – and the body tied to the cross, certainly lend themselves to that idea.' She turned back to the main gathering. 'This is a ritual, not a one off. Mistakes have been ironed out by practice. After the attack his behaviour patterns undergo a change. There might be some anxiety. He would work this off, perhaps in the garden or decorating, or with some other physical activity. The insertion of the dildo, if indeed that's what it was, and the destruction of her sex organs after she was already dead, was again planned in advance and features in his sick fantasy. The concept of insertion is tied up with male dominance. The bigger the tool used the more dominant the male. We'll probably find that the killer has an abnormally small erect penis. This goes some way to explain his use of a substitute. Two other things. Everything points to the fact that Jane West knew her killer. That she got into his car et cetera without being seen.'

If he was a copper, Baxter thought, getting Jane into the car would have been the easiest thing in the world.

Margaret continued, 'She was selected, certainly, but she knew him. The second thing is the smashing of her feet after she had died. We think that it was not part of the attack. That perhaps he went into a rage when she died before he had finished, picked up a weapon and hit out, crushing her feet. Perhaps the rage was a sudden expression of terrible guilt. It has even been suggested that the killer might be crippled, and this final act was in some way a revenge against nature itself, the destruction of something perfect. The final point is that he may have killed before and he'll kill again.'

Baxter's jaw took up some slack from under the chin. 'So we've got ourselves a serial killer?'

She glanced across and said, tersely, 'Did I say four? You

need four bodies before you have a serial.' She collected her papers together and sat down.

Baxter adjusted his spectacles and said, 'When? When will he strike again?'

'You've actually taken notice of me, Superintendent?'

'Don't let it go to your head, Margaret, but I always take note of what you say.'

'There'll be some kind of cycle, conscious or otherwise. If it's conscious, then it will be to do with the moon, the month, the year, some event, probably some astral, quasi religious event. If it's unconscious, then it will be after the wind down, and the necessary time to build up again. At that stage he'll start planning, watching, speculating. It won't be days, but it could be weeks, and going by experience, more likely months. Unless something triggers him. There's always that. But this is no opportunist.'

Baxter nodded thoughtfully. 'So we might be looking for some mad messiah. But why did he lead us to Jane West?'

'He's confident,' she replied. 'He's toying with you. He's enjoyed watching your people from a distance. He's getting a kick out of it. He's making it personal.'

'Watching us?'

'I'll guarantee it. From an upstairs window or a car or even wandering by on foot. Perhaps he's got binoculars.' She nodded absently and flicked him a worried smile. 'He'll be watching and enjoying every minute of it.'

Baxter and Cole watched the psychologist's trim behind as she walked away.

'Something's upset her,' Baxter said. 'I don't think it was me, but with women who can tell?'

'She didn't mention it at the briefing, Guv, but she's not happy.'

'That much is plain for all to see. I don't dare think what her problem might be.'

Cole smiled. 'With the case, Guv. She's not happy with the case.'

'Not her old man, then?' Baxter grunted.

'Some of it doesn't fit. *Modus operandi*. All that shit. This one's not following a pattern.'

'Go on?'

'Some of the injuries put there after death. It's almost as if the killer is trying to make it look even worse than it is.'

'Is that possible, Rick? It already seems pretty fucking nasty to me.'

'I know, but that's what concerns Ms Domey. It's almost as if there's another motive beside the sex attack and murder.'

'If, if, if,' Baxter groaned. 'It's all if, isn't it? If the profile had come up with an area, say, the houses overlooking the school, or the allotments, or even the Carrington, then we could consider a mass DNA screening. At least we'd be moving. We'd be doing something.'

Cole nodded glumly. 'With each test costing forty-five quid and the present deficit running into millions, the accountants would frown at even a moderate screening. I can't see the chief standing up to them. There's a maniac out there killing kids but he hasn't put the mileage back up yet. It's still fifty miles a shift. Can you see him standing for a screening programme?'

'You're getting cynical, Rick. We've got something in common.'

'I've been cynical for a long time.'

'If the worst comes to the worst we could even try a Warwickshire.'

Warwickshire was jargon for the threat of a mass DNA screening when there was no fragment that samples could be tested against. It was a bluff. The idea was that the killer would panic, move out of the area, thereby revealing himself.

Cole knew it was just talk. There were plenty of enquiries still to be made before they started grasping at straws. Baxter was just having a bad day.

Baxter made a contemptuous noise. 'Marsh wants to call in the experts from Bramshill. Coppers, yes, but they've been brainwashed by the psychologists. The place is swarming with them. Bloody deer grazing in the grounds, bowling-green lawns. The place costs a fortune and our mileage allowance has been cut. You know what it amounts to? A holiday, a piss-up for the boys.'

Cole pulled a disbelieving face. 'I've read through Scot's report on the stabbing. I'm not satisfied. This low-life, Pullin, must have seen something. I think we ought to have another go. I find it quite incredible that a man can park his vehicle, open up the doors to the theatre and carry out the girl, wrapped or otherwise, without being seen. It's not acceptable.'

'I was thinking along those lines myself.'

'I'll have a go personally. Scot can carry on with the witnesses. House-to-house in this weather will teach him to do better.'

Baxter saw what the DI meant. Sheets of rain pelted at the office window. It was the first rain since the weekend storms.

'There's one other thing,' Cole said. 'The mould under the girl's fingers. The conditions for it to grow – dark, moist, warm air – are found in a heated outhouse or garage, or more likely, a cellar. If it's a cellar that rules out the estate. The newer houses just don't have them. Chas is having a look at the town plans, coming up with a list. You never know.'

Baxter nodded thoughtfully. 'I'll be in my office,' he said and shuffled off down the corridor.

'Guessed you'd be back,' Pullin said from his hospital bed as he glanced at Cole's ID. 'Big guns, this time, is it?' He was in a private room.

Cole guessed that the man was in his sixties. His face glowed with the boozer's blush; patches on his cheeks were chapped and flaky. Long white hair hung in damp clumps from an uneven centre parting. A tube ran from his chest and curled to a container under the bed. He had a temperature, but that wasn't surprising. The hospital heating was full on. Everybody had a temperature.

'Mr Pullin, did DS Scot tell you why we're showing such an interest in you?'

'He mentioned that a young girl was imprisoned in the theatre before being murdered. Is that what you mean?'

Cole nodded. 'Living on the steps you must have seen a lot

of comings and goings. I doubt that much happened that you didn't notice.'

'So you're not interested in who stuck a knife in me, then?'

'That's true. I couldn't give a fuck. If you don't want to help us on that score then why should we care? That's unofficial. Officially, we're speaking to witnesses, but unless you tell us what happened, then we're wasting our time. The murder of a schoolgirl is a different matter. Surely you can see that?'

Pullin sighed. 'I've been thinking about it. Saw the news on the tele. It's a terrible thing, all too familiar. They bring a portable in now and again but we have to share it. If you were to slip them a few quid I could have it full time.'

Cole smiled vaguely. 'I'll give it some thought. I went over your interview with DS Scot. You weren't very helpful.'

'I wasn't. That's true. He looked a nice enough sort but, well, I didn't care for his attitude. I might be homeless and living rough, I might drink a little too much, and to be honest, I don't pay any taxes, but that doesn't mean that I should be treated with any less respect than your average Tory voter. Do we agree on that?'

'Yes, we do. In fact, I'd give you a lot more respect than I'd give the average Tory voter. Having said that, there aren't many of them left, are there? But I didn't come here to discuss politics. You were a school teacher. What made you give it up?'

'On the contrary, it gave me up. The children, more specifically one boy's unruly behaviour, made me snap. It didn't turn me into a child killer, though.'

'I never thought it did. What happened?'

'He was disrupting the class for weeks, totally out of control, and I was given absolutely no back-up from either the governors or the head teacher. They were terrified of parent power and complaints. In the end I thumped him, loosened some teeth. Of course, it was all swept under the extensive carpet. The boy stayed. I left.'

'Would you mind if I checked that story?'

'I wouldn't mind at all. Chances are you'll check it whether I do or don't.'

191

'Perhaps you'd give the details to the PC, later. Getting back to the present, did you ever go inside the theatre?'

'No. Not even when it was a theatre.'

'You didn't shelter when the weather got bad?'

'I said, no. Watch my lips if you have a problem with that.'

'Did you ever notice the security checks?'

'Some. If you can call them checks. They tried the front doors, kicked my gear off the steps, and sometimes me, too, and left. Is that security?'

'When was the last one?'

'They turned up about once a week on average. I couldn't be specific about the day. On the streets one day is pretty much like another. You tend to lose touch with time.'

'Did they ever go down the side of the building, by the alley?'

'I never saw them.'

'Did you see anyone going that way?'

'Are you kidding? That, dear boy, is where everyone takes a piss.'

'So you haven't seen anything suspicious?'

'On the streets everything is suspicious. But I know what you mean, and the answer is no. I really can't help you.'

'On the night you were stabbed someone broke into the theatre. Not the killer, or at least, we don't think it was the killer. He was using it well before the break-in. We think the killer had a key. But someone else got in through the back, and one way to the back is down that alley. Witnesses tell us that a man in his twenties, after doing what he could for you, went after your attacker down the alley. Who helped you?'

'I don't know, I'm sorry. I must have passed out. I didn't see anyone help me.'

'OK. Like I said, we think the murderer used a key to get into the theatre. Did you ever see anyone use a key?'

'I did, some weeks ago. They came in through the front. Cleared me off for over an hour.'

'Who were they?'

'The owners, or the agents, I assume. A man and a woman. He was in a suit, very young, a schoolboy really. She was older,

192

dressed like an executive.' He chuckled. 'She didn't think much of me camping on the doorstep. Promised me the police.'

'How did they arrive?'

'In a car. The lad was driving. He parked over the road, on a meter. All the way over, and even on the steps, he was using his mobile. Funny that, I always get the feeling that people are showing off when I see them with a mobile.'

'So, they had a key? Anyone else?'

'I imagine the security guys did. But I never saw them use it. No. There was no one else that I saw.'

'From where you camped you wouldn't see the side door, would you?'

'The stage door? No, that was well down the road. I wouldn't see that at all.'

'That's it. Thanks for talking to me. I take it you're still not interested in talking about your injury?'

'What injury is that?'

Cole smiled and left. On his way out he paid for a week's TV rental, then kicked himself back to the office.

Hazel McLintock met him in the IR, full of enthusiasm. 'Fingerprints have turned up a match. On the kettle. A Jason Hackett. And what's more, there's form. Plenty of it.'

Cole rubbed concentration into his forehead, then said, 'I know Hackett. A tealeaf. I sent him down a couple of times. Burglary, yeah, that's it. I seem to remember we threw in possession at the same time. We turned his place over. Have you got an address?'

'We had an old address and they gave us the new. Guess where it is?'

'I don't like games.'

'So I've been told. It's right opposite the—'

'Carrington theatre?'

'See, you do like them.'

Cole's face broke into a sudden smile. He punched the air. 'Barry's already over there doing a house-to-house. Pick him up, Hazel, and go and have a look. He'll be glad to get out of the rain. Ask John Knight for a couple of uniforms to back you

193

up. And make sure somebody's got the key!'

The key was what the coppers called the two handed ram that could smash open almost any door.

'Right, sir.'

He liked the sir. It tickled him. He narrowed his eyes slightly, on purpose, and said, 'I'm going to turn the car around and have another word in Mr Pullin's ear.'

'The low-life?'

'You'd be surprised. He's an ex-teacher, and there but for the odd bottle of Sainsbury's blended . . .'

'It's a sad world. In any case, you drink Teacher's.'

'Talking of which, are we having a drink after?'

'The White Horse?'

Cole nodded.

'I'll see you there,' she said.

Pullin paused for an instant too long. He tried to turn it into a grimace, but realised it didn't wash.

'So, Jason Hackett helped you out,' Cole said, 'then took off down the alley after your assailant.'

'Was it Jason? I didn't recognise him in the dark. It is awfully dark on those steps. He's not in trouble, is he? I'd hate to think he's in trouble.'

'Not that I know of. He might have seen something. I just wanted it confirmed that he was the one that went down the alley on Saturday night. You've just done that and I'm grateful.'

The old man shook his head. 'I must have done it without moving my lips. It's quite amazing the number of skills you possess that you're not even aware of.'

Cole had reached the door when Pullin said, 'If you see Jason, perhaps you'd thank him on my behalf. Meanwhile, I should thank you for the tele. But I won't. Bollocks to that.'

The policeman turned back and flashed a smile. 'That wouldn't do at all.'

Pullin nodded and returned the smile. 'That's what I thought.'

In the White Horse they were given the odd speculative glance from the uniforms, a sort of what-have-we-got-here look, half jealousy, half disapproval. Cole carried the drinks to a table in the corner, as far away from the uniforms as he could get.

Hazel had seen the glances and felt mildly uncomfortable. The last time they had been with DS Butler, at least for part of the time, and that had made it safe, above suspicion. Now tongues would begin to wag. To hell with them, she thought, and lit a cigarette.

'After tonight I've only got two more days of freedom,' she said. 'Nigel comes home on Saturday.'

'How have you found it?'

She laughed. 'Not a lot different. With the hours I've put in I've barely been home. But I've enjoyed the space, if that's what you mean.' She exhaled smoke and tapped her ash delicately into an ashtray. 'Ever since he told me he had a place on a course, I looked forward to him going. Can you understand that? I actually wanted to have the house to myself. Making decisions, silly things, like what I watch on TV, or even whether the TV is turned on at all, what time I eat and go to bed. Little things that get lost when you live with someone.'

'I know.'

'But somehow it hasn't worked out. I haven't missed him, not that, but I just don't seem to have done my own thing. It's almost as though the week's been wasted. I need another without a major, when the hours are regular.'

'Perhaps it's you that needs to get away.'

'Maybe you're right,' she said, softly. She glanced up with a question in her eyes.

'Go on?'

'No, it's not my business.'

'What isn't?'

'I wondered what went wrong with your marriage?'

He sighed. 'Who can answer a question like that?' He paused, then said, lugubriously, 'With hindsight it was probably just another case of marriage fatigue.'

'Do you still see her?'

'She moved out of town. I haven't seen her for a few months.'

Hazel nodded sombrely. Another question tightened her lips.

Cole smiled and waited.

'Listen, Guv, I don't want to pressure you . . .'

'For Christ's sake, Hazel.'

She gulped a breath and said quickly, 'If all things stay even, I knock off early on Friday. I don't suppose you'd like to drive out somewhere, have dinner?'

He didn't hesitate. 'I'd love to. What time?'

'I finish at four.'

'OK, if nothing breaks, let's say seven. I'll pick you up.'

Suddenly she felt easier, as though a weight had been removed from her shoulders. She finished her drink and in a flourish said, 'I'll get these. Is that ordinary bitter?'

Cole's gaze followed her to the bar. He watched the slight movement of her wide hips fighting the tight skirt, and for a moment he was captivated. He saw her eyes in the bar mirror, and saw the speculative look in them. He realised she'd seen him staring and for a moment felt a little embarrassed. He averted his gaze and looked at the other men in the bar. Some of them stood alone, leaning against the bar over a pint-pot, others were in small, quiet groups. They weren't all in the job, not by any means. There were a couple of suits, managers, civil servants with nicotine-stained fingers, and a few council workers, some of whom he vaguely recognised. He wondered what their day involved: paperwork, finances, decorating or building. Not murder of children, that was for sure. On the other hand, he could have been looking at the killer. Who would know? Most of the killers he'd known or read about showed no obvious signs, nothing strange or psychopathic, no sickness, no different to the average man. Looking at them, you'd say most were perfectly normal – they'd help an old lady across the road, cut their grass at the weekend, sit down to Sunday lunch with the family.

Cole sighed.

What he didn't know was that standing next to Hazel, looking at her through the huge mirror at the back of the bar, was Jane West's killer.

Chapter 20

Police work had led Cole to the altar.

There had been a break-in in the early hours. The house owners had heard the alley door open and gone to investigate. Their shed door had been forced; tools, bicycle and freezer food were either missing or scattered along the alley. He arrived with another PC. While her parents gave them details in the front room, Jenny made some coffee and carried it in. Even in her dressing-gown and without make-up he recognised her. He'd admired her through the windows of the Prudential building society where she worked. She responded to his smile. They went out. A year later they were married. A year after that he made CID and she made deputy manager.

Up until then he'd been a copper pounding a North London beat, picking and choosing, like they all did. Getting a result was too easy; toms and ponces and dealers, even illegal street traders, were easy game. And if things were quiet you could always visit the parks near the gents' toilets and stamp on the winking arses of the cottaging fraternity. If you didn't want a mountain of paperwork, looking the other way was an important lesson to learn. You approached them, warned them, gave them an occasional dead leg or a shove in the kidneys, and you let them go. As long as it was off your patch for the rest of the shift. They'd be back tomorrow, then it would start again. You only took it seriously if they started mouthing off or if the skipper was on the warpath.

And the low life had wised up too. They didn't upset you. Only the ethnics made a noise, shouted race while they blew sweet smoke in your face, forced you to take action.

Later, out of uniform, transferred to HQ, he was still on his own. It wasn't that he was antisocial, just that he found most of his immediate colleagues in CID bigger villains than the people they collared. He didn't join in, and was given the treatment. When the trouble started, half his colleagues were against his stand because of misplaced loyalty, and the other half through animosity. Even Jenny thought he was making a mistake. 'Walk away from it,' she had said. 'No matter what you do they'll never go down, you know that. What's the point in sticking your neck out?'

She had been right, of course.

There had been a number of resignations, golden handshakes, but no successful prosecutions. Since then he had wised up. He knew now that you couldn't beat the old school tie or the thumb-dominated handshake. But in those days he was still a dreamer. He thought he could make a difference. He stuck out his neck; he took on the system. He lost in more ways than one.

By Thursday morning, the theory that a policeman was involved had been all but exhausted. Helen Guest had been through photographs of every officer serving with the Metropolitan, City of London, Thames Valley, and Hertfordshire forces. She'd looked at regulars and special constables both past and present. It was a thankless task and even she was beginning to question her own memory.

As Baxter surveyed the stack of files in the incident room – statements, interviews and reports from security, residents, passers-by, allotment holders, Jane West's friends and teachers, neighbours, relatives, you name it – he knew in his heart that there wouldn't be a quick result. It was almost a week since Jane had gone missing. Before long, finances would dictate a scaling down of the inquiry.

He called Cole. 'If it's not a copper, we're still looking for a uniform: security guards, British Rail for Christ's sake, fancy dress hire.'

Security, especially the company dealing with the Carrington, had already been carefully examined. But Cole knew what he meant. It was back to the beginning, checking again to find out if they'd missed something. The slightest contradiction. Anything. He couldn't help feeling that they were being sidetracked by Helen's information. The photograph, supposedly found at the scene by an unknown person, was certainly damning, but there were too many questions left unanswered. Who found it?

Why did he or she post it to the police? Why was a photograph taken eight years ago there in the first place? It was almost as if they were being manipulated. That was the word Margaret Domey had used. Manipulation. He's playing with you, she had said. Perhaps the photograph and the idea that it was taken by a copper was a false lead. If that was the case, then Helen Guest had been misled too. Both Baxter and Cole were sure that Jason Hackett was the key to the inquiry. They could place him at the scene of crime. He had disappeared. And he had form. Not for sex-related crime, but form nonetheless. For the moment that was quite enough.

Scot's report about Hackett's bedsit lay on the top of the nearest pile, waiting for HOLMES to action. The door had been forced, signs of violence, used sticky tape, traces of blood – not Jane West's – on the bed, spilt milk by the door, and heroin on the carpet by the window. Along with Helen Guest's policeman, Hackett was a major suspect. Ports, stations and airports were on alert and every one of the forty-three forces in Great Britain was keeping an eye open for his face. Baxter was still undecided about giving it to the media. There was a negative side to posting a face in the papers. It could drive the man underground, take away the possibility of a beat copper turning him up. Still, if they hadn't found him in the next twenty-four hours, that would be the next step.

Helen Guest looked at Hackett's mug-shot and shook her head. 'That's not him,' she said. 'No way. But his face is familiar. Did he used to hang out? Juggle a little dope?' She glanced up and added quickly, 'Eight years ago, I mean?'

Cole smiled his indifference. 'When you were off-loading your prescriptions?'

'Yeah.'

'If I know anything about him, he still does.'

'That's probably where I know him from, then.'

'So he's out of the frame?' Baxter muttered.

'No, he's not,' Cole insisted. 'There's too much emphasis being placed on the photograph. Whoever dropped it in the Carrington probably bought the damn thing. A shop, by post, who knows?'

Helen threw up her hands. 'Oh my God,' she said. 'You mean they're on sale?'

'No, I don't mean that. We know sex offenders like to get off on porn. But we're jumping the gun. This might not have belonged to the killer at all. Hackett's still very much in the frame.'

'It's a bloody big coincidence,' Baxter said. He glanced down at Helen. 'You sure that face doesn't fit?'

'That's not the copper that took my picture.'

He glanced up at Cole again. 'Copper,' he muttered and sighed. 'That's where we came in.'

Margaret Domey's telephone rang three times before she set her Parker aside and carefully lifted the receiver.

'Ms Domey?' she heard.

'Yes?'

'Ms Margaret Domey?'

'Yes?'

'My name's Geoff Maynard. I'm from HOPE in Green Park. You might not have heard of us.' His voice was low pitched with a slight northern accent. His name rang a bell. 'The Home Office Psychological Experimental Unit. Somewhere along the line the unit part was dropped.'

'I read something,' she said. 'A paper.'

'I looked at the Catchem report along with your comments regarding the Jane West murder. It's still on-going, I take it?'

'Yes.' Margaret felt a little defensive.

'They're getting pushed through to us on E-mail. We tend to pick and choose. I wonder if I could come up and see you?'

'What do you have in mind?'

'Like I said, Margaret – can I call you Margaret?'

'No problem, Geoff.'

'We've been working along American lines with regard to profiling, and we're coming up with some quite different results. At the moment they've been one hundred percent successful. The thing is that the Home Office is quite keen for us to expand, so to speak, and the present inquiry seems right up our street. We've already been given the go ahead, so

200

I suppose, really, this is just a courtesy call, to let you know I'm on my way.'

'Does the chief know about this?'

'I understand he's being informed now.'

'I see.' She sounded deflated. Baxter was going to love this, she thought.

'I look forward to meeting you.'

'Likewise,' she said and put the phone down.

'Have you heard of an organisation called HOPE?' Chief Superintendent Marsh asked, while Margaret Domey hovered, tight-lipped, in the background.

'It sounds like some kind of charity,' Baxter snapped, irritated at being called to the top floor from the middle of a brain-storming session.

'Yes, I suppose it does. It actually stands for the Home Office Psychological Experimental Unit. Don't ask me what the devil it means. One of their chaps, Geoff Maynard, is on his way. We've been asked to accommodate him.'

'Who's asked?'

'Well, my chief has asked me, and his chief has asked him. Enough said?'

Baxter shook his head.

'We've been given no choice. It's not a request.'

The shaking continued.

'Perhaps you'd pass that on. He's to be given every assistance.'

Baxter shook his head all the way to the door. There he paused and glanced back. 'I'm not happy about this.'

'That much is obvious,' Marsh said. 'As it happens, I'm not either, and nor is Margaret.'

That upset Baxter even more – the thought that he had something in common with Marsh and Margaret Domey. He closed the door behind him with rather a heavy hand.

Marsh was dismayed by Baxter's attitude, but he was used to it and shrugged it off. 'What do we have on this Maynard chap?'

Margaret pulled a face. 'I had a word with Catchem. Jim knows him. He was regarded as exceptionally talented. By the

201

time he was thirty he'd already held top clinical and forensic psychologist posts in Staffordshire and the West Midlands. He moved south two years ago. He wrote a book on cognitive behavioural techniques. Do you want more?'

'Is there more?'

'He's a prominent member of the gay rights movement and until he took over HOPE at the beginning of this year, he was working with section fifty-three kids. You could say he switched from those doing the damage to the damaged. HOPE turned back the clock, put him back on his old trail.'

Marsh nodded. 'Well, Margaret, I don't know how long he's going to be with us, but I'll leave it to you to ensure he's looked after. And do try to keep Baxter happy.'

'With respect, sir, there's nothing that will keep the super happy. He has made tetchiness an art form. It probably has more to do with itchy haemorrhoids than dissatisfaction with his subordinates or peers. I have no intention of keeping the super happy. It's not in my job description and, anyway, happiness and the thought of being pleasant would destroy his image. And image is quite important to him. I think he sees himself as Jack Frost, David what's his name? Del Boy.'

'Get out of here, Margaret, before you start to get personal. Go and put out the welcome mat.'

She offered him her sweetest smile, which he accepted with the faintest of nods.

Sergeant Mike Collier thought he'd got a piece of low-life at the front desk. He sensed trouble. The man in front of him was confident and his smile a little too knowing.

'What can I do for you?' he asked.

'Geoff Maynard. I'm here to see Ms Domey.'

'Is that right? Take a seat, sir. I'll let her know.'

As the man turned to the row of seats the sergeant wondered what his business was with the diminutive psychologist from hell. Ms, he'd said. Not Miss or Mrs. Obviously a *Guardian* reader. One of those fucked-up liberals who believed in legalised shit and the banning of blood sports. Collier shook his head in exasperation.

He was big-boned, about six one or two, tanned, weathered face, firm chin covered with a grey stubble, greying, short hair, early forties. His eyes were faintly bloodshot and sleepless, brown and warm. They seemed to need spectacles – they had that distant look of the short-sighted. It was the face of a man who'd lived rough, burned too many at both ends, been there, and now wanted to be left alone. There was wisdom, a laid back philosophy, an easiness in both features and movement. He'd come to terms with himself, looked in the mirror and was content with what he saw.

Without so much as an introduction, Baxter felt that he could trust him. The thought was rare and unnerved him, made him feel slightly inadequate.

The man's clothes were comfortable and worn: faded jeans, wide black belt, checked cotton shirt rolled up beyond the elbows and hard-wearing brown shoes with thick soles and laces. He wore a gold watch and a dog chain.

He looked like a bloody cowboy, Baxter thought and self-consciously glanced down at his own working clothes – his dark-grey suit and tie, white shirt and polished slip-ons, the uniform that tied him to the system and the establishment, and again he felt a twinge of envy.

Against him, Margaret seemed to have shrunk. 'This is Geoff Maynard from HOPE. Superintendent Tony Baxter. He's SIO on the inquiry.'

Maynard's hand moved out. Baxter hesitated for a moment before shaking it and was surprised to find the grip slightly loose.

'I'm glad to meet you. Is Margaret taking care of you?'

'Fine, thanks. I'd like to follow the trail from beginning to end, if that's all right with you. I don't want to be gettin' in the way.'

He even sounded like a cowboy. One from the Midlands.

'The trail?'

'I'd like to start with the school, then the theatre, then the allotment. I'll come back and work through the files tonight.'

Baxter firmed up his spectacles. 'Whatever, Margaret will take care of it. If you need anything just shout.'

Once they had gone Cole knocked.

'Did you see him?'

'Yeah, Guv, I was introduced. Geoff Maynard.'

'A bloody cowboy.'

Cole grinned. 'The psychologists are taking over. We'll soon be redundant.'

'That'll be the day.'

'We've just had a call. The girl's clothes have been found on the allotment.'

Baxter balled his fist and hit the palm of his other hand. After a moment he said, 'How the hell did the search miss them first time round?'

'It's not quite like that. They've been hung out, like on a washing-line. In plain view. They weren't there last night.'

'Go on?'

'They were put there to be found this morning. Forensics are on their way.'

Baxter remembered Margaret's words and said, 'He's playing with us, Rick. The bastard's playing with us again. Could it be someone in the job?'

'Taking us on, you mean?'

That was too equivocal. 'Come again?'

'An ex-job, or someone who didn't make the grade, taking us on at our own game. Proving a point.' Cole sighed. 'I don't think so. My money's still on Jason Hackett. Find him and we'll wrap it up.'

'I hope you're right. I could do without these early morning briefings. So could the wife. When she doesn't get her eight hours sleep we all suffer.'

Baxter followed Cole back to the IR. At her desk, Hazel McLintock toyed with a pen and watched them enter. She exchanged a quick glance with Cole. The impending date was producing a curious chemistry between them. Scot brought up the rear.

'The clothes have been confirmed,' he said. 'School uniform, shirt, underwear, socks and shoes, even her bag. Everything but the underwear was put under the row of runner beans. Knickers were tied to the top. On show. Does that mean something?'

'Yeah, absolutely,' Baxter said. 'It means we're dealing with one sick son of a bitch.'

204

Chapter 21

Friday arrived with a buzz of excitement. Jim Gregory had agreed to a transfer, Sam Butler and his wife had agreed to give their marriage another go, the doctor had agreed to pass Butler fit for duty, and the top brass had agreed, for the sake of the job, to sweep the whole thing under the carpet. DS Butler arrived back to the sounds of applause and a nod of approval from Baxter. Before he was shunted into Cole's office, with Baxter right behind, Hazel gave him her best shot at a welcome home smile.

'We've basically run out of ideas,' Cole told him. 'HOLMES is still throwing out on-going inquiries and the search for Hackett is being stepped up. His mug-shot hit the papers this morning.'

Butler confirmed, 'I saw it.'

'Bits and pieces are still coming in from forensics, but basically, the results are disappointing. The labs have come back on tests on the girl's underwear. There was more than a trace of semen. The bastard had jacked off on it. I'm on my way to the Carrington. Apparently the SOCOs have come up with another entrance. They're convinced the killer used it to remove the body. He didn't need a key, after all. You and Hazel can tag along. I'd like you to update yourself.'

Baxter nodded his agreement. He and Cole had already discussed it.

In the theatre's gloomy dressing-room Margaret Domey was on her stomach on the floor in a chalked position that had once been occupied by the mattress. Her dark trouser-suit had picked up dust on the elbows and knees. The tall rangy figure of Geoff Maynard bent over her. A young uniformed policeman, standing to one side, coughed to tell them they had visitors. Maynard looked over his shoulder at the astonished faces and smiled.

'Now, this might seem a little odd, but it's not quite what it seems.' He pointed to the pile of A4 notes on the floor beside him. 'Come on in. It might interest you.'

Cole caught on and led the way. Butler and Hazel were still uncertain. They remained at the door.

Margaret moved beneath him. Her voice was tight as she said, 'Right, so you've buggered me, what's next?'

'That rape has caused the drops of blood here and here. Not much. Next, I turn you over and move to a position over your head, facing your feet, pressing your arms here and here. The finger bruises on your arms face that way. My penis goes into your mouth and down your throat. You suffocate.'

She snapped, 'I'll bite it off before I suffocate!'

'No, you won't. That's the whole point. You're terrified. He's got that far. All you can think of is to get it out of your throat. Not retaliation. You're unconscious before you can really think about it. He's probably not even aware that you're choking. So now, you're dead. Stay put.' Maynard moved his legs against her head. 'So, what's the bruise on the right side of your neck? When did I do that?'

'You gripped my neck when you raped me?'

'No, I didn't. I didn't have to. You weren't fighting me then. All the damage came after death. The threat of something, a knife maybe, or death, kept you quiet. No, something was sticking into your neck, perhaps while the oral sex took place.' He shook his head, then said to the uniform, 'You take my place for a moment.'

The uniform looked horrified. 'Not me, pal,' he said.

'Oh, get on with it,' Maynard snapped. Tiredness had sharpened his mood.

The policeman shrugged and reluctantly bent over Margaret's head. He was self-conscious and awkward.

'Move up,' Margaret insisted. 'You're supposed to be—'

'OK. OK.' He moved his knees either side of her head.

Maynard walked around, studying them from every angle. He stopped abruptly. 'Bend lower,' he said. 'Your penis is as far down her throat as it will go. So far, in fact, that I imagine your testicles are blocking her nose.'

The young PC reddened up.

Hazel felt a mixture of nervousness and embarrassment. It was cold and clinical. Maynard was oblivious to the horror. She exchanged a glance with Butler. He seemed to share her worries. This wasn't in codes of practice. She looked across at Cole. His expression was equally firm, but out of interest. He was almost as detached as Maynard.

The PC bent lower. Margaret had to turn her head so that she could breathe. She let out a sudden cry and the PC immediately backed up.

'Perhaps it was that,' she said, freeing her hand so that she could point to his baton. It was angled away, but the side-handle had caught her.

Maynard said thoughtfully, 'Yes, it's possible.'

'So's the end of a milk bottle, if he shoved it in her face,' Cole said, derisively.

Margaret struggled to sit up. She ignored him and looked at Maynard. 'My God,' she uttered. 'My God, if he used a truncheon instead of these new extended batons, it could easily have pushed into my neck. As he bent lower . . .'

Cole felt a rush of blood as a thought came at him from all sides. His earlier depreciation forgotten, he said, 'There was a trace of linseed oil found inside the girl. We thought it might be some kind of lubrication he'd used, but think about it. The bloody truncheon.'

Their gazes moved back to the PC who held up the end of the twenty-two-inch baton, still clipped to his belt.

Cole went on, 'Some of the older uniforms still carry the old ones. Some of them are dinosaurs, made of wood.' He glanced from Maynard to Margaret. 'Some of them used linseed oil to keep them from splitting.'

The PC shrugged. 'My old man was in the job. He had one of those.'

Cole nodded and turned back to Maynard. The man smiled, not smugly, and said to Margaret, 'So, we're agreed it might not have been a dildo? Right, back in position. You're dead. Remember? Now I'm angry. Or am I?'

Cole said, 'Maybe not. Maybe killing her then was your intention.'

'To save her from suffering, you mean? As Robert Black did?' Maynard looked mildly surprised and glanced at Margaret. 'You remember Black? He maintained that he didn't want to hurt the children, so killed them in order to save them suffering during the assault.'

'It's possible.'

'If it hadn't been for the way Jane West suffocated, I'd agree with you. Using his penis as a murder weapon would have been a first, and bloody dangerous for him. No, this was accidental. She was supposed to die later.'

'She didn't die here,' Cole said.

'What makes you say that?'

'It's in the notes. She'd been bathed, there was soap on her body and shit in her fingernails that wasn't picked up here. There was perfume on her body that wasn't on the mattress. Is that enough?'

'Is there more?'

'There was one tiny trace of semen on the mattress, perhaps a jerk off. But semen covered the girl from head to toe. There would have been more on the mattress.'

Maynard nodded. 'Didn't it cross your mind that he might have taken the body some place else after she died? That he still went ahead with his plan even though she'd died on him?'

'Getting off with the corpse, you mean? Necrophilia? That's pretty bloody far-fetched, isn't it?'

'You think so? Dennis Nilsen kept bodies hidden under his floorboards and brought them out occasionally to keep him company while he watched TV. A woman named Natasha Brauchitsch from former East Germany dug up the corpse of her husband and used the humerus bone from his arm as an artificial penis.'

'OK, point taken. There're some mad bastards about. But since when do dead bodies scratch at brick walls? That's what she was doing. That's where she picked up the crap, the lead, the brick, the mould. And that was after leaving here.'

'I can't answer that at the moment. But give me time and I will.'

Maynard turned back to Margaret. 'OK. For DI Cole's

208

benefit we'll make out that we are somewhere else. Same set up, you still die, but we've moved. You've died on me too soon. Too soon for what? What else had I got in mind? Nothing, I've done it all. So you dying didn't matter. Unless I wanted to kill you with . . . the truncheon? I'm going to wait a couple of hours now before taking you to the allotment. I've had two days to anticipate, do whatever I wanted, but I've waited until now, until the last few hours. OK. Now, here comes the curious bit. I'm going to put some marks on you. Rope burns. A little more damage. Make it look like you went through even more hell while you were alive. You've already got bruising to the wrists where I tied you up. Now I'm going to put bruises on top of bruises. Why? Am I trying to conceal that I tied you up? No. That's nonsense. Let's go ahead.'

He knelt beside Margaret again and went through the motions of tying her wrists. 'Now I tighten the ropes until the skin comes off. Now I take away the ropes. I'm still mad as hell at you for dying. That's just it, isn't it? You died. I was supposed to do all this while you were still alive. Your death was an accident. Of course it was. When I come back in two or three hours you're supposed to be alive. Why? I move you, where? Is there a plastic sheet on the floor? Here somewhere? There has to be. I was going to tape up your mouth to keep you quiet. But now I don't need it. I leave it on the floor. Now, let's move forward to the allotment. We'll go over there and go through it, but bear with me for a moment. I'm at the allotment. I smash your feet. So many blows. Stringing you to the cross and smashing your feet until they're unrecognisable, just stumps of meat. Why am I doing this? If I'm so mad at you for dying on me I would have done it at the theatre or wherever. I wouldn't have waited until now. And why don't I hit you somewhere else? No, that's just it. I'm in control or I would have done. I'm not mad. I'm not angry. It's part of it. You're dead. But you weren't supposed to die until now. You were supposed to die on the cross. But I go through with it anyway. I smash your feet and then I insert the truncheon to kill you. That was the idea.' Maynard's eyes moved back to the PC and down to the baton. He reached out his hand and said, 'Gimme.'

209

The uniform's frown looked painful. He released his baton and handed it across. Maynard smacked it against the palm of his hand then let it fall onto Margaret's thighs. There was no pressure but she flinched. Fear widened her eyes.

'Something like this. An old wooden one. You're hanging on the post. I ram it into your vagina, I destroy your sexual organs. Why? Am I trying to get rid of the evidence? Am I so horrified at what I've done I try to destroy all signs?' He shook his head. 'Then I move down and I smash your feet. Or do I smash your feet first? It doesn't matter. It's done.'

Maynard inhaled deeply and stood back. The PC helped Margaret to her feet. She began to dust her suit. Cole noticed her slender hands shaking, her wedding ring a golden blur.

She stuttered, 'So? Have I got it right so far?'

Geoff Maynard didn't acknowledge her distress. 'At first glance you were right. Most people would agree with you.'

Her voice still thick, she said, 'You're going to add a but, aren't you?'

Maynard grinned easily. 'Afraid so.'

'Go on?'

'On the face of it, it's a sex crime, we all know that. But I'm afraid sex isn't the main factor. It might even have been an afterthought. What's more, he hasn't done it before. You were wrong. There's too much experimentation. This was his first attack, and it went horribly wrong. This is no serial killer, Margaret. There's an ulterior motive.'

Cole growled, 'You're not making sense.'

Maynard addressed him. 'DI Cole, isn't it?'

Cole nodded.

'You want a motive, Inspector, don't be blinded by the sexual connection. The whole thing has been an act, the ritual, the performance, the additional injuries which weren't caused in the attack. An act. A performance to be discovered and understood. Whoever did this wanted someone to know exactly what the girl had gone through. It might be the girl's parents. Perhaps one or both of them had an enemy with a big enough grudge to do something like this. But I doubt it. I think you're looking for a policeman, one with a huge grudge.

210

What's more, he wants you to know he's in the job. It's almost a game. The police angle ties in with your other enquiries. All this is as personal as it can get. But believe me, it has been an act. A show, designed specifically so that someone will know exactly what to expect when—'

'When?'

Maynard met Cole's steady gaze. 'When it happens again. That's my guess. If the vengeance isn't directed against Jane West's parents, and I doubt that it will be – too easy to trace back – then the main act is still to come. It's ironic,' he waved his hand about, 'the theatre. An act. A stage show. This has been planned down to every last detail. This is personal. He's going to take another child and enjoy the spectacle of seeing the parents go through the agony, knowing what is happening moment by moment. The whole fucking thing has been about revenge.'

Cole narrowed his eyes in concentration. He didn't like it. It was pure speculation. 'What's the police connection?'

Maynard rubbed his stubble. 'You're looking for a copper. There's one in the frame. Helen Guest's photographer.'

Cole nodded and muttered gloomily, 'I wish we could find him.' He gave Maynard a thoughtful look, then joined Hazel and Butler and went to find the SOCOs.

The SOCOs were still working at the far end of the passage. One of them turned. 'It's where they used to bring in the larger stage equipment.' He pulled back a large section of chipboard and revealed a row of concrete steps that rose to a flat ceiling of what looked like concrete slabs. They peered after him as he climbed to the ceiling and pressed upwards with both hands. Very gradually, the slab gave way and bits of sludge fell in with a streak of daylight. 'It's at the back, near to the door that was forced,' the officer explained. 'Move just one slab from above and you've got yourself a ready-made entrance. A thick plastic sheet stopped any water seeping through, but that was moved. The entrance has been used recently.'

Hazel said, 'Not many people would know about this, Guv. Contractors, members of the theatre. I'll find out when these slabs were laid.'

Cole nodded.

She turned to face him. 'What do you think about . . . ?' She indicated the dressing-rooms. 'He seems pretty convincing.'

Cole shook his head. 'I'm not convinced. Not by a long shot. That wasn't police work. It was theatre, or rather a circus, and Geoff Maynard's a bloody clown. But just in case, when we get back organise another visit to Mr and Mrs West. Find out whether they've upset anyone.'

Butler cut in. 'It crossed my mind that if he's right, and it's not a grudge against the Wests, the final act will throw up the injured party. Getting his satisfaction, his revenge, will lead us to his door. We'll know who upset him.'

Cole flared, 'And while we wait to find out, another young-ster will be snatched. I don't want that,' he pointed back to the dressing-room, 'to happen again. I don't want to see another broken little body hanging on some fucking make-shift cross.'

'The point I'm trying to make is that if he follows the exact same pattern that chummy in there seems to think, then we'll have a couple of days. He'll use the same format, the same time-span. He'll want whoever it is to know the fate of his daughter right down to the last second. We'll have from a Friday night to a Sunday night to catch him.'

Hazel said, 'That's very mercenary, Sam. I'm surprised at you. Today's Friday, isn't it?'

Cole gave her a sideways glance. 'It hadn't escaped me,' he murmured.

The equivocation tugged her lips into a gentle smile.

They made their way back to the car. Cole climbed into the front passenger seat. Butler drove. From the back Hazel said, 'Did you see Margaret shaking? She was upset.'

'She had every right to be,' Sam Butler said. 'I've never seen a performance like it.'

'What do you think, Sam?' she asked.

'It sounded quite credible, in parts.'

'I wonder what the super will make of it. You know his views regarding psychologists.'

Cole nodded thoughtfully. 'On the other hand,' he put in, 'he'll he quite happy to hear that Margaret was distressed. As

212

far as the super's concerned, that'll be a feather in Maynard's cap.'

At four, Hazel McLintock began to pack up. Short of something breaking she was off until the morning. She caught Cole's eye and threw him a tiny smile, just a slight widening of the lips, and their date was confirmed. Seven o'clock. The prospect made her nervous. She had decided the day before that if he asked nicely, if the opportunity to sleep with him arose, she would play it by ear. The decision was a milestone and she had not reached it lightly. Being unfaithful was something she'd never even contemplated before. In her dreams perhaps, but that was all, and certainly not with Cole. The whole idea left her breathless and strangely high. It had happened so quickly. A week ago she had found him aloof and conceited, and suddenly her feelings were turned upside down. She wondered whether her disapproval, even dislike, had been a conscious barrier to her unconscious feelings. Some kind of protective shield. Perhaps she had found him attractive but fought against it, misinterpreting it as a sign of danger. Keep away. You don't like him. He is not a nice person. She watched him move into his office and enjoyed his movement. She found it difficult to keep her eyes off him.

There was a general feeling of disappointment and frustration in the office. They were a week into the investigation, five days into the murder but apart from the on-going search for Jason Hackett and Helen Guest's photographer, everything else had drawn a blank. The actions from HOLMES had become fewer as the weekend drew closer, and now they were left grasping at straws, waiting for a public response to the mug-shot of Hackett and the computer image of the photographer. Baxter was even considering *Crimewatch* and when that happened you knew the inquiry was in trouble. Fuck Jill Dando. They'd all like to do that. For the kozzers over twenty-five she'd become the locker-room pin-up.

The super was stealing coffee from Barry Scot's desk when Sam Butler waved a telephone at him and said, 'It's your wife, Guv.'

Baxter took another sip of coffee and carried the mug across to Butler's desk. 'I'll take it here,' he said. Butler handed him the receiver and moved away to give him privacy.

Everyone in the IR pretended to be doing something, but they were secretly listening. Baxter's wife calling him at the office was unusual.

'Hello, love,' Baxter said, easily.

Hazel sat at the next desk and was the first to notice there was something wrong. On the periphery of her vision, while she gathered her papers together, she saw Baxter's sudden seizure, as though he'd been kicked in the chest. She saw the mug bang down on the desk and the coffee spill, and when she looked up she saw his expression fall to a mix of disbelief and shock. She thought he was having a heart attack and made a sudden move towards him.

The others in the room seemed to freeze; files were suspended above cabinets, pens were held in the air. They saw Hazel's move, and then Baxter's hand rise to stop her approach.

Sam Butler leaned through Cole's door. 'You better get out here, Guv.' The tone of his voice brought Cole to his feet.

Baxter sank to the chair as Cole made the door. He whispered into the phone, 'Just stay put. I'll be there in five minutes.' He slowly replaced the receiver and looked up at the concerned faces of his colleagues. While he tried to gather his senses, while the freezing hand of panic gripped at his heart and the colour drained from his face, he said quietly, 'My daughter's missing. She was seen getting into a car with a copper.'

Chapter 22

By five, the abduction had still to be confirmed. Sketchy details began to emerge: a uniformed policeman in his late twenties or early thirties, a saloon car, differing makes and year and colour but certainly not new. Mary-Anne had known him. School friends had seen them chat on numerous occasions. She had been joking when she climbed into his car. There was still time, everyone said, but they secretly doubted it.

'A copper, a copper,' Cole murmured, as Chief Superintendent Marsh came in with his deputy. He had been with Baxter and organised an immediate response. Every vehicle in the area and some outside were on the alert. Every beat copper had his eyes open and more were sent out.

Marsh spoke in a severe voice. 'The super will be back later. Obviously he needs some time with his family. This is as bad as it gets, Rick.'

'Yes, sir. It is.'

'What's the situation now?'

'The entire team is out, taking statements from the kids. We need a description of the copper. Helen Guest's photofit is being flashed about. We're hoping like hell the kids don't recognise it. We'll see.'

'In the event that it's confirmed,' Marsh said, 'the super will obviously stay at home. You'll be acting SIO until things are clarified.'

Cole nodded reluctantly. He knew that someone more senior would be appointed quickly. The commissioner would take a personal interest. It would be out of Marsh's hands. The Yard would be crawling all over them. 'We'll see,' he muttered.

Deighton asked, 'Do you know Mary-Anne?'

Cole shook his head. 'No, I've never met his family.'

'She's eleven next month.'

Cole asked, 'Have you spoken to this guy Maynard?'

'No,' Marsh said, and raised an inquisitive eyebrow. 'Should I?'

'I was with him earlier. To be frank I didn't give him much credit. He seemed to be playing games. Now I have to admit that he got it right. He was pretty certain it was going to happen again. More to the point, he came up with the idea that it was personal, that Jane West was simply a trial run. The real motive was revenge. He was going to take another girl as revenge.'

'Revenge for what?' Deighton quizzed, a mark of irritation in his voice.

'He didn't say. But the parents would know what had happened before and therefore what was happening to their daughter. Something like that.'

Marsh said, 'So if Detective Superintendent Baxter's the target, we might be looking for someone with a grudge against him personally?'

'That's the bottom line.'

'For God's sake, he's a thirty-year man. There'll be thousands of them.'

Cole agreed.

Deighton cut in drily, 'There won't be that many coppers, though.'

Marsh saw his point. 'Still a few. He was attached to CIB in the seventies and early eighties. There're quite a few ex-coppers who might hold a grudge.' He glanced at Cole. 'Where's this Maynard character now?'

'I've no idea. He's not in the office. He and Margaret Domey seem to be doing their own thing. They were at the Carrington earlier.'

Marsh nodded. 'When he comes in, I'd like a word.'

'Right, sir.'

'Let me know as soon as anything is confirmed.'

Once they'd left, Cole made his way to Hazel's desk. She was one of only three people left to man the IR.

'That's the end of my early night,' she said, wistfully. The shock of Baxter's phonecall had still not worn off. It left a horrible churning sensation in her stomach. She exhaled smoke and stubbed the end of a cigarette, her seventh since the news came in.

'And dinner, too, I'm afraid.'

She'd already accepted it. She gave him a regretful little smile and glanced at her watch. 'Maybe I've been saved by the bell. Anyway, there's still time.'

'It's been ninety minutes. Mary-Anne's never done anything like it before. It's not a quick spin around the block. There is no more time. The son of a bitch, whoever it is, copper or not, sane or insane, has got Baxter's little girl. And we're all running around in circles.'

Baxter caught his brother just as he arrived home from work. It crossed his mind how odd, and yet, how perfectly natural it was, to turn to family when everything else failed.

There was surprise in Henry's voice when he answered, 'Tony, what's happened?'

'I need your help.'

'Name it? Anything.'

'The case I told you about on Saturday. The bastard that took Jane West.'

'I remember. I saw in the papers that he murdered her. I wouldn't like your job, Tony. Not a bit of it.'

'Right. And now I think he's got Mary-Anne.'

Silence, a long silence, then, 'I'll be with you in ninety minutes. Two hours at the outside. I'll bring June.'

Baxter choked on his next word. 'Thanks,' he muttered and replaced the handset.

His wife sat on the sofa, waiting, her face blotchy yet composed. The boys were upstairs, whispering. They had been told, and sensed more than understood the seriousness. Their immediate reaction was that Mary-Anne was going to be for the high jump for getting into someone's car. Baxter fought his own impulses. The most natural thing in the world was to go rushing out to search for her, even though in his heart he knew that it was a complete waste of time. It was panic. The sudden uncontrollable fear that got in the way of rational thinking. The same could be said about his need to get back to the office. His place was at home. There was nothing he could do that wasn't already being done. In truth, he would probably be in the way. How many times in the past had he insisted an officer went home? An interested party could never be involved in an investigation. And this was only the beginning. If he felt so utterly useless now, the feeling was only going to get worse. He'd shed his tears already. When he got home he comforted his wife, then hid in the bathroom and sobbed until there was nothing left but a terrible hole in his heart. Now he had composed himself and gone onto auto. The years in the job had trained him to do that. He had to reason things out logically, sanely, put aside his feelings of panic and despair. He'd go over every action made during the last week, searching for something they'd missed.

'I can't believe that Mary-Anne would get in someone's car,' his wife said, repeating the words she had uttered when he'd first arrived. She seemed amazingly composed.

He could scarcely believe it either. They had drummed in the dangers ever since Mary-Anne was old enough to walk.

His wife went on, panicking a little, feeling that terrible fist tighten in her gut, 'I must ring Kay and Julie. They must know . . .'

Baxter steadied her. 'No, sweetheart, not yet. And then not by telephone. I'll deal with that if and when the time comes.'

Kay and Julie were their eldest daughters. God knows how they would take the news. Silly things came to mind. Kay was in the middle of writing a module. How would she be able to complete it once she heard the sickening details?

He heard a car pull up. He glanced from the bay-window and saw Sam Butler climb out.

'Guv,' Sam said on the doorstep, holding back so that he was out of earshot from anyone inside.

'Sam,' Baxter said, gravely.

'Rick asked me to have a word. He talked to you about Geoff Maynard's idea and thought it might be worth following up.'

'The revenge business? I'd more or less dismissed it.'

'The DI hasn't, Guv. He's taking it seriously. He wonders whether you'd start to put a list of likely contenders together, keeping the police link in mind. He mentioned your time with CIB.'

Baxter considered the request for some moments. He thought

it was a waste of time but at least it was something he could do. He nodded. 'Tell him I'll work on it.' He glanced at his watch. 'I'll pop back at about nine. Meanwhile . . .'

'Don't worry, Guv. You'll be the first to hear anything.'

Baxter watched the DS down the path and closed the door as he climbed into the car.

Back at the office, the atmosphere was intense. There was an urgency in the voices, a rush to answer the phones. When Sam Butler walked in he recognised immediately that there had been more bad news. The expressions were even darker than when he'd left. A layer of grey smoke spread out below the strip lights. Hazel told him, 'Two of the kids identified Helen Guest's photofit. It's the same guy. Older, of course, but the same guy.'

'Shit,' he said. He glanced at the drawn faces in the room. They'd been brooding on the implications.

'Yeah,' Hazel muttered.

Behind her, Scot came in with some hurried copies of Mary-Anne's photograph. While he pinned one to the board next to the shot of Jane West he said to no one in particular, 'You know, there's a likeness between the two girls. Look at this, not at their bodies, one's tall and one's short, but their faces. They could easily be taken as sisters.'

Butler said, seriously, 'Shall I tell the super it's the same guy?'

'No,' Cole said, firmly. 'It'll keep for a while yet. I'll deal with it when it's necessary, when he comes in.'

From the theatre the psychologists motored across to the Wests'. While Mrs West poured yet more strong tea, they had gone through every snap that Mr West had ever taken of his family. Jane featured in most of them. From baby shots right up until a few months back, hundreds of them, beach, bath, or just plain fooling around. They watched an hour-long video of the last holiday. A Spanish beach, a red-hot sun. Jane, peeling skin on her shoulders, running up and down a beach, riding a horse, taking part in a talent contest at the hotel. By the time they'd finished they knew the family history. A family photo album was a hidden drawer of secrets. They showed relationships and friends, they caught the unguarded moment. They showed who was close, and who wasn't, the clothes and decorations, the genuine smiles and those that were forced. They gave details, responses, they told you about the family and even more about the photographer.

From there they went to Barnwall School and parked on the road opposite the bus-stop. They sat in the car taking in the details. Maynard had his eyes half closed. Margaret wondered if he was dozing off.

Eventually she said, slightly disgruntled, 'I've followed in your footsteps for the best part of a day and I'm exhausted. The least you could do is tell me what you're trying to achieve here.'

He smiled an apology. 'The killer has left a trail, fleeting it might be, so vague even the dogs couldn't pick it up, but it's here, in front of us. We know he took the girl from somewhere in this area, and we know she ended up on the allotments. We know he took her to the theatre and we know he bundled her out again. No one saw a thing. Not her abduction, nothing. If we are to find him, recognise him, then we must do so through reconstructing what Jane West saw. What did she see? Did she see the car pull over, did she struggle or simply get in? See what she saw, Margaret, know the victim as well as you can, go through her emotions, her fears, become her for a while, and see what happens.'

Margaret nodded thoughtfully. She was trying to like Geoff Maynard, but found it difficult. He lived on another planet, as far removed from her cosy world as Buckingham Palace was from a two-bedroom terrace.

'Most victims belong to one of three groups – young gays, prostitutes and runaways. What do you think the link is?'

Margaret coloured slightly. She should have known the answer, but tiredness got in the way. She was going to kick herself.

'Don't worry. This isn't a quiz. The link is their availability. The most difficult thing for the killer, once he's crossed the line, is to get the victim into a vulnerable position. Prostitutes ask to get in the car, as do runaways – for that read hitch-hikers – and young gays want privacy with a stranger. What made Jane West get in the car?'

'Right,' she said, through tight lips.

Maynard settled down again.

Jane West had been a likeable girl, that much was established, but she wasn't pushy. If anything, the opposite was true. Attractive, in a boyish sort of way, yet she was very much a little girl, fragile in both mind and body. She wouldn't have been led, exactly, but she wouldn't have been the first with an idea. That fell to Jenny, the dominant force in the small group of school friends.

Come with me, Jane. The words went through his mind.

What do you want?

Get in the car.

Please don't hurt me.

Get in the car or I will.

He didn't like it. Not on this stretch of road at that time of day. A struggle would have produced a witness. All she had to do was scream. She knew him. She got in the car out of her own free will.

Once Jane West had been aware that getting in the car had been a terrible mistake, her fear would have left her unable to move. Had the opportunity to escape or call out arisen, Jane would have been incapable of grasping the chance. Two days later, just a few hours before her death, she had been able to eat a small meal. Perhaps it had been the first meal offered to her. Somehow, Maynard doubted it. Until that time, she had been unable to eat. The killer had talked to her, had, to some little degree, gained her confidence. That's why she was able to eat her last meal. Perhaps he had promised her freedom. Any threat would have had her retreating again, unable to function, and that included the ability to eat. If not traumatised before the rape, she certainly was after it when the killer put his penis down her throat. No sign of foreign skin or blood meant that she hadn't used her teeth to defend herself. Fear might have stopped her, as he had suggested earlier. The emotional shock had left her incapable of fighting back.

He looked out across the road and pictured the scene, Jane West's confrontation with her attacker. He had a car or a van. He'd used it to move the girl to and from the theatre. It was inconceivable that she'd walked with him or been carried. So he used the car for the initial meeting. Was he in uniform? It made sense. Everything was pointing to a copper.

He'd got past the child's first defence. Somehow, he'd gained her trust.

Not that difficult for a copper.

Seeing a uniform, kids of that age did what they were told. Unless they were streetwise, which Jane West wasn't.

'OK,' he said suddenly, and Margaret jumped. 'Let's take the direct route back to Richmond Park, into Churchill Place, the way she would have walked. Drive slowly.'

Margaret Domey nodded, glad to be on the move.

He relaxed back, letting his knees slide forward to the dash, and watched the road in front, concentrating on the pavements.

Jane West would be walking along in front; her friends had already left her, or she was hurrying ahead. They were in a hurry to finish their homework, get out again. She was the one hurrying. The others weren't that committed. She rounded the bend first. Now, apart from the traffic, she was on her own. The man had seen her on her own, waited until she had rounded the corner, then pulled up. No, he didn't like it. It was too well planned. He wouldn't take the chance that she left her mates, even if it had happened before. No, for some reason he was absolutely confident she'd get in the car, whether she was with her mates or not. The car was parked, he was waiting for her.

They continued along the road until they reached the edge of the estate. Now the roads narrowed and there were a lot more people about. Adults. He'd run out of time. It happened back there, on the bend.

The man felt at ease, knew where he was and knew exactly what he was about. He was absolutely certain that Jane would get in his car without a struggle. OK, leave that for a moment.

'Drive on, Margaret, head towards the Carrington. Take the quickest route.'

So, he had her in the car. He was excited now. He could actually see her close up, perhaps for the first time, he could see her knees and legs. Obviously he was concentrating on driving. She would realise, if she hadn't already done so, that he wasn't taking her home, and now she might struggle. Or would she? Would the fear get in the way? Was he acting out the usual role of the abductor, explaining in graphic detail what he planned to do? Now, left in no doubt about her mistake, would Jane make a challenge, or would she fall into submission? It had to be submission. There were no marks made at this early stage. There was no way he would have stopped to bind her arms and legs. If he had hit her it wasn't forceful, perhaps a slap, nothing more, nothing that caused any bruising. The marks at the side of her neck and just below her elbows had, according to the pathologist, been newer, caused no more than a few hours before her death. So perhaps there was something else. Now that she was in the car a threat alone would be enough to control her. The sight of a knife maybe. This would make the danger quite clear, and her impulse to struggle or scream would be controlled.

Margaret drove into the main road leading to the theatre. It was busy with early evening traffic. What time did he arrive here? Indeed, did he drive straight here or stop at some intermediate place until the traffic had eased? Perhaps until darkness had fallen? No, he wouldn't take that chance. The police would then be out in force. Knowing something about the police he would have guessed that. He drove here straight from the school, and parked at the back of the theatre, hidden by the high walls, his entrance already open and waiting.

Now she was at his mercy, totally compliant, unable to function for herself. He had to lead her into the theatre, down those dark steps. The more submissive she became, the more dominating he was. Dominance, the concept behind ninety per cent of sexual assaults.

'Let's call it a day,' he said at last, taking Margaret by surprise. He wanted to be alone with his thoughts. He'd get rid of her, grab a bite to eat and then return to the scene alone, when he would immerse himself further, become the girl, feel what she felt. Then he would go over it again, and this time he'd be the killer, and through his actions he'd sink into the murky depths of the killer's mind. He would excite himself, bring to mind the photographs of Jane West he had seen earlier, think of her as something he must have, build up an uncontrollable urge. If he could do that, become the killer, then he'd have the bastard.

Baxter shouldered his way into the IR. The others stopped work to greet him, feeling terribly self-conscious. As he crossed the room he paused momentarily at the incident board. Catching sight of Mary-Anne's photograph pinned next to that of Jane West chilled his heart. 'Oh Jesus,' he uttered. He looked desperately at his colleagues.

He moved across to Cole's door. Cole looked up from the papers on his desk.

'Hello, Guv.'

'Rick, tell me?'

Cole nodded slowly as he came to terms with Baxter's wretched look. 'They matched. At least two of the girls recognised Helen Guest's photofit. We're looking for the same guy, a copper.'

Baxter slumped against the door frame. 'I don't know if I can handle this.' He felt smashed into little pieces. He inhaled deeply and let automatic pilot lead him into records.

He tried to concentrate, but found it impossible. He hung around for an hour, then went home. At something after ten Cole found the rest of the team packing up. The sense of disbelief and anger was mixed with disappointment and failure. They needed a break. Night duty had arrived. The uniforms were being briefed in their parade room. The obligatory CID man sat at the end of the management table. It was the start of the weekend. Other things went on. One murdered girl and one missing didn't stop the drunks getting out of hand, or the pushers and pimps and robbers carrying on their trade. Other people, innocent people, were still getting hurt. That never stopped. On their patch there were over thirty boozers, any one of which could be the scene of a brawl; there were hundreds of miles of track waiting for an accident to happen. The 999s continued to ring. Domestics, burglaries, assaults, you name it, on Friday night it happened. The briefing would go on for another thirty minutes or so, then the corridors would be busy with heavy plods making their way to the exits. In the car-park, the pandas would pull out. Clockwork. Superintendent Billingham's well-oiled machine.

Sam Butler said, 'Some of us are knocking off for a few hours. We're into a swift half before we fall down.'

Cole was slightly surprised that the DS wasn't rushing home to work on his second chance.

'Yeah, Sam, that sounds good. Unless anything breaks, we'll meet up here at eight in the morning.'

Butler yawned and said, 'When this is all over there'll be a lot of people taking a rest. Are you coming?'

'I'll be over shortly. You can get them in. Where's Hazel?'

'She was in records with the super. She's probably still going over his list.'

Cole nodded. 'I'll walk her over.'

Butler locked his drawers and followed the other exhausted bodies to the door.

Mike Collier emerged from the gents wiping a splash from his fly. He saw Cole and grunted, 'All over?'

'Will be in a minute. For a couple of hours, anyway.'

'Bad news, all this. Fucking bad news. It's still sinking in. I can't believe it. Nobody can.' He shook his head. 'The super's about the only one of your lot that our lot even remotely admire.'

Cole nodded. Collier headed to his desk in reception where he had a secret kettle on the boil. Cole watched him go, then headed the other way, up three flights of steps, to the collator's office. It was a square room, one wall covered with bookcases packed with lever-arch files, the others with four-drawer filing-cabinets. Two Kodak micro-film viewers stood on a far table and just inside the door a single pedestal desk was piled high with grey folders. Hazel sat at the desk with one of the folders open in front of her. Her elbow was on the desk, her chin resting on the palm of her hand. A cigarette drooped from her fingers and smoke curled up to the fluorescent strip. Her back was to him. He closed the door. She turned suddenly.

'Guv?'

'Hazel, haven't you had enough? We're calling it a day. The duty team can take over for a few hours.'

She stubbed the cigarette but left a lazy smoke trail. Her swivel seat swung his way. Her black clad knees were held together. The edge of her skirt fanned over them.

'The others have gone. I said we'd see them over the road. That all right with you?'

She nodded but stayed seated. Her eyes held onto his before she turned back to the desk and fumbled among the papers. She found the door key and paused.

'Did the super put his list together?'

'He made a start,' she said. 'Just a dozen or so names.'

'Is that all?' Cole flared. 'I was hoping for more than that. Perhaps he doesn't realise that time is against us. For Christ's sake, what's he been doing?'

Hazel stood up and turned on him, responding impulsively, 'How can you be so cold? The poor man doesn't know what day it is.' She shook her head angrily. 'You are a callous bastard; the others were right.'

She swung past him towards the door. He grabbed her hand and the key flew to the floor. He knew it was a mistake but it was too late. She faced him. Surprise brought a gasp and her eyes widened. Their lips locked. They tasted smoke, slightly bitter and familiar. She broke free and said, 'This isn't a good idea.'

'I'm due a bad one.'

She reached up and kissed him again. For a few seconds they were in a different place, nothing else existed. Her hand slid inside his jacket; his beneath her shirt. He felt her silky skin and soft breasts; she went between buttons into the hair on his chest. Suddenly, she was at his fly and he was under her skirt. She freed him and held onto his testicles and only let go as he bent to push down at her tights and pants. She stepped out of her shoes and pulled her underclothes free of her feet. Their lips glued together again. She felt his hand between her thighs.

226

Her legs went weak. She guided him, forcing him to bend his knees, and he straightened inside her, surprised at how easy the insertion had been. She moaned delightfully in his ear, a tiny little laugh that came with a gasp.

'Oh, Rick,' she uttered.

He backed her against the side of a four-drawer and she raised her elbows onto it in order to lift herself against him. He placed his hands beneath her bare buttocks and her legs wrapped around him. She felt him pulsating inside her. The feeling of pleasure made her moan again and she brought her legs up further. His thrusts became harder, his pelvis ground against her. His breaths became ragged. Hers came with every thrust. She shut her eyes tightly as she felt a wave of heat beginning to build. She arched her pelvis higher, clamping her legs to hold him in, her body quivering under the exquisite torture. Her climax came on, releasing a coil of wonderful heat. She hadn't experienced the sensation in many months. Now it came, turning her body into a shaking jelly. Her mouth opened in a silent cry. It looked like pain. Suddenly she was whispering into his ear, 'Shit, shit.'

It might have been the clenching of her muscles that sparked him, but maybe not; he was well on the way. They'd had two days of foreplay. He came with a final thrust that slid her up the steel cabinet until she was all but sitting on top. The sensation rocked him; it felt like lava pouring out of him, going on forever. It was almost painful. He stayed motionless, inside her, not daring to move, feeling the throb as his ejaculation continued. She lowered herself gently, tentatively, feeling the pressure stretching her inside and the hot flow of semen spread out. Slowly her legs relaxed from around him and slid down his body until her feet touched the cold floor. She gazed up at him and raised her hands to his face, pulling him down to kiss her again. When they parted she whispered, 'There, it's better now. Let's go and get that drink.'

In the White Horse, with the heat of their bodies still burning through their clothes, they met Butler and the rest of the team. The gloom was overbearing, the voices kept low and indistinct.

Hazel acknowledged Butler with the faintest of smiles. Butler noticed the look of her skin; it seemed softer and radiant, and he felt a slight stab of jealousy. Or was it disappointment? Either way, they were ludicrous sentiments and he shook them off. As Cole drew up a chair, he asked, 'Everything all right, Guv?'

'I don't know, Sam. You tell me.'

Butler finished his drink and nodded. 'We'll have this bastard tomorrow. We'll find Mary-Anne.'

Cole nodded stonily.

Hazel felt the wetness between her thighs and pressed her legs together. Her body was trembling. Over her glass rim, as she drank, her eyes locked onto Cole again. There was no one else she wanted to see. She gave him a small knowing smile. Her body felt bruised and wonderful, her lips swollen. She saw Sam Butler's speculative glance and shrugged. For the moment, she no longer cared.

The detective sergeant glanced at his watch and reluctantly said, 'I'll be getting off, then.'

DS Barry Scot and Sergeant Wilson joined him. They moved to the door together. That left James and Walker sitting with Cole and Hazel. Single people with nowhere to go.

After a quick drink, Hazel said goodnight and left them to it. When Cole pulled onto his drive at midnight she was waiting for him, her car bathed in the vulcanic light.

'Surprised?'

'A little.'

'Do you mind?'

'Mind?'

'Well, you're the senior officer. You're the one compromising your rank.'

'I don't mind.'

'You knew I'd be here?'

He inserted his key in the door and said, 'That's a bit strong. I hoped. There's a difference.' He shut the door behind them and switched on the hall light. She'd changed and showered; her hair was still damp. He indicated the living-room. 'Go on in and pour some drinks. I'll be five minutes.' On the bottom stair he hesitated.

'What is it?'

'You shouldn't be here.'

'D'you think I don't know that? I feel shell-shocked, numbed. I'm still tingling from before. Now I need to be held. Is that so bad? It's a war zone out there. What's right and wrong seems to go by the board. You find comfort where you can; you live while you can. That's how I feel. In any case, I'm in love with you.'

'That's a bit sudden.'

'Does there have to be a time scale?'

'Pour the drinks.'

She watched him up the stairs then went into the living-room. The curtains were still open, flooding the room with street-light. She felt strangely giddy and elated, detached, as though she was watching herself go through the motions. She left the light off and opened his scotch, then stood by the window gazing out into the quiet street. She needed to be joined, filled with him again, feel his throb against her own. She needed the physical comfort of someone close, hot breath on hers, arms wrapping her in an easy embrace, her chest flattened snugly against his, sharing breaths, somewhere painless, warm and peaceful. Euthanasia. That was it. She needed a gentle death; the heat spreading from her groin, wave after wave of it, would carry her away into another world.

He came up behind her, wet, a towel around his waist. She turned to face him and he kissed her gently, lips parted. He tasted of Colgate. She felt him stir beneath the towel. When they parted she held the glass out towards him and he swallowed a measure.

He said, thickly, 'Come on, you're absolutely right, let's forget it all for a couple of hours. Talk about whatever normal people talk about. Do whatever normal people do.'

'That's the problem. We're not normal people, are we? Nobody understands.'

'Come upstairs to bed. Under the covers there's a certain security.'

In the deep shadows she reached up and kissed him again.

'Your husband is back tomorrow,' he said awkwardly.

'Yes,' she confirmed. 'Late morning. He'll be pretty pissed off when he realises I've got to work. He's arranged a meal out with some of his colleagues and, unusually, partners are included.'

'Social workers? It sounds as though you've got out of it by the skin of your teeth.'

'I'd already resigned myself to an evening of shop talk, with me and the other partners looking at our watches.' She sighed. 'It's not as bad as it sounds.' She stroked the hairs on his chest. 'What am I saying? It's worse than it sounds, believe me.'

'I believe you.' He leaned to the bedside table and lit a cigarette. He settled back against her. She borrowed a drag and exhaled toward the ceiling.

'This is a disgusting habit, smoking in bed after making love. It stems back to the old black-and-white movies. The fifties and sixties. *Room at the Top*, *Saturday Night and Sunday Morning*.'

'They're before my time.'

'Mine too. I caught them on the box. They're still better than some of the crap they serve up today. Oh God, I feel wonderful. I'm still throbbing. I love you, Rick.' She punched his arm gently and handed back the cigarette. 'And I'm leaking like the Yorkshire Water Board. It was wonderful.'

He was taken by the curious intimacy of Hazel sleeping quietly beside him. It wasn't the inches between them, or the incredible gentleness of what had gone before, but the impression of trust, the sense of how natural it had been. Little things, removing her skirt and pants and displaying herself unashamedly before sliding into his bed, the first contact again, the curious spark of skin against skin, the touch of her subtle perfume, the feel of her soft breasts and slightly rounded stomach, the little catches of her breath as she moved easily beneath him, the ease with which he slid smoothly inside her, the slippery heat; they came back now to produce a warm contented glow.

Before he slept he set the clock for seven, and hoped an hour to get ready would be enough.

Part 4

Chapter 23

Weekdays, days when cabbying was a waste of time, he'd go to the White Horse. The police were always in there, drinking and laughing, their voices thunderous, booming and hollering. They were surprisingly friendly towards him, unlike other places where no one spoke a word to him. 'Hello, David, how's your mum?' they used to ask, and their concern seemed genuine. And then, after, they made a special point of saying, 'I'm sorry to hear about your mum, David. It must have been a terrible shock for you.'

Stupid. It wasn't a shock at all. The doctor had told him to expect it. He'd been waiting for it to happen for ages. That's how much the coppers knew.

But they all knew him.

He'd been in the pub a lot during the week, picking up bits about Jane West's murder. The coppers in there had been affected by it. They were quieter than usual, and often in a hurry. They seemed tired, strained, bags under their eyes. He remembered one night in particular, last Saturday night, just after he'd moved her. The girl had only been missing for a day. But the coppers had been searching for her, and the concern was showing. It had been late, well past closing, but he'd been allowed to stay with the other regulars. He had become a regular. The landlady had taken to him. She probably felt sorry for him because his mum had died. Lots of people did. They seemed surprised that he was still coping after three months. On that night some of the plain-clothes cops were in, sitting away from their uniformed colleagues. Not that they wore their uniforms in the pub, but you could tell which were which. The plain-clothes strutted, as though they were special. He found that interesting. It was like a barrier between the two groups. He realised then that they weren't all in one team. There was animosity between them. Maybe it was jealousy. Something like that. He'd looked through the mirror at the back of the bar. He'd seen the plain-clothes man buy a round of drinks and carry them across to a table where two others sat. The woman seemed nervous and unhappy, chain-smoking. She was all right, fairly attractive, but he liked the one he'd seen in uniform better. She was with other colleagues at the bar, close to him. They were obviously due back on duty and hadn't bothered to change completely. Their shirts were a giveaway. He'd seen her often. Her name was Wendy. She always saved him a special smile. He was surprised to see her. It was her long weekend off. A couple of days earlier he'd heard her saying how much she was looking forward to it. Maybe, because of the missing girl, all police leave had been cancelled. He chuckled. The thought pleased him. Gave him a warm feeling in the chest. But Wendy. She was different. She had big tits. Like his mother's. He liked to see her in the uniform. In the street, sometimes it was trousers. That night she had changed into a skirt. A tight black skirt. She was different to the plain-clothes woman, or the other women he'd seen. She'd been used, yeah, but not as much as the others. Sort of half and half. He supposed that if he'd been forced, like, say, if the other coppers in there had been drunk and got hold of him and forced him to stick it into a used one, then he would have chosen Wendy. Being forced he wouldn't have had a choice. He would have had to do it. It wouldn't have been his fault. He'd struggle against it a bit. He'd have to do that. But it would be useless and he would have been forced to watch his own cock sink into her pus hole. Oh God, it was wide open, horrible, oozing with filthy cock come from one of the other coppers; used, yeah, but not worn, only a bit, not smelly and filthy. But there were still cobwebs up there, and slippery things like eels with razor-sharp teeth. Waiting to snap bits of flesh off the incoming cock. Off the coming cock! But he was being forced. He had no choice. So he had to do it. Oh God. God, what a horrible thought. Being forced like that. He felt the wet patch on his groin and finished his drink quickly. Outside he felt himself. He was sticky without even getting a proper stiff on. Just a half stiff while he pictured himself being forced. That was amazing, like a waking wet dream. That had been the first time he'd thought about himself sinking into a used slit and he'd come a bit without even wanting to. Just shows you what they could do. Bloody dangerous. Suck the cream out of you without you even trying. When he got home he scrubbed himself clean. He had to get rid of the evidence. He sprinkled Ajax onto his cock and used a nail brush. Bastards, those coppers, forcing him like that. That's probably what happened to his dad. Something like that. Being forced. That's probably why he turned to drink.

One night he drove the gollywog called Moses home from Benny's. Moses sat in the back. Lights from other cars skidded across his face so that he could make out the worry lines.

'This ain't good,' Moses said, taking him by surprise. He checked out the face in the mirror to make certain that the black man was talking to him. He gripped the wheel tighter.

The mouth went on, 'In all the time you worked for us, you ever seen such worried faces?'

He hated questions when he was driving. He shook his head.

Moses answered for him. 'No, you haven't. It's down to women. Isn't it always? I've gone and done it, that's what. Got myself fucked up.'

He managed to find his voice. 'What's happened?'

'Man, I'll tell you. I've fallen in love, that's what, and it ain't a good feelin'. Might have been, but she's up and gone. Run away. Now that's a fucked-up start to a relationship, ain't it?'

He nodded. He'd agree with anything the black bastard wanted. Black men were dangerous, particularly at night.

Moses continued, 'And now this other mother, the one who's took the girl, causin' more coppers on the street than I've ever seen. It ain't healthy out here. It ain't good for Benny's business.'

Moses gave him a tenner and said, 'Keep the change. Man, if you'd got any sense, you'd move. Me too. That's what we should do. Get the fuck out of it. Some place in the sun.'

He watched Moses move off towards his tower-block flat, then opened the windows to get rid of the black smell.

Friday night, when Benny's car hire was short of drivers, they gave him the fares. Benny's regular drivers were black.

That meant they weren't reliable. Either too stoned or getting their end away with one of the white girls that hung around the office. Anyway, it meant weekend work for him, ferrying couples from the pubs and clubs. Most of them were loud on alcohol, dressed up to the nines, trendy suits and short skirts. He knew what they were up to. Feeling each other in the back. In his car. Touching their stiffs. Touching their cunts. Syphilitic pus-filled holes. Cocks dripping with sticky. Disgusting. Sometimes he'd see the girls disappear from his mirror. When that happened he knew what they were doing. Ugh. Getting their red lying mouths full of it. That's what.

That night he made some good fares, one all the way to Gatwick. He knocked off at dawn, when the crowds had dwindled and the fares dried up. No one had thrown up in the back or come on the seat. That was a bonus. It usually happened on a Friday. He drove in a daze to Richmond Park and turned off just before it into Wellington Avenue. The back gardens of the houses on his side bordered the playing fields of Barnwall School. The houses in Wellington Avenue were mostly terraced but, at the top end, where he lived, they were detached, much older, some in desperate need of renovation. Render was crumbling to leave patches of bare brick, paintwork was blistered and flaking, some of the window frames were rotten. The big bay-windows were dark, the nets at them grey and fraying. A small driveway at the side of his overgrown front garden led to a lean-to at the side of the house. He pulled up beneath it. It was reasonably secluded. A six-foot fence ran down the drive between his property and the next. His back door was at the side of the house, the other end of the lean-to.

He didn't like the ghosts in his mother's room so he used the boxroom that had been his since the day he was born. He didn't mind going in his mother's room. But he wouldn't sleep in there. When nan had come to stay, before she went mad and was carted off, she shared his mother's bed. That close, she could see to her needs when she woke up during the night. Once nan had gone, he didn't bother. His mum often woke and called out but he didn't go in to see her. He lay in bed listening to her cries, trying to blank them out by pressing the pillow against his ears. By then, of course, towards the end, he had begun to resent her, the fact that his life had been stolen. It was only after she died, the sudden release behind him, that guilt began to twist his gut. It was about that time, just a few weeks ago, that mother came back. She was a ghost, of course, in the dressing-table mirror, taking over the reflection of his own image, but she was real enough. She laughed out loud as he stretched the child's soft, white bra across his naked chest; her eyes sparkled as he wrapped the cool material around his penis. Eventually her lips drew back and she sighed as he masturbated into one of the small cups.

Chapter 24

On the Monday that Jason Hackett did a runner, Keith Mason called his men together. 'This is a major fucking crisis I've got here,' he said in his high, effeminate voice. It was chalk on a blackboard. No one liked an effeminate voice on a man; it sounded like the fucking Bee Gees were at it again. But when it belonged to Keith Mason you listened. 'The sparklers do not belong to Jilly Jackson. They are on loan from a very tasty Bond Street store for her next assignment. We're not talking fucking Ratner's here. She's gotta have 'em back. Understand? She's threatenin' all sorts of fucking nightmares. Where she was, what she was doing, all that shit. She's threatenin' fucking Fleet Street, or worse, Canary fucking Wharf! Now, my old lady's back on Monday and I really don't feel like comin' up with an explanation. Get it? That's seven short days. You find out where this cunt-faced fuck-faced Hackett is, and you tear the fucker into little pieces. But you get hold of the sparklers and you get them back to me. Before Monday. Got it? I don't care what the fuck you've got to do, or how much it fucking costs. My life's at stake here. You all know what my fucking wife is like!' His pop eyes bulged, ready to explode. There was real fear behind them. 'Get in touch with that fuck-faced detective inspector. We pay the bastard enough. He might know where the little toerag is!'

That's how it started. The faces went out. People on the street were hauled in and given a slap and a nasty fright. Before long, Martin Brookes's name, Jesus, was mentioned. Sunday morning, almost a week later, Mason paid him a call.

'I've heard of you, Jesus,' he said. 'Now, I'm not going to fuck around here. Normally I bring a few things with me, food, make a meal. But in this situation I don't have the time. Do you understand that? I'm running out of time. I'm beginning to fucking panic. When I panic it ain't healthy for people around me. Monday's on its fucking way. And that means my wife is too. The thought is fucking terrifying.

I haven't been able to sleep and my mood is not good. Understand?'

Brookes looked at him wide-eyed and bemused. It was clear he didn't understand. He hadn't got a clue what the man was talking about. But he sensed heavy drama. He could smell danger. It made him nervous as hell.

His wife lolled on the sofa. Brookes said nervously, 'That's the wife, man. Help yourself if you like. Take her next door.'

Mason's minders gave her the once over, fidgeted with their sawn-off shotguns, powerful phallic symbols, and decided against. Her face dropped, hurt.

Mason pushed his wrist in Brookes's face. 'See that? That's a fucking Rolex. Two and a half fucking grand's worth. And do you know what? Because of that toerag dog shagger I've had to have it fumigated and still it don't feel right. It still smells, for Christ's sake. I can't get rid of the smell. It's the same in the bedroom.' Mason sighed. 'You can see that I'm pretty pissed off, can't you? Now I ain't going to hurt you permanently, Jesus, on account of that being bad for business. You stayin' in business is good for me. Percentages, all that. But what I am going to do is tip a little bleach into your left eye. It hurts like fuck and it'll blind you in that eye. But it won't stop you weighin' out. It won't get in the way of business. But I guarantee you'll tell me what I want to know.'

'Man, Mr Mason, sir, you don't have to tip any bleach. All you gotta do is ask.'

Mason smiled. 'I know that. I know I don't have to. But I like to see people in pain. Now,' he said, holding up the supermarket own brand bleach. 'Hackett. Jason fucking Hackett. Ring any fucking bells with you?'

When Johnathan and Big Billy Moses arrived two hours later, Brookes's eye was still dripping blood and a lane through his beard had turned white. He was blind in his left eye. It looked a mess, red instead of white and white instead of blue. He'd injected heroin into the corner to ease the pain. It helped. Now he was snorting to help some more. It went against one of his principles. He didn't believe in using his stock.

'That's the wife, man. If you fancy it . . .' He waved a hand towards the bedroom. 'Know what I mean?'

Moses said, 'Well, if it's on offer, I ain't fussy . . .' He glanced at Johnathan for confirmation.

'Go ahead,' Johnathan said. 'But don't take too long.'

Moses nodded, grabbed a hand and pulled the spreading smile towards the bedroom door.

'That eye of yours does look sore. Yes, sir. I'd say you'd been called upon by a certain Mr Mason. That is his trademark you're winking at me. The eye, the hole in the needle through which the thread is passed, the calm region at the centre of a storm, the organ of sight. Yes, sir, it's an important thing. I don't suppose for one minute that, with your good eye, you saw which way Jason Hackett went, did you?'

Brookes hesitated and wondered whether to tell him the same question had been asked by Mason. Eventually he thought bollocks. He could find out for himself. Johnathan took Brookes's pause as reticence. He listened to the moans coming from the open bedroom door, then said, 'Without any doubt at all, Martin Brookes, Jesus, or whatever else they call you, if you want to save yourself from more injury, then you should talk to me.'

Brookes threw up his hands. 'Man, I'll talk to you. I'll tell you my whole fucking life story.'

'No, no, that won't be necessary, Jesus. I'm sure it's real interesting, but right now just tell me which way Jason Hackett went. That's all I ask.'

Five minutes later, Moses appeared at the bedroom door. Johnathan nodded his satisfaction and they left. Five minutes after that, Connie appeared, her knees quivering and held a foot apart. She collapsed on the sofa and her dressing-gown parted. Her smile remained fixed in two places.

'Man,' Brookes said. 'I'm getting fed up with all this shit. We should change the fucking locks. We should go ex-fucking-directory.'

The golden beach at Perranporth, just south of Newquay, seemed to go on forever. Even mid-afternoon, as hot as it was, there were acres of uninhabited sand. Enough space to lose yourself, if that was your bag.

Jason Hackett didn't like the water, he couldn't swim and even three feet of it, particularly the things that might be crawling beneath its surface, filled him with dread. He was quite content to lie on a towel stamped with the words DO NOT REMOVE, and watch Greg splashing and whooping in the surf. She had bought herself a tiny blue bikini, discarded the top the day before, and was now something right out of a holiday brochure. He would have been content to watch her forever, or at least until the sweating started.

It was Sunday, the day of rest. They had been resting for six days, and he still hadn't slept with her. That wasn't strictly true. They'd slept together, went in for some heavy petting and she'd jerked him off almost every day, but they hadn't made love. That was still to come. The business in London had brought on an early period and for three days she had been feeling decidedly ill. A doctor who made money out of holiday-makers prescribed some antibiotics to deal with an infection. She was now well on the mend and the sun and sea had worked wonders. The bags beneath her eyes had disappeared and the odd freckle had sparked on her nose and across her shoulders.

The day they arrived they had booked into a small B&B just over Fistral Bay in Newquay, and Hackett had left Greg in bed while he went out to search for a supply. Priorities. He'd found one within an hour, in a pub overlooking the beach. It wasn't anywhere near as good as Martin Brookes's gear, it was cut down to criminal, sold to the tourists and the surfers who wouldn't complain, but it would do until he could find his way about. He purchased a little weed at the same time, to use on the beach. It meant that he didn't have to go running back for his cooking pots.

After that, mindful of what the girl had said, he found a dentist who agreed to treat him privately and immediately. As well as the cleaning and scaling he was talked into an X-ray and two fillings. It would be a long time before he visited one of the robbing bastards again. Even so, for most of the way back to

241

the B&B, before the injection wore off and he began to curse, he wore a wide grin, flashing at everyone in sight, and lingered at every shop window to clock his own reflection. It was quite remarkable how clean teeth changed a man. His face seemed to have filled out and his broad smile had become engaging.

On his way back, thinking she might find it tricky, he bought himself a pair of Botham look-alike bins at Boots and an Alba portable CD player from Dixon's and a dozen top-ten CDs from Smith's. Nicking them never even crossed his mind. He was a changed man. The CD was the business and blasted thirty watts over the sand.

When he got back she waved at him from the bed, not even noticing the player or the bins. 'Oh my God, Jay, you've had your teeth done. Come here and kiss me, quickly.'

She even let him touch her tongue with his. Not much. She tasted of sweet tea and hamburger relish. He could have lived on it for ever. Right?

Greg shared his spliffs but she kept well away from the other stuff and had made him promise to give it up. He'd already cut down in case he got a chance at a real poke. He kept some coke handy to make up the difference. They'd agreed he would quit at Christmas. He knew he wouldn't. No way. But he was all for the quiet life. Almost married already.

On the Tuesday, he'd caught a bus to St Austell and nicked an old blue Maxi. They'd been using it to motor down to the beach every day. Since Friday, they'd chosen a more secluded spot. That was the day his photograph hit the tabloids. He hadn't recognised it at first. Greg had pointed it out. The police at Sheerham wanted to interview him in connection with a break-in at the Carrington. He was surprised. They didn't usually go to such lengths for a minor incident; what the hell did they care about a piss-poor theatre that hadn't been used for over a year? Nevertheless, he was there, head and shoulders for all to see. Fortunately, it didn't resemble him much. Since he was taken to Sheerham nick by a certain DI Cole and charged with burglary and given a conditional discharge by a sympathetic magistrate, his face had grown fatter and his hair longer. The mug-shot didn't do him justice. He hadn't read on, and neither had Greg; they had caught a glimpse of the paper when stocking up on cigarettes. Buying it might have alerted the newsagent. But if they had, they would have learnt about the possible link with the murder of Jane West. Then he would have worried.

'I've been thinkin',' he said when she approached. The soft sand fell into her footprints. She stretched beside him on the sand, arms thrown above her head, the tiny drops of water on her body shimmering in the sun. Her stiff nipples drew his gaze. Her eyes were closed so he was able to stare.

'You'll hurt yourself,' she said, light-heartedly.

'Maybe I will, but I've been thinkin' about the chips. Right?'

'Ah, ah.'

'Earlier, at lunch, you said they didn't taste the same as when you were a kid, right?'

'Mmm.'

'They used to cook 'em in fat. Proper fat, white stuff. Now it's all the common market crap, sunflowers, olive oil, stuff like that. It's probably got nothin' to do with the potatoes at all.'

She opened her eyes. They twinkled. He pulled his gaze off her breasts.

'I think you're right,' she said.

'Right. Right. But it could be the potatoes, if they're using new ones, or red ones. Go to a Wimpy or a Mac's, taste the chips in there, nothin' like chips, right? That's 'cos they're French. French fries. They don't even use potatoes. I don't know what it is. Somethin' European, not British. Not English. So maybe it ain't the stuff they cook 'em in, after all. Take the fish. Cod. Right? That tastes the same and it's cooked in the same stuff. There's no difference there. Think about it.'

He opened a can of Coke, guzzled some and passed it to her. 'Have some real thing,' he grinned.

'Jay, you made a joke.'

'Right.'

She took a gulp. It ran down the side of her mouth. She wiped it on her bare arm and left the tiny hairs sparkling.

'The fish,' he began. 'That comes from deeper water now. You don't get it round the coast any more. The old Spanish

243

bastards have taken all that. They use it in their paella. I had that once, in a Chinese. Fuckin' joke, isn't it, really? We go over there and spend our money on holiday, keep them afloat, and they come here and nick all our fish. So we have to go all the way to bleedin' Canada to catch ours. Not likely. I wouldn't have it. I don't know why we joined the bleedin' common market, really. But that's it, common. Everyone can help themselves to everythin'. They can come and nick our fish. The French bleeders nick our lamb, and all our prices go up 'cos there ain't enough to go round. What a way to run a country.' He shook his head. 'Maybe we should get off, emigrate. Those South Sea islands, that Tahiti place off Pakistan. That'd be nice. There's plenty of fish there.'

She gave him a strange, thoughtful look. Her dark, oval eyes blinked quickly as curiosity marred her brow.

'I don't think your money would run to the South Seas, Jay.'

'That's what you think. There's quite a few grand stashed away in the bag. Right enough.' He patted the bag he used as a pillow. 'Enough to get there for a while.'

Once he'd got established in the B&B he'd made a call to Jesus. Brookes had told him that the old Jew had been in touch. The trinkets that Hackett had left were worth a cool thirty grand. Big money. They'd talk again once the Jew coughed up. Hackett contained his excitement. Things were getting better by the day. He still had most of the original money left. Soon, he would have enough to take them anywhere in the world. But first things first. He had to be sure of her. He didn't want her staying with him for his money. And at the back of his mind there remained the worry that Mason would be less than happy with him. A couple of grand and shitting on his lover's slip was bad enough, but nicking a small fortune meant that he wouldn't stop looking. Maybe Newquay wasn't far enough.

'You'd need passports,' she said, shaking him from his thoughts.

'That's true. But we could get 'em. Everybody does.'

'You need your birth certificate and all that. I haven't got mine.'

He frowned. 'I ain't got one either. Maybe we'll have to give that a miss. This isn't a bad little place, is it? Or we could go to Scotland.' He raised his head as a group of people wandered by to the sea. Skimpy beach-wear, bare breasts, tanned muscles. He concentrated on the breasts and forgot his concern. 'That's me in a month or so. Go for some body-building, get a job on *Baywatch*. Right?'

She touched his arm. 'I like you just as you are. I don't want you to change, except for—'

'I know. Christmas. We agreed. I might need some help.'

'I know. But we can get it. Arm patches or something.' She hesitated, then said, 'When we get back, I thought . . .'

'Yeah, what?'

'You know, we might slip into bed.'

His eyebrows rose and his mouth opened. He glanced at his watch. 'It's four now.'

'Have you had enough?'

'Right. I'm startin' to catch the sun, you're right. Certainly don't want too much of it in the first few days. Next week we can stay longer.'

She smiled, stood up and dusted sand. She slipped into her bikini top and hooked it.

He rolled his jeans down from his knees and forced into his new Nike trainers. All of a sudden the prospect made him nervous. What he'd told her before, in London, was crap. The girl who'd stayed with him for a few nights, off and on, had never sat on his face; she'd never even flashed her goodies. He'd sussed that she was playing him a line and once he cut her free digs she was off like a light. Faster than a black man who owed you money. That taught him a lot about women. Since then there hadn't been many opportunities. He never fancied approaching a tom. Somehow that didn't appeal.

He followed her along the soft sand, treading in her footprints. His thoughts were hyper, beginning to hurt.

'We'll go out later,' he said, breathlessly. 'Maybe have a few drinks, then a restaurant. Not fish and chips. Somethin' proper, pie and three veg, and maybe afters, a puddin'.'

'We'll see.'

'Then we could do a club, maybe. Right?'

'Jay.'

'What?'

'Just shut up and follow me.'

'Right.'

In the hall, the landlady saw the towel bulging out of the bag on Hackett's arm and said abruptly, 'You're not supposed to take the towels to the beach. The sand stains them. I'll have to charge you extra.'

Hackett nodded and checked her arms for swastikas, then continued up the stairs, catching up with Greg as she reached the top. He was excited. Too excited. If he wasn't careful he'd come in his pocket. In their room she said, 'Calm down, will you. I'm going to take a quick bath to get rid of the salt and sand. Then you can. I want you clean and soft.'

'Bloody hell,' he uttered, and was left gazing at the bathroom door. He heard the water splash and the girl's voice as she began to sing.

'Oh God,' he said, not knowing which way to turn. He glanced in the mirror to check that his tongue wasn't hanging out. He heard the faint tap on the main door and guessed it was the landlady come to collect for the towel. If she wasn't a neo-Nazi there was definitely a lot of Yid in her.

He opened the door and looked into two black faces. His breath was sucked out of him and he felt himself buckling to the floor. The shock drained his face.

'Now, I hope you're not going to come out with another missing link joke,' Johnathan said, and walked in. Behind him, Moses waved a black snub-nosed handgun, and gently closed the door behind him. Johnathan brushed past Hackett and walked to the window.

'Nice view,' he said. 'Nice room. As a matter of interest, how much do they charge for a room like this?'

Hackett gulped and surprised himself by finding his voice. 'Twelve quid a night.'

'And does that include a full English breakfast complete with toast and marmalade and a choice of cereal?'

Hackett nodded like a brain-damaged pigeon.

'That is reasonable. I've always promised the wife that one day we'd do these B&Bs. Now that the kids are older I might just give it a try. They have an oldie worldy charm about them, don't they? They hark back to the days when Britain ruled the waves, George Fifth, empire, all that shit. Before women got the vote and ruined it all. And speaking of women, or rather, girls, spunk hoovers, where is she?'

Hackett had fallen in on himself. He stood head bowed, shoulders sagging, his chest deflated.

Johnathan heard the gurgle of water emptying from the bath and smiled. 'Ah, I see. No need to answer that, Jay. I appreciate it was a difficult question.'

She came out naked, drying her hair on a small hand towel. 'Your turn—' Her mouth fell open and she stood poised, not knowing whether to run or cover herself. She saw Johnathan first, then Hackett, then Moses with his gun. She saw the flash of Moses's teeth as he threw her a broad smile of acknowledgement. She dropped the towel to her groin.

'Don't bother,' Johnathan said. 'It's still fresh in the mind. You're forgetting we've seen it from every conceivable angle. Just get dressed. We're in a hurry.'

'Where are we going?' she snapped.

'Home, Greg, home. You'll have to work your butt off to make up for the expense you've caused Black Benny.' He turned to Hackett. 'And as for you, Jay, croaking a good customer is not a good idea. No, it isn't. That's not the way to keep your business ticking over at all. Now, if a customer croaks while he's on the job, a heart attack or stroke, well that's not a problem. But if he croaks because some thoughtless son of a bitch fuck-face has stuck a fucking hammer up his nose, that's different. But don't worry. We are under strict instructions to deliver you back safe and sound. Black Benny wants to discuss things with you when he gets out of hospital. The weather, the England cricket team, the dangerous release of radioactive isotopes, your extremely slow death, that sort of thing.' He turned back to the girl. 'Greg, Greg, if you want to walk out of here naked as the day you were born, that's fine by me, and I don't think Moses will

247

object either, but if you don't, then you better put on some clothes.'

She made a move back into the bathroom. Johnathan followed to keep an eye on her.

She had just about finished – short black skirt, sweater, sandals – when the main door crashed open and an explosion rattled the windows. Johnathan crouched low, whipped out his gun and peered around the bathroom door.

Moses stood beside Hackett with his Smith and Wesson handgun pointing at the open door. In the doorway lay a man Johnathan vaguely recognised. He had a serious chest problem caused by a .357 slug, and it was spreading out on the carpet beside him. A sawn-off double-barrel lay near his motionless hand. Johnathan stood up and pulled the girl into the bedroom.

'What the fuck happened?'

Moses stuttered, 'There were two of them. It wasn't my fault. I saw the gun. It was instinctive.'

'OK, OK, don't panic. Do you recognise him?'

Moses pulled a blank face and shook his head.

'I do,' Hackett said. The others looked at him, amazed.

'You do?' Johnathan said.

'Yep, that man is Keith Mason's brother. Simon Mason. Right?'

Moses caught Johnathan's falling expression. 'Oh shit! That ain't so cool.'

'I told you to get your eyes tested. Did I not tell you to get your eyes tested? How long ago did I tell you? Tell me?'

'I know you did.'

'If you'd done like I said, got them sorted, wore spectacles or contacts, then you might have recognised Simon Mason before pulling the trigger.'

'I went to the eye man, I really did. Two for the price of one, he said on tele.'

'And?'

'I didn't understand it, boss. He said something about a lazy

248

eye, worse at ten o'clock. Tell me what the time has to do with your eyesight? I gave it up.'

'Moses, I do believe the ten o'clock might have had something to do with the plane, the angle of vision, and not the time of day it was or the time of day you were born.'

'It was a mistake, boss, how was I to know? Burstin' in, wavin' a gun. It coulda been anyone. It all happened in a split second. Seeing clearly wouldn't have made a difference. You see the barrel and bang, you go for it. It wasn't my fault. No, it wasn't.'

'I know that, Moses, I know you didn't recognise Simon Mason. Hell, I know that. And I'll do my level best to explain it that way to Black Benny. You're not usually trigger-happy. Hell, you're no Roy Rogers or Buck Jones. But he won't be happy. Keith Mason will hit back with all his might and Benny's not in the ideal place to wage a war. A hospital bed is not the place to direct operations. Especially when you're having a job to think straight. And especially when you know that if you take off the bandages your head will split in two like a fucked-up coconut.' Johnathan paused to overtake, then continued. 'If you had managed to get the other guy as well, it would have been better. At least it would have given us time, and we could have denied we were ever in the vicinity. As it is, the news is going to spread faster than clergy spunk on a choirboy.'

Moses grunted and said, 'Anyway . . .'

'Pardon me?'

'Anyway, we didn't recognise Simon Mason, did we? Not even after I'd shot him. Hackett came up with the name.'

'Ah, the present occupant of our boot. You're right. It was Simon's hair. He'd had a restyle. That's the trouble with change. Change brings trouble.'

They were on the A303 moving east across the undulating downs of Salisbury Plain. The troughs of the plain were filled with dark shadow, deep purple, massive ocean waves held back by clusters of mysterious bushes and trees.

'News – BBC, ITV, Sky News – it's the main problem of the twentieth century, believe me. A bomb goes off in London and within seconds it is flashed right around the world; rag-heads around the Ganges look up from their curries and Abos around Ayers Rock from their fried lizard and they say, "Fuck me, those fucking Irish bastards have bombed London again". They hear about it at the same time we do and we live just six miles up the road. Ain't that a thing? The point is, because of the news, Keith Mason is more than likely goin' to hear about his brother before we can get the same info to Benny. That ain't so good.' Johnathan shook his head.

Moses sat in the back with his thick arm circling the girl's shoulders. She seemed to shrink against him.

'Still,' Johnathan went on, at least we've got Jason Hackett safely tucked away and our reputation is back to something like reasonable.'

Giving Hackett up to Keith Mason hadn't gone down well in the street. No, sir. People were even suggesting that Johnathan and his assistant were losing their bottle. That sort of comment was bad news when your business was built on fear.

'What did the boss mean about Gregory's terminal illness?'

Johnathan shrugged. 'It's only rumour. Apparently, one of Keith Mason's people mouthed off. These white fuckers cannot hold their drinks. But it means the detective inspector has been transferred; he's redundant. He's no use to Keith Mason in Yorkshire, is he? It's an evil fact of life, Moses. Redundancy. The word was created by the Tories. Remember those days? A nasty little word. It means you're worthless. And worthless things get buried on some council tip. Indeed, it's ironical and rather pleasing to know that many Tory candidates, ex-MPs, now have a real grasp of what redundancy really means.'

'Johnathan?'

'Yes, Big Billy Moses?'

'I'm gettin' myself steamed up in the back here with thoughts that ain't so holy. You do remember that I was interrupted before? Do you suppose you could pull over for a while? It is getting mighty uncomfortable.'

'I can see that. The rear window has misted over. The lights from passing traffic is blasting it like nuclear explosions. If I didn't know better I'd think the French were doing some more testing. But yes, I can pull over for a while, I need to relieve myself as well. But make it short and sweet. Black Benny will be frettin'.'

Johnathan took the next left, travelled a short distance further and pulled into an empty car-park. He climbed out of the car, stretched his back, and wandered casually towards a line of trees. He took his time, enjoying the freedom of movement and the slow emptying of his bladder. It was a pleasure to shake the last drops without some bastard watching from the next urinal. He'd been driving for most of the day. He was beginning to feel it. He peered at his watch. With a little luck they'd be back around ten.

Moses had the girl perched on the edge of the boot, her feet off the ground, her legs, white even in the dark, splayed either side of his. Her hands gripped his arms, trying to stop herself sliding further onto him. Her face jerked up and down on his shoulder. Her grimace was fixed but her eyes were open, staring at him as he approached. Moses's trousers were around his massive thighs, his black ass pumping away like something on an old gas turbo, shining in the light from the passing traffic.

Johnathan wondered whether Hackett could hear her bare ass slapping on the boot.

He looked out beyond the deserted car-park at the ancient monuments, powerful ghosts against the night sky.

'Stonehenge is one weird fuckin' place,' he muttered. 'Those Druids are certainly a strange bunch of mother-fuckers. Did you know, Moses, that most people consider it to be an ancient calendar? Dates can be worked out by the alignment of the stones. Some experts believe that it was a sanctuary for worship, perhaps to the sun or the moon. Well, now, I happen to disagree with them. Yes, sir, I do. I personally believe that that is so much shit.'

Moses's breaths began to shorten and the girl made little squeaking sounds that seemed to catch in her throat.

'I happen to believe that the whole area, including all the Bronze Age barrows around here, and believe me there are many of those, is just a thing. An abstract monstrosity. I know the barrows are graves and therefore functional, but it's their position I'm speaking of. Experts are always reading meanings

251

when none exists. Think of the other great monstrosities: the pyramids, the civil service, the royal family, all of them at one stage or another considered burial places. For the sane, and I consider myself sane for most of the time, they don't make any sense.'

Moses was grunting louder, like a pig under an apple tree the morning after a storm. A high-pitched 'Ah' emerged from the girl's wide open mouth. It went on and on. Then Moses caught up with her. 'Oh, oh, oh, mother-fuckin' Jesus! Christ! Oh Christ!'

Over his shoulder the girl's voice grew stronger. 'Ah, ah, ah!' Her eyes widened and her breaths came in little bursts. She continued, 'Ah, ah!' She let go of Moses's arms and fell back over the boot and rear windscreen, her arms outstretched. Her legs stiffened and her toes turned up.

Johnathan said, 'Now that is a surprise. Yes, I admit, in these days of political correctness, when that sort of thing is pure male fantasy, derided and spurned by women from all sides, that is a fuckin' surprise.'

In the car again, underway, Moses gripped the girl closely and said, 'I'm thinkin' of keepin' this girl all to myself.'

'Now I can't see Black Benny being altogether happy with that. She's merchandise, a money machine. A feel-good dispenser. I think you're going to have to be happy with takin' a turn now and again.'

'Hell, I know that, boss. I'm only joking. I ain't ready to settle down yet. There's too many shores to see and hills to climb and urinals to piss against.'

'Why Moses, that's almost poetic.' Johnathan smiled into the rear-view mirror.

Moses was stroking her hair, holding her against his chest. The son of a bitch had fallen in love.

Chapter 25

They took the side streets to the back of Benny's Mini-cabs and parked beneath the flight of steel steps. Johnathan tossed the keys to Moses, who opened the boot. He hauled Hackett out and waited a moment while Hackett got used to the dim street light and found his legs again. He'd been bent double for five hours.

Johnathan led the way up the steps, pushing the girl in front. He held her aside and knocked loudly on the door at the top. It was opened by the black woman Hackett had seen before, plaits and bright red lipstick and black fuzzy hair that reached right up to her navel. For just an instant she was taken aback, and as she looked up at Johnathan there were questions all over her face. She glanced at the others, recognised Hackett and gave him a sweet smile.

'My, my man, I didn't expect to see you here again. You're gettin' to be a regular. Did you bring my dress back?' She stood aside while they trooped into the passage, then closed the door.

'What's happening?' Johnathan asked.

'We've got ourselves a full house and people waitin' on. Hell, we's busy, for a Sunday, too.' She moved past and sashayed on in front.

'How's Benny?'

'He's gettin' a final check tomorrow. Hopes to be home in the mornin'.'

'That's good,' Johnathan muttered. 'Yes, indeed, that is good.'

'Yeah, it's cool. Now what did you bring him here for?'

'Well, now, Benny made it clear he wanted to see him, and I'm not taking him to my place. No, sir. Putting up toerags like this is not part of the contract.'

She moved forward and flicked a finger against Hackett's chest. 'Well, honey, it seems that I've got you for the night. Now ain't that a treat? I hope you haven't brought that tool

253

along. We cater for most things, but not that kind of fetish. No, sir, we draw a line at puttin' holes in a customer's head.' She smiled quickly and turned to Johnathan. 'Put him in the end room. Somebody'll have to watch him. That's your responsibility. Security.'

'Moses will watch him, no problem.'

'Listen, honey,' she flicked Johnathan's lapel, 'when I hear the words "no problem", I just get a funny feelin' in the ass.'

Johnathan nodded to Moses, who started to shunt Hackett back the way they'd come, to the room next to the fire-escape door, and turned back to the woman. 'Now, listen here, there might be some bother later.'

'I knew it. I just knew it. What happened?'

'One of Mason's people turned up and Moses had to put him out of commission, so to speak. It turned out to be permanent.'

'One of Keith Mason's men?'

'Yes.'

'Jesus, that ain't so hot.'

'It does get worse.'

'Go on?'

'It was his brother.'

'Simon? Simon Mason? Moses killed Simon Mason?' She shook her head. Plaits fanned the air. 'There's somethin' you can guarantee . . . shit!'

'I know. We'll get some people together downstairs, tool them up, just in case.'

'You better have some heavy artillery, honey, 'cos popguns don't scare Keith Mason's boys. You better deal with it, pronto.' The woman glanced at Greg, then said to Johnathan, 'She's got some catching up to do. I've got a dozen punters waitin', and only four girls on. Put her in room three. She can start right away.' She opened a small box-table by the wall and took out a syrette. It came ready for use, an automatic one-time injector, expensive as hell, but time-saving. When time cost even more, that was important. 'Hold her arm,' the woman said. She smacked for a vein, found one, and pushed the needle. Greg drew in a sharp breath. She felt the heat creeping up her

254

arm, just like before. 'That'll take just about two minutes, that's all, then she won't be going anywhere, just putty in a man's arms.' She dropped the syrette in a waste-bin by the table. 'Room three,' she repeated to Johnathan. 'I'll go and line up the punters.' She headed for the stairs and disappeared.

Johnathan opened a door and turned on the light. The room was an eight-by-eight, no window. It contained a single bed, an upright chair, some hangers on a rail, and some rubbers on a side table. The girl's legs began to buckle. He held her up and sat her on the bed.

'I feel so hot,' she said. She felt the sweat on her forehead. 'Oh, is it me? Or is it hot in here?'

Johnathan grunted. That was some good shit. Two minutes ago the girl had been strung out tighter than a wallet made in Scotland, now she was acting like she lived in the place. She lay back, looking up at him without a care in the world. She smiled. A pretty smile. She raised her hands above her head. Her short black skirt moved up her thighs flashing a V in his face. Christ, if he wasn't happily married to a black piece of ass made in heaven, he could almost be talked into it himself. For the first time he saw what Moses saw in her.

The woman appeared at the door. Two punters, tongues lolling, followed her in and gazed drunkenly at the girl. She turned to Johnathan. 'That's it, she's happy. Everything's under control. You can go and sort out your army now. I got me a feeling you're going to need it.'

He nodded slowly and glanced at the punters. They were in their thirties, well-dressed, one mixed up with some white shit, the other Nigerian. Both of them were spooked as they drooled over the girl.

'Well?' the woman asked, looking from one to the other. 'Will she do, or not?'

The Nigerian gave a stupid smile of approval.

She saw Johnathan's concern and waved it away. 'They's regulars. Benny's friends from way back. They believe in togetherness. And since they pays the money, they gets the service.'

The Nigerian threw Johnathan a big white- and gold-toothed grin.

'Oh,' Greg said. 'It's so hot in here.'

'If I wasn't in such a hurry I'd have me an inkling to stay and watch,' Johnathan said.

'Hell, I never thought I'd hear you say that, honey. This is strictly a sad man's game.'

'That is true.'

'Be careful, Keith Mason does not play by the rules.'

He nodded and muttered, 'Nor do I.'

Hackett sat on the floor with his legs straight out in front of him, his back resting against the wall. Moses was next to him on an upright chair he'd salvaged from the pile of rubbish. His gun was held loosely, kept upright by the barrel forced into Hackett's ear. The street light shone through the window. There was no curtain and Moses didn't want to chance the light, not with Mason's people on the prowl.

Moses seemed glum. 'I sure ain't happy about what's goin' on down the corridor. It almost makes me wish we'd never found you. That girl's too good for all this. And she's too good for you. She's got the sweetest ass I've ever come across.'

'You don't have to let it happen. You got the equipment to stop it. Right?'

'That's true. But that would mean goin' against Black Benny, Johnathan, too, and I sure wouldn't recommend that. Hell, no.'

'Then you'll have to watch her turn into a scaghead, watch her arms fill up with bruises and scabs. See her used by twenty guys a day. Right?'

'I know it all, man. I've seen it. I don't need a description. I'm findin' it hard enough as it is.'

'Well, let me go and get her out then. You could say I hit you with somethin' while you weren't lookin'. They'd believe you.'

'No, they wouldn't. That you could take me is inconceivable, just not possible. That idea just wouldn't pass go.'

'I've got me thirty grand comin'. You let us go, it's yours.'

'Huh. Since when have you had thirty grand? I ain't stupid, Jay, so don't insult me. Anyway, it wouldn't be for the money. Did she ever mention me?'

Hackett thought hard. He knew she hadn't. She'd done her best to forget the man and wipe the scene from her mind. 'Well, she was pretty impressed with your dick. You name me a girl that wouldn't be. She never came near me, that's for sure.'

'You ain't fucked her?'

'No. We're more like, you know? Brother and sister. That kind of relationship.'

'Well, I never did.'

'Anyway, I ain't so hot in that department. Not any more.'

'Scag fucks up your love life. I heard that. You should sniff the snow instead. They tell me that's different. A stalk for a week. Is that true?'

'It's bollocks. It's no more than twenty-four hours.'

Moses chuckled. 'Anyway, it don't matter to you. Your sex life is the last thing that matters. What else did she say?'

'She said that Johnathan was the one that frightened her. She thought you held back, like, tried to be gentle. You could have caused her serious grief with all those diamonds.'

'She said that?'

'Yeah, why?'

'Well, 'cos it's true. I didn't want to hurt her. Anyway, the sparklers are polished right down to smooth. The backs are little plastic pellets. I got 'em done in Amsterdam. They don't cause no damage.'

'That's what she said.'

'I am surprised she noticed, bein' so frightened an' all.'

'Well, she did.'

'I believe you.'

'There's another thing.'

'What's that?'

'Keith Mason's goin' to be comin' after you with everythin' he's got. You should put a lot of space between you and Keith Mason, right?'

'I been thinking hard on that. It seems to me I'm best off stayin' put, with friends, then we can put up a fight.'

'That's if they will fight. They might not like the odds. Think about that. Will Benny like the odds? He might cut his losses. That'd leave you right out in the cold. How much does Benny think of you, Moses? How much are you worth to the main man?'

'He thinks a lot of Johnathan, and I'm his partner.'

'Right. So you'll all go down together, like Davy Crockett at the Alamo.'

The light from the window glistened on Hackett's forehead. 'You're startin' to sweat,' Moses said. 'You gettin' bad?'

'Startin' to? I was gettin' bad when you were knockin' hell out of the boot. My bag's still in the car.'

Moses nodded reflectively. 'You should cut that shit out. It ain't cool.'

'But you don't mind Greg gettin' filled with it?'

'I know. I know.'

Hackett's chosen profession had tuned his ear to slight changes in background noise and footsteps blasted his ears like armour piercing shells. He stirred against the gun.

'What is it?'

'Outside, on the steps.'

Moses withdrew the gun and eased up to the window. Hackett was at his shoulder.

Another car had parked next to theirs. Two men, dark shadows, stood at the bottom of the fire escape. One of them had a foot on the bottom step. The car door opened and another man climbed out. In that instant, as the interior light went on, they caught the unmistakable, round, white face and pop eyes of Keith Mason in the passenger seat.

'Oh, shit,' Moses said.

'I told you he'd come. Right?'

The car door closed and the man joined the others and started slowly up the steps. They drew sawn-off shotguns from beneath their jackets.

The car moved off, slowly, to the corner.

'My guess is,' Moses said, 'they're going to hit front and back at the same time. These guys will hang on until the car gets round the front.'

'They don't seem to be hangin' on to me,' Hackett said, as they continued to climb.

'Listen, brother,' Moses said. 'We's in this together now. Live or die. You get the girl. As soon as they open the door, I'm going to shoot the mother-fuckers. Somehow, we've gotta get to the car. We can take it from there.'

'Right. I'm with you.'

Hackett selected a leg from one of the broken chairs, then moved into the corridor. He'd heard the woman say room three. He found the door just as another opened and a man came out. He was dressed casually, bomber jacket and jeans. His face was flushed. If he noticed the chair leg that Hackett carried he didn't show it. Instead, he winked at him and headed for the stairs. Hackett breathed relief and reached down for the handle. As he pushed open the door he heard a crash of glass from the shop down below. A woman screamed and men shouted. In that same moment the back door flew open and Moses fired his gun. The explosion ripped down the corridor, making the bare hanging lights jump. A shotgun roared. The far wall the other side of Hackett lost some plaster and the man who was heading for the stairs was flung forward, the back of his jacket pitted and torn. The man who'd fired the shotgun groaned and fell over in the doorway. Hackett shoved the door wide open and leapt into room three.

The explosions and screams had stunned the two men, frozen them to the spot. Their eyes were wide, their mouths open. He couldn't see the girl's face. All three were naked.

The cross-breed sat on the edge of the bed. Greg faced him, in a kneeling position, her legs either side of his. The Afro was standing behind her, his knees bent like a Japanese Sumo, his hands on her shoulders. Both of them were giving it some, caught mid-stroke.

Hackett smacked the standing man square across the head. He crumpled in a heap, his shaft still upright. Hackett pushed the girl aside and swung the length of wood again. The second man tried to move away and it thudded into the side of his neck. He yelped, then lay groaning.

Hackett caught hold of Greg's hand and pulled her to her

feet. Her knees buckled immediately. He reached for her sweatshirt, found the neck hole and pushed it over her head. The skirt gave him more trouble. He left the buttons undone, lifted her onto his shoulder and headed for the door.

Grey smoke poured along the passage, coming up the stairs in a dense cloud. Out of it came a lick of orange flame. The passage had filled up with panicky people, some still dressing, some not bothering. Screams and shouts rang out. He stooped by the box-table and filled his pocket with syrettes, then let the crowd carry him to the back door. By the time he reached it he was bent double under her weight. Johnathan's voice came from behind.

'Hackett, stop right there!'

Johnathan stood by the stairs, the flames and smoke billowing just behind him, only his head and shoulders visible. His gun was raised, held two-handed. Hackett watched terrified as the gun exploded. A woman pushing to the door next to him suddenly cried out and fell face down.

As he went through the back door he caught sight of Moses. The man sat beneath the window. His head was bowed, his white shirt turned red.

He clattered, stumbled, ran and crawled down the fire escape, not daring to look back. Other people fell in front of him. There were still a few behind. He leaned the girl against the car while he kicked in the side window. He had the door open in moments, beating his own record. He pushed her into the seat then climbed across her to the wheel. He saw Johnathan on the steps. He wrenched out the wires.

'Come on, come on,' he cried, searching for a spark. Suddenly it took and the engine kicked. 'Right,' he said. 'Right!'

Even in her confused state Greg saw the flash of blue and gave him a spaced out smile. 'Hey, Jay, don't let anyone ever tell you that you ain't a hero. You're cool, man, real cool.' She sank back into the seat, chewing on the front of her sweatshirt.

Johnathan was racing along the pavement, catching up with them, threatening the smashed side window with the gun, but too late. Hackett was grinding into third, screaming on the corner, swerving to miss another car. From the passenger seat, Keith Mason recognised him the moment their eyes met.

In the rear-view mirror, Hackett saw Mason's car come to an abrupt halt, then begin to turn. He drove past the front of the shop and saw flames and smoke pouring out. Petrol-bombed, Hackett guessed. 'That is one serious fuckin' blaze,' he muttered, and glanced at the girl. She was out of it, sinking into the warm embrace of the shit cruising through her veins.

Pedestrians flashed by, shop windows became a blur. The car behind was gaining, using the path bored by Hackett, and they had shooters. He had to get off the main road, lose them in the back streets. He made a sharp turn, heard the tyres screaming rubber. Greg was thrown against him. She giggled, completely out of it. As far as she was concerned they were on the waltzers. They were heading to the estate. It wasn't a bad idea. He knew it well. If he could lose them anywhere, it would be in those narrow, criss-crossing, dimly lit roads. He took two more turns. A lamp-post took the paint off the passenger door and the silver hub cover hit a fence. He came out of the last turn fighting to control a skid, and in correcting took the next right hander. Even as the car roared into the new road he realised his mistake. It was a dead end, a private road rising to Barnwall School.

'Shit, shit, shit,' he heard his own voice. The rear-view confirmed that the car behind had turned his way, accelerating now, eating up the space between them, its twin beams exploding in his mirror.

He followed the narrow drive between bushes and trees and pulled up at the back of the school, behind a row of steel waste-bins.

'Come on, girl, quick! Out!' He ran round the car and wrenched open the passenger door. He caught Greg's hand and pulled her from the seat. She went down on her knees. For a moment he considered leaving her, then dismissed the idea. He'd never get her back a third time. He pulled her to her feet, put one of her arms around his neck, and started across the playing-field. She got the idea and tried to get her legs functioning. They were approaching the fence when the headlights swept the field and picked them up. He heard a shout and the slamming of car doors, but didn't look back.

He pushed Greg into the fence and begged, 'Climb. Please climb.' She grabbed at the wire and slipped. He caught hold of her by the waist. 'Grab the top, for Christ's sake.' He lifted with the last of his strength. If she didn't make it in one they were finished. Suddenly her weight eased from his hands as she bent over the top of the fence. 'Keep going,' he shouted, as he began to climb. He could hear the footsteps thumping across the playing-field. He was over in seconds, and pulled the girl after him, bearing her weight as she fell onto his shoulders. He hit the grassy verge, rolled from beneath her and yanked her to her feet again. With her arm around his shoulders, his arm around her waist, he took her weight and ran into the narrow road bordered on one side by the school fence, the other by a long wooden fence leading to the back gardens of the terraced houses. He raced along to the end of the road towards the detached houses, trying the garden gates as he went. Even as he rattled the gates he was struggling with a vague thought. There was someone up here that he knew. Back in the old days Hackett had juggled him a bit of weed. A taxi driver, that was it. The thought had barely registered when he recognised the second detached along, a run-down affair, with an awning of sorts and a car parked beneath it. He said a silent prayer and tried the gate and almost jumped for joy as it opened. He pushed through and closed the gate behind him, hoping for a bolt, but found it hanging uselessly from one screw. He dragged her along the path to the side of the car. The footsteps grew louder, and he heard a voice, 'In here.' The latch of the gate rattled.

'Jesus,' he muttered, as he realised there was no time to get into the car.

Another car pulled up in front of the house, washing the front garden with light. They were trapped. Panicking, without giving it a second thought, he broke a pane of glass in the back door. The key was in the lock. In an instant he had the door open and was pushing her through the dark kitchen towards the faint outline of another door. She tripped over a swing-bin and sent the contents flying. He hauled her up and shoved her into a passage. It was faintly illuminated by the headlamps from the car at the front of the house shining through the glass in the front door. He took the first door on the right and pushed her through it before diving in behind her. She shouted out as she fell painfully down the cellar steps. He landed on top of her.

'Quiet!' he snapped, and dragged himself back to the door. He flicked his lighter.

The steps led down to a murky brick-walled cellar where dusty cobwebs hung from the uneven crumbling walls and lines of dark fungus grew around the edges. The fetid smell of damp and decay filled their noses. The floor of the room was black, covered in what looked like mud. Some old grey pipes rose from it and curled into the festering brick. But for a blanket spread on the floor, it was totally bare.

His lighter went out.

'Hush,' he said, as he heard the faint sounds of the back door opening again.

Johnathan had climbed into one of Benny's cabs that had swerved to miss Hackett's car as he sped onto the main road. They followed behind the car chasing Hackett. Johnathan had picked up the shotgun by the door and filled his pocket with cartridges. As he saw Hackett turn into the school, he said, 'Keep going. Take the next road. There's only one way out for him, and that's on foot.'

They cruised up the road, searching between the houses. Short of breaking into a terrace, they had to head for the group of detached. He saw them, just shadows by the car under the lean-to, and pulled up. 'Wait here,' he said to the driver. He moved quickly across the garden and was into the kitchen just as he heard the back gate close. He opened the cellar door just as he heard a girl's cry, faint and muffled but unmistakable, coming from above. He closed the cellar door and climbed the stairs, his long legs carrying him up three at a time. He opened the bathroom door. The light was on. Soap hung in the air. He heard another sound, a strangled sound, a girl's voice. He couldn't make it out. Then a man spoke. He reached down and opened the bedroom door.

Out of the darkness came a scream that froze him to the spot. He caught the glint of a long serrated knife as it swept towards him, and gasped as it hit him in the chest. Even as he fell forward, wondering what the fuck had hit him, he unloaded one of the twelve-bore barrels. Flame lashed out from the explosion, shook the windows and cracked through the house. A burning pain shot through his lungs and he dropped the gun. He grabbed it instinctively and fell back just as the door slammed shut in his face.

Hardly daring to breathe, the knife still embedded to the hilt in his chest, he pulled himself upright and staggered back to the stairs. He was on fire, stunned, waiting for the pain. He had to get out. He felt the warm blood beneath his shirt.

As he hit the stairs, shotgun poised, Keith Mason was starting to climb them. They clocked the surprise on each other's faces. Both guns went off simultaneously, three barrels in all. The front door blew out, the plaster in the landing blew off, Mason was all but cut in two, carried onto the doorstep. Johnathan bounced off the landing wall, his side ripped out, and hit the stairs again, head first. The knife twisted round, slicing through his ribs. He came to a stop half-way down. He felt a numbness spreading. The pain would explode about him at any moment. He helped gravity and hauled himself further down. A lick of flame came from the kitchen, the crash of another barrel, then splinters from the banister tore into his face, and the wall over his shoulder was pitted. Some lead, not much, buried into his shoulder. He barely felt it. He pulled out his handgun and fired three times through the banister. Someone yelped in the darkness. He reached the bottom of the stairs and hauled himself through the front door, over Mason's body. In the distance he could hear the wailing sirens. He staggered across the overgrown lawn towards the waiting car. From the corner of the house another shotgun roared. It caught him in the back and threw him forward. He twisted round and fired again. The man at the corner of the house fell back onto the boot of the car; the other barrel exploded into the air. He rolled off the car, a black motionless shape on the gravel drive.

Johnathan reached up to the car door. The sirens got louder. He looked into the horrified face of the driver. 'I can't make it, brother. No, sir. Catch me for a tip next time, will you?'

The driver nodded, slipped into first and roared off. He was into third before he reached over and pulled the door closed. In his rear-view he saw a car pulling up beside the still figure of Johnathan and, in the distance, turning into the road, the flashing blue and white lights of a panda.

Hackett waited until he could count to twenty between shots, then eased open the cellar door. He saw the body lying on the front porch and heard the police sirens approaching. He pulled the girl through the kitchen, and made the door just in time to see the flashing light illuminating the drive. He clocked another body lying at the back end of the car in the drive, then half carried Greg across the path to the back gate. He closed it behind them, taking his time now. To any witnesses they might have been a courting couple. The girl had had too much to drink and he was helping her along. He didn't fancy the fence again, so walked the long way round to the school entrance. By the time they got there Greg had come round a bit. The night air, the exertion, and the passing time had all played a part. Mason's car was in better nick. He forced the boot of his own car with a section of the school fence and reached for his bag. He was about to pull the wires on the Jag when Greg tapped the ignition and rattled a full set of keys.

'Where do you want to go?' he asked. 'Anywhere particular?'

'Sun, sea and . . .'

'Go on, finish it.'

'Sssseafood.'

'In that order, right?'

'Right.'

'Right then, hold on tight.'

He turned the key, heard the engine purr, and rolled her

out. 'Always wanted a Jag,' he said. 'A midnight-blue Jag. This is class. We're goin' up the world, girl. Right?'

'Right,' she giggled and leaned over against his bony shoulder. 'But don't call me girl.'

Part 5

Chapter 26

His mother used to love chocolate. Milk Tray, not that horrible dark stuff. Between the pills and gin she used to get through a box every day, except for the strawberry creams. She didn't like those. The chocolate made her teeth fall out or rot away, so in the end she didn't have any of her own. Before she sucked him, she'd take her false teeth out and drop them in a tumbler on her bedside table.

Saturday night, late, he found himself rubbing shoulders in the White Horse again. He could still taste the girl. Yes, he had to admit that he'd had a little taste. He hadn't hurt her. He hadn't done that. Just a little tongue job, just to get the feel. But the thought of what tomorrow would bring, the anticipation of actually emptying into her tight little body, left him dizzy and hanging onto the bar for support.

The place was crowded with policemen trying to wind down. They were stressed out, breaking; you could see it in their hollow faces. Through the mirror above the bar he watched the two men carry drinks to their table. A policewoman sitting there jumped to her feet and followed one of the men to the back door. They were at it. He knew. There was a secret look in their eyes. They couldn't fool him. The police were all the same. They were all at it. Dirty bastards.

When they came back she had pinked up. She'd probably gone down on him in the car-park. Her mouth was still full of his spunk. Yeah, no doubt about it. He could tell. Just by looking at her face he could tell. After a while the plain-clothes police were joined by another couple, a tall gangling man dressed in casuals, and a short, rather business-like woman. They didn't fool him either. They were at it all right. He probably bounced her on his knee. On his cock. She'd be bouncing while his big hands were squeezing her tits. The difference in their sizes, well, it was like father and daughter, really. Man and child. No difference. Just the same, really, except for holes. Hers would be covered with disgusting hair. Ugh.

His favourite was in there again, Wendy, close to him, talking quietly to other uniforms. So close he could actually reach out and touch her. She flashed him a quick little smile, but it wasn't humorous and her face firmed up quickly. They were all worried. Even Wendy. You could see it in their tired eyes. They were losing and they knew it. There was the awful resigned look of failure in their grey faces.

He spent an hour in there, enjoying his superiority, before taking to his cab. He had a routine to keep. Nothing would change it. He wouldn't give them the slightest hint. You just couldn't be too careful. If his father had taken care they wouldn't have kicked him off the job. Turned him into a boozer. That's why his father turned violent. That's probably why his father hit him with the truncheon and broke his arm.

The pavements thronged with late revellers. In the safety of his cab he loved the atmosphere of colour and movement. Noise came from all directions. Mixing with the tourists were born-again Christians, Hare Krishnas, Jesus freaks with their tambourines, black guys in fancy clothes, buskers, beggars, crazies; they were all there. It seemed like an unhealthy place. Ungodly. He could pick out the bag-snatcher and the pick-pocket. He could mark the pusher and the prossie. He should be a cop. No problem. But what was he saying? Should be! Should be! He was a cop, no difference, not really. Just like his old man. Undercover most of the time, but sometimes, on special occasions like tomorrow, he'd wear his uniform.

The night went quickly; his mounting excitement had something to do with it. He parked with the dawn and went straight to bed without checking her. When he woke, darkness had fallen again. He was a creature of the night. He forced down some food even though he wasn't hungry then ironed the uniform as though he had all the time in the world. Everything had to be right. He stroked the uniform. His mother had kept it hanging in the wardrobe. His father had looked so good in it.

He caught sight of himself in the kitchen window. He smiled and stroked his dark wig. Or rather, his mother's hair-piece. He'd started using it to be like Jesus, he supposed, all those years ago. He wondered what became of that little pusher.

270

Since she was young, his mother suffered from a problem with her endocrine system, whatever that was. An underactive thyroid gland, or something. It made her hair fall out. That's why she got the wig in the first place. After the accident she never went out, so she didn't need it. He borrowed it. He wore it all the time, except when he put on the uniform. That wasn't often.

He climbed the stairs to his mother's room then took off the dark wig and combed his short hair. He dressed slowly, methodically, enjoying the feel of the warm material, watching his reflection in the mirror as he buttoned the jacket. The uniform was slightly too big across the chest, but if he inhaled deeply and held it in, it was a perfect fit. His black lace-ups were polished, his tie crisp and double knotted. Everything was ready. He picked up the truncheon, his father's old wooden truncheon, and attached it to his belt. It was a trophy, battered, worn, the grain of the wood standing out like little veins to make it unique, nothing like the black polypropylene batons being issued today. There was something very special about it, perhaps its history. Perhaps the number of black heads it had smashed in. His father never liked the blacks. He used to say that unless you hated the blacks you couldn't get into the job. He gave himself a final studied inspection and nodded his approval. He looked perfect. Like a copper. The image of his father.

It was time.

The final act, then it was over, then he'd live on memories. Maybe. But this one had got under his skin. He liked her. More even than that. She was a fighter. How that bastard spunk-sucker had fathered her, he'd never know. But as much as he wanted to keep her for himself, he had his plan. The man had to pay the full price. Nothing less. But he wasn't going to enjoy it, not like the last time. Not that. Not that. He'd enjoy that all right. But later, smashing her, killing her with the truncheon, he wouldn't enjoy that. Not now. Not now that he'd come to like her. Pity. That bit had been ruined, really. She'd messed it up by messing with his thoughts, by flirting with him. Even at her age they were dangerous. You had to be

271

careful. Christ, he could understand how Samson was fucked. Get rid of your hair and you're in trouble.

In the kitchen, while he heated up a slice of pizza, he admired his reflection in the window. He looked younger with short hair, and cleaner. Funny what a uniform could do. Maybe that's why women, the slags, went for men in uniform. Maybe that's why they went for the blacks. After all, black skin was a uniform.

He caressed the truncheon again. He could feel the veins, like his dad's big cock. From the drawer beneath the drainer he took out a long serrated fishing knife, a roll of bright red sticky tape and a small bottle of oil. The bottle was faded now. His father had used it on the truncheon to stop the wood splitting. He'd found another use for it, to stop something else splitting. He hid all three items in the deep pocket of his jacket.

So that was it. The food was ready. He was ready. It was time to feed and bathe her and lead her to his mother's room.

He placed the pizza on the tray along with a glass of wine and some of his mother's left-over Milk Tray and carried it to the cellar door.

Chapter 27

Saturday dawned and promised a bright day. Heads were thick, like the morning after a party, but there'd been no celebration.

Cole was in by eight and, after a canteen briefing, he addressed the team in the IR.

'I want some more bodies on the screens,' he said, as though it hadn't been planned, and indicated the bank of VDUs that had been installed overnight. 'Sam, I'll leave it to you. Sharpen up your office management techniques. I want every name that Tony Baxter has ever come across, living or dead, put on file. There are some more indexers coming in at nine. You'll have to contact the Yard, CIB and records. Not a single name missed. Every bloody thing you can get hold of.'

'That's a request and a half, Guv.'

'That's why you're in charge of it. You've got a head start with the list that the super has already drawn up. So, let's get them working, round the clock if necessary.'

'It will be,' Butler muttered. He knew just how slow the civvies in records responded, especially at weekends. They didn't have the same commitment. They were a law unto themselves. Frankly, the only thing the civvies were concerned with was their wage packets. They didn't give a fuck about police work. That was the difference. There were a lot of reasons kozzers did the job but the main one was catching villains. No one could take that away, not even from the bad ones.

Scot walked in. 'I've just been talking to one of the wooden tops. He's been on duty at the Carrington. Apparently, the psycho was there all night, sitting bunched up in the corner, staring into space. I tell you, our Mr Maynard is spooking the hell out of the uniforms. They've started to call him Norman Bates.'

A few chuckles broke through the atmosphere of gloom. Scot took off his jacket and hung it across his chair. 'The guy never seems to sleep. They're certain he's spaced out, puffing on weed.'

'Then they should arrest him,' Butler quipped. 'That would please Margaret. When she came back last night after spending the day with him, she was pretty upset. His methods are not bound by police procedure.'

Cole looked on thoughtfully but made no comment. He caught Hazel's look. They hadn't spoken since she drove off from his house at just after seven. He shivered at the memory of waking next to her. Her body had been warm and relaxed, her breasts quite magnificent.

Last night it had all seemed right, as natural as it could have been, but the sober dawn and strong coffee had brought with it a mild feeling of regret. It was two-fold, firstly that his thoughts hadn't been totally concentrated on the case and, then, that he'd taken advantage of her when she was at a low ebb. Of course it had been her decision, but he knew also that the inquiry had blasted her emotions wide open. She hadn't been in any fit state to think straight. He should never have followed her into records and later, he should have packed her off back to the safety of her own bed. But it was too late now. He couldn't shake a terrible feeling that it had all been a mistake and that sooner or later someone was going to pay for it.

Butler said, 'What about the super? Is he going to finish this?' He waved the list.

Cole nodded, mindful of Hazel's passionate outburst the night before. 'Give him time, Sam. He'll be here.'

Hazel flashed him a little smile of intimacy.

Butler caught the mild rebuke. He thought quickly and said, 'Wasn't it Lamartine who said that sometimes when one person is missing, the whole world seems depopulated?'

Hazel gave him a quizzical look. She laced her fingers beneath her chin and waited for Cole's response.

'I take it you're referring to the super and not his daughter?'

'I don't know what I'm referring to, Rick. I feel like I've taken a kick in the guts. I feel deprived, without even knowing what's happened. Jesus, I'm taking this personally.'

'We're all taking it personally. That son of a bitch has made it personal.'

Half an hour later, Cole caught up with Geoff Maynard in the theatre dressing-room. The psychologist still wore the same clothes that he'd arrived in, his face was haggard and his stubble longer.

'Geoff.'

'DI Cole.'

'It's Rick.'

'OK, Rick.'

'How are you getting on?'

'It's not something I log as I go along.'

'Perhaps you should, then everyone could share your insight.'

Maynard grunted. 'Do I detect a little hostility?'

'I saw your performance yesterday. You seem to have upset Margaret.'

'If I did, then she's in the wrong profession. Did it upset you?'

'Not a bit. I'm used to seeing women used as props. We do it all the time. Haven't you read the newspapers?'

The sarcasm wasn't wasted.

Maynard threw him a knowing glance. 'You're missing the point, Rick. Although most of it was for my benefit, some of it was for hers. I wanted her to understand exactly what Jane West went through, to understand how helpless she was. University is fine, but all those mortar-boards don't mean a thing without experience. And every experience is different. There simply aren't enough child killers to go round. Margaret might have been blooded in the field of murder, but child murderers are a law unto themselves. What's more, she's too middle-class, and middle-class people don't like to get their hands dirty. And you've got to do that. For hands read mind. It's all very well for the psychologist to come up with a profile based on case histories, you get all that out of books, anyone who can read can do it. Fuck *Cracker*. That was the failure in Margaret's profile, she'd read too many books. Picked up on any similarity without thinking it through. Her profile touched on every child

275

killer there ever was and gave us nothing, not even a ghost. Understanding why and how, and the relationship between the killer's methods and motive, only comes from acting it out, getting under the skin of both parties. That's why I manhandled her. I was trying to shake her out of her starchy underwear.'

'And you're doing that, getting under the skin of Jane West and her killer?'

Maynard didn't respond. There wasn't any need.

'I'm trying my best to believe that we should take note of what you say. For instance, this revenge scenario. I'm pulling people out of other areas of the inquiry to look into it. They could be employed elsewhere.'

Again there was no response.

'Talk to me,' Cole insisted. 'Convince me.'

'I'm not in the business of selling myself. I'm not here on approval. Like you, I'm doing a job. Unlike you, I enjoy my work. What the fuck is it that makes you people so opposed to us?'

'It's the fear of science,' Cole said, reflectively. 'The fear of experiments. You're not interested in catching this son of a bitch. It's a game to you. You'd like to see him do it again, wouldn't you? So you could fill another book with more theories.'

'My interests don't come into it. What I think, whether I treat it as a game or not, whether I'm more interested in the why than the apprehension of the killer, that's not what really bugs you.'

'You're going to tell me what does, aren't you?'

'It doesn't make good listening.'

'Go on?'

'You don't like the idea that people's motives are on show. Because that means your own are as well. On a personal level, you don't like the invasion. You think we're looking at you, at everybody. You think it's second nature to us. On a petty level, you think I might have noticed your interest in a particular detective constable whose wedding ring glints in the office light. You might think I've noticed her interest in you. You think that I might cut through that cold, formal skin of yours, and see into

276

your soul. That you have the capacity to be a bent cop. That you have even thought about it. That you don't give a fuck about your colleagues, they're just things around the centre, the self-centre of DI Rick Cole. Is that close enough?'

'Is that all?'

'It gets better. This case is personal. Even before last night and Mary-Anne, your red warning-light was blinking. There's something wrong in the engine room. It's not just the animosity between you and Baxter, is it? It's deeper. Dark. It's this case. Rape. Little girls.'

'I think you've said enough.'

'Do we like little girls? Is that it? We all like little girls. But it's a secret, isn't it? The idea horrifies us. But put us in contact, get the subconscious churning over, the photographs and porn the job throws up, the idea, the power we can have over innocence, the taking away of innocence, the unblemished skin, tight little bodies, long slim legs, little pussies with their swollen pubescence, the soft down along their stomachs, domination. They'll do anything. Smiling little faces. What's the matter, Inspector, am I hitting a nerve? Is it getting to you?'

Cole clenched his fists. 'You're getting to me, pal.'

'Ah, the veiled threat, the auto-defence. When did you realise they turned you on? A few cases back? Months, years? It goes away, doesn't it? Once a job is finished you can put it away, return to normal. It takes a few days to wipe out the dreams, but they do go. We actually start dreaming about fully grown breasts again, women. The other images are locked away, until something jolts them out again. A case. More photographs. Or even something innocent like the little girl next door skipping in her garden. What do we do? Watch her from behind the curtain? The artistic quality of her movements, her innocent beauty. Nothing wrong in that, is there? So why are we hiding, why are we taking furtive glances as we try to get a look up her skirt? We are looking, aren't we? Is it then that we start to conjure up little fantasies?'

Cole's jaw had firmed up. He wasn't angry. He remained in total control. He wondered how much of it Maynard really believed. He recalled Paul Baker, the Ice-cream Man, saying something similar during the interview. *You know, don't you? You can't fool me*, he had said. *I can tell you know. Once you've been with 'em you'll never be satisfied with anything else. It's like a magic potion, a drug. Don't tell me you ain't thought of it!*

Cole smiled thinly at the memory and said to Maynard, 'You've convinced me. If you come up with any other ideas, don't keep them to yourself.'

Maynard looked surprised. He lit a French cigarette, the wooden top's spliff. 'I heard about you, Rick. I read the reports on the Ice-cream Man. In my department you're something of a fucking hero. What I've just given you was a load of crap. Jealousy. I'd have given up the pension to have cracked that one.'

'Didn't you finish the report? I was three hours too late.'

'Too late for Sharon Keaton, maybe, but dozens of others were saved.'

Cole grunted contemptuously. 'There aren't heroes any more. We're just part of a system. And most of that's paper-work.'

'When I believe that, I'll give it up.'

'And for your information, not all of it was crap.'

'Shit, I know that. But there is a difference. It's to do with being one step ahead of the animals.'

'Animals don't fuck their young.'

'Yes they do, as soon as they're big enough.'

'There is one thing,' Cole said, seriously. 'Can we be certain that Mary-Anne won't be physically harmed until tomorrow night?'

'I think we can. The timing seemed to be important. There's some kind of ecstatic anticipation in the build up. He's savouring each moment, watching her and so on. In his mind, Baxter's – assuming I'm right – Baxter's agony will be prolonged for as long as possible. The first act, Jane West, was Sunday night. He'll keep to the timetable. There's just one snag.'

Cole frowned.

'The venue has been changed, obviously. That might have upset him, changed his plan. If we assume that he's managed to find another place at short notice, and that he's equally happy about security, then it'll be the same, Sunday night. We know he moved her from the theatre some time before taking her to the allotments so I think it's safe to assume that his other venue already exists. It's probably his own front room. We've got until Sunday night.'

'I'll see you later,' Cole said.

Maynard watched the policeman walk off. At that moment he decided that Cole was safe. He liked him. The door swung shut, leaving him alone in the room where Jane West was imprisoned.

Throughout the dark hours he had absorbed every detail of the dressing-room, from every position. He had seen Jane struggle, heard her cries, and crawled into the mood of her killer. He went over the events, changing the sequence but always within the parameters set out in the pathologist's report. He had aroused himself, both mentally and physically, by the destruction of the girl, forcing himself into an outburst of fury as she died before he was ready. He could no longer enjoy the terrified look on her face, the look that meant she was completely at his mercy. But then, faced with the corpse instead of a breathing, struggling girl, he went through with it anyway, touching the limp body, tying it up, fixing tape around the cold lips. He looked over every part of her, moving her limbs, pulling back the lips of her vagina, perhaps even penetrating her again, feeling the sensation of cold flesh. On the very edge of his consciousness, as he toyed with the body, an idea came to life. He could move her at will, touch her without her flinching, he could do anything without being watched by her sad eyes. Anything. She was a doll. She belonged to him alone. He was all powerful. A god! The Christ. An angel. The religious connection came tumbling back. The ritual. The cross.

Revenge. The need to hurt Baxter. That was the key. Take it from there. In some way, imagined or otherwise, Baxter has caused me grief. The need to take revenge is paramount. I follow him, find out about his family. Yes, I follow him home, perhaps in the car. Park up and watch his children play in the garden. Or I might creep up to the windows, see them in the living-room. I see Baxter's playfulness with his youngest daughter. The boys are older, they don't join in so much. The caress, the hug, is saved for Mary-Anne. Perhaps she sits on his lap and snuggles up to him while they watch TV. Father and daughter, the strange bond, a closeness I've never felt. But she is his weakness.

So, plan, plan. He must know what I'm going to do, must witness it first hand. See the mutilation, the horror, grasp the idea that I have forced into every hole. I need a victim, someone to model the atrocities for Baxter. Someone who resembles Mary-Anne. I find her. OK, stop there.

I couldn't go through with this attack, this rape of a young girl, unless I had the urge for young girls anyway. And this has built up over the years. I've got pictures, one of Helen Guest, and they've been exciting me, but she was older, developed. This is paedophilia. I'm in contact with girls of ten, eleven. Am I a policeman? Am I with CPU? No, no. I don't like that. Do I visit schools? Not enough. I need to see them, regularly. A club, a paedophile ring. I've got books and tapes. I'm a policeman. They're easy enough for me to get hold of. I'm a policeman with a grudge against Baxter and now I've taken Baxter's daughter and because I'm a policeman I know that HOLMES will make the link and . . . I'M NOT A POLICEMAN!

I'm dressing up in a police uniform, impersonating a police officer. What am I? Where did I get the uniform? Here, dammit. The stage. It's a costume. Another link with the theatre. I was linked to the theatre before it closed. Amateur dramatics, professional. An actor. It doesn't matter. Come back to it.

Where am I meeting the girls? Am I a teacher, a swimming instructor, or do I just watch them? Do I live near a school? I know Jane West, or at least, I've seen her. She got into my car. She knows me. For fuck sake, I'm a teacher. It fits. Go on. Don't stop. Never stop. Get back to the girls. You've been watching them. Little fantasies on the verge of sleep or in the bath, anywhere warm where they are easy to conjure. Hang on. I'm her teacher. I'm intelligent – am I? I'll be interviewed. My name would be on file, spilled out when I take Baxter's daughter. I'm linked with Baxter. Am I? Is this revenge? Shit, maybe it's not after all. No, it is, it's got to be. The feet, the destruction. Right, accept revenge, lose the teacher. I'm not a teacher. Feet, dance, dance instructor. Did Jane take dance lessons? Same problem. I'm not a teacher. Or maybe once the deed is done I expect to be caught. In which case the links to Baxter don't matter. I could be a copper or a teacher or a dance instructor. Shit, if that's the case we're nowhere. Forget it, madness lies down that path. I'm not prepared to be caught, so the link matters. Concealing the link is important. Go on from there. How do I know Jane? Where have I seen her? Where have I seen the other girls? Jane goes to school, she goes home, she occasionally goes out with friends, the movies, or to the shops, nothing planned. Where do I see her? I'm a neighbour. No, impossible. The council houses around the Wests' home have been checked and re-checked. Nothing there. So, where do I see her? It has to be the school. Barnwall School. It's my only opportunity. I'm not on the staff. The connection would be too easy. I live there. My house overlooks the school. I can see the playground. Yes, I can watch the girls. I've been watching them for months, years. Those houses have been checked, certainly, but not with the same attention given to the neighbours.

But that's not good enough. My interest could have been aroused by any school. It doesn't have to be Barnwall. My house might have overlooked any one of a dozen schools. It might even have been Mary-Anne's school and that's miles away. But Mary-Anne is the real target. It's too much of a coincidence that I live by her school. And choosing someone similar in looks, Jane West, was no spur of the moment thing. I know her routine; I've watched her for a long time. Go with Barnwall. It's got to be. I live adjacent to Barnwall School.

Which came first, watching them, or being turned on by them? It was probably always there, hidden, watching them brought it out. I've chosen Jane because she looks like Mary-Anne. Any other reason? No. Not at the moment. So, my sexual longings have been fed by watching the girls. Why do I feel this way? My grievance with Baxter has nothing to do with this. This is something from the dark past. Physical or sexual abuse when I was a kid. Women are dirty, impure, their characters are overwhelming. That's why I need them young, before they develop. My father was overbearing, he humiliated me, put me through torments. I've grown up sexually dysfunctional, yet I remain in control, am able to plan and carry it through. I've prepared for this moment. I'm not married, my work is flexible, time off during the day to watch the girls. Perhaps I'm unemployed. Come on, come on. Father is abusive, violent, absent, a religious man with a strong belt that he uses on me. I've disappointed him. Mother has indulged me, made up for it. Yes. She glorifies me. I'm angry with my family, my anger burns into fantasies of revenge. Revenge is everything, revenge against the girls for my own sexual impulses, revenge against the church and therefore against my father, revenge against Baxter for something in the past. It comes down to detachment. As a child, faced with the endless abuse, I detached myself emotionally and psychologically from the violence. It's the only way I can survive. Into adulthood my detachment and dissociation are pushed under the surface, but they're there, multiplying beneath the consciousness, nurturing a desire for revenge. All they need to erupt is some event, however unlikely, to stir the memory.

Maynard felt exhausted, desperate for something to eat and drink. He stood up and rubbed at his stiff muscles, then lumbered into the passage. A uniform nodded.

'Can I use your mobile to speak to DI Cole?' Within moments he was through and Cole came on. 'It's not a copper.'

'What?'

'It's not a copper.'

'You're certain?'

'Ninety per cent. Yeah.'

'You're beginning to irritate me.'

'That's the way I work. Take down these headings. Theatre connection, actor, copper's costume. Number two, house in the vicinity of Barnwall School, almost certainly overlooking playground or road outside. Number three, the house will have a garage, or a concealed place for the car. Number four, new venue will be room in the house. No time to arrange for alternative he's comfortable with. Got it? Tie that lot up with a name from Superintendent Baxter and you've got yourself a killer.'

'We've already interviewed everyone in those houses.'

'Then you've missed something.'

'You're pretty sure of yourself, aren't you?'

'That's the way I work.'

'Margaret is on her way. Try not to upset her too much.'

'Lighting the touch paper and standing back to watch the result is—'

'How you work. Yeah, I guessed. Catch you later.'

DS Barry Scot looked up from the map. 'There are a total of thirty-six houses that have some glimpse into the school playgrounds or playing-fields, eighty if we include the school drive and the road the drive turns off. Three hundred and twenty-one if we include all the houses that Jane West passed on her way to school. Every occupant has been TIED.'

'OK, we'll do it again, and again. Get some uniforms to assist. You, Martin and Jock Wilson.' Cole turned to Walker. 'You and Hazel concentrate on the theatre angle. Who used it? Local groups, whatever. Lists of members. They've been checked once. Let's do it again. Go back until records began. The local rags might help. Get everything back to Sam as soon as you can. Get everything onto those bloody boxes.'

He made his way to Baxter's office and tapped lightly on the door.

'Guv?'

'Come in, Rick.'

'I won't ask you how you are.'

'Good.' Baxter looked grey. His face was blotchy, his eyes sunken. He waved a hand as Cole sat opposite. 'I feel totally bloody useless. Absolutely wiped out. It feels like someone's reached inside me and pulled my bloody guts out. There's a bloody great hole and yet I feel sick all the time.' His gaze reached across; it was almost begging.

Cole nodded and sipped at the drink he'd brought in. He placed the plastic cup on the desk and lit a cigarette.

Baxter continued, 'I saw Marsh. He's ordered me home once I've finished with the list.'

'That's what I would have done.'

'Me too,' Baxter agreed. He indicated the door. 'What's happening out there?'

Once Cole had explained, Baxter said, 'Do you give this guy much credit?'

'I do actually, Guv. He makes a lot of sense. Margaret's with him now.'

Baxter nodded and flicked the papers on his desk. 'This will take me another half hour or so, then I'll get back.'

'I'll be in touch.'

'Anything at all, Rick. Please.'

'Yeah.'

'Call me anyway, will you? Last thing?'

'I hope to have something positive before then, but yeah, I will.' He looked around for an ashtray. There wasn't one. He stood up and headed for the door.

'I'm going to have this bastard. I'm going to tear his fucking head off,' Baxter said from behind him.

Cole paused at the door. 'I'll hold him down while you do it.'

Sam Butler saw Cole's glance towards Hazel and read something into it. 'You're dragging on that cigarette as though you're taking it down to your bollocks.'

'Maybe I am.'

'They still need a stimulant, do they?'

Cole shot him with a back-off look, left him at the bar and moved across to Hazel. Scot acknowledged him with a nod. Hazel refused to meet his gaze and toyed with the stem of her glass.

'Can I have a word?' She gazed into the golden liquid without looking up.

Butler came up behind him with their drinks.

Suddenly Hazel pushed back her chair and walked swiftly to the door. Cole followed her.

Butler stood holding both glasses.

'What's all that about?' Scot asked.

'Unhappiness,' Butler answered, sadly.

'Is that all? I thought it was something serious.' Scot watched the door close then, speculatively, 'Are they—?'

'Did I say that?'

'No, skipper, not that I heard.'

'Well, then, forget it.'

In the darkness of the silent car-park she stood with her back to him, arms crossed, as she gazed at the lights of the city.

'I didn't get a chance in the office. Not with everything going on.'

'Well, now you've set tongues wagging.'

'They'll think it's business. I'm having a go. Something.'

'You reckon?'

'How's Nigel?'

'Pissed off at having to go out alone.'

'But really?'

'All right, I suppose. No problems, if that's what you mean. He didn't notice my bow legs.'

'That's not what I meant.'

She turned to face him. 'I know,' she said.

'I wanted to—'

'Can I come back to your place?'

'Nigel will be waiting for you.'

'I've wanted to touch you all day. I wanted to come over to your desk and just look at you.'

'Me too,' he whispered. That sense of regret was still hanging over him. 'I don't know what the hell's happening to me.'

'Let me come back, please. Just for a little while.'

'What's the point?'

'I'll settle for anything. A coffee, if that's all you're offering.'

He nodded. 'You can stay as long as you want, you know that. But don't compromise yourself, not on my account. I don't want you to look back and blame me.'

'I won't.' She took a step towards him and drew his lips to hers. Her quick tongue fluttered. A noise at the door separated them and they stood aside while two men left with unsteady steps and moved to a car.

'Do you want an arrest?' she asked, smiling.

He grunted.

'Come on,' she murmured. 'Let's finish our drinks and make some excuses.'

He followed her back into the pub. Butler recognised Hazel's slight blush. 'Everything OK?' he asked, looking from Hazel to Cole.

'Everything's just fine, Sam,' she said. 'Just fine. So stop worrying. I'm a big girl now, Skippy.'

'Don't call me Skippy. Sam, Sergeant, bastard if we're on first name terms, but not Skippy.'

Scot and Hazel spoke together. 'We've heard it before.'

Butler smiled genuinely and gulped at his drink.

Geoff Maynard arrived with Margaret Domey and joined the group. They had obviously made up. She moved a chair to tuck in beside him.

Margaret, more at ease than the others had ever seen her, said, 'Geoff was telling me that in Tokyo the age of consent is twelve. Sex with schoolgirls is a big thing; they even have a name for it. *Rori-con. Lolita* is back in business, complete with pleated skirts and ankle socks. And it's all perfectly acceptable.'

'It's all bloody disgusting,' snapped Butler.

Maynard gave him a thin smile. 'Disgusting to you, perhaps. But like the rest of us, you've been conditioned. A few individuals set the limits for the rest of us. They may be wrong.'

Butler's frown deepened and spread to Scot. 'You're saying it's all right?'

'No. But my opinion is irrelevant. Keep in mind that just a few generations ago, even in this country, the age of consent was ten. The brothels were full of girls as young as that. It was only raised from twelve in 1929. Is it right now? It's a matter of opinion. Some people would like it to be higher.'

'It *is* right now,' Butler said. 'Christ, you've got to be sick if the thought of sex with a girl of ten turns you on.'

Maynard grinned. 'That thought doesn't turn me on. Nor does the thought of sex with a girl of twenty.'

Butler reddened. 'You know what I mean.'

Maynard relented. 'Yes I do. But most men can see the woman in girls of school age. They have tremendous appeal. They're not threatening, physically or intellectually. They're subservient, innocent, everything that men desire. The whole point of paedophilia is that the child is not developed. And it's pretty common. It's about power over the powerless.'

For a while they let the alcohol do the trick, smooth out the edges, take away reality. It helped them put aside the fact that in the morning, early, they had to get back to Mary-Anne Baxter and that, unless they found her, in less than twenty-four hours she would be dead meat on a post mortem slab.

They made love in the dark and he forgot what she looked like. Afterwards, they blew white smoke into the darkness. She drew deeply on the cigarette and for an instant the glow caught the curve of her breasts.

'All my life I've been in control,' she said, quietly. 'That's the one positive thing about me. I walked a narrow path, never taking chances, but it was straight. It meant I never had to make difficult decisions. Dammit, I like being in control. But now I want someone else to tell me what to do.'

'I can't—'

'Not you. Someone on the outside. A parent, a teacher, someone to put their foot down and say, "No, you can't have that", or "Yes, that's all right". I want to turn back the clock and not be responsible any more. Just for a while. It's such a mess.'

'Maybe this wasn't a good idea. You're tired.'

'Hold me. I'll sleep. No, I won't. I'm too tired to sleep. Talk to me, Rick. Tell me a story.'

'I'm not very good at stories.'

'Yes, you are. You're unbelievable at everything.'

'And you're beautiful. Even in the dark.'

'Tell me a story.'

'About?'

'Anything. No, London. Tell me about London, your time at the Yard. Why you left. What's your deep, dark secret?'

London? God, where did it start?

Hendon was light years away. He'd spent seventeen weeks in those north London suburbs, sitting in the centre of a class of thirty or so aspirants, each face bright with expectation. They were going to stick on a sheriff's badge and change the world. They knew about as much as *The Sweeney* had shown them. John Thaw knocking shit out of the low-life; Diane Keene giving them a flash of dark silk. Then it was out to division, Bow Street nick to begin with, the learning beat, pounding the streets of a sub-division under the watchful eye of his parent constable. Now they were called street duty PCs or street duty sergeants or bastards. In those first few months the glamour died; you learned about tedium. You updated the manuals, the IBs, for anyone who asked, inserting six months' worth of amendments. Everyone's IB waited for a newcomer, a fresh recruit who hadn't learned to say bollocks. In those days it was an eight-day working week. Eight days, one off, eight days, one off, eight days, then a three-day weekend. Leave had always been uncertain. There had always been some bastard thing going down, a bomb, a procession, something like that. London coppers soon got to hate the royals almost as much as they hated the Irish. They caused more cancelled leave than anything else.

Over the years, you became immune to the public, indifferent to their rights. You began to think that they were all guilty of something. You saw them as a hindrance, and you began to look down on them. The indoctrination, the psychology of it all, the frightening reality of power, led you to think that you were superior. It became a battleground.

A way of life.

'So, what happened?'

He reached under the sheet and gently stirred her clitoris.

'Oh, Rick, don't change the subject. You're not getting away without telling me.'

Under cover of darkness he grinned and withdrew his hand. She caught hold of it and put it back.

'You can tell me at the same time.'

'OK, what do you want to know?'

'The whole lot. Why you left. You don't strike me as the sort to run away, so what happened?'

'It started a few months after the Ice-cream Man went down. I was still with the Child Porn Unit, attached to Vice. CPU in Manchester were investigating reports of child abuse at a local Chinese. The owners were adamant they didn't know the children. They were panicked, shouting and screaming. If they'd come up with a reasonable story, that might have been the end of it. But CPU weren't satisfied. No one seemed to own the children involved. No one came forward to collect them. No parents or relatives. Nothing. Eventually, through an interpreter, they led us back to a restaurant in Soho's Chinatown. The Vice squad were already interested in the place. Their opposite numbers in Kuala Lumpur and Hong Kong had tipped them off. A guy named Hing was bringing in kids from all over the Far East, supposedly to stay with relatives for two or three months at a time. They were sent all over the country, mostly to Chinese take-aways. It gave the notion of take-aways a new meaning. The kids were taken away overnight and returned the next morning, just like renting a video. Boys and girls, any age, some as young as six. Some were stitched up again to make them seem like new. It was called the Birds Nest Run and it was big business.'

Out of the darkness she said flatly, 'I didn't hear about it.'

'You wouldn't. Some of the customers had influential friends and very dodgy handshakes.'

'Senior coppers?'

'Yeah, senior coppers. And magistrates and civil servants and honourable members.'

'There was a cover up?'

'What do you think? We didn't pull a single name. Plenty of resignations, but no arrests. A few take-aways were closed down.'

'And Hing?'

'He disappeared somewhere in Hong Kong, probably into Kowloon Harbour. The triads don't like failure.'

She moved closer, if that were possible. 'So what happened? Why you?'

'I was the only one to make a noise.'

'It's awful. I'd have quit, gone to the papers.'

'I thought about it. I'm still thinking.'

'But you moved?'

'It wasn't by choice. I didn't request a transfer. But it was pointed out that my prospects at HQ were somewhat limited.'

After a few moments she said, 'That's not a nice bedtime story. I wish I hadn't asked.'

Across town, dirty yellow light shone into the third-floor window of a poor man's hotel. Standing there, his naked body bathed in the filth, feverish in the oppressive heat, Geoff Maynard fought an old battle. He was tainted, outside of society. Alone. His mind hammered with images of the young boys and girls he'd lost. He'd moved away from this business because of them. His mind blown, shell-shocked. It'd taken him two years to recover. But he'd done it alone, in the fresh air, away from the corruption of the city. Now they'd talked him back, given him a new department and free rein.

The images caressed him with their ghostly hands, feather-light, butterfly wings. Their perfect shapes draped themselves before him; he reached out between their shoulder blades to the sweep of their backs, the rise of their buttocks. He felt the weight of his celibacy, the pull of heavy blood. It came on, unstoppable, and fell, wasted, to the carpet. He took a deep breath of corrupt air; some of it, perhaps, had been breathed out by Jane West's killer. Now it was inside him. He held onto it, wanting it to filter into every part of him.

'I know you,' he said into the flickering night. 'And tomorrow, you're mine.'

Chapter 28

Sunday. Not surprisingly, Baxter looked as though he hadn't slept for two nights. Once he'd finished the list of possible contenders he was left hovering within earshot of the ringing phones, wanting to be there the instant any development came in. He kept out of sight of Marsh who'd ordered him home the day before. The others didn't mind. They understood. Somehow, it was easier than being at home. There, the sense of security and order had been smashed. It had become a cold, unfamiliar place, like a prison cell. He recognised a devastating accusation in his wife's eyes that left him feeling bewildered and inadequate. It wasn't obvious, there was no outburst of reproof, but it was there nevertheless, hidden away behind the taut features. He had been the guardian of the family and he had failed. And now she blamed him. It was a ludicrous sentiment, maybe even imagined. In reality, his wife was too shattered to feel anything but bereavement. The anger and hatred towards the perpetrator and the institutions – government, police force and the like – that had allowed it to happen, would come later. She moved in a daze, numbed, driven by instinct alone.

Officers from South Wales had visited his daughters at the university and were arranging transport to get them home. They would be arriving around lunch-time. Baxter would get back to meet them. Then he would face the agonising wait with his wife and family.

Sam Butler caught Cole waiting for a plastic cup to fill from the machine that was gurgling like a blocked drain. 'Maybe the super's sabotaged it,' he said. 'He was in for most of the morning.'

'I think he's got other things on his mind, don't you? But you're right. He should have been at home. Marsh would go spare if he knew. What time did he leave?'

'Just before lunch.'

'Still, he might as well wait here as there. That's all we've been doing, isn't it? The whole morning has been a wasted effort.'

'There's still time,' Butler said, reassuringly. 'We're still working on the info from CIB.'

Cole nodded thoughtfully. Butler was right, of course. At any moment the computer could spill out a name. It only took seconds. Through the partition he searched for Hazel's face. She was at her desk, concentrating on a screen. It didn't surprise Cole to see her looking washed out. Neither of them had slept more than an hour or so. She hadn't left his place until breakfast, and they were back in the office an hour later.

At the front door she had kissed him.

He said, apprehensively, 'Is this it, then?'

She flashed him a quick little smile. 'I don't think so, do you?'

He watched her climb into her car. He didn't know whether it was relief or fear that fluttered in his gut.

They were all conscious of the clock, and the afternoon flashed by. They watched the screens, waited for calls, snatched at every ringing phone. But nothing. Tempers frayed, resignation set its ugly cast. Lips tightened, eyes narrowed, sweat began to trickle. Clothes became uncomfortable, foreheads shone, hands became moist and swallowing became difficult. Everyone was thinking of the super and whether he'd ever get over it.

It was late when Butler perched himself on Cole's desk.

'Sam.'

'Rick.'

Cole drew deeply on his cigarette before stubbing it in an overflowing ashtray. Two or three dog-ends squeezed out onto his desk. He made an effort to clean them up and blew the residue ash to hell. He shook his head and said, 'We're losing.'

Butler shuffled his backside off the corner of the desk to find a more comfortable position. 'If our policeman friend, or whatever the hell he is, knew of Helen Guest's connection with the prescription pads, someone told him. Maybe Helen or one of her friends.'

'That is a point.' He was surprised it hadn't been thought of earlier.

'Do you mind if I follow it up? We're more or less finished with the listings. I'll leave Chas Walker to tidy up with the indexers.'

'You go ahead,' Cole replied. 'Take Hazel with you. Helen might be more forthcoming.'

'Are you kidding?'

'Yeah, but it'll do Hazel good to get out.'

Helen Guest opened her door to DS Sam Butler and DC Hazel McLintock. Her surprise vanished in an instant. She wore a pair of plum-coloured stirrup pants with a matching tunic and not much underneath. Butler seemed impressed. She showed them into the hall. In the next room a television blared. She went to the door and said, 'It's the police, darling. More of the same, I imagine. I won't be long.' She pulled the door closed and, all poses and long legs, turned to the detectives. Her lips pouted in a sham sulk. She looked at Butler, then spoke to Hazel. 'Where's the gorgeous detective inspector?'

Hazel shot her a poisonous glance.

Helen chuckled and moved across to one of the chairs by the table. 'My, constable, your eyes have turned green. Just like mine. It must be the light in here.' She laughed out loud. 'For goodness sake, can't you recognise a wind-up?'

Hazel's cheeks flared. She hadn't realised her feelings were so apparent. Butler cleared his throat. He felt a little uncomfortable, overwhelmed.

'Mrs Guest,' he said. 'We've come up with an idea. Eight years ago the man who took your picture—'

'Oh yes, that reminds me. Can I have that back? My husband would like it.'

Butler was momentarily flummoxed. 'I don't see any reason why not—'

'Can we keep to the point?' Hazel cut in. 'The guy who took your picture must have known about the prescriptions. Can you remember who you told?'

Helen raised her pencil-thin eyebrows. 'Well, I didn't spread it around.'

'Did you mention it to anyone other than the guy you gave them to?'

She shook her head. 'Maybe a school mate. That's all.'

'Who was your supplier, Helen?' Hazel asked.

'I can't tell you that. That would be unfair.'

'You're still chilling out, I can see that. It's more than weed now, isn't it?'

Helen shrugged.

'Do you want me to have a look around?'

Butler took a step forward. 'Helen, we're not interested in you, or your supplier. Take my word for it. If he comes up with the information it'll go no further. That's a promise. There's a girl's life hanging in the balance. We're not after a two bit pusher, believe me.'

Helen took a deep breath. Butler watched her chest rise and shook admiration from his eyes.

'A guy named Brookes. We used to call him Jesus on account of his goatee and long blond hair. Do you know him?'

Butler nodded. 'On the estate?'

She nodded.

'Yeah, we know him. Thanks a lot.'

Helen stood up and walked them to the door. 'If you see the DI, will you give him my—'

'Yeah, yeah,' Hazel said, and stepped out into the night.

Butler pushed Brookes aside and forced the door open. The scales glinted as brightly as the stoned smile on the face of the woman lying on the sofa.

Brookes staggered back and collapsed in an armchair. 'I'm having a real bad day here, man.'

Hazel followed Butler into the room and shut the door. She stood by it, arms folded, legs braced.

'What happened to your eye?' Butler asked.

Brookes fingered the angry flesh and shrugged weakly.

Butler moved across to the coffee table and dipped a finger

294

into white dust. He rubbed it into his lower gum. 'Good,' he muttered, then raised his eyebrows.

'I'm a class act, man. Anyone will tell you that.' Brookes sighed and threw the woman a glance. 'That's the wife. She's got nothing to do with all this. She thinks I'm a fucking chef, baking a cake.'

The woman gave them a stupid smile. Her robe opened and Butler clocked some springing hair.

Brookes noticed Butler's tongue and began, 'You can take her in the back—' He remembered the DC at the door and cut himself short and sighed. 'Well, I get my rights, or what?'

Butler waved a hand. 'Make you a deal, Jesus. Answer some questions, move out of my area, we'll call it quits. Understand?'

'Man, that sounds heavy, but I like it. But if you want my supplier, no deal. I'd lose another eye, and I'm getting short of them.'

'Nothing to do with this shit.'

'Well, then, I'm all ears.'

'We know you're juggling a bit with Helen Guest.'

'Helen Guest?'

'Don't give me—'

'Oh, that Helen Guest. Man, a bit of weed, maybe.' He shrugged.

'Yeah,' Butler said. 'Yeah, yeah. And the coke. Last time I saw her she'd forgotten to wipe her nose. But we're not interested in that. Eight years ago she came to you with some blank prescription pads. Remember?'

'It's ringing a distant bell.'

'In those days her name was Helen Klincewicz. You told someone about her selling prescriptions.'

'I did?'

'She gave you the prescriptions in exchange for a few joints. You used them.'

'I did? Yes, I did. They were too good a gift to pass on.'

'Then you must have told someone about them. You're the only one that Helen told.'

'Yeah, a guy, man. His mum had some long-term illness.

He used to buy a little weed for her to ease the pain. I remember now. Because he was always going to the chemist for his mum's pills, I got him to change the prescriptions.'

'Who was it?'

'I don't remember his name. Not sure I ever knew it, man. He was thin, long dark hair. He lived over the back some place. Near the school.'

Butler drew out the photofit drawn by the girls from Mary-Anne's school.

Brookes's good eye blinked as he studied it. 'Not much, although put some long black hair on him, thin him up a bit, man, and maybe . . .'

'Right,' Butler said.

'Is that it?'

'That's it,' Hazel said, and opened the door.

Butler paused. 'Jesus, you've got until nine in the morning. Is that long enough?'

Brookes rubbed his hands together. 'That's cool, man. I'll be gone.'

At the door Butler said, 'If I were you I'd get someone to look at that eye. Casualty.'

Brookes nodded.

In the car Hazel spoke into the mobile.

Back at the office, Cole turned from the phone. 'Long, dark hair, thin-framed, medium build, lives in Wellington Avenue.'

'Yes, Guv, that's David Orbach,' Walker said. 'You know David, from the boozer?'

Cole frowned. 'David. I know David. He drinks in the White Horse. Slightly backward.'

'Well, he was forward enough to buy dope and cash in the prescriptions. That's not so backward.'

'He's not daft at all,' DC Wilson put in. 'He does some cabbying. You need your wits about you in a mini-cab. It was a cabby who won *Mastermind* that time. Remember that?'

Cole said, sharply, 'Who interviewed him?'

Walker read from the screen. 'DC James.'

Martin James glanced up sheepishly from his desk. 'Yes, Guv. He's as good as gold. We've all known him for years.'

'Didn't his mother die recently?'

'That's right. We held a collection at the White Horse.'

'You eliminated him?'

'Yes, it's there. On HOLMES.'

'Come on, Martin, why?'

'Christ, we know the man. His old man was in the job,' he said defensively and fingered a copy of the photofit on his desk. 'Since when has he had short fair hair?'

'You didn't know that at the time,' Cole snapped. 'In the job. A fucking police connection?' Cole turned to Walker, who was coordinating the input of Baxter's names. Walker raised a hand for calm as he waited for the girl sitting at the monitor.

'Just a minute,' she said, as the screen filled with characters.

Maynard came up behind Cole's shoulder.

Suddenly the name was there, blinking in green.

ORBACH. ALFRED MATTHEW. DECEASED SEPT 20 1976.

Cole turned on James. 'As good as gold, eh?' He turned back to the screen.

Walker read from the screen. 'His old man, Alfred Orbach. A sergeant. Retired through ill health. 1975. Died in car crash 1976. Suspected heart attack. Wife severely injured in same accident. She pulled his pension till she died earlier this year. Two dependants at time of death. His wife Millie, an actress, and David Orbach.'

Cole thundered, 'A police connection, a theatre connection. What the hell have we been playing at?'

'We know him, Guv,' James responded quickly. 'Anyway, the hair's all wrong. It's not making sense.'

Cole steadied himself. The situation needed diffusing. He asked, calmly, 'Where does he figure with Baxter?'

Walker said, 'Baxter was CIB. The word retirement might have come from him.'

'The super forced him to resign or else?' Maynard asked.

'That's the top and bottom of it.'

'Shall we talk to the super?'

'No need. It'll be booze, or caught with hand in till, or planting evidence, or any one of a thousand things. If we can keep it quiet, we do. Public relations, all that. If he goes quietly he gets to keep his pension.'

Maynard struggled into his jacket. 'Rick, his mother was an actress. The theatre's the clincher. He's our man. No doubt at all.'

Cole nodded and said, tartly, 'I don't know. But we'll go and have a word.'

'Do you want some back-up, Guv?' Walker asked, hopefully.

Cole shook his head. 'Get Butler to meet us there. You carry on with this lot, just in case it blows out. Like Martin said, the description doesn't fit. The girls at the school were pretty adamant about short blond hair.' He glanced at his watch, then moved in front of Maynard. 'Come on, Geoff. Let's put your theory to the test.'

On the way, they heard the radio.

'Sierra Oscar to Charlie Bravo One, receiving?'

'CB one receiving. What is it, Mike?'

Cole recognised PC Wendy Booth's voice.

'Reports of a disturbance in the High Street, Benny's Mini-cabs. Can you respond?'

'Will do. I'm on Empire Road, about two minutes away.'

'Hold on, CB one . . .' There was some indistinct but excited chatter then, 'Charlie Bravo One?'

'Still here, Mike.'

'There's all hell breaking loose . . .'

Maynard glanced across at Cole as he heard the scream of sirens. The DI concentrated on the road, his face set in determination. The radio chattered on. A fire-bombing of Black Benny's mini-cab shop, shootings, bodies.

'What do you reckon?' Maynard asked.

Cole shook his head. 'Are you kidding? It sounds like gang war. Black Benny's in it up to his eyes. Him and a guy named Keith Mason. They're probably having a pop at one another. It happens every so often. Territorial disputes, dope, you name it.

But there're enough wooden tops out there. We've got another priority.'

'I hadn't forgotten.'

They'd gone another mile, approaching the school road, when the radio spluttered again. The shooting had moved north after a car chase. Neighbours had complained with 999s. Bodies in front of the house. Wellington Avenue. DC Wendy Booth, 7231, in CB1, was asked to respond with back-up. An urgent assist went out to other vehicles and an armed response vehicle was on its way.

Cole glanced at Maynard and flipped his mobile. 'Mike, it's Rick. I'm thirty seconds away from your last call. Check with DS Walker for details.'

'OK, Rick. CB one should be just behind you. DS Butler is five minutes away. He was on his way back when the call went out. I'm sending in all the spare back-up I can. We've got our hands full. There's bloody mayhem in the High Street.'

'Understood, Mike.'

Cole flicked off and put his foot down.

Chapter 29

Cole and Maynard pulled up just in front of Wendy Booth. Sergeant Mike Wilson, white-faced and wide-eyed, sat in her passenger seat. His knuckles were rigid. He had never known her to take the corners so quickly. He thanked God that he was still alive.

Cole took in the three bodies. The huge black man near the road was obviously dead. So was the fat man, face up in the doorway. His lips were drawn back over some expensive bridge work and his eyes were open, counting the stars.

'That's Keith Mason, the local gangster,' he told Maynard.

In CB1, PC Booth was coolly confirming urgent assist and ambulances.

Sergeant Wilson called over from the car parked round the side of the house. 'This one's dead.'

Cole stepped over the body at the door.

'We've got an ARV on the way, Rick,' Wilson shouted. 'Let's wait for them.'

Cole ignored him and crunched over glass to the stairs. He pointed down the passage and said to Maynard, 'Check down there. Be careful.'

Maynard grunted, then went ahead. In the last few moments he'd changed his mind about the police carrying arms.

Cole climbed the stairs three at a time. He saw the mess at the top. The missing plaster, the pitted walls. The bitter smell of cordite burned the air and collected in the throat. It made you want to cough and spit. He saw the trail of blood along the landing.

Crouching low, he pushed open the bathroom door, then the one to the single room. Nothing. Maynard came up behind him and whispered, 'Nothing down there, Rick. The cellar's been used. This is it.'

They moved either side of the remaining door. Cole reached down to the handle, exchanged a quick glance with Maynard, then turned the handle and threw open the door.

They piled in together, crouching certainly, but to hell with safety first. They took in the scene instantly.

'Jesus F Christ!' breathed Maynard.

Cordite hung in the air along with something else, raw sewage.

Their eyes followed the slimy trail of brown and red on the carpet to the twisted shape of a man lying beside the bed. His face was a mask of agony. His police uniform was torn from groin to midriff and his guts had spilled onto the carpet beside him. One bloody hand held onto a wooden truncheon that he was attempting to lift towards the bed. With the other he tried to hold in his bowel.

Maynard's massive strides carried him across the room in three. He kicked the truncheon out of the man's desperate hand and it hit the carpet and disappeared under the bed.

Cole was almost as fast. He reached the bed and pulled the girl away from danger. He saw the relief in her eyes and held her close. Very gently, he peeled away the strip of tape from her mouth and let it drop to the carpet. She let out a long cry.

'I'm dying,' the man groaned. 'I can't stand the pain. Please help me.' His uniform was soaked in blood.

Maynard stood over him. 'I'll help you,' he said, contemptuously. 'No problem. But first tell me about the cups in the theatre.'

The man's features spread in confusion.

'You had coffee, milk, but no cups. What happened to the cups?'

Eyes fell in. He shook with another bout of pain. 'I brought them home. They're part of a tea-set. My mother's china.'

Maynard smiled. He glanced across at Cole and exchanged a secret message. It was all in the eyes.

Cole understood, or thought he did. He took off his jacket and wrapped it around Mary-Anne's shoulders. She faced him, her legs dangled over the bed. He saw the streak of oil which he took for semen and pulled the jacket together, bunching it in front of her. She shivered. He reached behind her, beneath the jacket, to unfasten her wrists. 'It's all right, sweetheart, you're safe now,' he said. He glanced over her shoulder at Maynard and offered him the faintest of nods.

Maynard placed his heavy shoe across the man's windpipe. He saw the look of shock, then horror in the man's eyes and watched his mouth open to scream. He increased the pressure. A sound emerged, half-strangled in his throat, and then a tiny bubble burst on his lips. The disbelieving eyes slowly slipped upwards and began to bulge.

'Is he dead?' Cole asked.

'Yes.'

Cole flashed him a curious look. 'Is that what you people call exorcising a demon?'

They heard the sounds of an ambulance drawing up. Sergeant Wilson appeared at the door.

'OK?' he asked, then took it all in. 'Jesus Christ.'

Maynard nodded.

'The ambulance is here.'

Mary-Anne clung to Cole, and whispered into his chest, 'I want my dad.'

'Don't worry, Mary-Anne, we'll find him together. He's been worried about you. He's been right off his food. Good thing. He needed to lose weight. In the office we call him a fat bastard.'

He heard her faint giggle. 'I'll tell him that.'

'Does it hurt anywhere?'

She shook her head. 'No, not really. Just funny, in my tummy, you know?'

'We'll get it sorted. Just hang on to me. If your dad sees you clinging to me like this, he'll be really upset. I'd like that.'

Surprising him, she said, 'There was a black man. He shot him. But he got hurt with a knife. Is he all right?'

Cole held her close. ''Fraid not, sweetheart. He didn't make it. But let's worry about you, eh?'

Sergeant Wilson held open the door and Cole carried her along the passage, shielding her eyes with his hand. Maynard followed behind.

Cole said, gently, 'I'll take you to the ambulance and we'll call your dad from there. OK? I'll use the mobile. You can talk to him if you like. He can meet us at the hospital.'

She gave him a little nod of agreement. 'Please will you come with me?'

Cole glanced across at Maynard who gave him a shrug.

''Course I will. I'll hold your hand all the way. Got to come for my jacket.'

'I've got . . . stuff on it,' she said, remarkably composed.

'Don't worry about that. Your dad can have it cleaned for me. I bet he doesn't even know how to use the washing machine.'

He saw the tug of a smile. 'He doesn't. He's useless in the kitchen.'

'Yep, that's what I figured.'

Carefully, he started down the stairs. The body on the front doorstep had been covered with a coat. Beyond it, flashing lights flooded the lawn, turning the grass into ash. Two paramedics met him at the bottom. They reached out to take the girl but she drew back, and tightened her hold around Cole's neck.

'I'll come with her,' he said firmly.

They nodded and stood back. On his way through the hall he said to Sergeant Wilson, 'Mike, give Detective Superintendent Baxter a call, right now. Tell him we'll meet him at the North Mid. Tell him . . . tell him that Mary-Anne is safe . . . and making eyes at me.'

He heard her giggle again.

The uniform sergeant nodded. It was one task he didn't mind at all.

There were two ambulances in the front. Another panda pulled up and more uniforms piled out. A crowd of onlookers were being kept at bay by more officers. DS Butler parked behind them. Hazel was in the passenger seat. Cole saw her look of concern as he climbed into the ambulance. The skidding blue light flashed across her face and turned her lips black. One of the paras followed him in and the doors closed, cutting out the sounds of confusion.

The paramedic moved up next to him on the seat. 'Mary-Anne, can I just check you to make sure you're OK?'

She shook her head and desperately clung onto Cole, her spindly arms taut around his neck.

Cole smiled at the woman and said, 'It's my uniform. All the girls love it.'

'What uniform?'

'You might think we're out of it. But we never are. Not really. We wear it in our eyes. I'm surprised you didn't know that.'

She returned his smile, then sat back as the ambulance accelerated through the outskirts and raced towards the city.

Chapter 30

When Cole arrived back at the IR, he found Maynard briefing Marsh and Deighton, both of whom had rushed back from the violent scenes in the high street. Margaret Domey stood with them.

'So one of the villains shot him? That's a turn up,' said Marsh.

'It was a shotgun, close range, full in the belly. Orbach had been planning it for years,' Maynard said to the small assembly. 'Since before he went out to buy dope for his mother.'

Cole settled at the back of the room. He shared just the faintest nod of acknowledgement with the stiff-backed assistant chief super.

Without noticing his presence, Maynard continued, 'That's when he first started to wear the wig, his mother's wig. He even used it on the cabs. His neighbours were convinced that it was his real hair. In fact, the only time he didn't wear it was when he impersonated a police officer. Putting on the uniform began as a game, until he realised that people accepted him in it, and that he could get away with what coppers can get away with.'

Deighton interrupted. 'But why did Mary-Anne get in the car?'

'Coming to it. He was dressed as a copper. The cab radio off station sounded right. He'd been down at the school all week, patrolling because of Jane West. The kids got to know him. Mary-Anne accepted a lift home. Probably thought the super had arranged it.'

Deighton shook his head.

'So, he could get away with being a copper. Enter Helen Guest. At that time the motive might have been illusive. He was desperate for a young girl, but the concept disgusted him. He needed an excuse to carry it through. When he saw the super and his family at the shops one day and saw Mary-Anne for the first time, the concept of revenge provided the excuse. Raping the girls was no longer seen as a weakness.'

Marsh raised an eyebrow. 'You got all this from his diary?'

'Most of it,' Maynard agreed. 'Soon, of course, revenge took over, became even more important than his sexual gratification. Once his mother died and his plan to get even with the super became paramount, he took the uniform with him and changed at the theatre. He'd drive over there in his new car, change, then use his old car to drive to the school. Although he's been watching the girls, including Mary-Anne, for some time, he started to get serious when his mother died. Since that time, he's been patrolling the schools, getting to know Jane and Mary-Anne, gaining their confidence. His mother's death changed him from being a daydreamer, a fantasist, to actually carrying out the attacks. For the first time in his life he was totally alone. Take away a month or so after her death for things to settle, the will and so forth, and that leaves just a month before Jane West was abducted.

'We're still looking at his plan. He wrote everything down. Without any doubt at all he was sexually abused by both his parents. It appears that his mother called him angel, God's little angel. The abuse went on with the mother long after she was incapacitated. The religious connotation must have been born with this. He was going to hang Mary-Anne on the cross on his parent's grave, a gift, if you like, yet still convinced that this wouldn't lead you to his door. You'd be looking for a serial killer. The name on the cross would be irrelevant. The destruction of the body, sex organs and feet, part disgust, part revenge, partly so that the super would know what to expect. There'll be books, a whole shelf of them, by would-be psychologists, the true-crime writers. You'll become household names.'

Marsh allowed himself a small smile. Deighton looked horrified and took a step back.

Maynard went on, 'But they'll come up with a dozen answers. The *Mirror* will blame TV or the movies and the *Guardian* the inner cities. The *Sun* will blame everyone except page three. That's it. You'll have to be patient for more. It's been an interesting few days.'

'What did the super do to deserve all this?' Marsh asked, seriously.

'Probably nothing,' Maynard put in quickly. 'That's the ludicrous part, and why it was so difficult to put the two and two together. Twenty-one years ago Superintendent Baxter was the shoulder Alf Orbach used when he was hitting the bottle. It was Alf's own decision to quit and get some medical help. The super even smoothed things over so that the pension was paid in full. But to David's mind, the job had turned his father to drink, had caused his father's violence towards him, and the super was the job. For the next twenty years, while David looked after his mother, the fantasies and the hate built up. Sooner or later it was going to blow.'

Marsh turned to Cole. 'Is it good news?'

'It could be worse. Physically, Mary-Anne seems OK. She's a tough little kid. They're keeping her in overnight, just to be on the safe side.'

'Was she raped?'

'They say not, but they're waiting for a paediatrician to make the final examination.'

'That is good news. What about Tony?'

'He's relieved, Guv. He's staying at the hospital with the rest of his family.'

Marsh nodded. He exchanged a casual glance with his assistant, then looked again at Cole before he said, 'Well done, everybody. Excellent result. I think the rest can wait until morning.'

Mary-Anne had insisted that Cole stay with her. The doctor in casualty helped her dress in a sterile gown.

'I had better hang on to your jacket,' she had said to Cole.

'No need. No prosecution. Not unless they move the court to the mortuary.'

She looked calm as she handed him his jacket. The examination had barely started when Baxter arrived with his family. They crowded into the cubicle, taking turns to hug Mary-Anne. There were tears all round.

Cole backed out; no one noticed. He rang a cab from reception, then waited outside so that he could smoke. Baxter arrived at his side.

'Guv.'

'Rick . . .' he began, but lost it.

The mini-cab pulled in.

Cole nodded, flicked the cigarette butt into the road and opened the car door.

'I'll see you later, Guv.'

He slammed the door and told the driver, 'Sheerham nick.'

The driver started the meter and pulled out. Cole looked straight ahead, not giving Baxter the chance to thank him. He didn't want it; it wasn't necessary. It was just a job, a shit job, nothing more than that.

Shifts hadn't meant a damn lately, but the night duty was left to pick up the pieces. Overtime had already gone through the roof and the accountants were having nightmares. Deighton, responsible for the local budget, was a nervous wreck. Of the others, some went home to sink into exhausted sleep and some went to the White Horse. They were on a high, euphoric, putting off the tail-spin of the sober aftermath. Alcohol splashed and raised voices. They relived it all, now able to joke, like a huge family at a wake, expounding the virtues and eccentricity of the deceased. In this case the deceased was the incident. It was a necessary part of putting it to bed.

Counselling would be offered over the next few days, but not many would take it up. Counsellors were fat dogs or dandruff storms. They knew fuck all about real life. Instead, they would work it off under the car, in the garden, or down the pub. Mostly down the pub. Watching the England cricket team was always good. Made them realise that some things were worse than the job. They would get to know their wives and families again and they would read more than the headlines in the tabloids. They were heroes, all of them, but no one ever mentioned it. Worse than that, come the dawn they were the bastards again, interfering with the rights of the common man.

Cole, with Maynard and Margaret Domey at his side, arrived an hour or so after the others, and was surprised at how many people had stayed behind. Dawn was not far away. Hazel's dark eyes fastened onto him as she shot him a wan smile. He paid for drinks and they shouldered their way across.

Maynard said, 'Cheers. Until the next time,' and sank half his golden short.

Cole grunted. 'Don't take this the wrong way, but I hope not. Not through business anyway.'

'You can guarantee it, Rick. There's dozens more David Orbachs out there, waiting to be discovered. Some of them will never be investigated. If they prey on missing people we don't even know there's a crime been committed. Think of Fred and Rose West. Think of community care, the closure of secure accommodation, people controlled with pills, sent out to live in your street, or mine. There're enough David Orbachs out there to give every town, village and hamlet, perhaps even every community centre, their own version. We already know that every twenty-five houses throws up one point two paedophiles. We know that one in twenty-five men is an abuser. We know that more than that number dream about abusing. Social services don't confide in the police, the police don't tell the council, councillors are mostly buffoons, amateurs anyway, and doctors and priests hide behind their creed and the whole fucking world is going up in flames. Your children aren't safe any more. Don't let the experts blind you with figures. They're paid by governments, the biggest lying bastards on earth. Lock your kids up, meet them from school. The age of innocence is fucked. Now it's down to the parent. You have to accept that no one else is going to help you.'

Someone put another glass in Maynard's huge hand, perhaps hoping he'd go on.

Cole said, 'I don't have kids.'

'You're probably lucky. In the next few years, unless there's a change of policy, bringing them up is going to be a nightmare. Nursery education is going to be the least of your worries.'

'They tell me it always was.'

'Yeah, but when they told you that they were only concerned with the measles jab and post-natal depression. You've seen nothing yet, believe me. Just wait until the pills start running out, until there's a glitch in the system, until the cost-cutting government accountants get their way. If you want a reason for all this, they're it. If ever there's a fucking revolution, they're the people to string up first. Know what I mean?'

'You are a depressing bastard. I thought that things were going to get better. Do we need this at four in the morning?'

'There's a bright side. You can always think of it this way. You lot are never going to be short of work, are you? Come to think of it, that goes for us as well.' He nudged Margaret's shoulder. Somewhere there, deep down, was something more than work.

Cole and McLintock edged to a corner and found themselves out of earshot. Only Butler noticed them. And Maynard, of course. He noticed everything.

'You're very beautiful, do you know that?'

'I don't feel it. I'm pale, washed out, and my eyes are so deep they need digging out.'

'What happened?'

'Nigel waited up. I tried to catch you during the day.'

'He knows?'

'No names, don't worry.'

'I'm not worried.'

'He knows.'

Cole sighed. 'Would you like a refill?'

'No, I'm going now. I only waited to see you.'

'That sounds a bit final.'

'It is, Rick. The war's over. It's back to normality. The old customs, what's right and wrong. There's no longer an excuse.'

'But we're not normal people.'

'I said that.'

He smiled. 'I remember. And the war goes on. It's just the battle we won.'

'If you watch me walk away you'll embarrass me.'

'In that case I'll look the other way.'

'I can't imagine a future without you, but I've got to try. I love you. Does it make any sense?'

'No. None at all. Not to me. But then, I'm only a simple copper. Go on, get out of here before you change your mind and mess it up completely.'

310

She threw him a quick smile and said, 'That easy?'

'Yeah. You've got to let some things go.'

'Dreams and things like that?'

'Yeah.'

She whispered, 'Thanks.' Then she was off, struggling through the tightly packed bodies.

He watched her until the crowd got in the way, then caught Butler's eye. 'Drink?' he mouthed.

Butler nodded his satisfaction, content that his friend had seen the light, that propriety had been restored, and held up his empty glass.

'Life's a shit, Sam.'

'It's a fucking joke. I know that much. You know what they say about a copper, don't you?'

'They say a lot, most of it not very nice. What did you have in mind?'

'Open him up and there's nothing there. Just a shell. Take away the job and there's nothing left. We're all fucked-up. And we fuck up everyone around us.'

Cole finished his drink in one. Jenny had said something similar. A lifetime ago. He muttered, 'That's crap.'

'I thought so.'

'What're you drinking?'

'Bitter.' He threw a rueful smile. 'But if you're buying, I'll have scotch. Lots of it.'

One of the PCs standing behind Butler overheard and said, 'Is this a celebration, Skipper?'

Butler snapped, 'Don't call me Skipper.'

The PC shrugged. He had found another job, in security, and had already written out his resignation. He'd also had a mite too much to drink. He said, 'How about bastard then, will that do you?'

Chapter 31

The week had gone quickly, in a spaced-out sort of haze. Not much was clear. Martin Brookes, Jesus for short, and his wife, Connie, had joined them on Wednesday, shortly after his release from casualty. Supermarket bleach, the consultants agreed, wasn't like the real thing, and they managed to save his eye. He would have blurred vision for a while, see three tits instead of two, that sort of thing, but it wasn't life threatening. They booked into the same B&B, same floor, next-door room. Brookes had brought his stock with him, so Hackett floated down to the beach and back. Greg had to visit the doctor again. Another infection, more antibiotics. This time he gave her a lecture about protection. Rubber. Wetsuits. Hackett was kept at arm's length. Brookes recognised his friend's frustration and suggested his wife as a substitute. The strands of dark hair, sprouting out of the white bikini briefs, were one hell of a temptation, the wilderness itself, but knowing that Greg was only dozing and was likely to be listening in, Hackett politely declined. It was just as well he did, for as soon as Brookes had joined his wife in the surf, expertly riding on flashy boards, Greg leaned over, brushed some sand from Hackett's white chest and whispered, 'I've finished the tablets. I think I'm all clear. Just in case you're interested, that is.'

That did it. Within two minutes Hackett had packed up and was treading sand. Lawrence of fuckin' Arabia. Right? Half an hour later they had undressed, showered at her insistence, and got into bed to share a prelim heavily loaded spliff. Skunk, nothing less. For the nerves. This was sixties-style. Jesus had got to them. Free love, all that Woodstock shit. It gave him a chance to cool down and steady himself. He was threatening to explode.

Six uniformed officers of the Devon and Cornwall constabulary burst into the bedroom.

Jason Hackett and Greg, naked but still unattached under the single sheet, were taken quite by surprise and made no attempt to move.

The officers crowded into the room. They had been tipped off by the landlady that funny smells were seeping under the door. A young PC moved to the bedside table and sniffed at the smouldering joint while his colleagues looked on. He pulled open a drawer and examined some digging equipment, syringe and rubber and burned teaspoon. 'Oh dear, oh dear,' he said, lifting a small plastic sachet of scag. He gave the girl a curious look of disapproval. 'How old are you?'

Greg shrugged and held the sheet to her shoulders.

The PC turned to his colleagues. 'I recognise his face. He's on a sheet. They want him in London. What's more, I think she's under age.' He turned back and addressed Hackett. 'You've written Smith in the register so that'll do for the moment. Mr and Mrs Smith, I'm arresting you both for the possession of illegal substances. And Mr Smith, I'm also arresting you on suspicion of unlawful sexual intercourse and indecent assault. You don't have to say anything, but it may harm your defence if you do not mention when questioned something you might rely on in court. Anything you do say may be given in evidence. Something like that. Fuck knows. Got it? Now you can get dressed.'

Their clothes were piled on a chair some distance from the bed. No one made a move to pass them across. The officers simply waited with smug anticipation, hoping for a quick peep at the girl's frills.